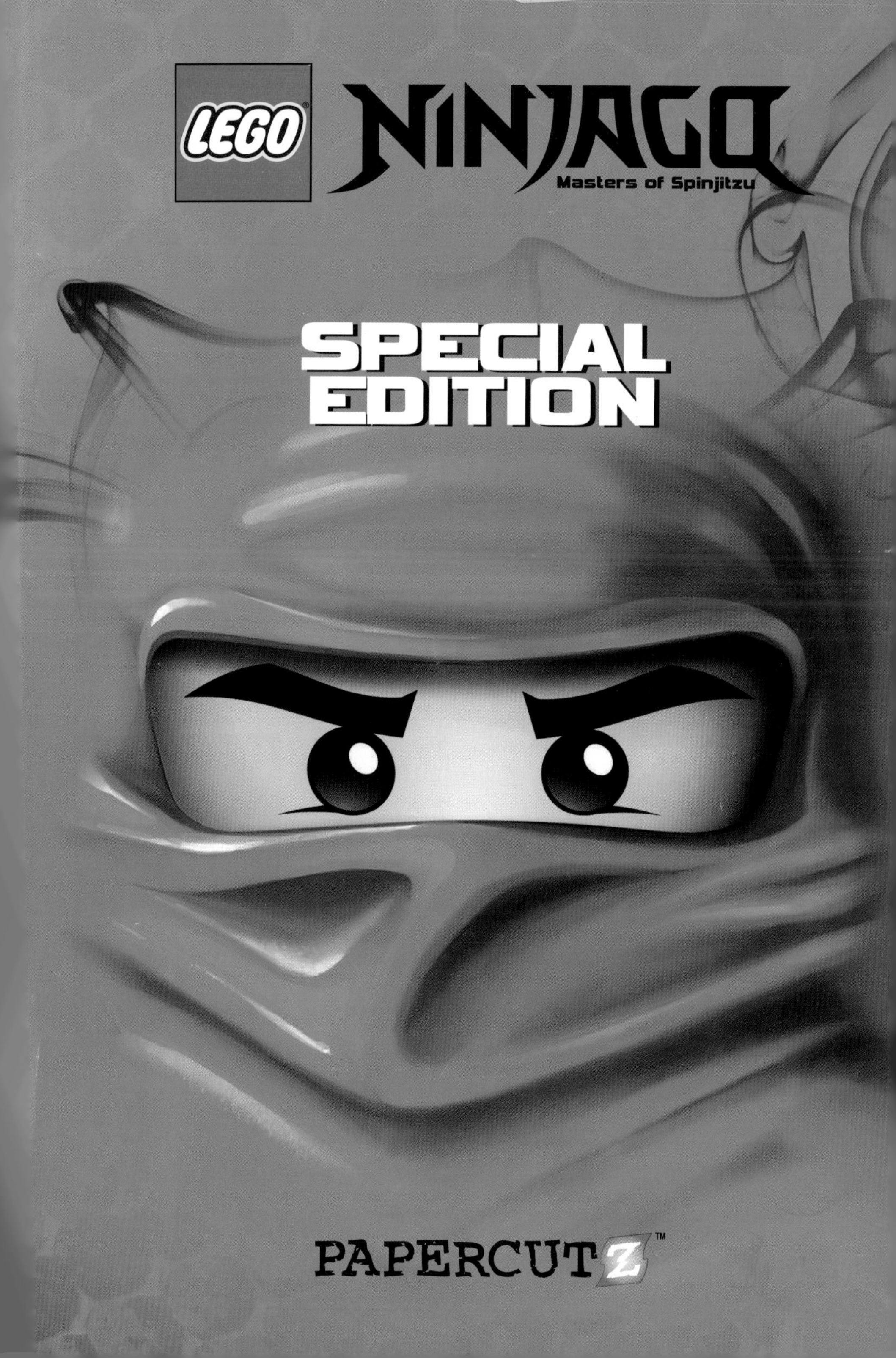
LEGO
NINJAGO
Masters of Spinjitzu
SPECIAL EDITION
PAPERCUTZ™

LEGO® GRAPHIC NOVELS AVAILABLE FROM PAPERCUTZ™

LEGO NINJAGO #1

LEGO NINJAGO #2

LEGO NINJAGO #3

LEGO NINJAGO #4

LEGO NINJAGO #5

LEGO NINJAGO #6
Coming Soon!

LEGO NINJAGO #7

LEGO NINJAGO SPECIAL EDITION #1
(Features stories from NINJAGO #1 and #2.)

LEGO NINJAGO #8

LEGO® NINJAGO graphic novels are available in paperback and hardcover at booksellers everywhere.

LEGO NINJAGO
Masters of Spinjitzu

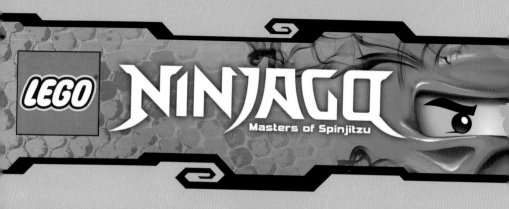

SPECIAL EDITION #3

"KINGDOM OF THE SNAKES" AND "WARRIORS OF STONE"

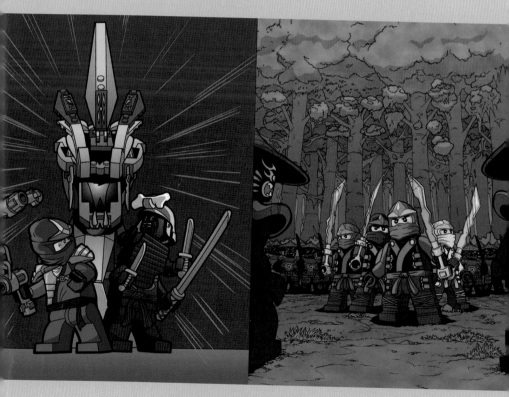

Greg Farshtey • Writer

Jolyon Yates • Artist

JayJay Jackson • Colorist

PAPERCUTZ™

New York

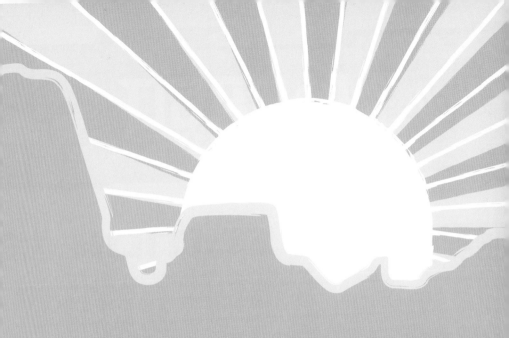

LEGO ® NINJAGO Masters of Spinjitzu
SPECIAL EDITION #3
"KINGDOM OF THE SNAKES" and
"WARRIORS OF STONE"

GREG FARSHTEY – Writer
JOLYON YATES – Artist
JAYJAY JACKSON – Colorist
BRYAN SENKA – Letterer
PAUL LEE – Cover Artist (LEGO Ninjago #5)
PAULO HENRIQUE – Cover Artist (LEGO Ninjago #6)
LAURIE E. SMITH – Cover Colorist (LEGO NINJAGO #5 and #6)
MICHAEL PETRANEK – Production
BETH SCORZATO – Production Coordinator
MICHAEL PETRANEK – Associate Editor
JIM SALICRUP
Editor-in-Chief

ISBN: 978-1-59707-699-9

Printed in the USA
June 2013 by Lifetouch Printing
5126 Forest Hills Ct
Loves Park, IL 61111

Papercutz books may be purchased for business or promotional use. For information on bulk purchases please contact Macmillan Corporate and Premium Sales Department at (800) 221-7945 x5442.

Distributed by Macmillan

First Printing

FSC
www.fsc.org
MIX
Paper from responsible sources
FSC® C112431

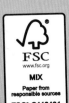

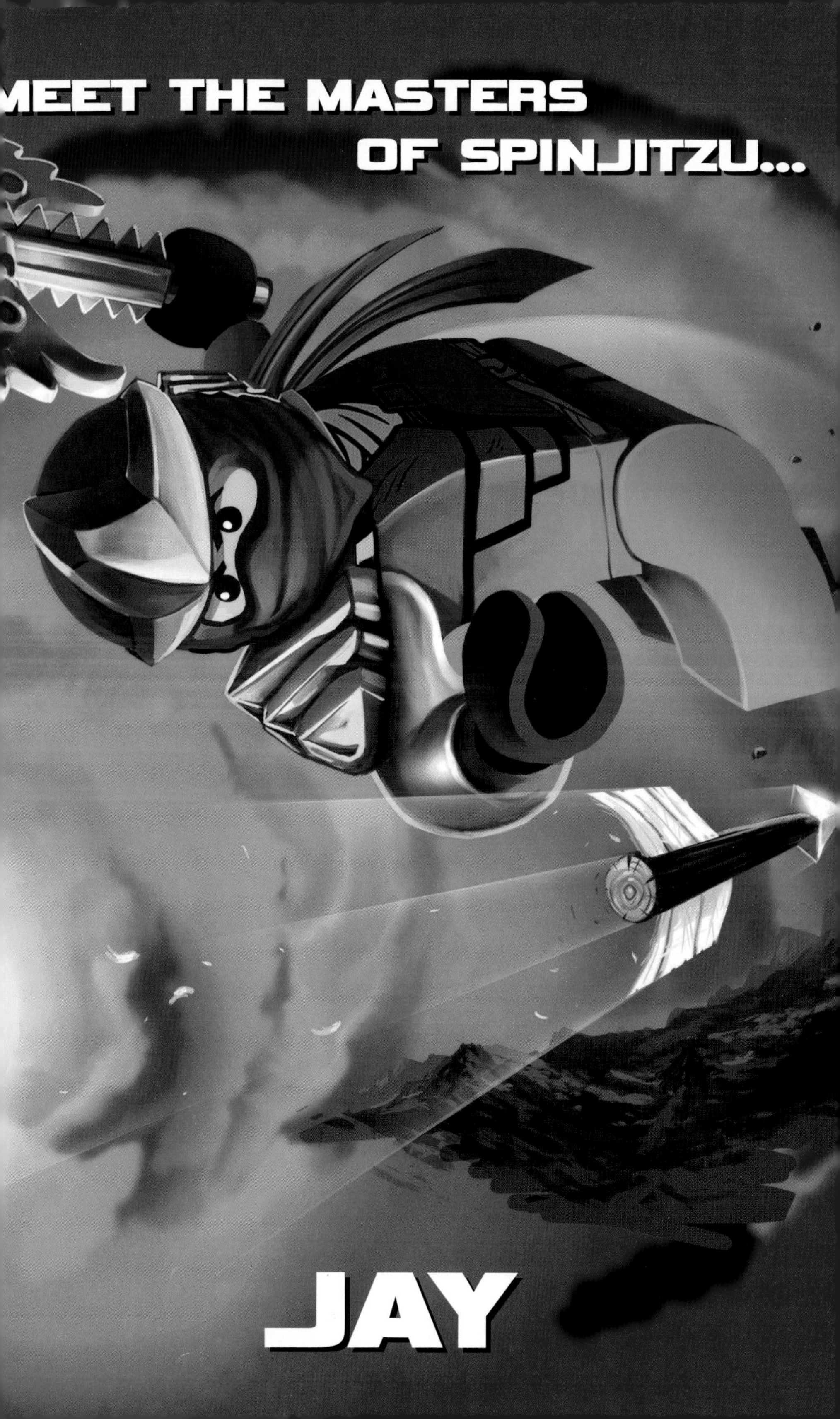
MEET THE MASTERS
OF SPINJITZU...
JAY

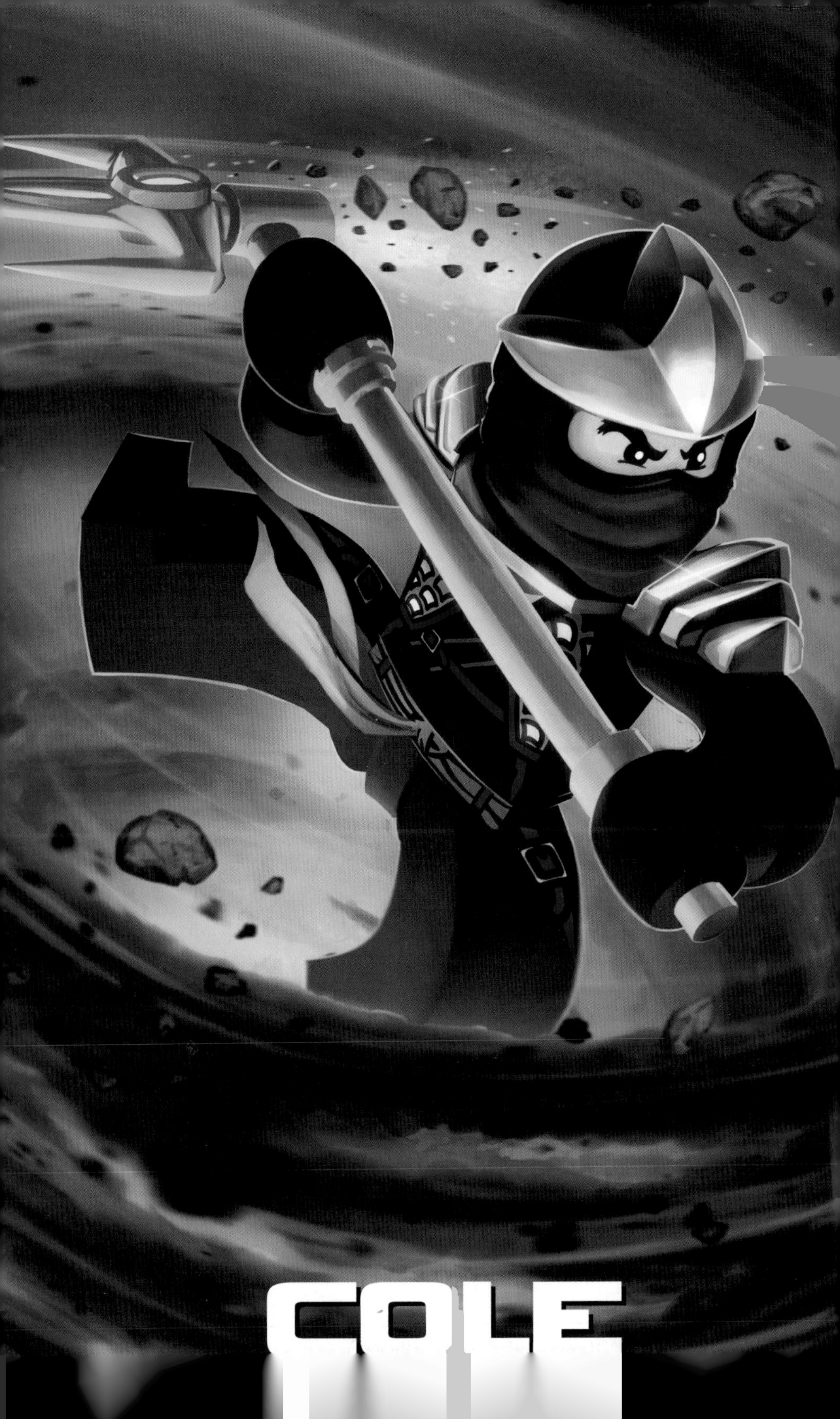
COLE

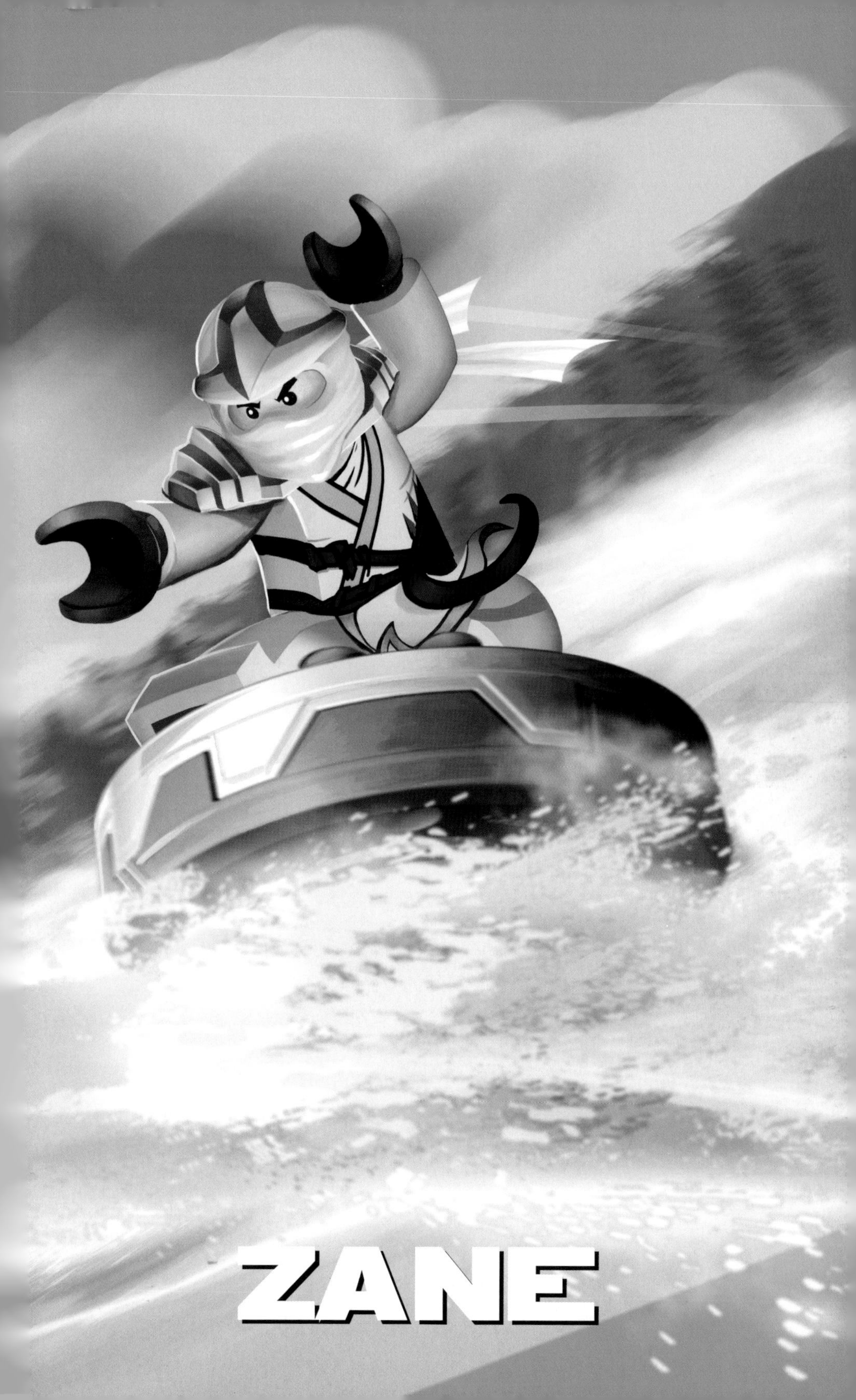

ZANE

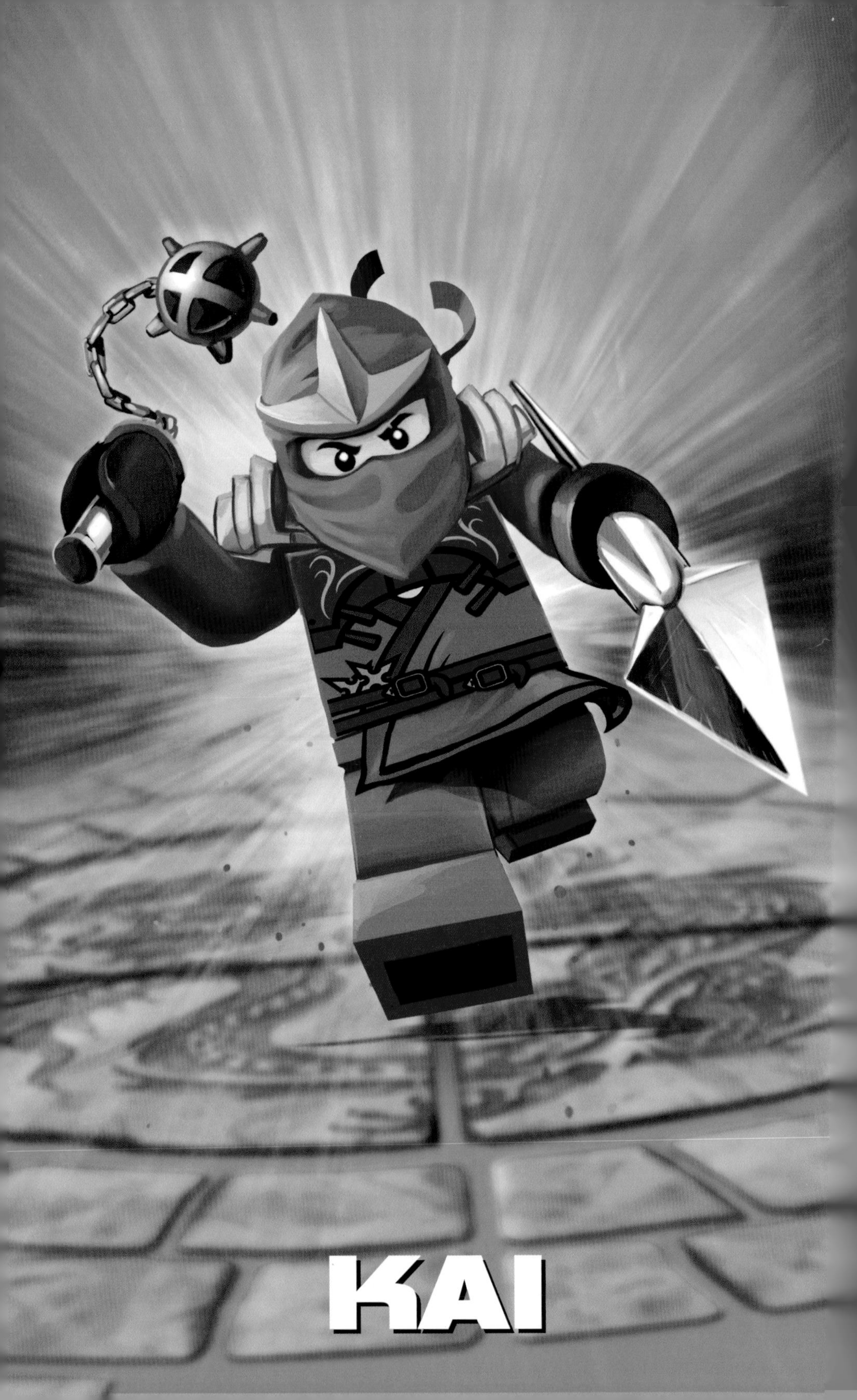
KAI

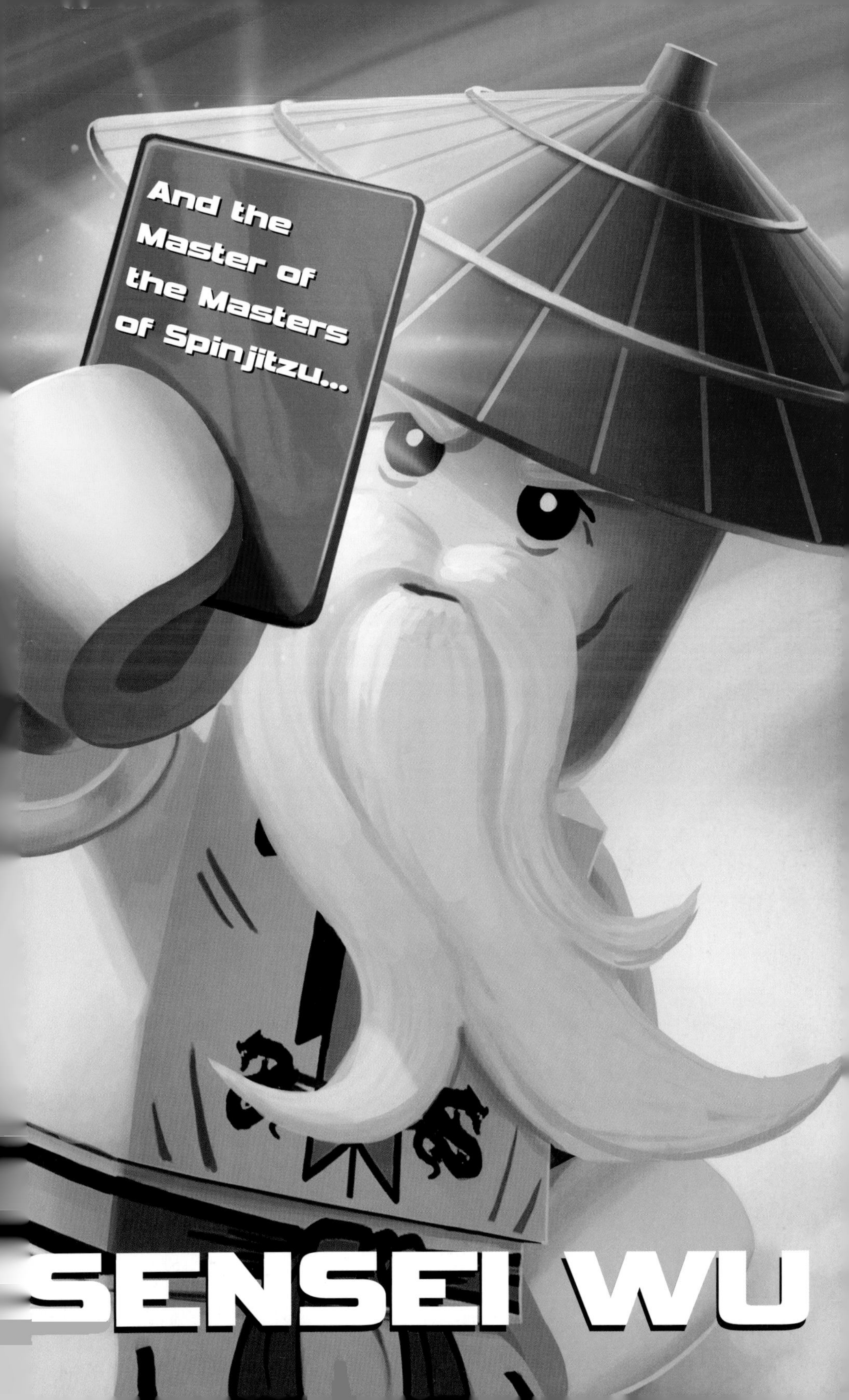
And the Master of the Masters of Spinjitzu...
SENSEI WU

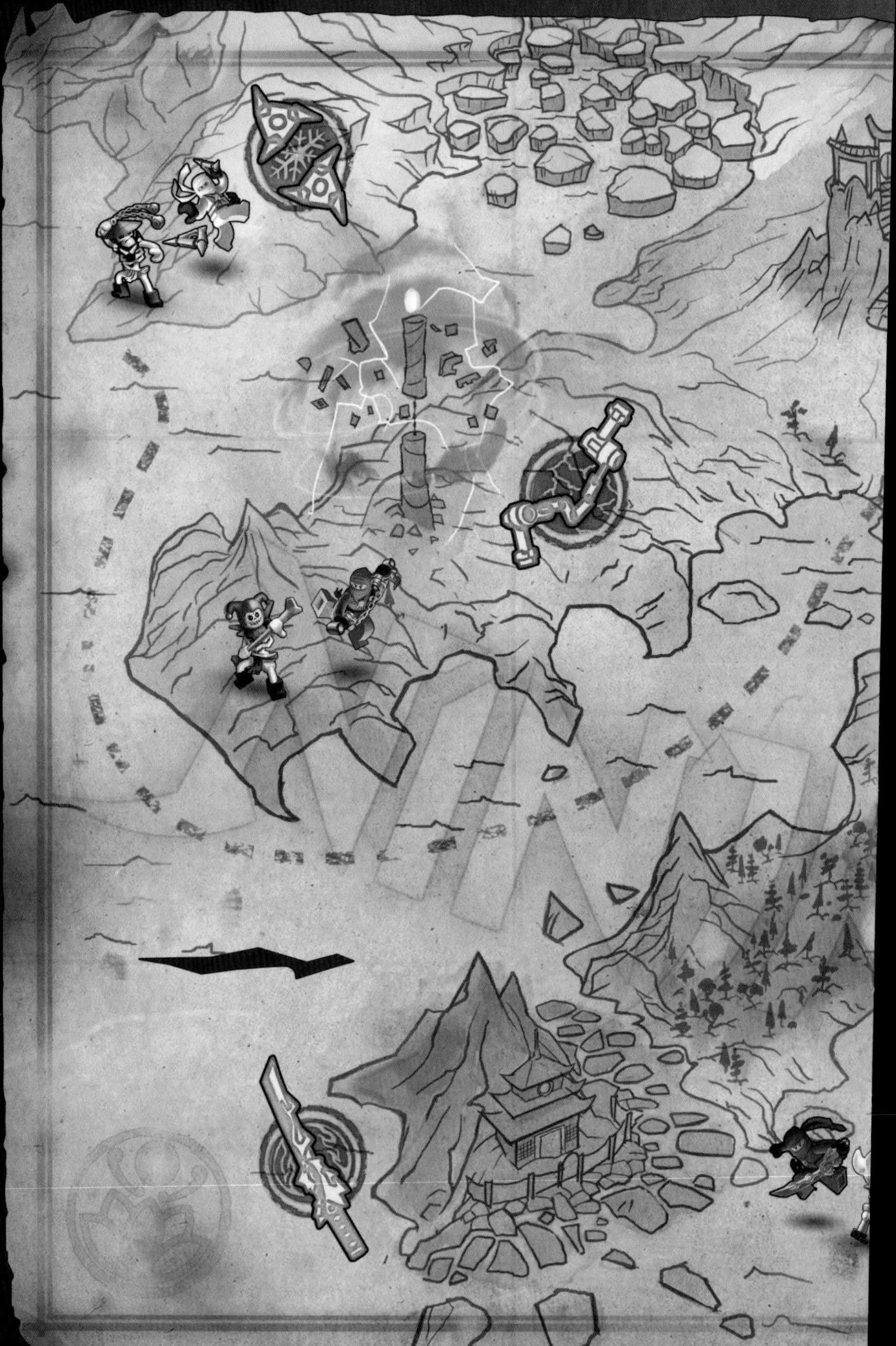

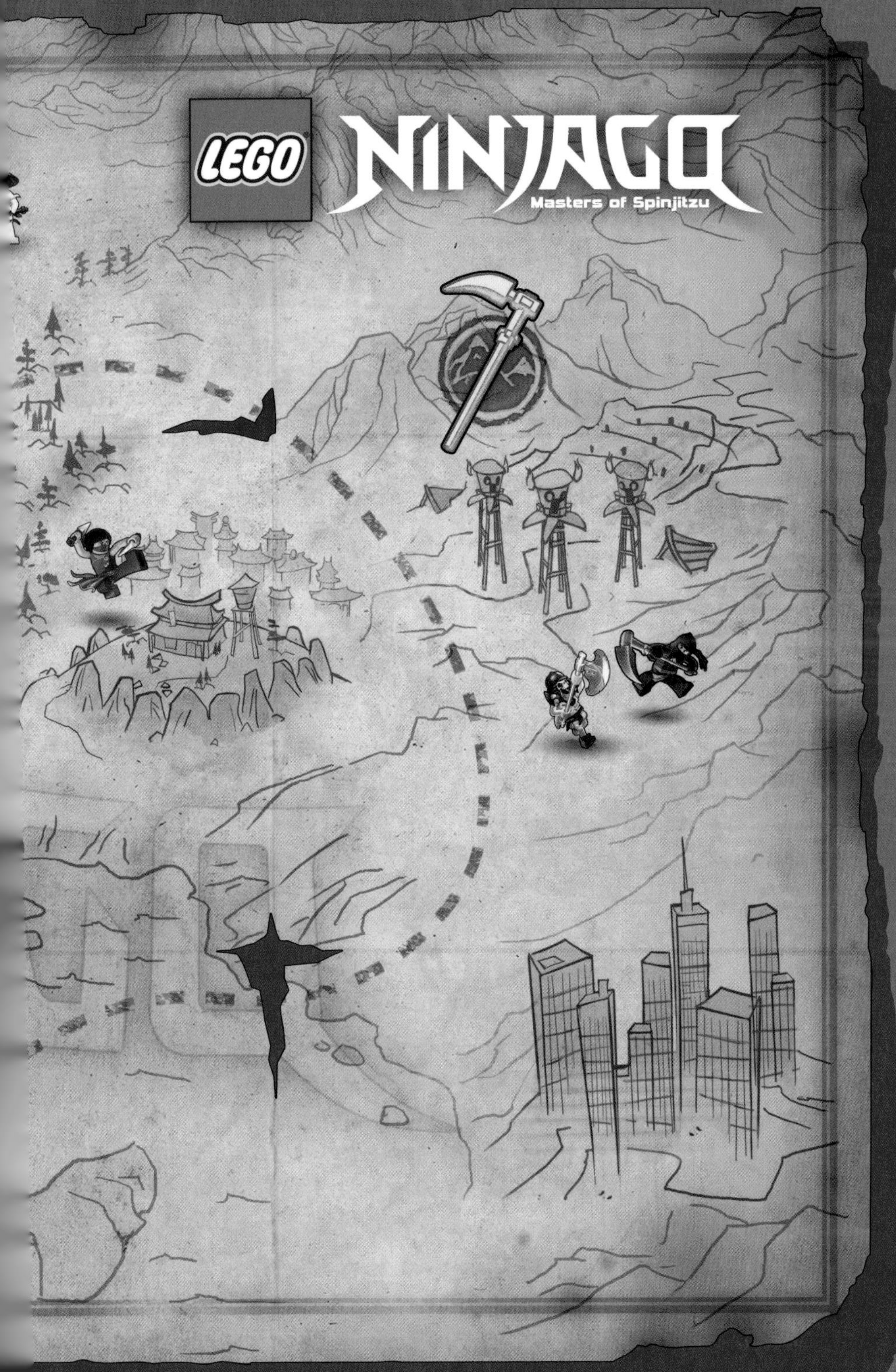
LEGO
NINJAGO
Masters of Spinjitzu

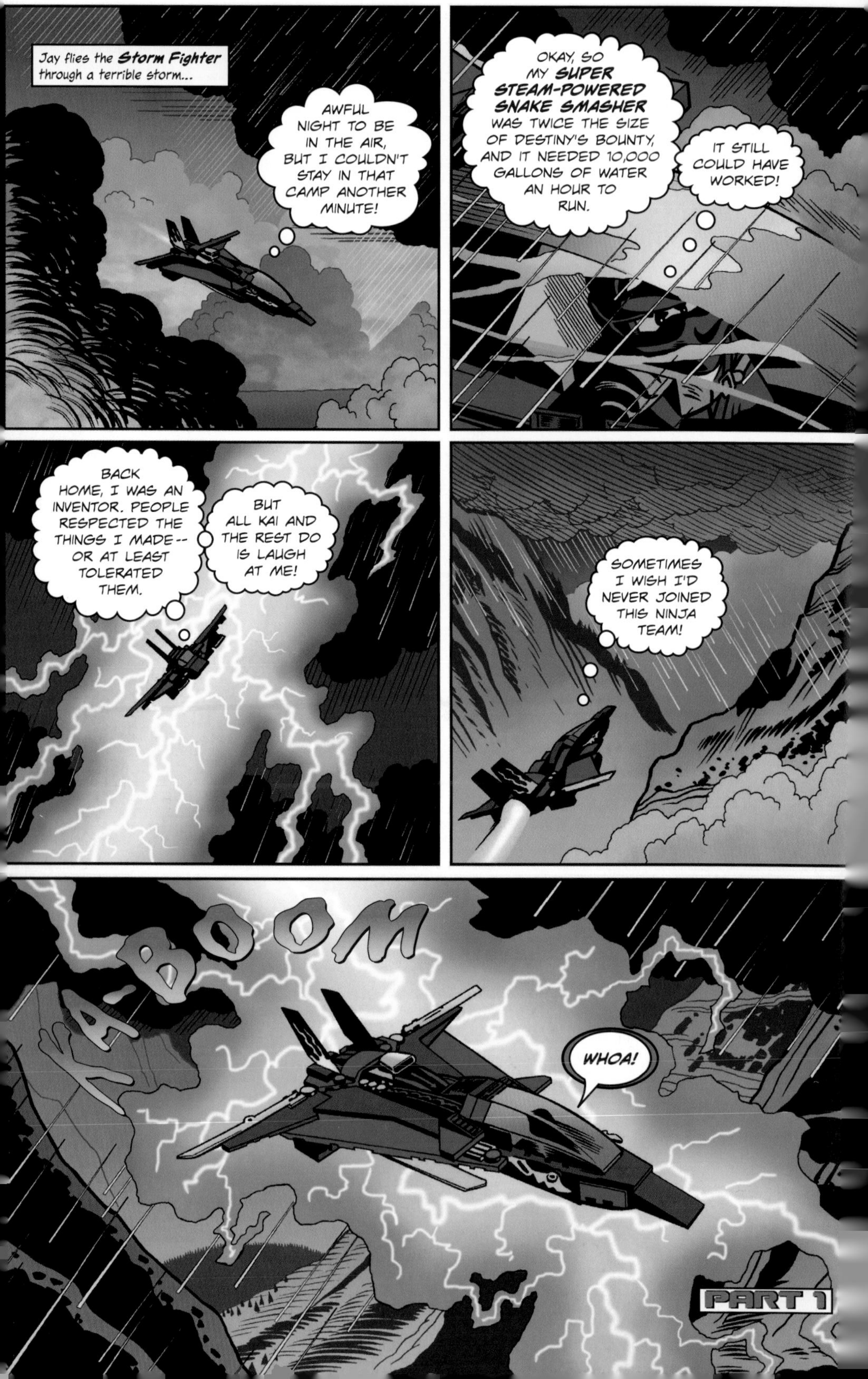

Jay flies the **Storm Fighter** through a terrible storm...
AWFUL NIGHT TO BE IN THE AIR, BUT I COULDN'T STAY IN THAT CAMP ANOTHER MINUTE!
OKAY, SO MY **SUPER STEAM-POWERED SNAKE SMASHER** WAS TWICE THE SIZE OF DESTINY'S BOUNTY, AND IT NEEDED 10,000 GALLONS OF WATER AN HOUR TO RUN.
IT STILL COULD HAVE WORKED!
BACK HOME, I WAS AN INVENTOR. PEOPLE RESPECTED THE THINGS I MADE-- OR AT LEAST TOLERATED THEM.
BUT ALL KAI AND THE REST DO IS LAUGH AT ME!
SOMETIMES I WISH I'D NEVER JOINED THIS NINJA TEAM!
A-BOOM
WHOA!
PART 1

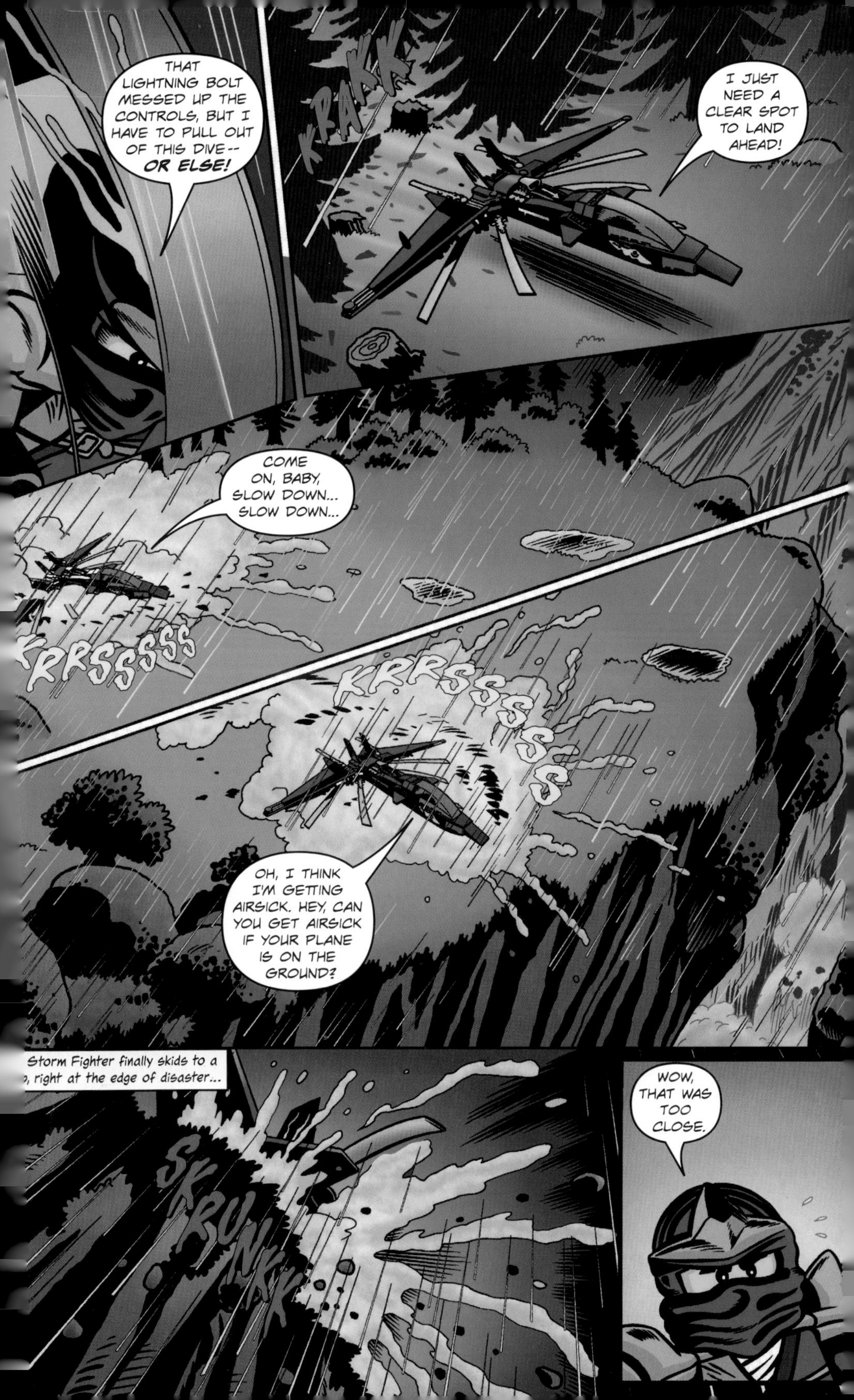
THAT LIGHTNING BOLT MESSED UP THE CONTROLS, BUT I HAVE TO PULL OUT OF THIS DIVE-- **OR ELSE!**
KRAKK
I JUST NEED A CLEAR SPOT TO LAND AHEAD!
COME ON, BABY, SLOW DOWN... SLOW DOWN...
KRRSSSSS
KRRSSSSSS
OH, I THINK I'M GETTING AIRSICK. HEY, CAN YOU GET AIRSICK IF YOUR PLANE IS ON THE GROUND?
Storm Fighter finally skids to a
, right at the edge of disaster...
SKRUNKK
WOW, THAT WAS TOO CLOSE.

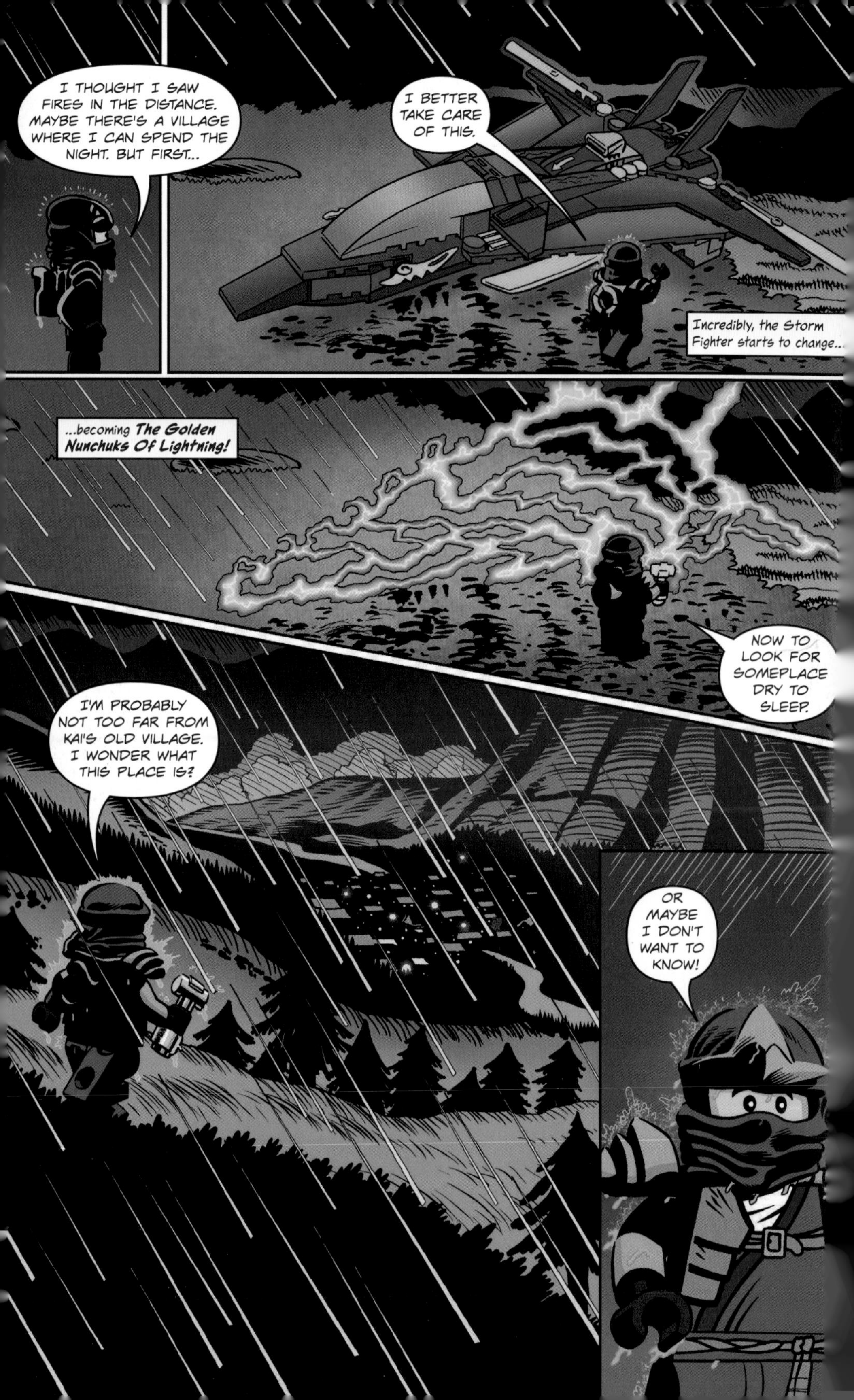
I THOUGHT I SAW FIRES IN THE DISTANCE. MAYBE THERE'S A VILLAGE WHERE I CAN SPEND THE NIGHT. BUT FIRST...
I BETTER TAKE CARE OF THIS.
Incredibly, the Storm Fighter starts to change...
...becoming The Golden Nunchuks Of Lightning!
NOW TO LOOK FOR SOMEPLACE DRY TO SLEEP.
I'M PROBABLY NOT TOO FAR FROM KAI'S OLD VILLAGE. I WONDER WHAT THIS PLACE IS?
OR MAYBE I DON'T WANT TO KNOW!

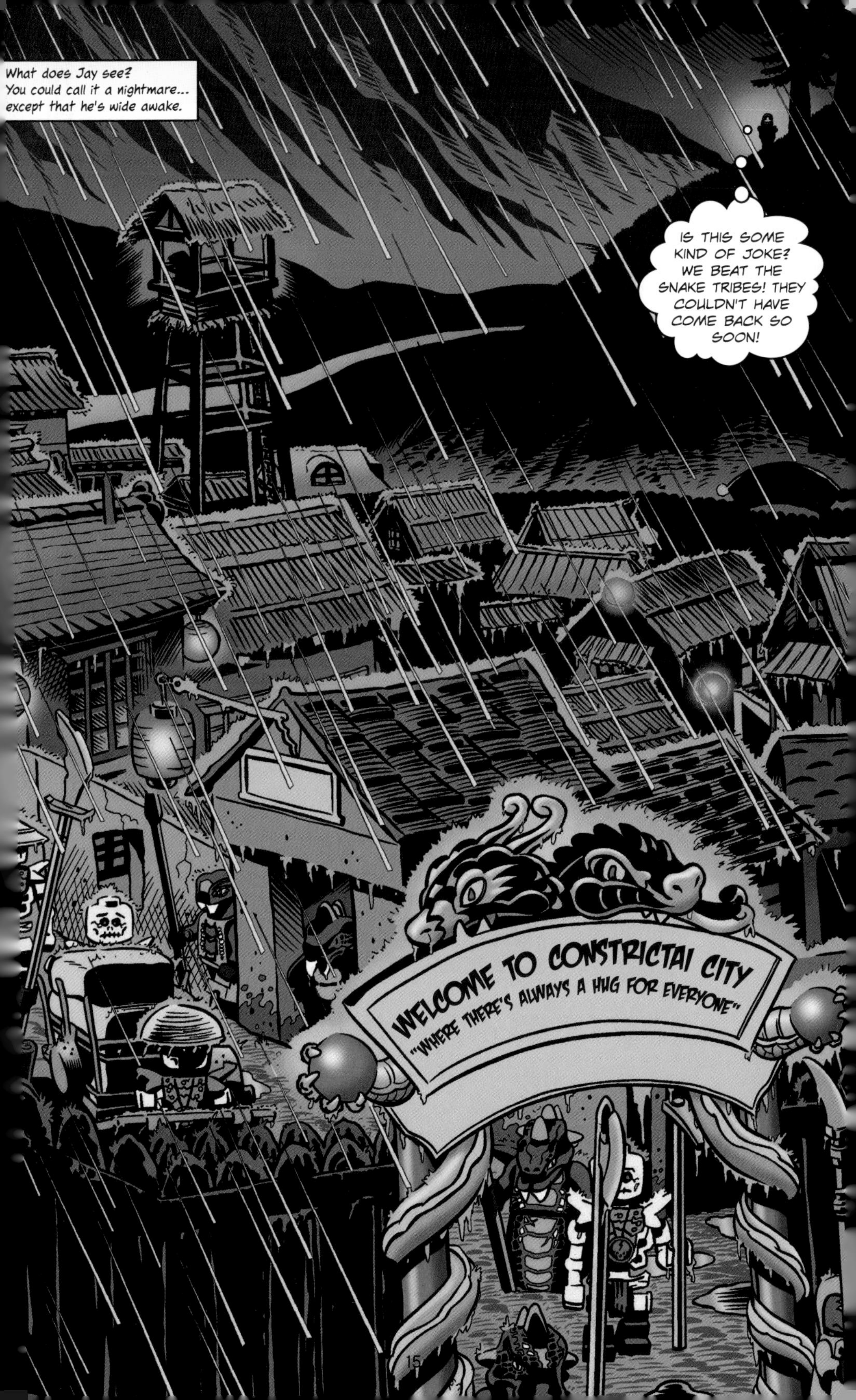
What does Jay see?
You could call it a nightmare...
except that he's wide awake.
IS THIS SOME KIND OF JOKE? WE BEAT THE SNAKE TRIBES! THEY COULDN'T HAVE COME BACK SO SOON!
WELCOME TO CONSTRICTAI CITY
"WHERE THERE'S ALWAYS A HUG FOR EVERYONE"

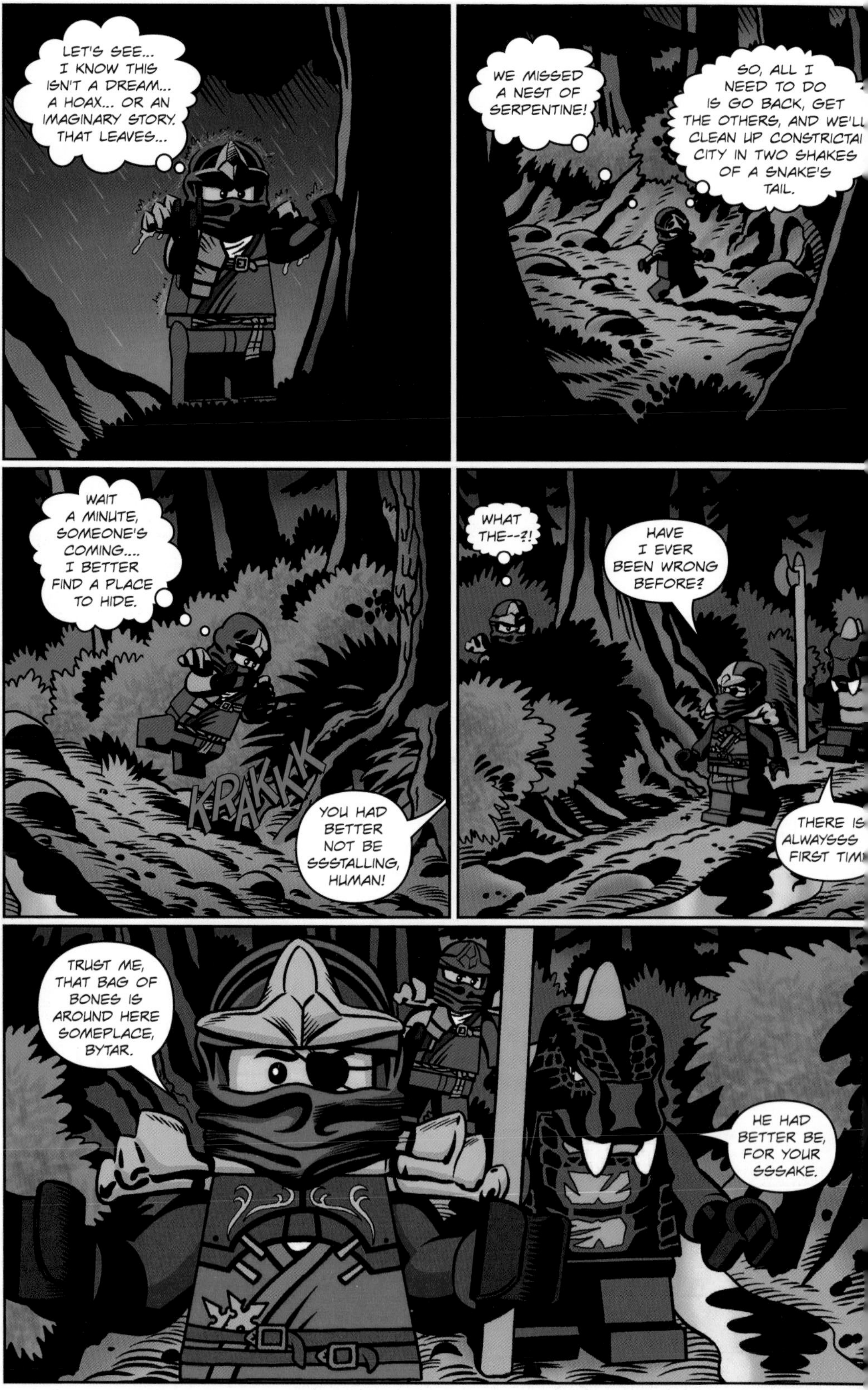
LET'S SEE... I KNOW THIS ISN'T A DREAM... A HOAX... OR AN IMAGINARY STORY. THAT LEAVES...
WE MISSED A NEST OF SERPENTINE!
SO, ALL I NEED TO DO IS GO BACK, GET THE OTHERS, AND WE'LL CLEAN UP CONSTRICTAI CITY IN TWO SHAKES OF A SNAKE'S TAIL.
WAIT A MINUTE, SOMEONE'S COMING.... I BETTER FIND A PLACE TO HIDE.
KRAKKK
YOU HAD BETTER NOT BE SSSTALLING, HUMAN!
WHAT THE--?!
HAVE I EVER BEEN WRONG BEFORE?
THERE IS ALWAYSSS FIRST TIM
TRUST ME, THAT BAG OF BONES IS AROUND HERE SOMEPLACE, BYTAR.
HE HAD BETTER BE, FOR YOUR SSSAKE.

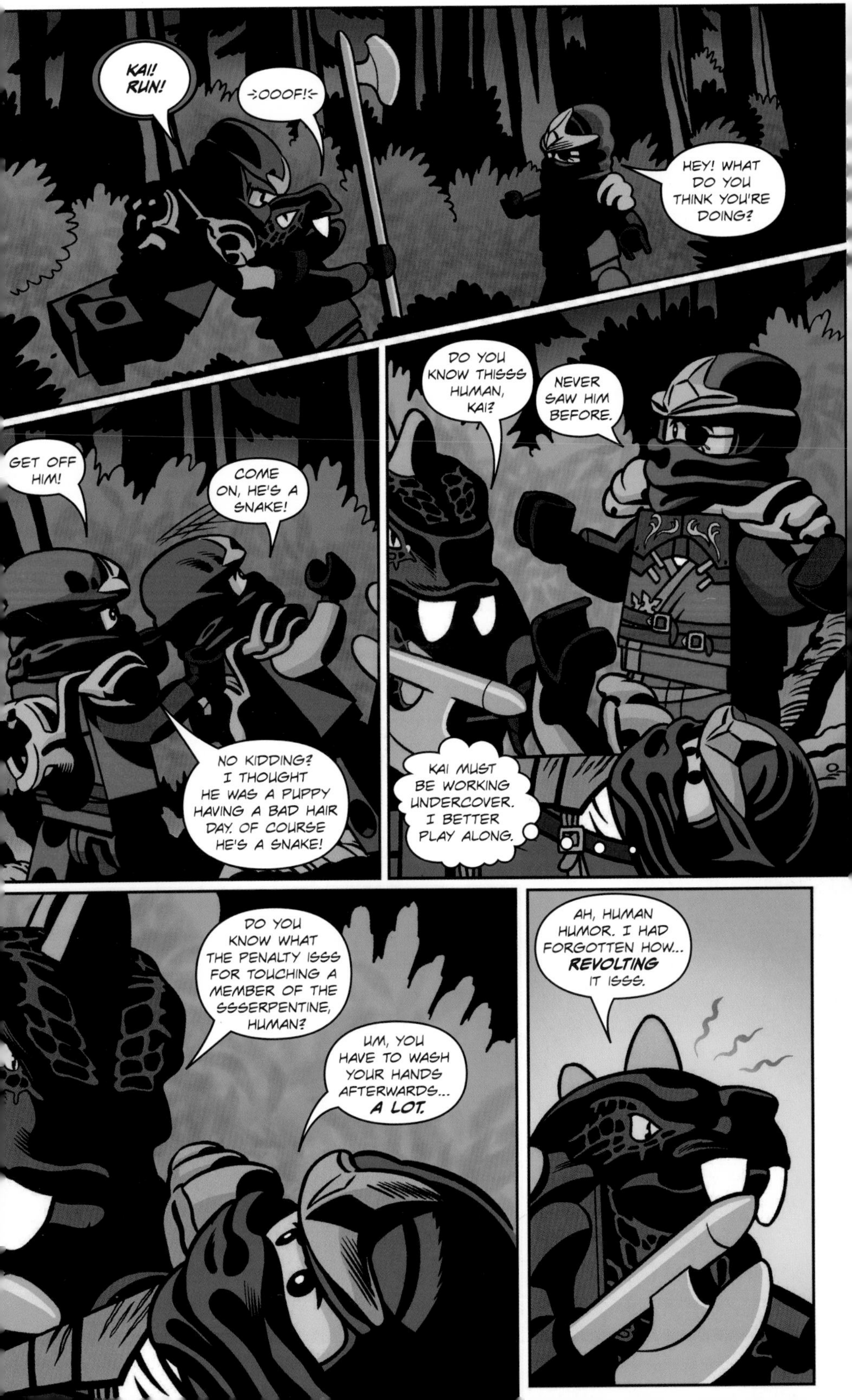
KAI! RUN!
OOOF!
HEY! WHAT DO YOU THINK YOU'RE DOING?
GET OFF HIM!
COME ON, HE'S A SNAKE!
NO KIDDING? I THOUGHT HE WAS A PUPPY HAVING A BAD HAIR DAY. OF COURSE HE'S A SNAKE!
DO YOU KNOW THISSS HUMAN, KAI?
NEVER SAW HIM BEFORE.
KAI MUST BE WORKING UNDERCOVER. I BETTER PLAY ALONG.
DO YOU KNOW WHAT THE PENALTY ISSS FOR TOUCHING A MEMBER OF THE SSSERPENTINE, HUMAN?
UM, YOU HAVE TO WASH YOUR HANDS AFTERWARDS... A LOT.
AH, HUMAN HUMOR. I HAD FORGOTTEN HOW... REVOLTING IT ISSS.

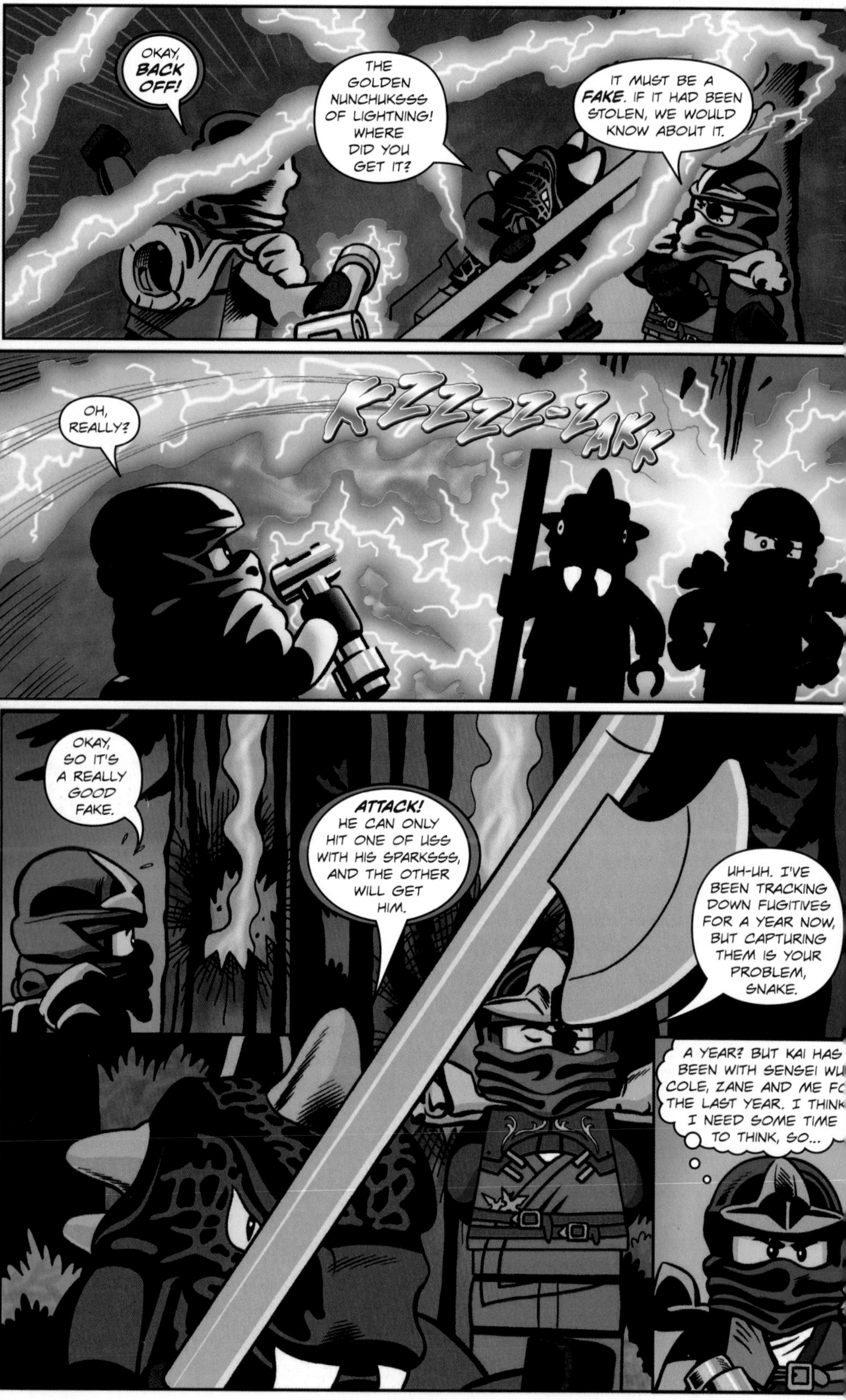
OKAY, BACK OFF!
THE GOLDEN NUNCHUKSSS OF LIGHTNING! WHERE DID YOU GET IT?
IT MUST BE A FAKE. IF IT HAD BEEN STOLEN, WE WOULD KNOW ABOUT IT.
OH, REALLY?
KZZZZZ-ZAKK
OKAY, SO IT'S A REALLY GOOD FAKE.
ATTACK! HE CAN ONLY HIT ONE OF USS WITH HIS SPARKSSS, AND THE OTHER WILL GET HIM.
UH-UH. I'VE BEEN TRACKING DOWN FUGITIVES FOR A YEAR NOW, BUT CAPTURING THEM IS YOUR PROBLEM, SNAKE.
A YEAR? BUT KAI HAS BEEN WITH SENSEI WU COLE, ZANE AND ME FO THE LAST YEAR. I THINK I NEED SOME TIME TO THINK, SO...

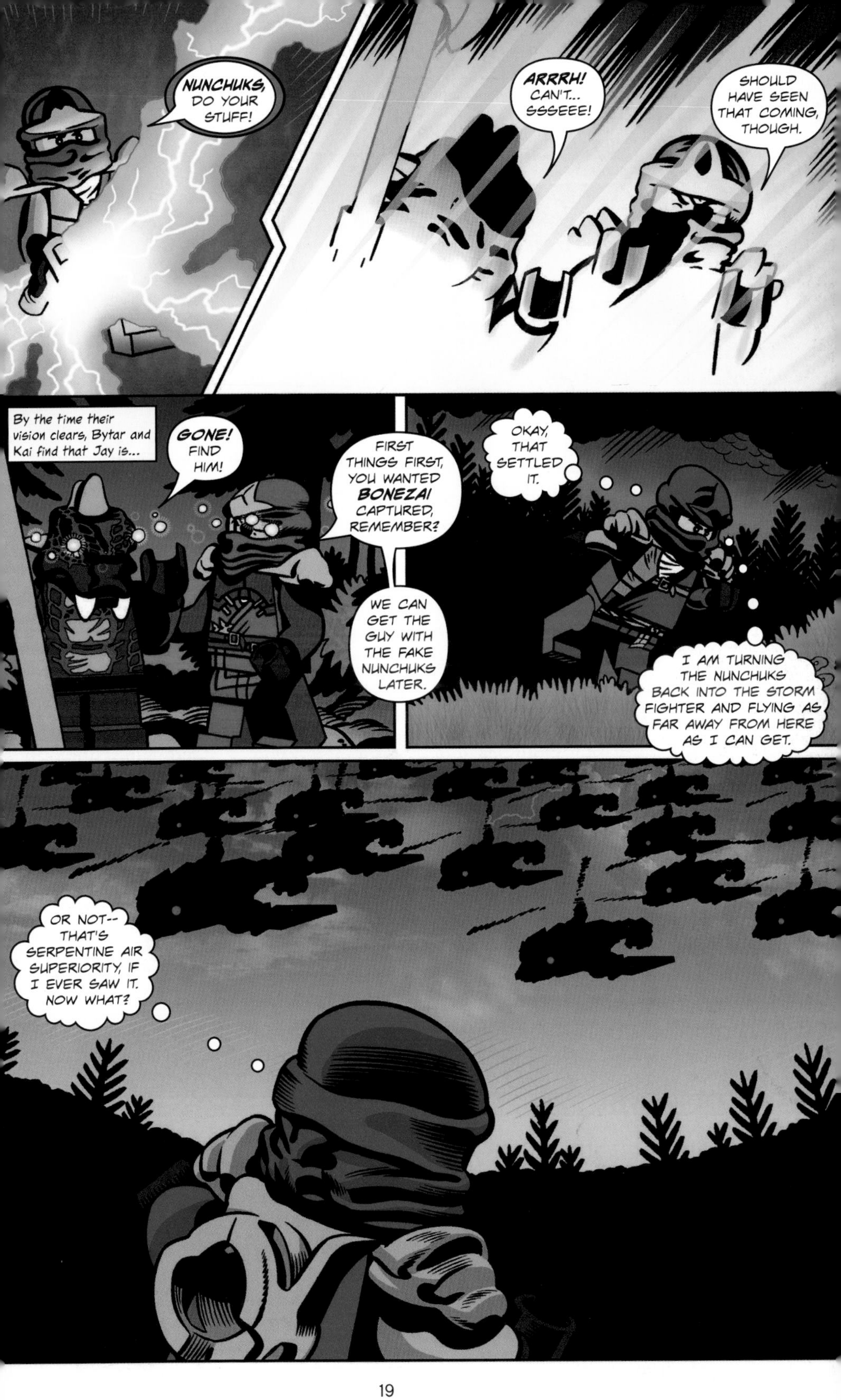
NUNCHUKS, DO YOUR STUFF!
ARRRH! CAN'T... SSSEEE!
SHOULD HAVE SEEN THAT COMING, THOUGH.
By the time their vision clears, Bytar and Kai find that Jay is...
GONE! FIND HIM!
FIRST THINGS FIRST, YOU WANTED BONEZAI CAPTURED, REMEMBER?
WE CAN GET THE GUY WITH THE FAKE NUNCHUKS LATER.
OKAY, THAT SETTLED IT.
I AM TURNING THE NUNCHUKS BACK INTO THE STORM FIGHTER AND FLYING AS FAR AWAY FROM HERE AS I CAN GET.
OR NOT--THAT'S SERPENTINE AIR SUPERIORITY, IF I EVER SAW IT. NOW WHAT?

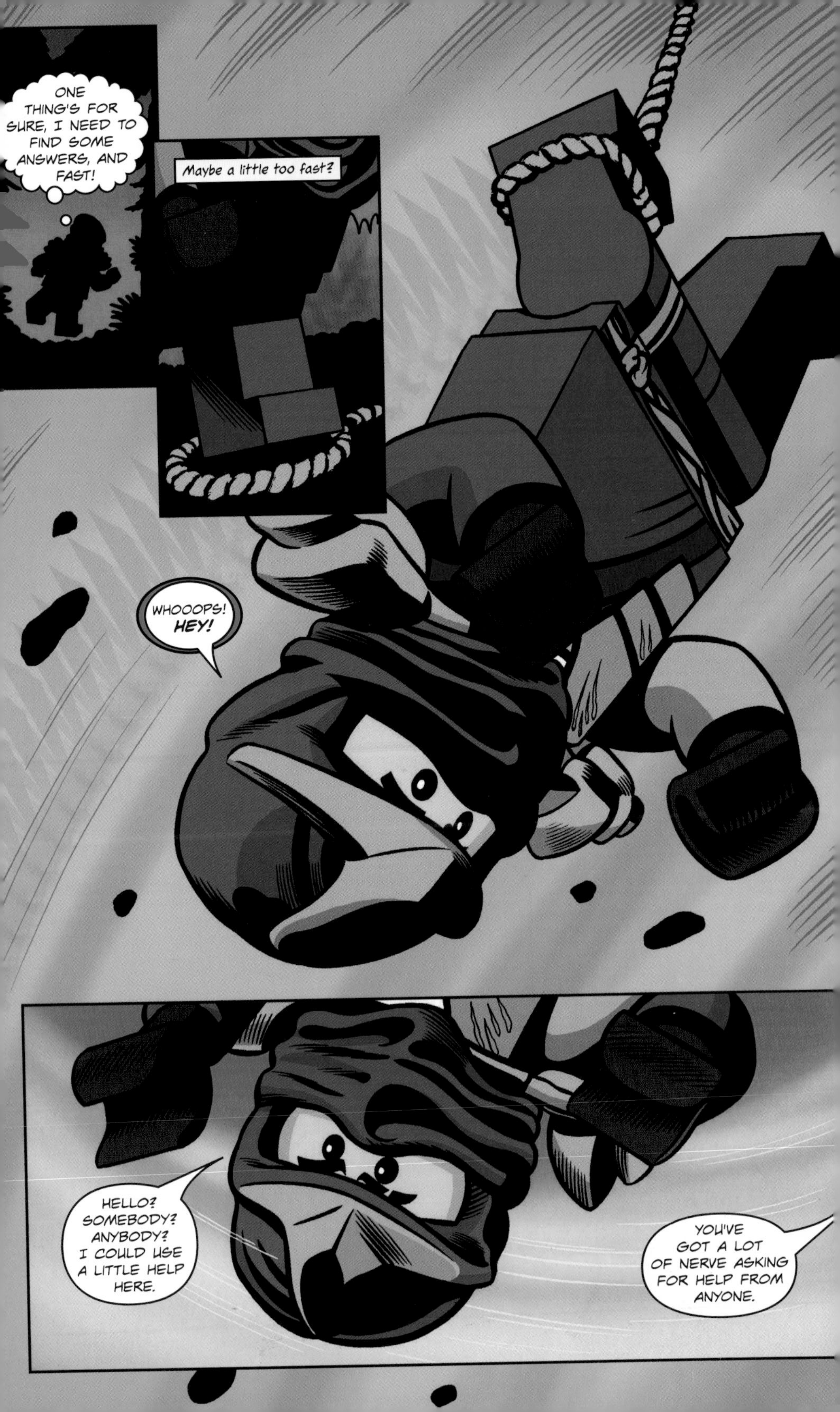
ONE THING'S FOR SURE, I NEED TO FIND SOME ANSWERS, AND FAST!
Maybe a little too fast?
WHOOOPS! **HEY!**
HELLO? SOMEBODY? ANYBODY? I COULD USE A LITTLE HELP HERE.
YOU'VE GOT A LOT OF NERVE ASKING FOR HELP FROM ANYONE.

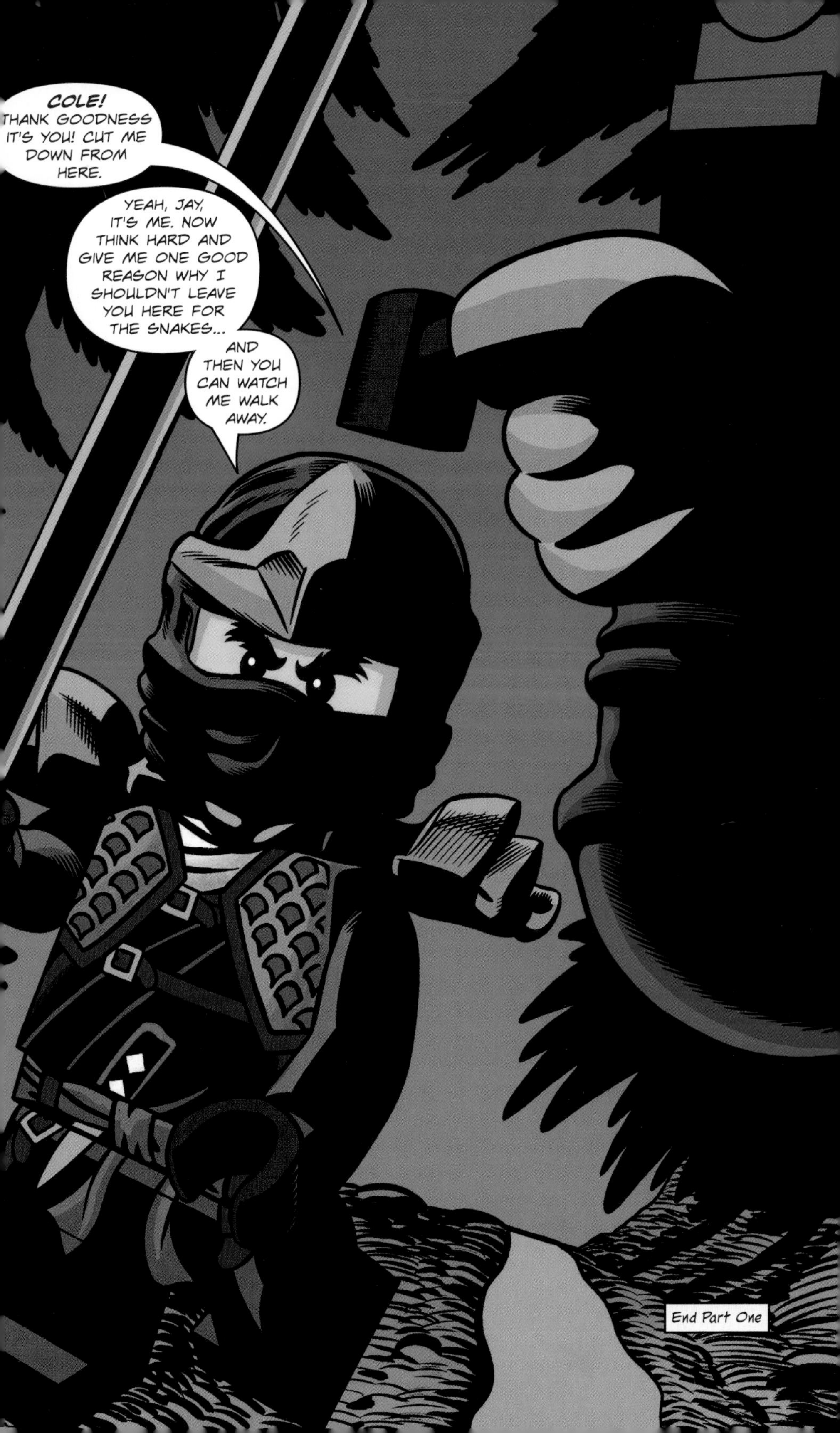
COLE! THANK GOODNESS IT'S YOU! CUT ME DOWN FROM HERE.
YEAH, JAY, IT'S ME. NOW THINK HARD AND GIVE ME ONE GOOD REASON WHY I SHOULDN'T LEAVE YOU HERE FOR THE SNAKES...
AND THEN YOU CAN WATCH ME WALK AWAY.
End Part One

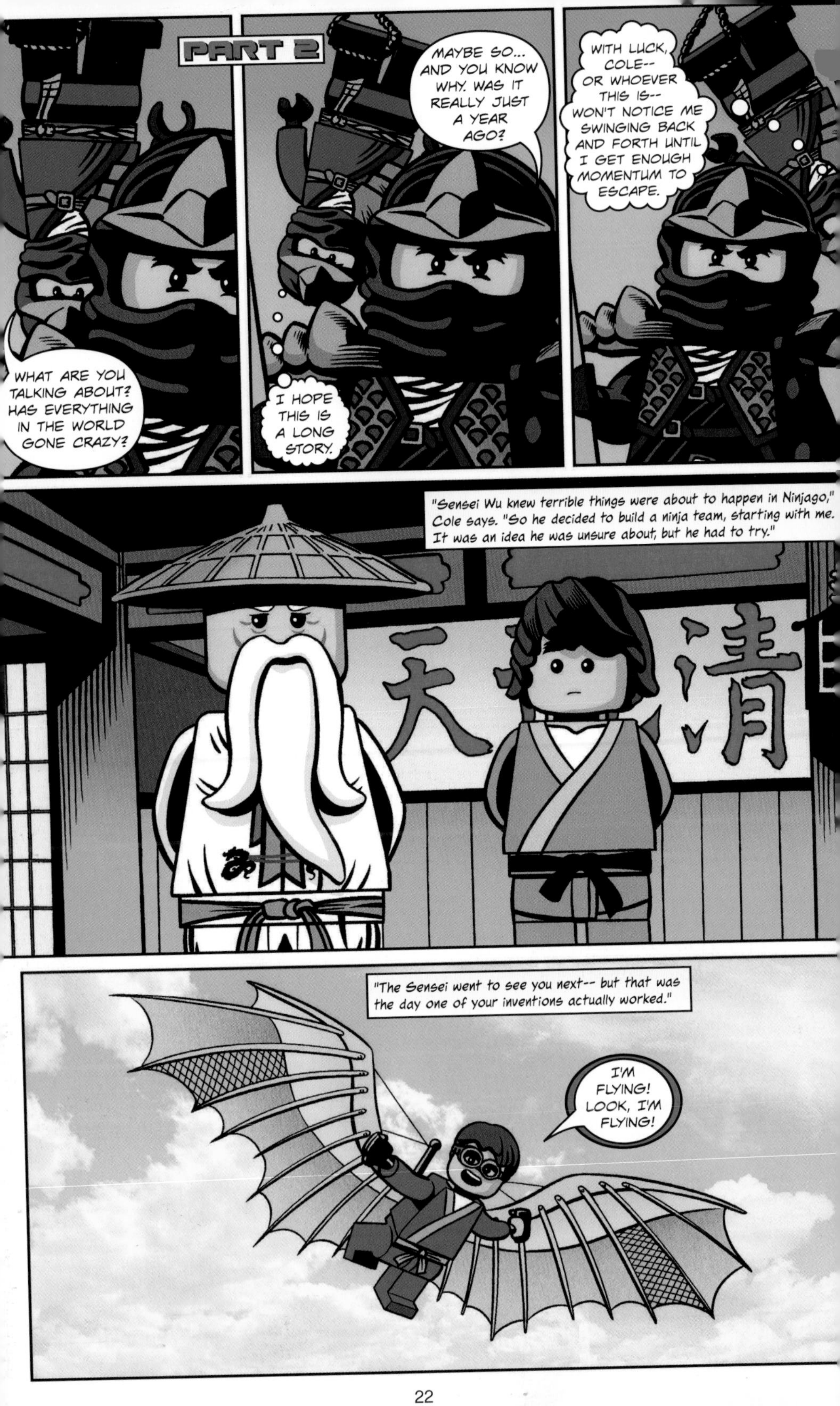
PART 2
WHAT ARE YOU TALKING ABOUT? HAS EVERYTHING IN THE WORLD GONE CRAZY?
MAYBE SO... AND YOU KNOW WHY. WAS IT REALLY JUST A YEAR AGO?
I HOPE THIS IS A LONG STORY.
WITH LUCK, COLE-- OR WHOEVER THIS IS-- WON'T NOTICE ME SWINGING BACK AND FORTH UNTIL I GET ENOUGH MOMENTUM TO ESCAPE.
"Sensei Wu knew terrible things were about to happen in Ninjago," Cole says. "So he decided to build a ninja team, starting with me. It was an idea he was unsure about, but he had to try."
天 清
"The Sensei went to see you next-- but that was the day one of your inventions actually worked."
I'M FLYING! LOOK, I'M FLYING!

"...you finally came down, you weren't mood to listen to Sensei Wu."

...T THIS ...JA TEAM ...BE VITAL ...INJAGO'S ...AFETY!

SKELETON WARRIORS? YOUR NASTY BROTHER COMING BACK FROM THE UNDER-WORLD?

AND YOU'RE GOING TO STOP ALL THAT WITH JUST FOUR GUYS?

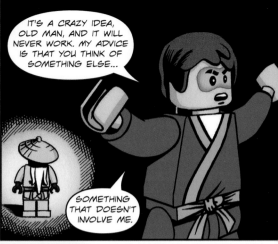

IT'S A CRAZY IDEA, OLD MAN, AND IT WILL NEVER WORK. MY ADVICE IS THAT YOU THINK OF SOMETHING ELSE...

SOMETHING THAT DOESN'T INVOLVE ME.

...ei Wu was so crushed by your response that ...ve up the idea of recruiting a ninja team."

HE'S RIGHT.

FOUR YOUNG MEN, WITH BARELY ANY TRAINING IN SPINJITZU, AGAINST GARMADON AND HIS SKELETON HORDE?

IT WOULD HAVE BEEN A DIS-ASTER.

HUH? NONE OF THAT EVER HAPPENED.

MY WINGS, WELL, HAD A GLITCH, AND I JOINED SENSEI WU'S TEAM RIGHT AWAY.

...TIME TO ...ET OUT OF ...S TRAP AND ...GURE OUT ...AT'S GOING ON.

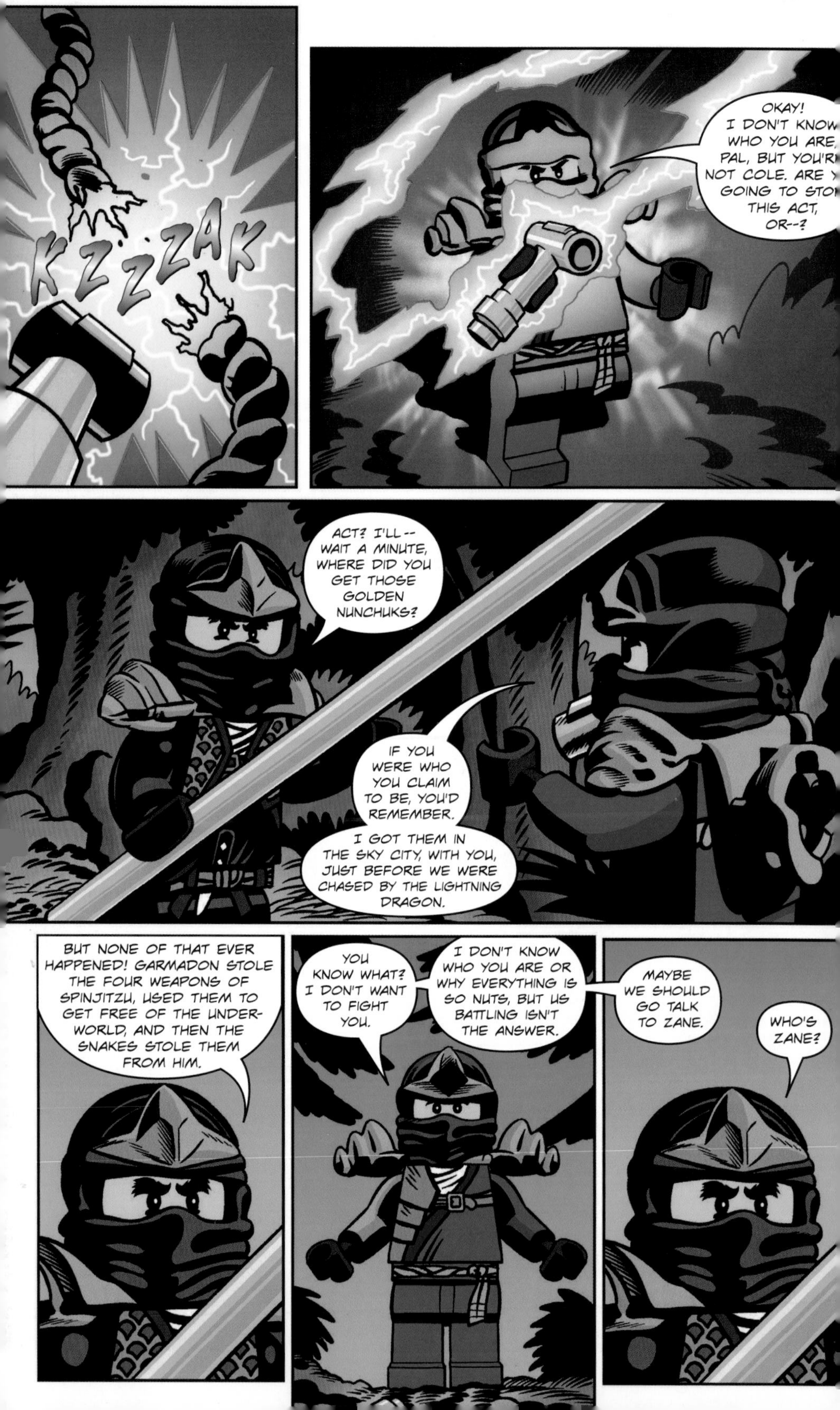
KZZZAK
OKAY! I DON'T KNOW WHO YOU ARE, PAL, BUT YOU'R NOT COLE. ARE Y GOING TO STO THIS ACT, OR--?
ACT? I'LL -- WAIT A MINUTE, WHERE DID YOU GET THOSE GOLDEN NUNCHUKS?
IF YOU WERE WHO YOU CLAIM TO BE, YOU'D REMEMBER.
I GOT THEM IN THE SKY CITY, WITH YOU, JUST BEFORE WE WERE CHASED BY THE LIGHTNING DRAGON.
BUT NONE OF THAT EVER HAPPENED! GARMADON STOLE THE FOUR WEAPONS OF SPINJITZU, USED THEM TO GET FREE OF THE UNDER-WORLD, AND THEN THE SNAKES STOLE THEM FROM HIM.
YOU KNOW WHAT? I DON'T WANT TO FIGHT YOU.
I DON'T KNOW WHO YOU ARE OR WHY EVERYTHING IS SO NUTS, BUT US BATTLING ISN'T THE ANSWER.
MAYBE WE SHOULD GO TALK TO ZANE.
WHO'S ZANE?

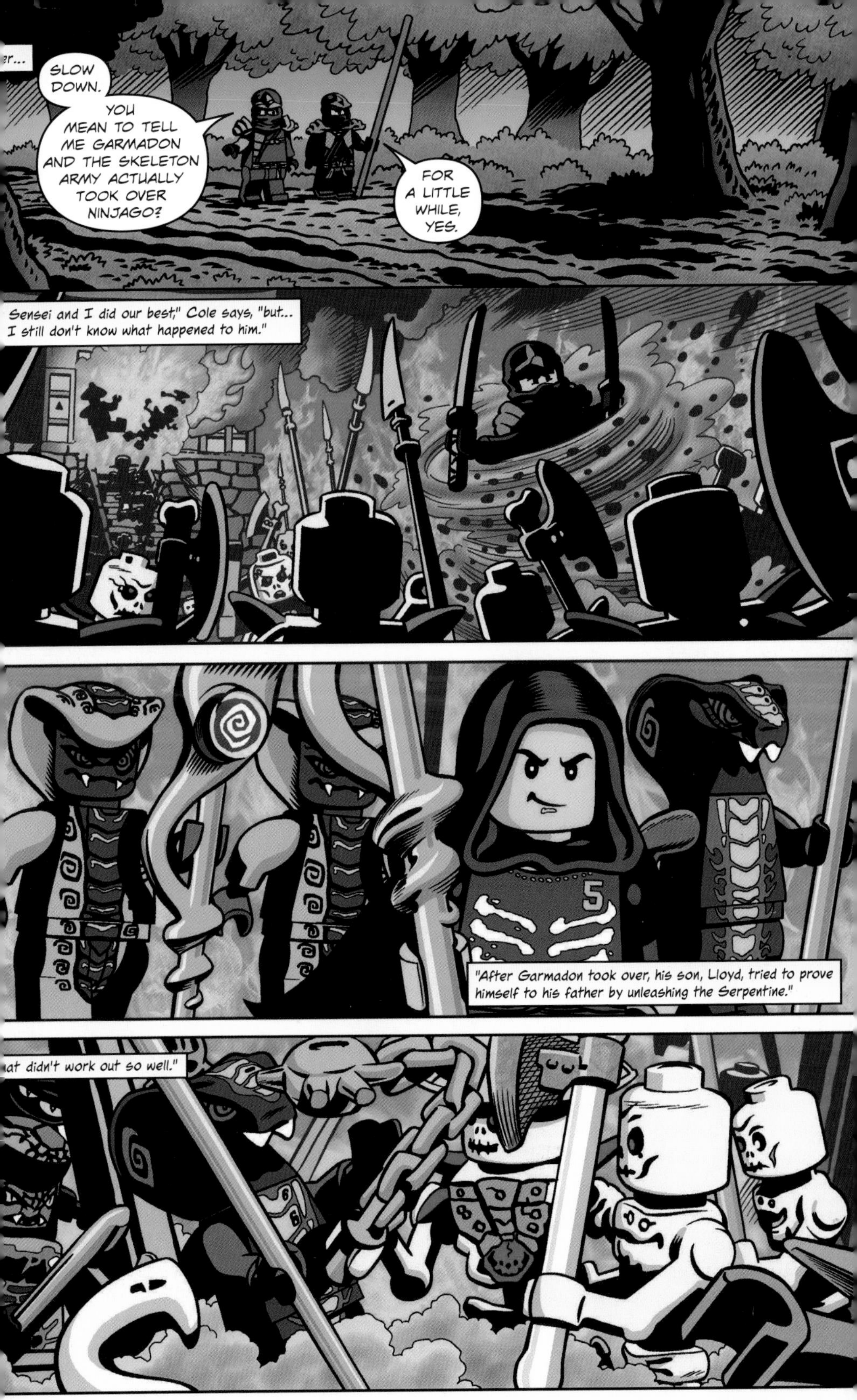
er...
SLOW DOWN.
YOU MEAN TO TELL ME GARMADON AND THE SKELETON ARMY ACTUALLY TOOK OVER NINJAGO?
FOR A LITTLE WHILE, YES.
Sensei and I did our best," Cole says, "but... I still don't know what happened to him."
"After Garmadon took over, his son, Lloyd, tried to prove himself to his father by unleashing the Serpentine."
at didn't work out so well."

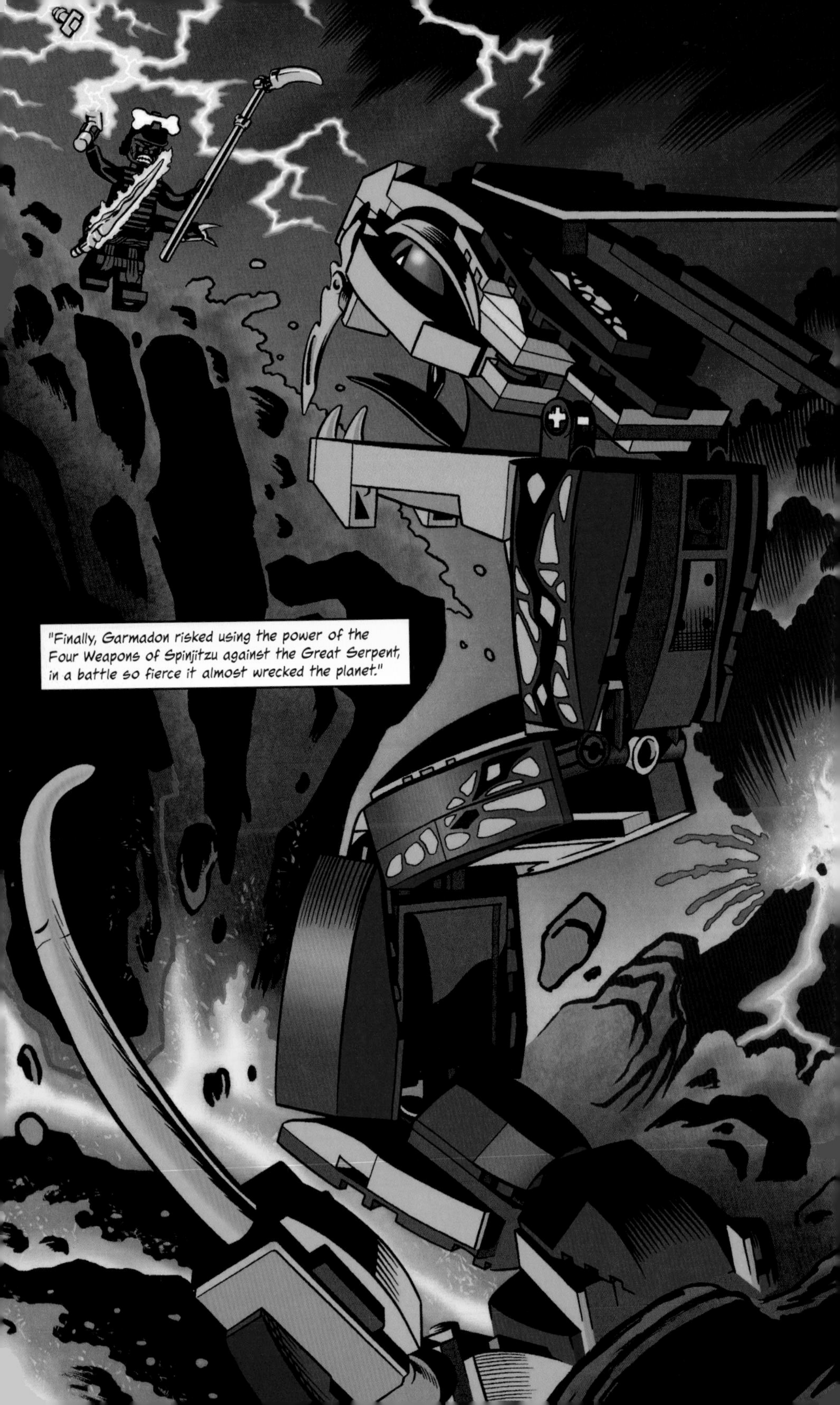
"Finally, Garmadon risked using the power of the Four Weapons of Spinjitzu against the Great Serpent, in a battle so fierce it almost wrecked the planet."

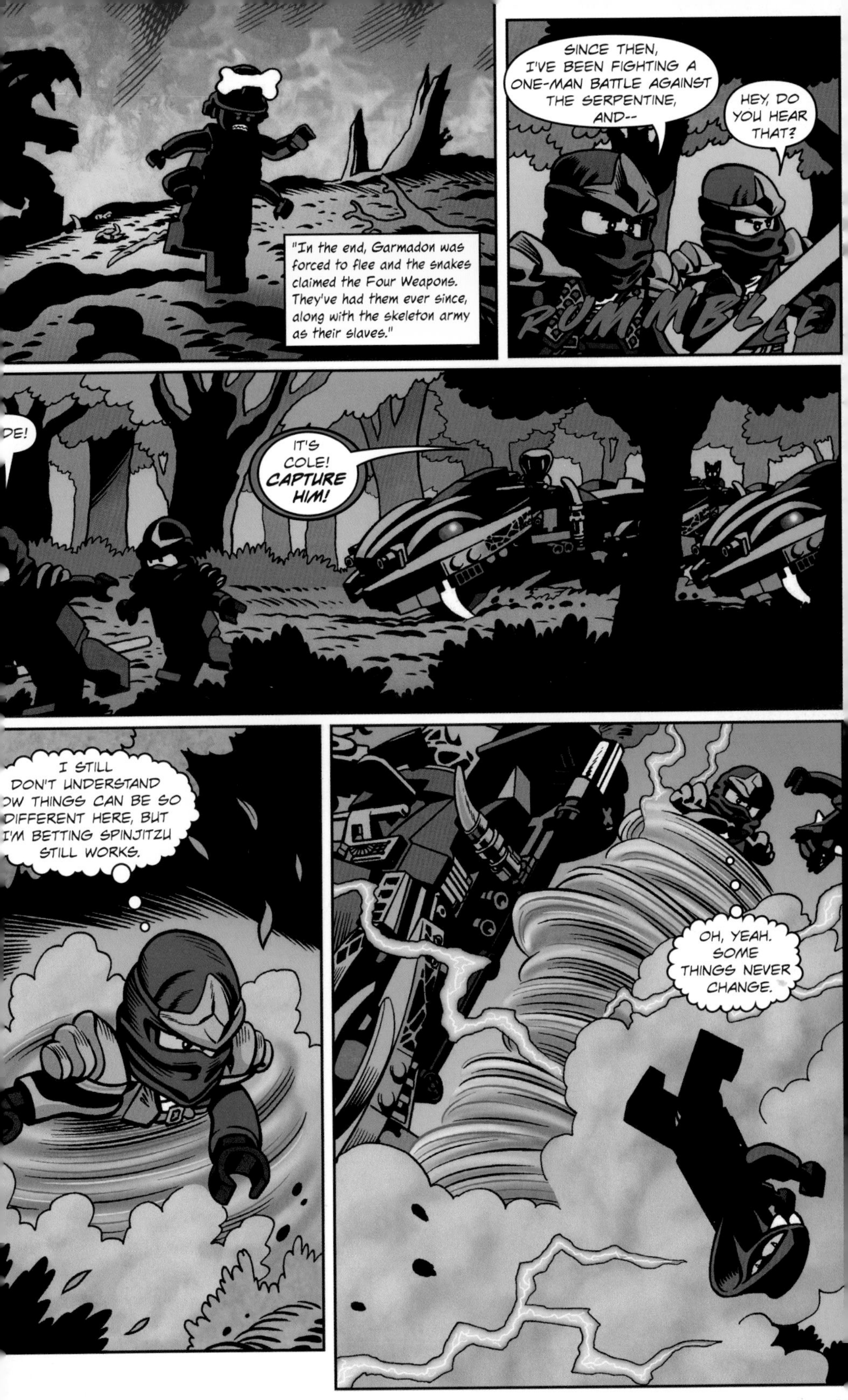
"In the end, Garmadon was forced to flee and the snakes claimed the Four Weapons. They've had them ever since, along with the skeleton army as their slaves."
SINCE THEN, I'VE BEEN FIGHTING A ONE-MAN BATTLE AGAINST THE SERPENTINE, AND--
HEY, DO YOU HEAR THAT?
RUMMBLLE
DE!
IT'S COLE! CAPTURE HIM!
I STILL DON'T UNDERSTAND OW THINGS CAN BE SO DIFFERENT HERE, BUT I'M BETTING SPINJITZU STILL WORKS.
OH, YEAH. SOME THINGS NEVER CHANGE.

YOU HAVE INTERFERED WITH THE SSSERPENTINE TOO OFTEN, HUMAN!

IT'S NICE TO KNOW YOU CARE, SNAKE-BREATH.

PYTHOR WANTS YOU TAKEN ALIVE SSSO THE GREAT SSSERPENT CAN DECIDE YOUR FATE... BUT HE SSSAID NOTHING ABOUT YOU BEING UNHARMED.

HE'S ALL HEART-- AND YOU'RE ALL MOUTH.

YOU'VE NEVER BE ABLE TO S ME, EVE WHEN KAI HELPIN YOU.

BAH! YOU CAN'T TRUSSST A HUMAN TO DO A JOB RIGHT, EVEN IF HE IS FIGHTING FOR HISSS SSSISTER'S LIFE.

THAT'S RIGHT, YOU WERE THE ONE WHO CAPTURED KAI'S SISTER, NYA, WEREN'T YOU?

THEN THIS ONE IS FOR HER!

BAMM

WARRIORSSS, TO MY SSSIDE!

UH-OH, LOOKS LIKE COLE IS IN TROUBLE. I BETTER GO HELP.

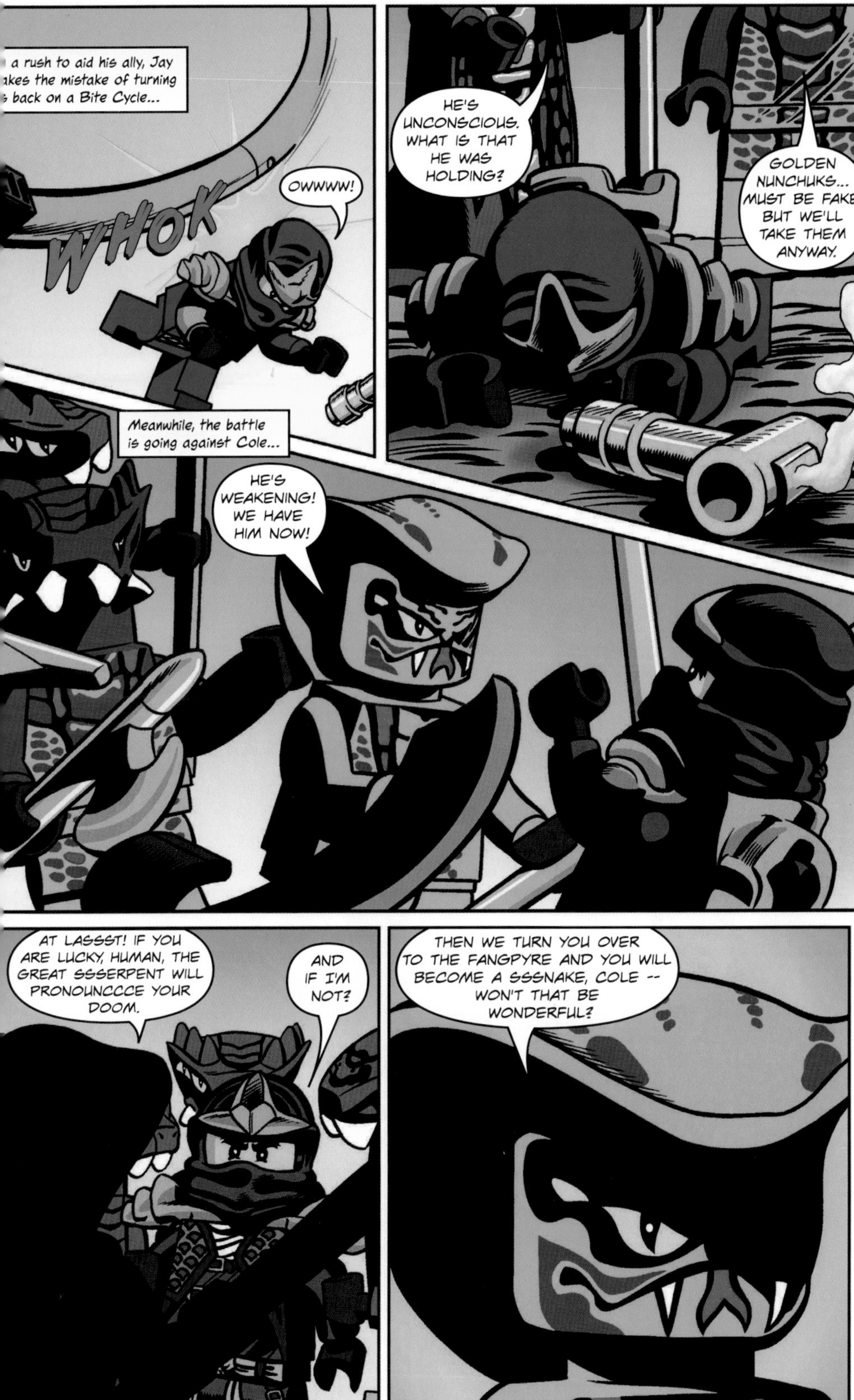

a rush to aid his ally, Jay akes the mistake of turning s back on a Bite Cycle...
WHOK
OWWWW!
HE'S UNCONSCIOUS. WHAT IS THAT HE WAS HOLDING?
GOLDEN NUNCHUKS... MUST BE FAKE. BUT WE'LL TAKE THEM ANYWAY.
Meanwhile, the battle is going against Cole...
HE'S WEAKENING! WE HAVE HIM NOW!
AT LASSST! IF YOU ARE LUCKY, HUMAN, THE GREAT SSSERPENT WILL PRONOUNCCCE YOUR DOOM.
AND IF I'M NOT?
THEN WE TURN YOU OVER TO THE FANGPYRE AND YOU WILL BECOME A SSSNAKE, COLE -- WON'T THAT BE WONDERFUL?

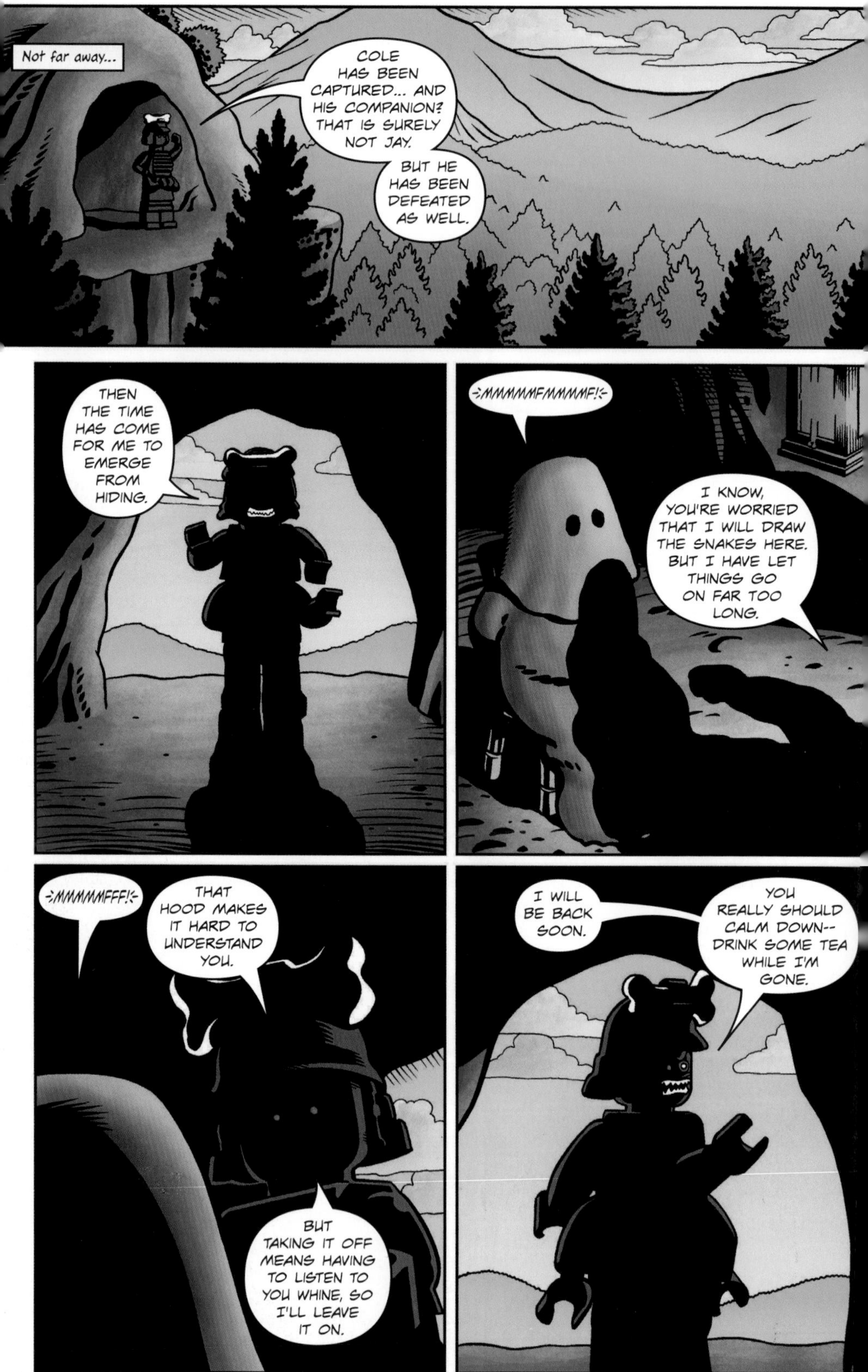
Not far away...
COLE HAS BEEN CAPTURED... AND HIS COMPANION? THAT IS SURELY NOT JAY.
BUT HE HAS BEEN DEFEATED AS WELL.
THEN THE TIME HAS COME FOR ME TO EMERGE FROM HIDING.
-MMMMMFMMMMF!-
I KNOW, YOU'RE WORRIED THAT I WILL DRAW THE SNAKES HERE. BUT I HAVE LET THINGS GO ON FAR TOO LONG.
-MMMMMFFF!-
THAT HOOD MAKES IT HARD TO UNDERSTAND YOU.
BUT TAKING IT OFF MEANS HAVING TO LISTEN TO YOU WHINE, SO I'LL LEAVE IT ON.
I WILL BE BACK SOON.
YOU REALLY SHOULD CALM DOWN-- DRINK SOME TEA WHILE I'M GONE.

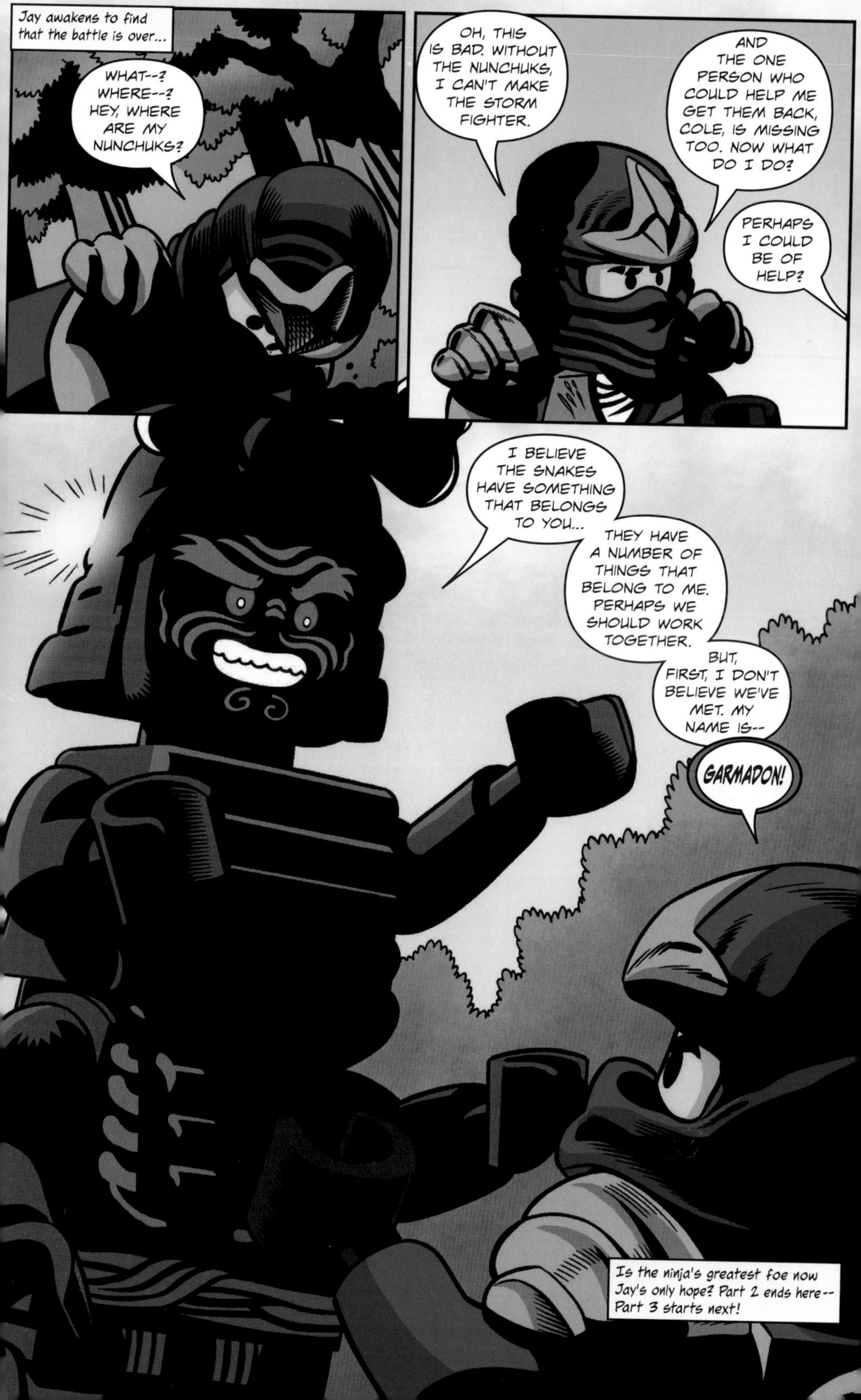
Jay awakens to find that the battle is over...
WHAT--? WHERE--? HEY, WHERE ARE MY NUNCHUKS?
OH, THIS IS BAD. WITHOUT THE NUNCHUKS, I CAN'T MAKE THE STORM FIGHTER.
AND THE ONE PERSON WHO COULD HELP ME GET THEM BACK, COLE, IS MISSING TOO. NOW WHAT DO I DO?
PERHAPS I COULD BE OF HELP?
I BELIEVE THE SNAKES HAVE SOMETHING THAT BELONGS TO YOU...
THEY HAVE A NUMBER OF THINGS THAT BELONG TO ME. PERHAPS WE SHOULD WORK TOGETHER.
BUT, FIRST, I DON'T BELIEVE WE'VE MET. MY NAME IS--
GARMADON!
Is the ninja's greatest foe now Jay's only hope? Part 2 ends here--Part 3 starts next!

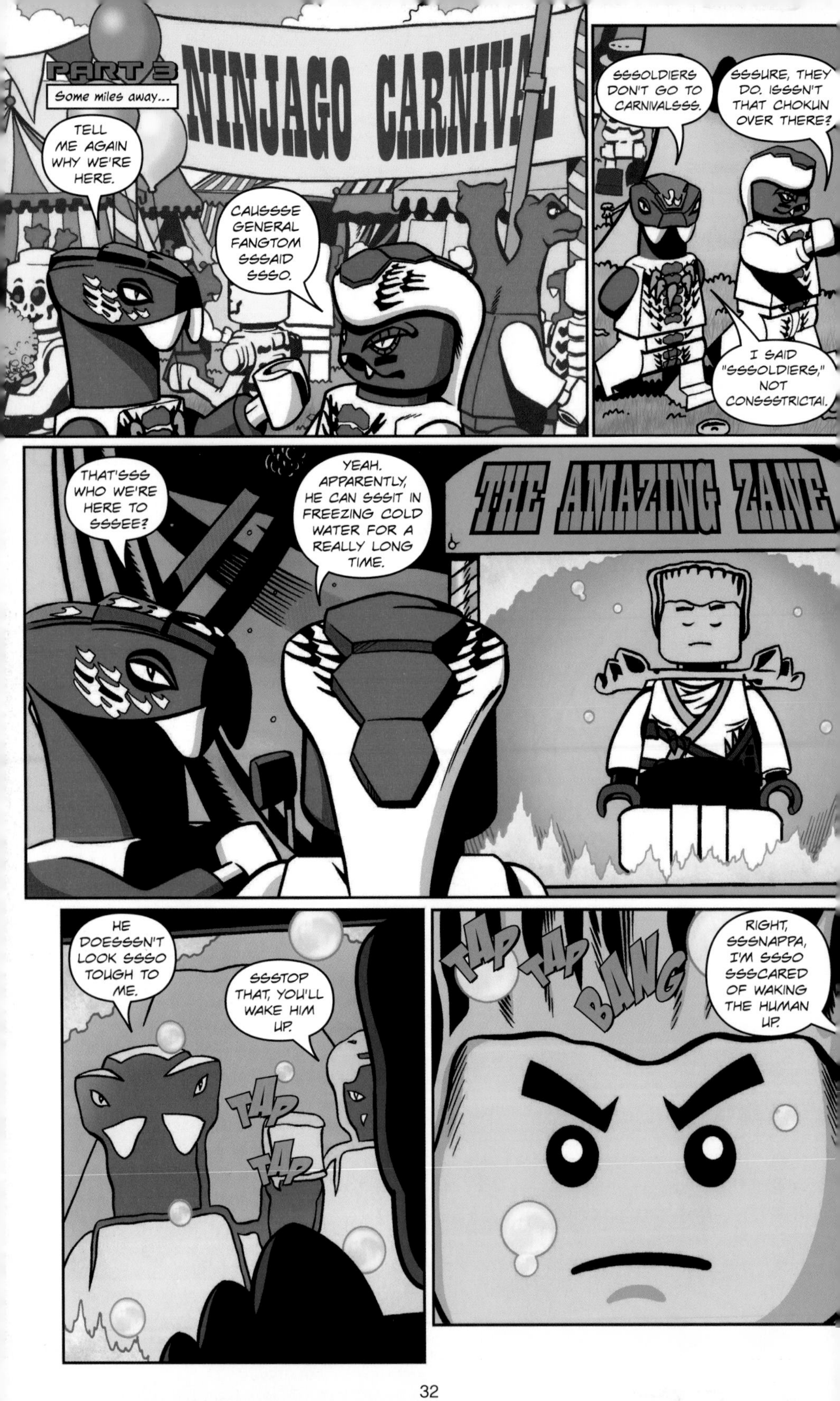
NINJAGO CARNIVAL
PART 3
Some miles away...
TELL ME AGAIN WHY WE'RE HERE.
CAUSSSE GENERAL FANGTOM SSSAID SSSO.
SSSOLDIERS DON'T GO TO CARNIVALSSS.
SSSURE, THEY DO. ISSSN'T THAT CHOKUN OVER THERE?
I SAID "SSSOLDIERS," NOT CONSSSTRICTAI.
THAT'SSS WHO WE'RE HERE TO SSSEE?
YEAH. APPARENTLY, HE CAN SSSIT IN FREEZING COLD WATER FOR A REALLY LONG TIME.
THE AMAZING ZANE
HE DOESSSN'T LOOK SSSO TOUGH TO ME.
SSSTOP THAT, YOU'LL WAKE HIM UP.
TAP
TAP
TAP TAP BANG
RIGHT, SSSNAPPA, I'M SSSO SSSCARED OF WAKING THE HUMAN UP.

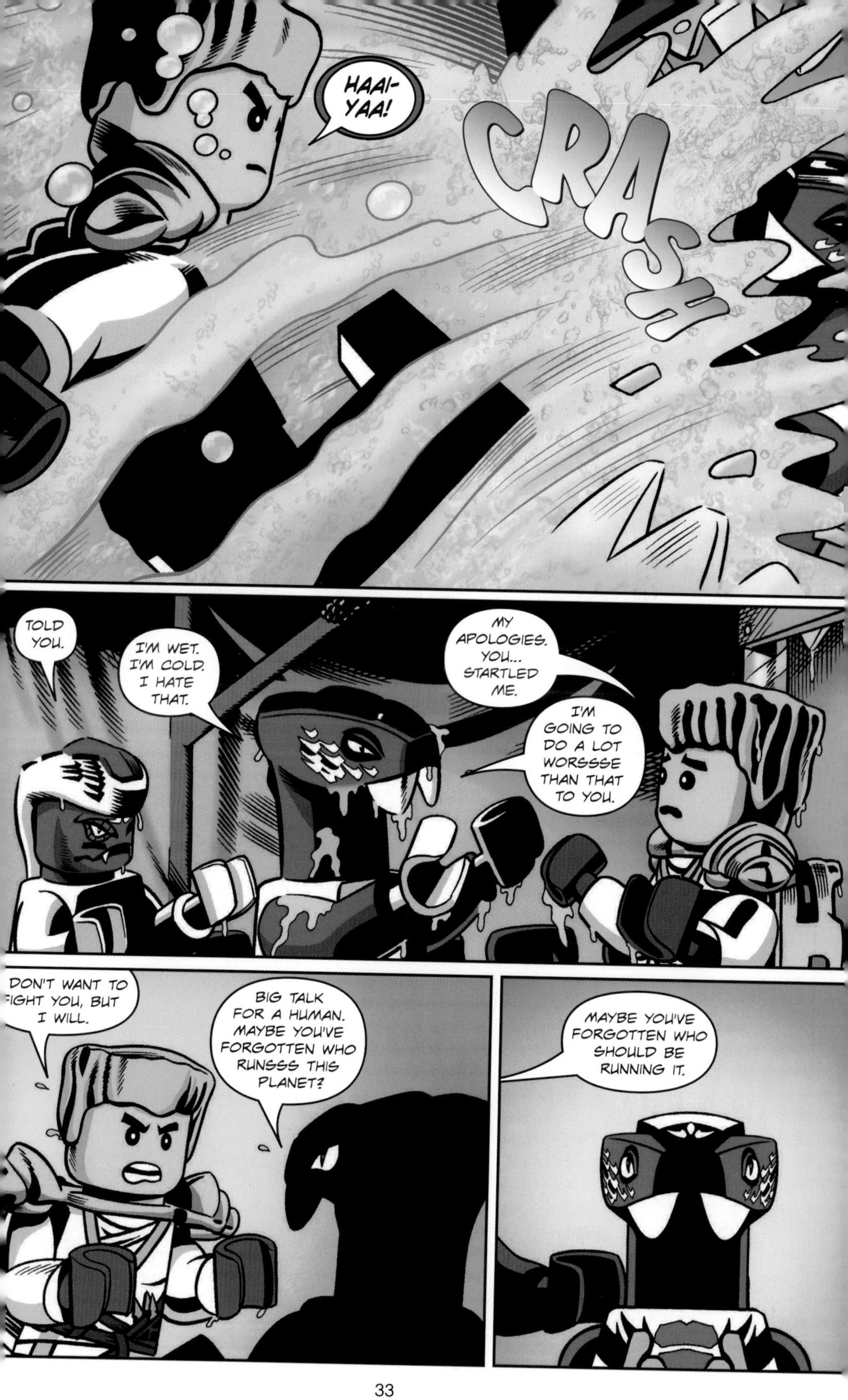
HAAI-YAA!
CRASH
TOLD YOU.
I'M WET. I'M COLD. I HATE THAT.
MY APOLOGIES. YOU... STARTLED ME.
I'M GOING TO DO A LOT WORSSSE THAN THAT TO YOU.
DON'T WANT TO FIGHT YOU, BUT I WILL.
BIG TALK FOR A HUMAN. MAYBE YOU'VE FORGOTTEN WHO RUNSSS THIS PLANET?
MAYBE YOU'VE FORGOTTEN WHO SHOULD BE RUNNING IT.

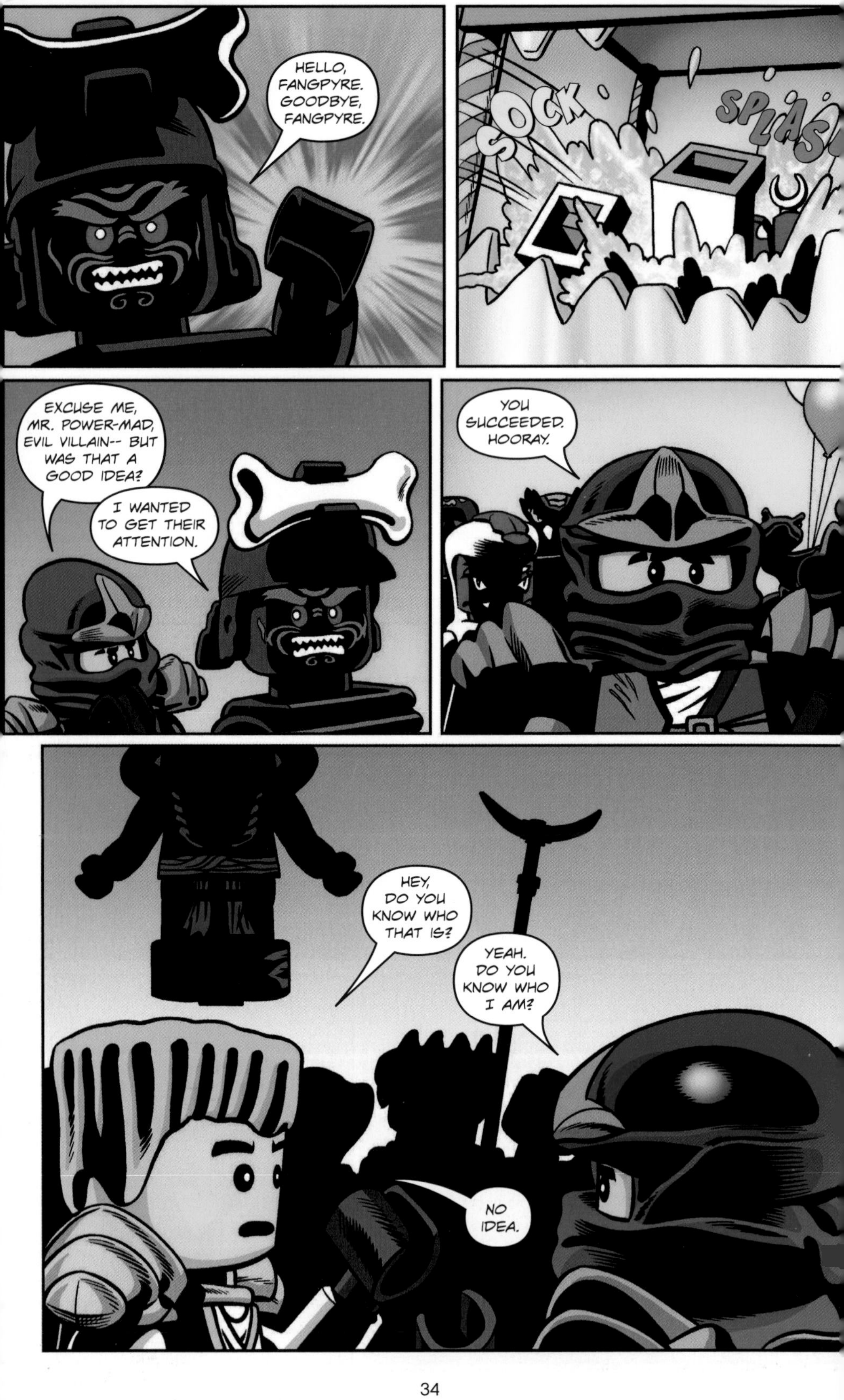
HELLO, FANGPYRE. GOODBYE, FANGPYRE.
SOCK
SPLAS
EXCUSE ME, MR. POWER-MAD, EVIL VILLAIN-- BUT WAS THAT A GOOD IDEA?
I WANTED TO GET THEIR ATTENTION.
YOU SUCCEEDED. HOORAY.
HEY, DO YOU KNOW WHO THAT IS?
YEAH. DO YOU KNOW WHO I AM?
NO IDEA.

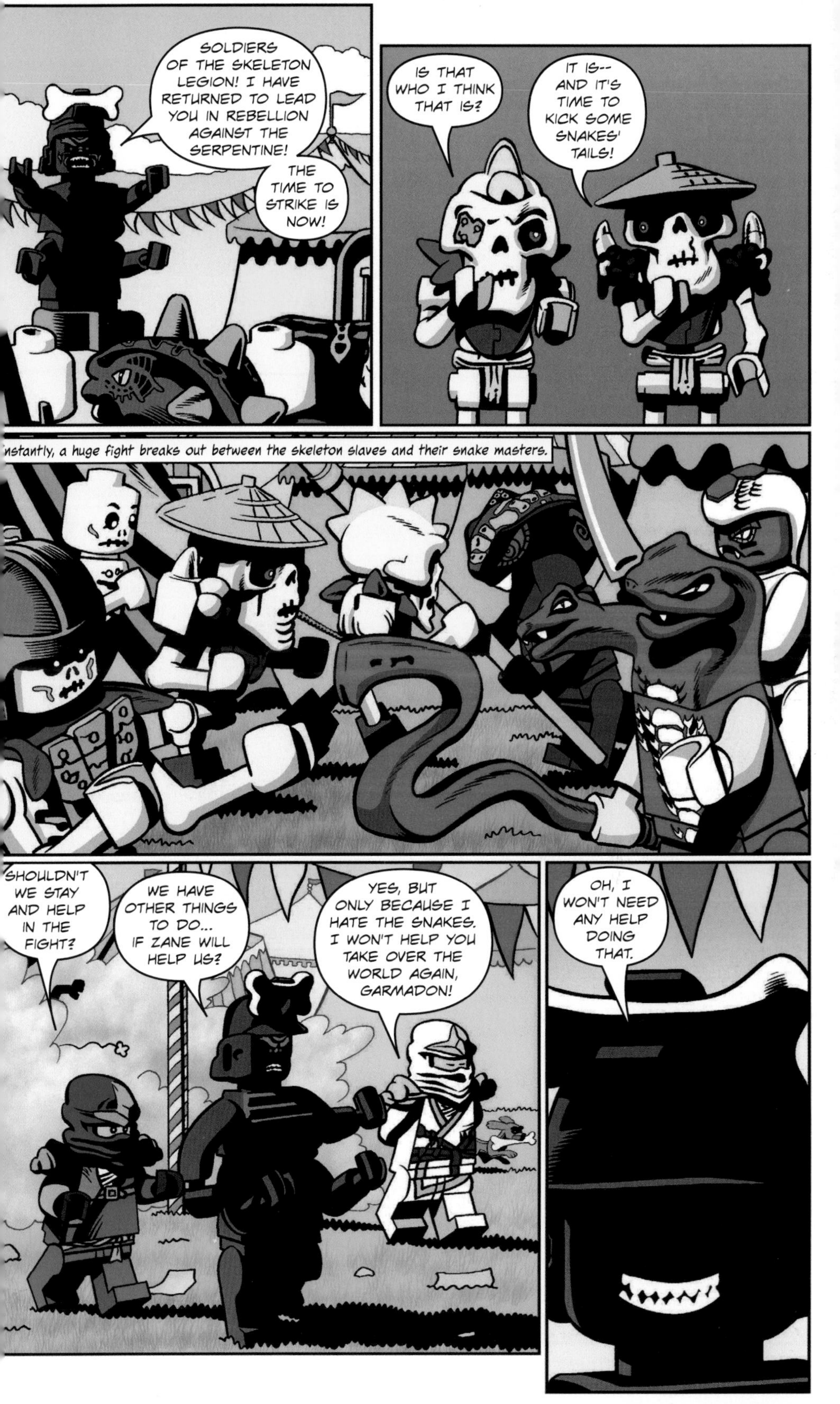
SOLDIERS OF THE SKELETON LEGION! I HAVE RETURNED TO LEAD YOU IN REBELLION AGAINST THE SERPENTINE!
THE TIME TO STRIKE IS NOW!
IS THAT WHO I THINK THAT IS?
IT IS-- AND IT'S TIME TO KICK SOME SNAKES' TAILS!
nstantly, a huge fight breaks out between the skeleton slaves and their snake masters.
SHOULDN'T WE STAY AND HELP IN THE FIGHT?
WE HAVE OTHER THINGS TO DO... IF ZANE WILL HELP US?
YES, BUT ONLY BECAUSE I HATE THE SNAKES. I WON'T HELP YOU TAKE OVER THE WORLD AGAIN, GARMADON!
OH, I WON'T NEED ANY HELP DOING THAT.

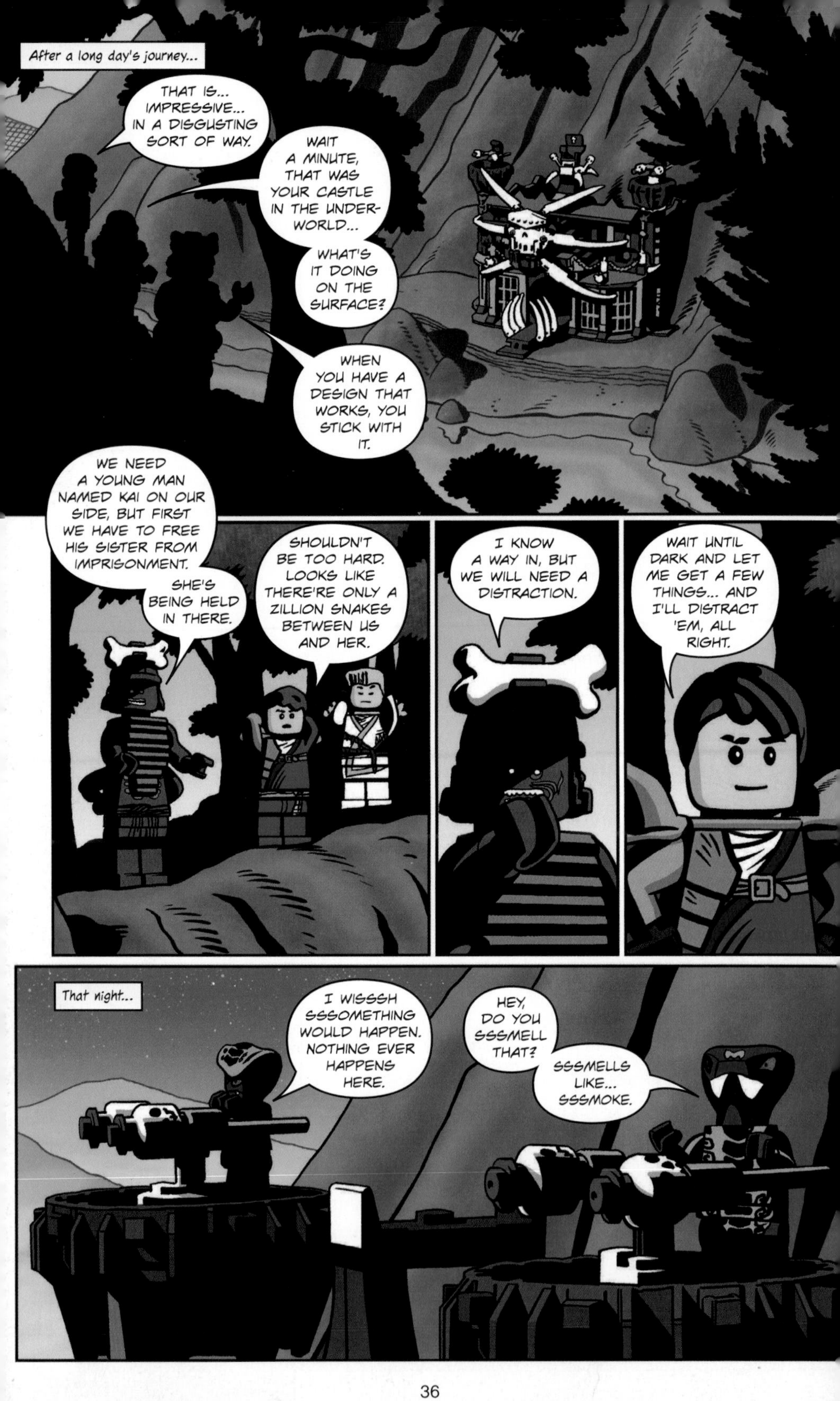
After a long day's journey...
THAT IS... IMPRESSIVE... IN A DISGUSTING SORT OF WAY.
WAIT A MINUTE, THAT WAS YOUR CASTLE IN THE UNDER-WORLD...
WHAT'S IT DOING ON THE SURFACE?
WHEN YOU HAVE A DESIGN THAT WORKS, YOU STICK WITH IT.
WE NEED A YOUNG MAN NAMED KAI ON OUR SIDE, BUT FIRST WE HAVE TO FREE HIS SISTER FROM IMPRISONMENT.
SHE'S BEING HELD IN THERE.
SHOULDN'T BE TOO HARD. LOOKS LIKE THERE'RE ONLY A ZILLION SNAKES BETWEEN US AND HER.
I KNOW A WAY IN, BUT WE WILL NEED A DISTRACTION.
WAIT UNTIL DARK AND LET ME GET A FEW THINGS... AND I'LL DISTRACT 'EM, ALL RIGHT.
That night...
I WISSSH SSSOMETHING WOULD HAPPEN. NOTHING EVER HAPPENS HERE.
HEY, DO YOU SSSMELL THAT?
SSSMELLS LIKE... SSSMOKE.

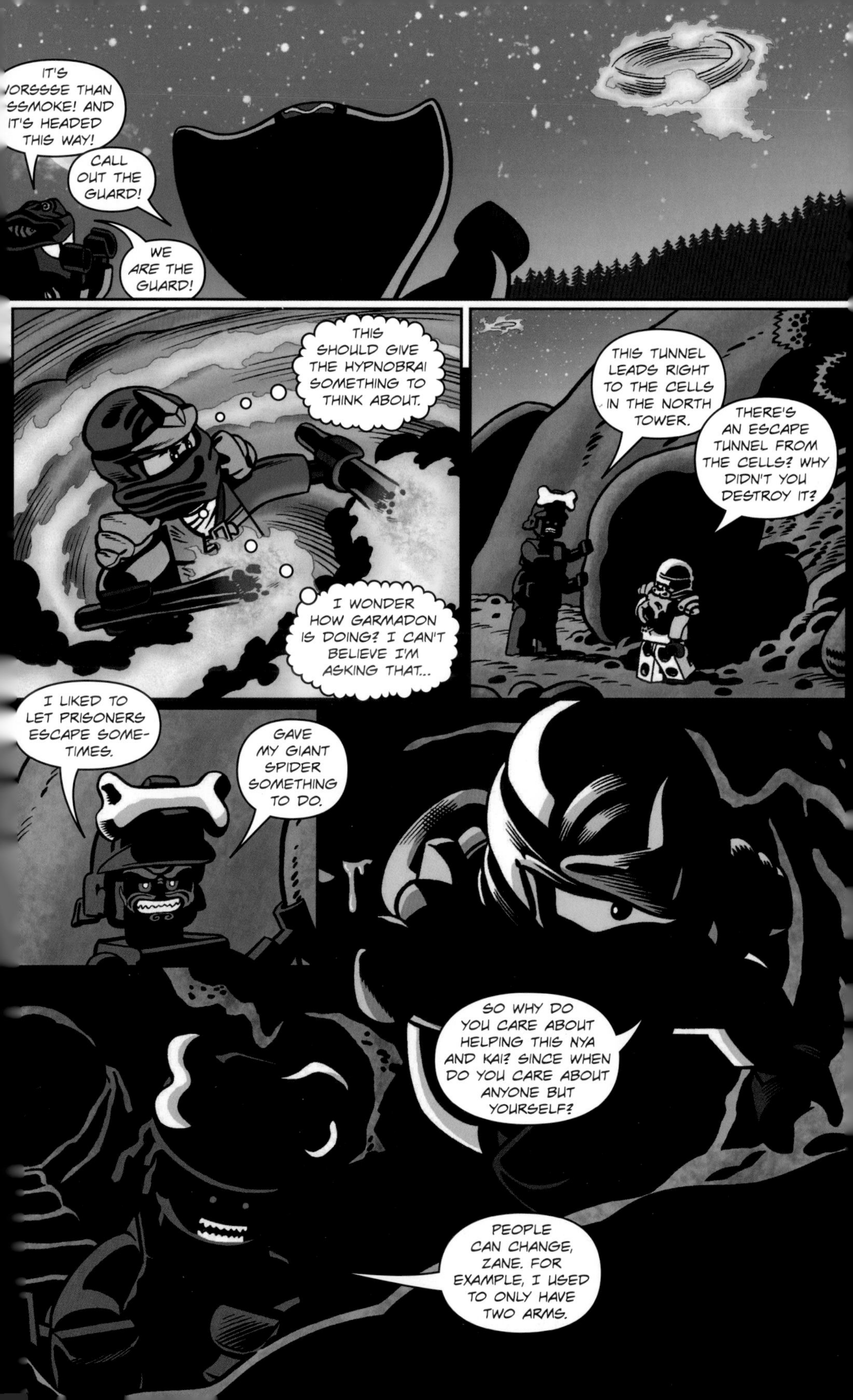
IT'S ORSSSE THAN SSMOKE! AND IT'S HEADED THIS WAY!
CALL OUT THE GUARD!
WE ARE THE GUARD!
THIS SHOULD GIVE THE HYPNOBRAI SOMETHING TO THINK ABOUT.
I WONDER HOW GARMADON IS DOING? I CAN'T BELIEVE I'M ASKING THAT...
THIS TUNNEL LEADS RIGHT TO THE CELLS IN THE NORTH TOWER.
THERE'S AN ESCAPE TUNNEL FROM THE CELLS? WHY DIDN'T YOU DESTROY IT?
I LIKED TO LET PRISONERS ESCAPE SOME-TIMES.
GAVE MY GIANT SPIDER SOMETHING TO DO.
SO WHY DO YOU CARE ABOUT HELPING THIS NYA AND KAI? SINCE WHEN DO YOU CARE ABOUT ANYONE BUT YOURSELF?
PEOPLE CAN CHANGE, ZANE. FOR EXAMPLE, I USED TO ONLY HAVE TWO ARMS.

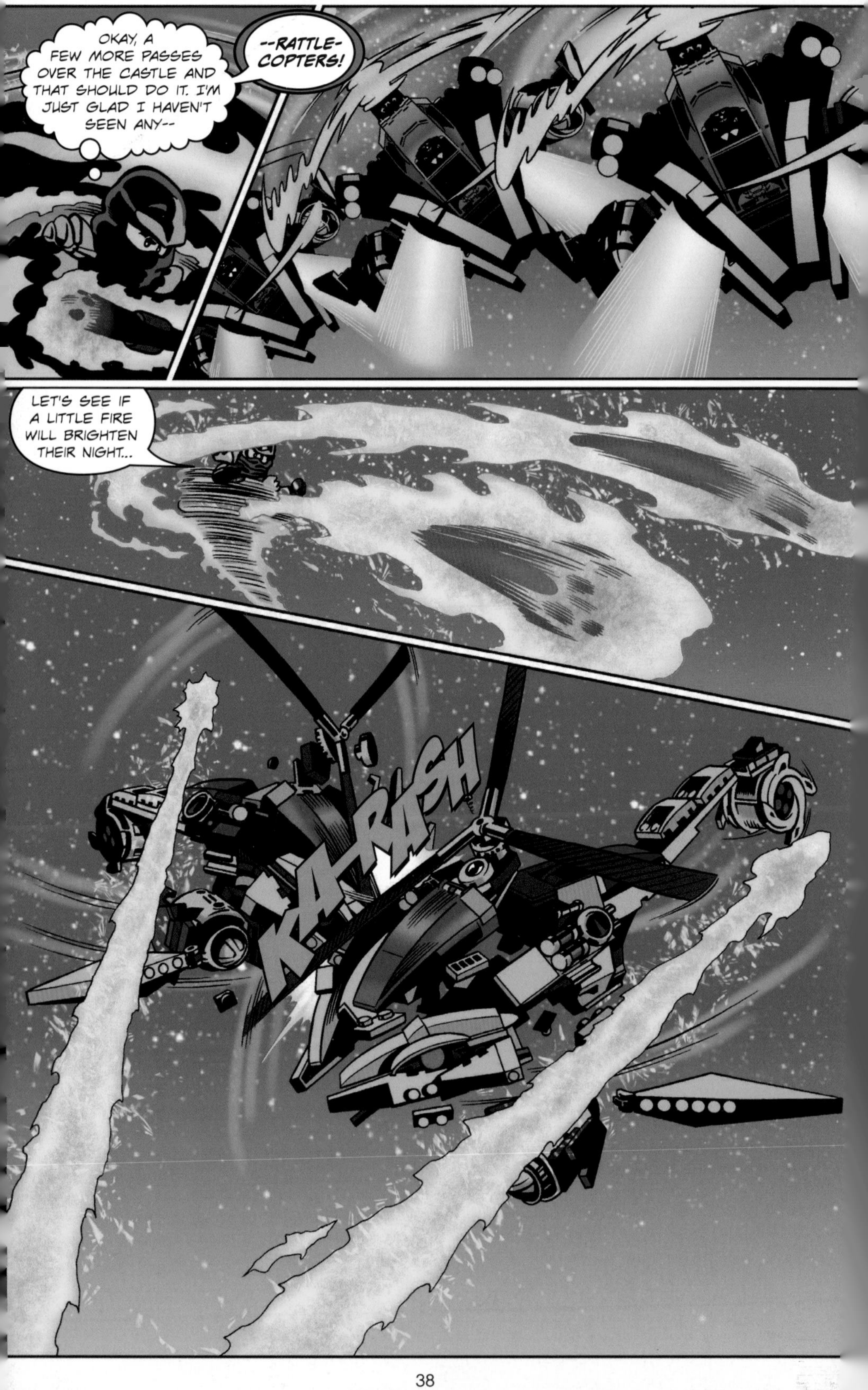
OKAY, A FEW MORE PASSES OVER THE CASTLE AND THAT SHOULD DO IT. I'M JUST GLAD I HAVEN'T SEEN ANY--
--RATTLE-COPTERS!
LET'S SEE IF A LITTLE FIRE WILL BRIGHTEN THEIR NIGHT...
KA-RASH

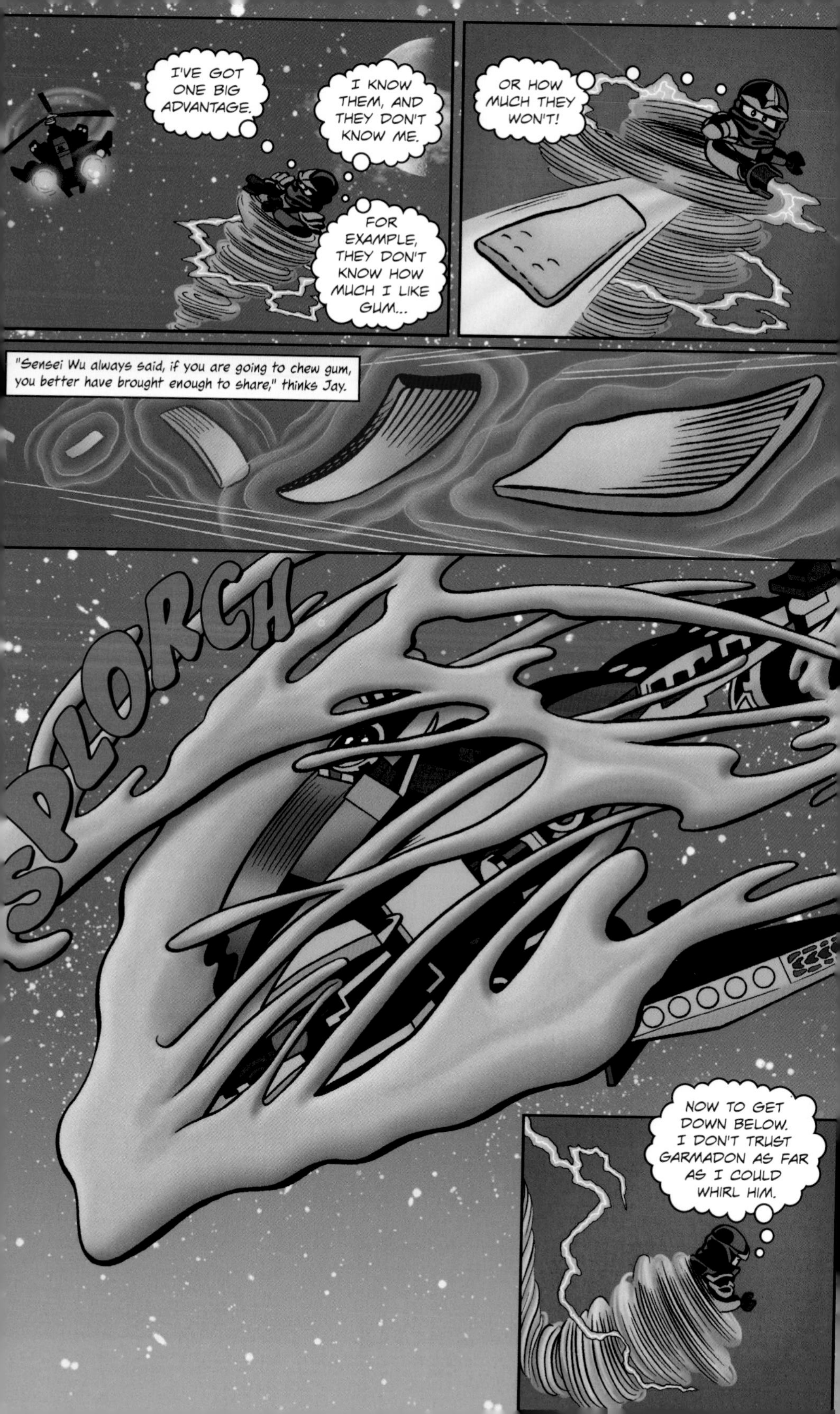
I'VE GOT ONE BIG ADVANTAGE.
I KNOW THEM, AND THEY DON'T KNOW ME.
FOR EXAMPLE, THEY DON'T KNOW HOW MUCH I LIKE GUM...
OR HOW MUCH THEY WON'T!
"Sensei Wu always said, if you are going to chew gum, you better have brought enough to share," thinks Jay.
SPLORCH
NOW TO GET DOWN BELOW. I DON'T TRUST GARMADON AS FAR AS I COULD WHIRL HIM.

WE'RE HERE.

HEY! WHO ARE YOU? HOW DID THAT TUNNEL GET THERE?

HOLD ON, I REMEMBER YOU-- YOU'RE GARMADON. WELL, YOU CAN JUST CLIMB BACK INTO WHATEVER HOLE YOU'VE BEEN LIVING IN, AND--

DO YOU ALWAYS TALK SO MUCH DURING A RESCUE?

IT'S TRUE. WE'RE HERE TO HELP YOU ESCAPE THE HYPNOBRAI.

YOU THINK I NEED HELP? HA!

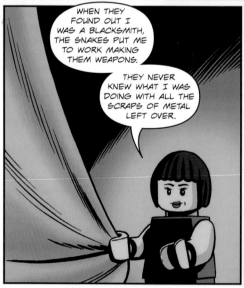

WHEN THEY FOUND OUT I WAS A BLACKSMITH, THE SNAKES PUT ME TO WORK MAKING THEM WEAPONS.

THEY NEVER KNEW WHAT I WAS DOING WITH ALL THE SCRAPS OF METAL LEFT OVER.

I'LL ESCAPE, ALL RIGHT, BUT NOT THROUGH A TUNNEL--

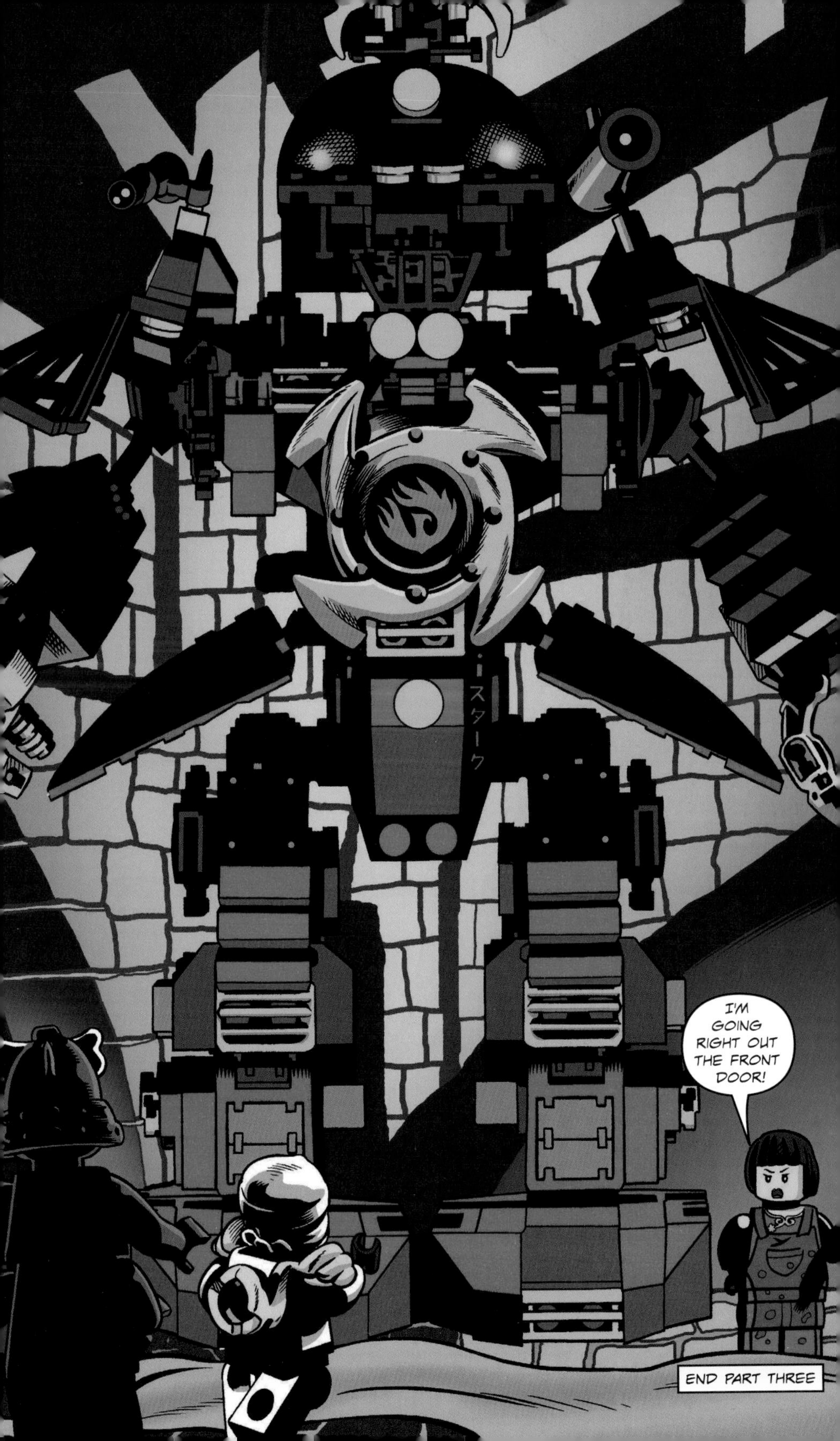
スターク
I'M GOING RIGHT OUT THE FRONT DOOR!
END PART THREE

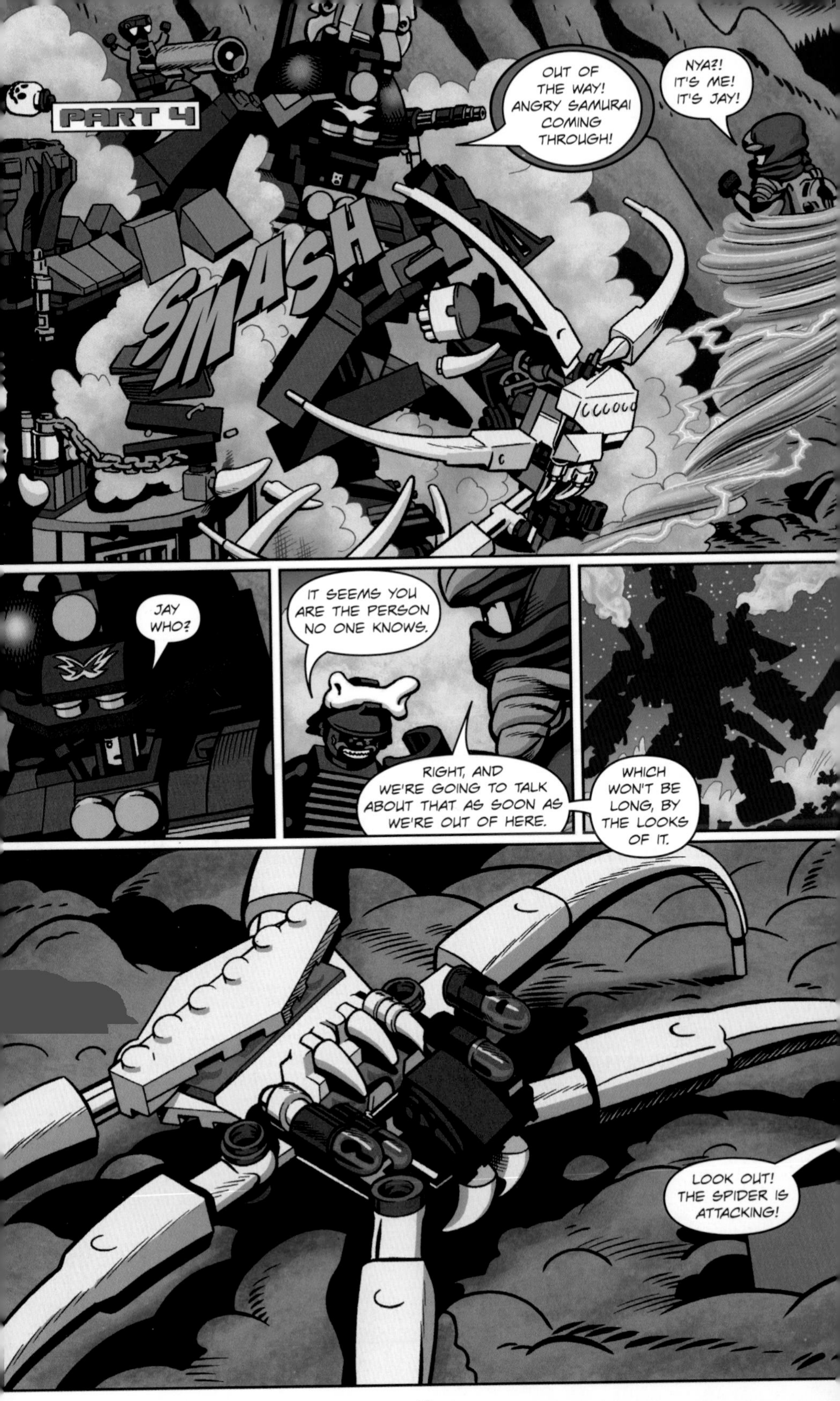
PART 4
OUT OF THE WAY! ANGRY SAMURAI COMING THROUGH!
NYA?! IT'S ME! IT'S JAY!
SMASH
JAY WHO?
IT SEEMS YOU ARE THE PERSON NO ONE KNOWS.
RIGHT, AND WE'RE GOING TO TALK ABOUT THAT AS SOON AS WE'RE OUT OF HERE.
WHICH WON'T BE LONG, BY THE LOOKS OF IT.
LOOK OUT! THE SPIDER IS ATTACKING!

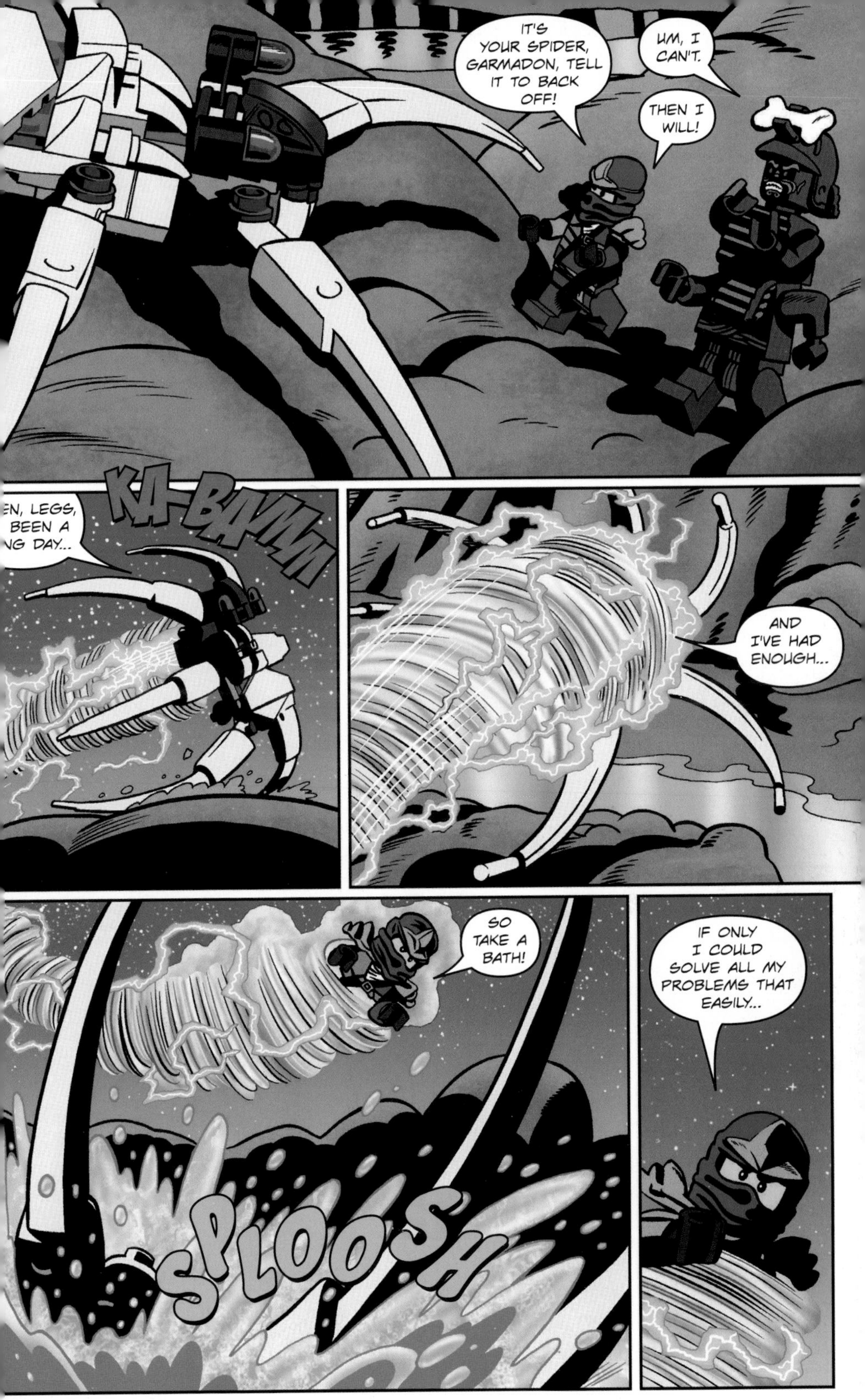
IT'S YOUR SPIDER, GARMADON, TELL IT TO BACK OFF!
UM, I CAN'T.
THEN I WILL!
KA-BAMM
EN, LEGS, BEEN A NG DAY...
AND I'VE HAD ENOUGH...
SO TAKE A BATH!
SPLOOSH
IF ONLY I COULD SOLVE ALL MY PROBLEMS THAT EASILY...

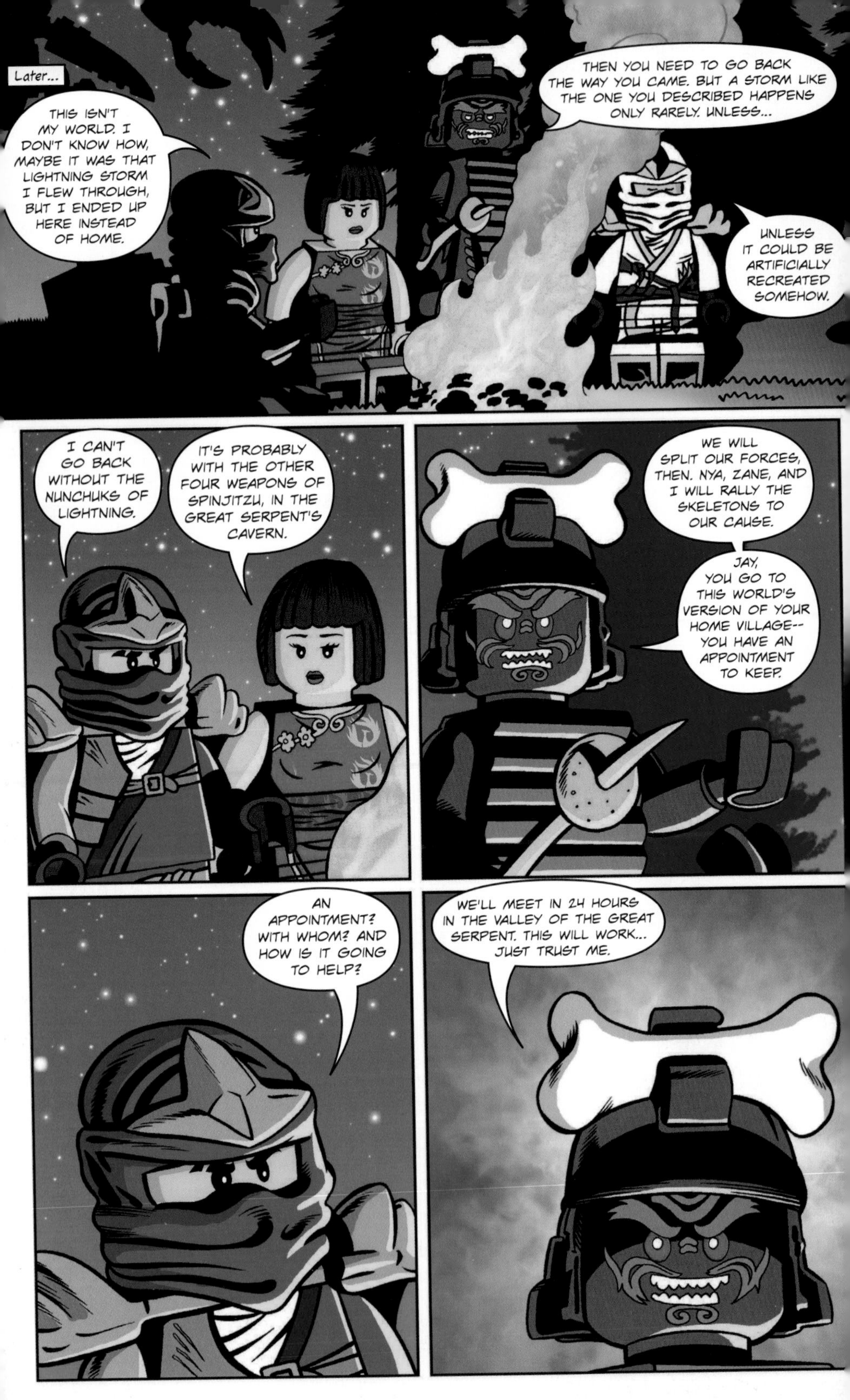
Later...
THIS ISN'T MY WORLD. I DON'T KNOW HOW, MAYBE IT WAS THAT LIGHTNING STORM I FLEW THROUGH, BUT I ENDED UP HERE INSTEAD OF HOME.
THEN YOU NEED TO GO BACK THE WAY YOU CAME. BUT A STORM LIKE THE ONE YOU DESCRIBED HAPPENS ONLY RARELY. UNLESS...
UNLESS IT COULD BE ARTIFICIALLY RECREATED SOMEHOW.
I CAN'T GO BACK WITHOUT THE NUNCHUKS OF LIGHTNING.
IT'S PROBABLY WITH THE OTHER FOUR WEAPONS OF SPINJITZU, IN THE GREAT SERPENT'S CAVERN.
WE WILL SPLIT OUR FORCES, THEN. NYA, ZANE, AND I WILL RALLY THE SKELETONS TO OUR CAUSE.
JAY, YOU GO TO THIS WORLD'S VERSION OF YOUR HOME VILLAGE-- YOU HAVE AN APPOINTMENT TO KEEP.
AN APPOINTMENT? WITH WHOM? AND HOW IS IT GOING TO HELP?
WE'LL MEET IN 24 HOURS IN THE VALLEY OF THE GREAT SERPENT. THIS WILL WORK... JUST TRUST ME.

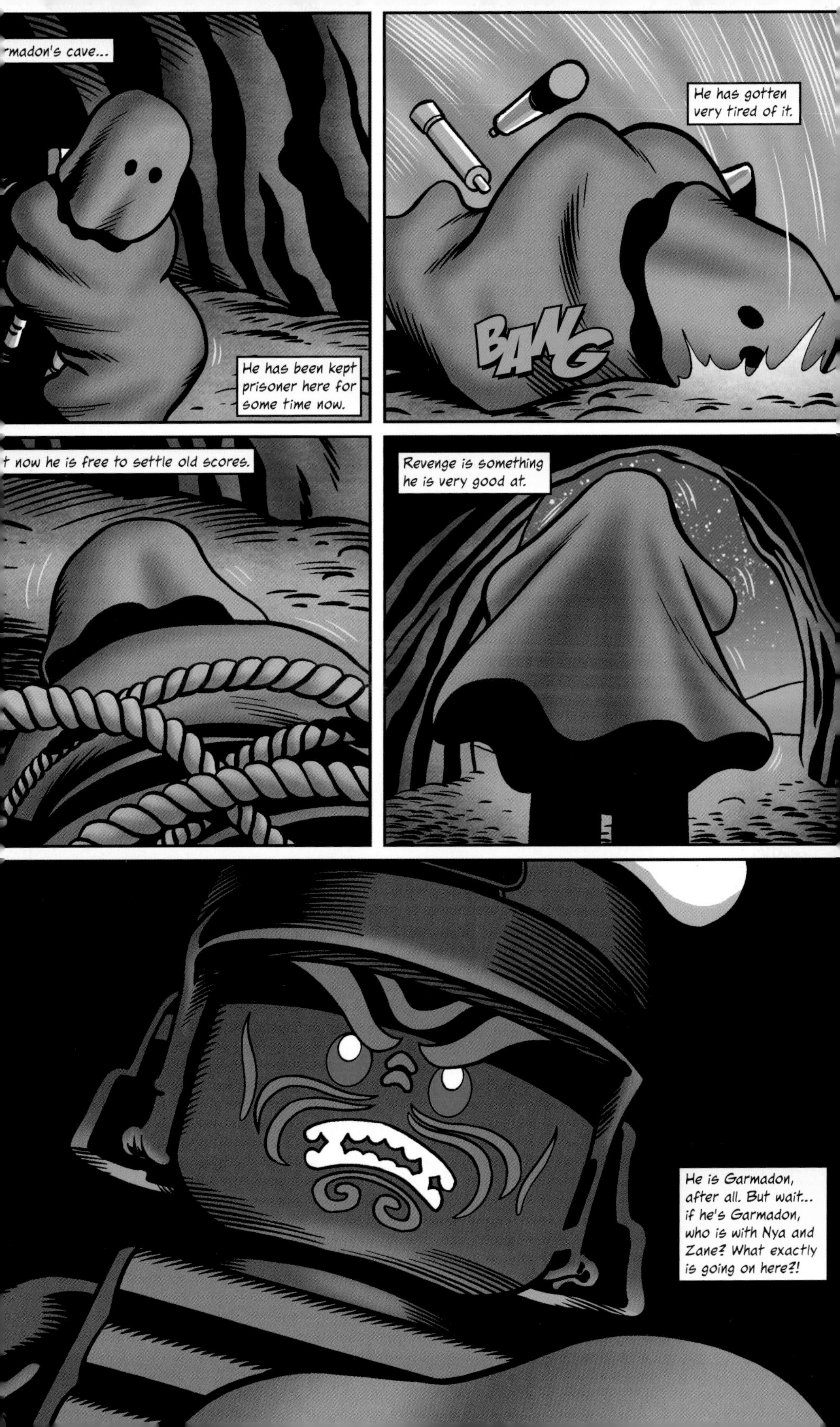
rmadon's cave...
He has been kept prisoner here for some time now.
He has gotten very tired of it.
BANG
t now he is free to settle old scores.
Revenge is something he is very good at.
He is Garmadon, after all. But wait... if he's Garmadon, who is with Nya and Zane? What exactly is going on here?!

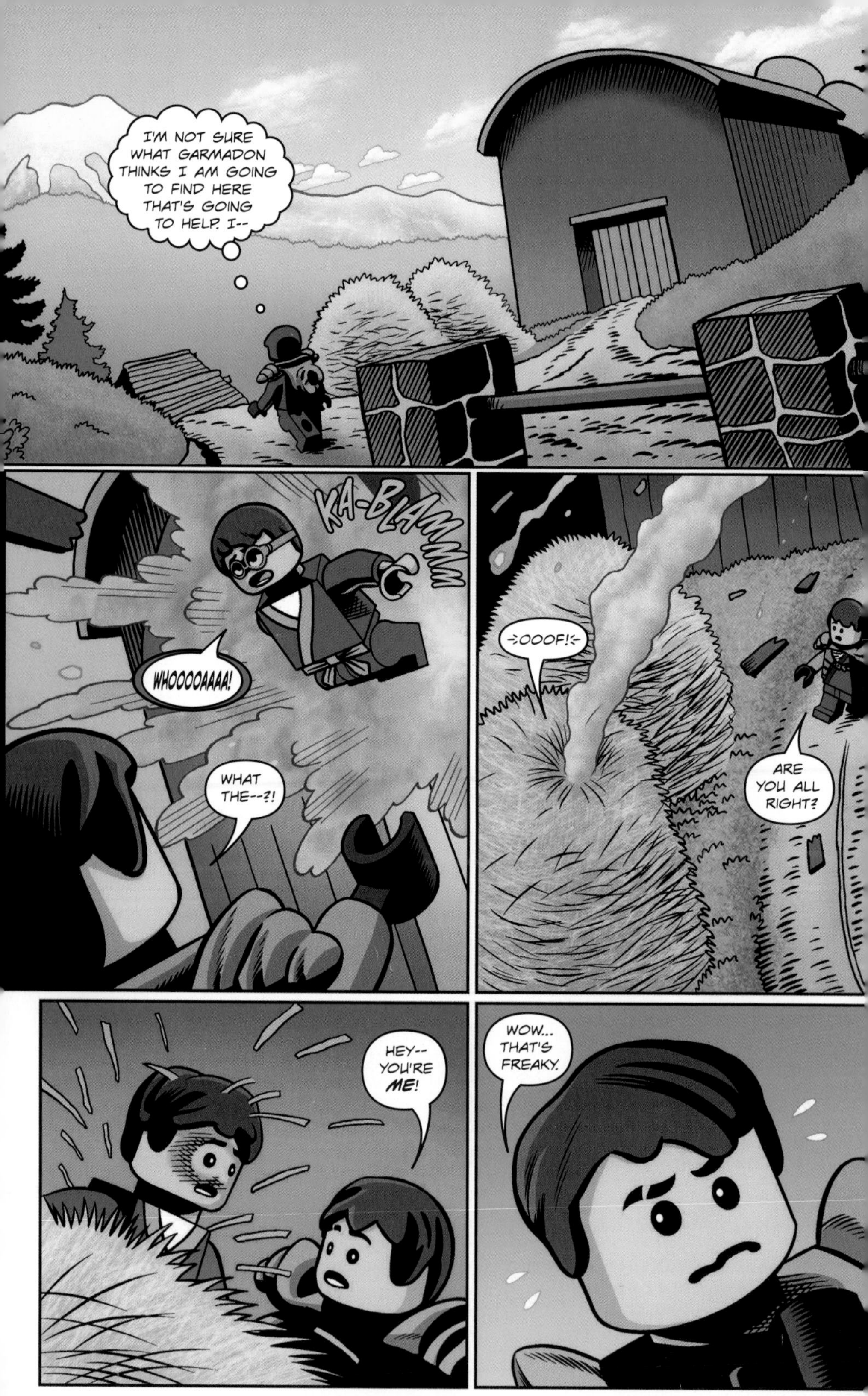
I'M NOT SURE WHAT GARMADON THINKS I AM GOING TO FIND HERE THAT'S GOING TO HELP. I--
KA-BLAMMM
WHOOOOAAAA!
WHAT THE--?!
OOOF!
ARE YOU ALL RIGHT?
HEY-- YOU'RE ME!
WOW... THAT'S FREAKY.

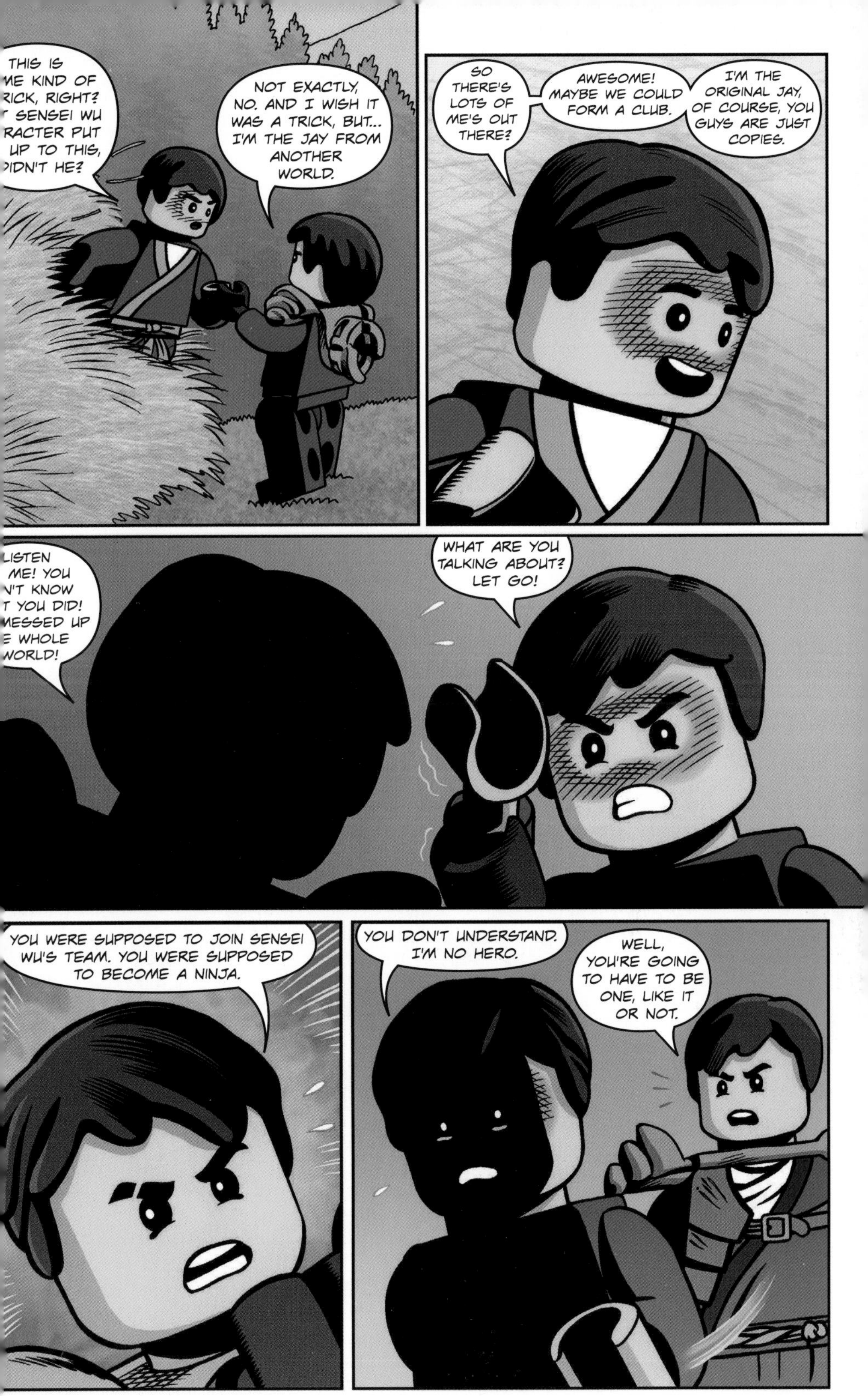
THIS IS ME KIND OF RICK, RIGHT? SENSEI WU RACTER PUT UP TO THIS, IDN'T HE?
NOT EXACTLY, NO. AND I WISH IT WAS A TRICK, BUT... I'M THE JAY FROM ANOTHER WORLD.
SO THERE'S LOTS OF ME'S OUT THERE?
AWESOME! MAYBE WE COULD FORM A CLUB.
I'M THE ORIGINAL JAY, OF COURSE, YOU GUYS ARE JUST COPIES.
LISTEN ME! YOU N'T KNOW T YOU DID! MESSED UP E WHOLE WORLD!
WHAT ARE YOU TALKING ABOUT? LET GO!
YOU WERE SUPPOSED TO JOIN SENSEI WU'S TEAM. YOU WERE SUPPOSED TO BECOME A NINJA.
YOU DON'T UNDERSTAND. I'M NO HERO.
WELL, YOU'RE GOING TO HAVE TO BE ONE, LIKE IT OR NOT.

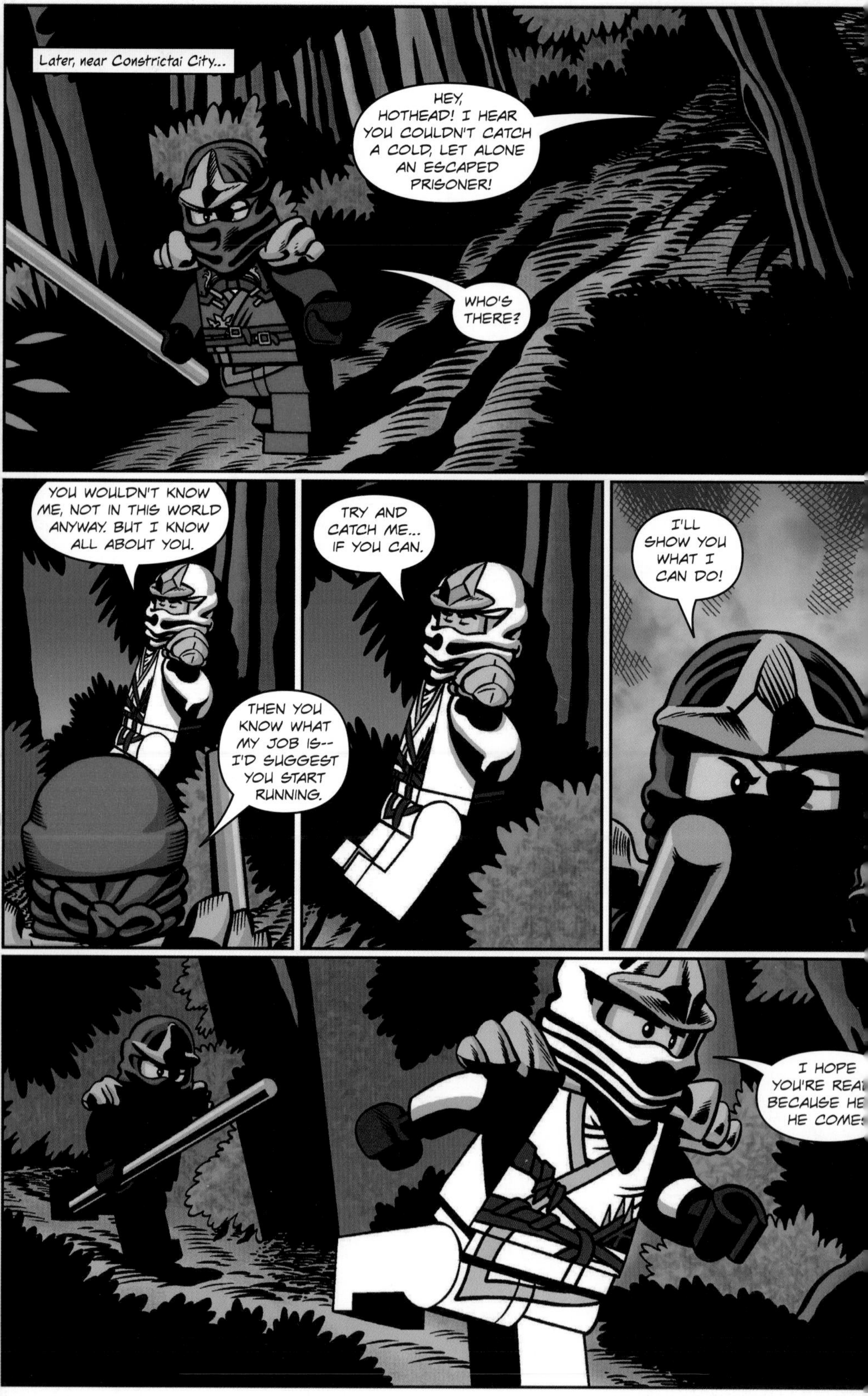

Later, near Constrictai City...
HEY, HOTHEAD! I HEAR YOU COULDN'T CATCH A COLD, LET ALONE AN ESCAPED PRISONER!
WHO'S THERE?
YOU WOULDN'T KNOW ME, NOT IN THIS WORLD ANYWAY. BUT I KNOW ALL ABOUT YOU.
THEN YOU KNOW WHAT MY JOB IS-- I'D SUGGEST YOU START RUNNING.
TRY AND CATCH ME... IF YOU CAN.
I'LL SHOW YOU WHAT I CAN DO!
I HOPE YOU'RE REA
BECAUSE HE
HE COME

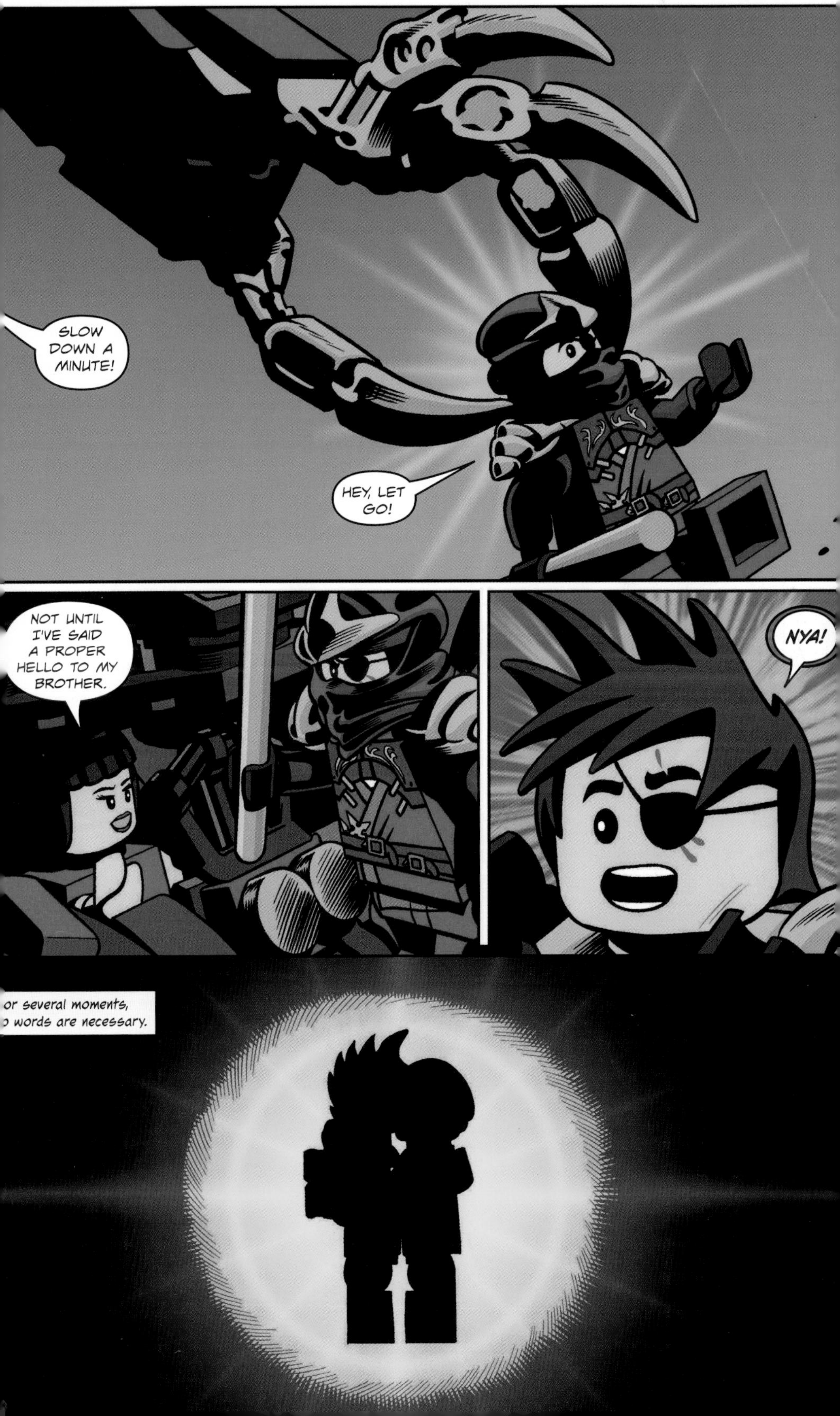
SLOW DOWN A MINUTE!
HEY, LET GO!
NOT UNTIL I'VE SAID A PROPER HELLO TO MY BROTHER.
NYA!
or several moments,
o words are necessary.

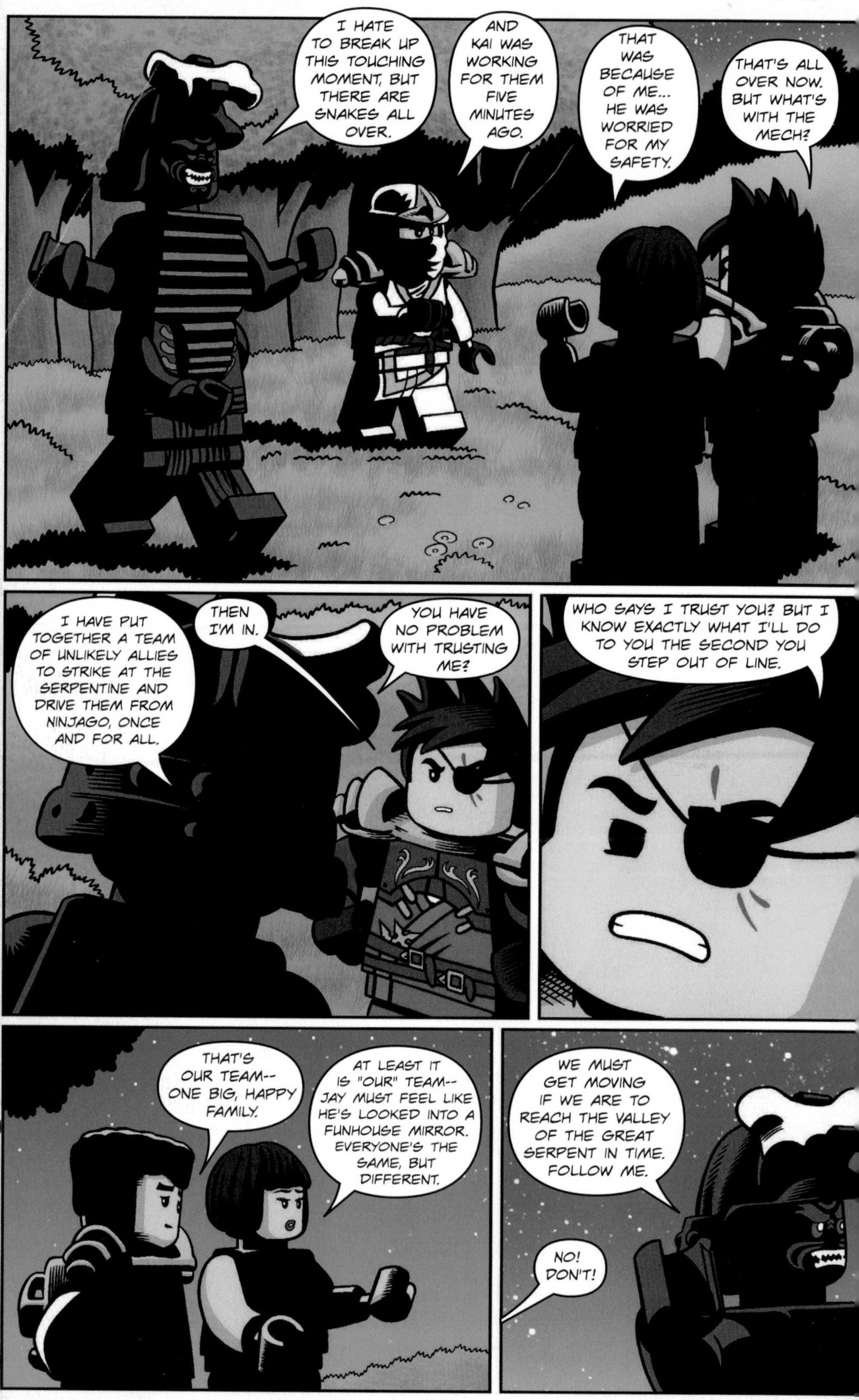
I HATE TO BREAK UP THIS TOUCHING MOMENT, BUT THERE ARE SNAKES ALL OVER.
AND KAI WAS WORKING FOR THEM FIVE MINUTES AGO.
THAT WAS BECAUSE OF ME... HE WAS WORRIED FOR MY SAFETY.
THAT'S ALL OVER NOW. BUT WHAT'S WITH THE MECH?
I HAVE PUT TOGETHER A TEAM OF UNLIKELY ALLIES TO STRIKE AT THE SERPENTINE AND DRIVE THEM FROM NINJAGO, ONCE AND FOR ALL.
THEN I'M IN.
YOU HAVE NO PROBLEM WITH TRUSTING ME?
WHO SAYS I TRUST YOU? BUT I KNOW EXACTLY WHAT I'LL DO TO YOU THE SECOND YOU STEP OUT OF LINE.
THAT'S OUR TEAM-- ONE BIG, HAPPY FAMILY.
AT LEAST IT IS "OUR" TEAM-- JAY MUST FEEL LIKE HE'S LOOKED INTO A FUNHOUSE MIRROR. EVERYONE'S THE SAME, BUT DIFFERENT.
WE MUST GET MOVING IF WE ARE TO REACH THE VALLEY OF THE GREAT SERPENT IN TIME. FOLLOW ME.
NO! DON'T!

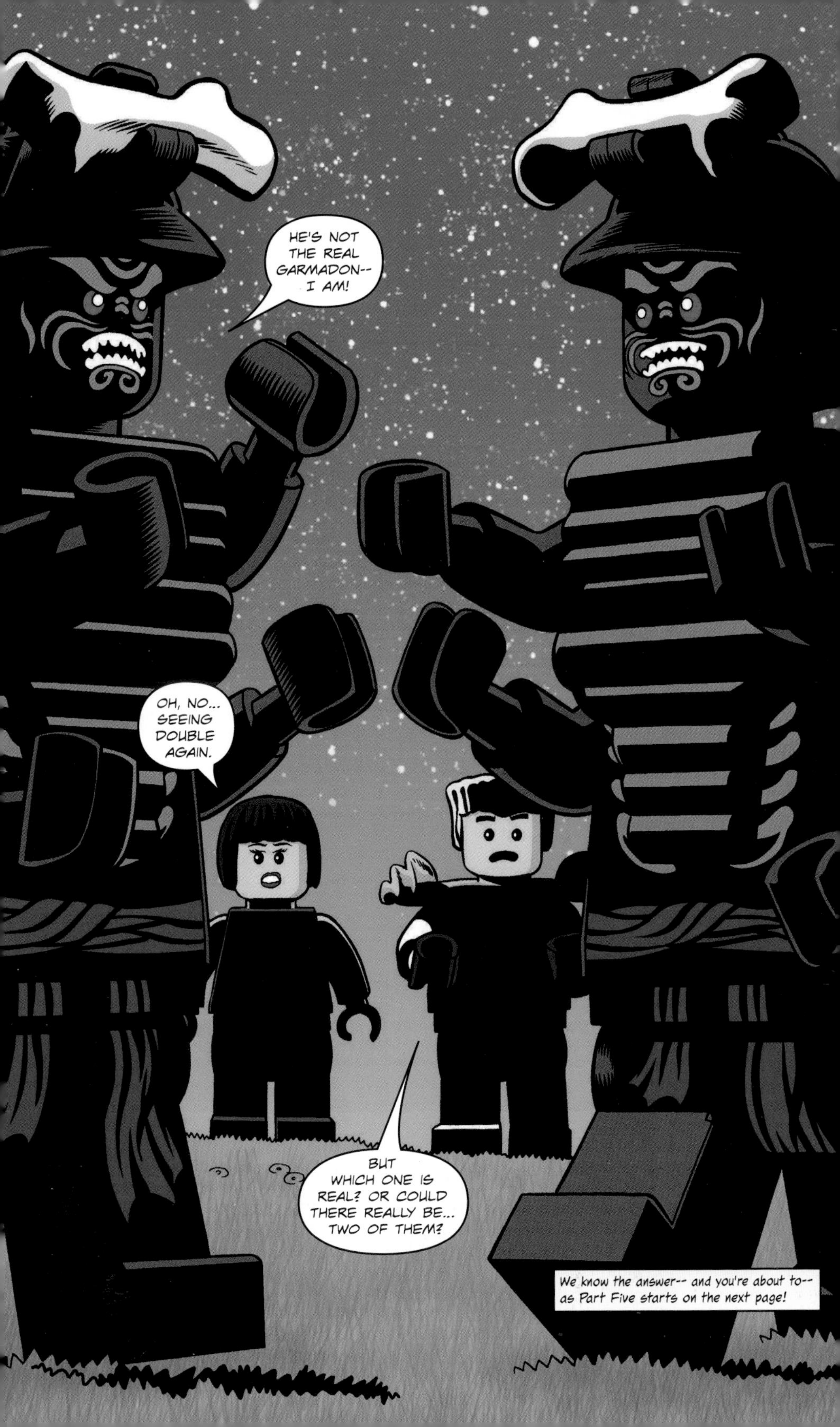
HE'S NOT THE REAL GARMADON-- I AM!
OH, NO... SEEING DOUBLE AGAIN.
BUT WHICH ONE IS REAL? OR COULD THERE REALLY BE... TWO OF THEM?
We know the answer-- and you're about to-- as Part Five starts on the next page!

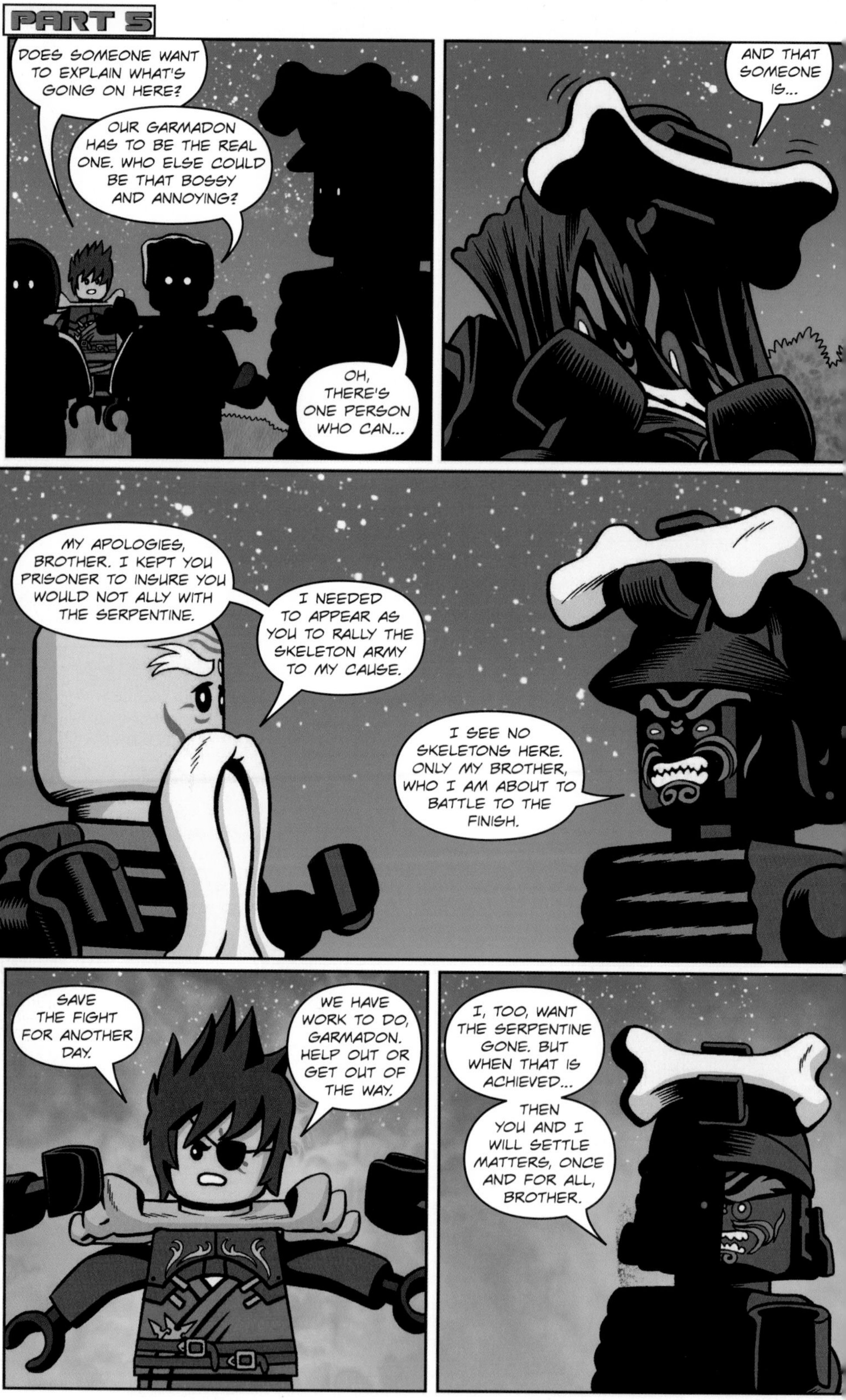
PART 5
DOES SOMEONE WANT TO EXPLAIN WHAT'S GOING ON HERE?
OUR GARMADON HAS TO BE THE REAL ONE. WHO ELSE COULD BE THAT BOSSY AND ANNOYING?
OH, THERE'S ONE PERSON WHO CAN...
AND THAT SOMEONE IS...
MY APOLOGIES, BROTHER. I KEPT YOU PRISONER TO INSURE YOU WOULD NOT ALLY WITH THE SERPENTINE.
I NEEDED TO APPEAR AS YOU TO RALLY THE SKELETON ARMY TO MY CAUSE.
I SEE NO SKELETONS HERE. ONLY MY BROTHER, WHO I AM ABOUT TO BATTLE TO THE FINISH.
SAVE THE FIGHT FOR ANOTHER DAY.
WE HAVE WORK TO DO, GARMADON. HELP OUT OR GET OUT OF THE WAY.
I, TOO, WANT THE SERPENTINE GONE. BUT WHEN THAT IS ACHIEVED...
THEN YOU AND I WILL SETTLE MATTERS, ONCE AND FOR ALL, BROTHER.

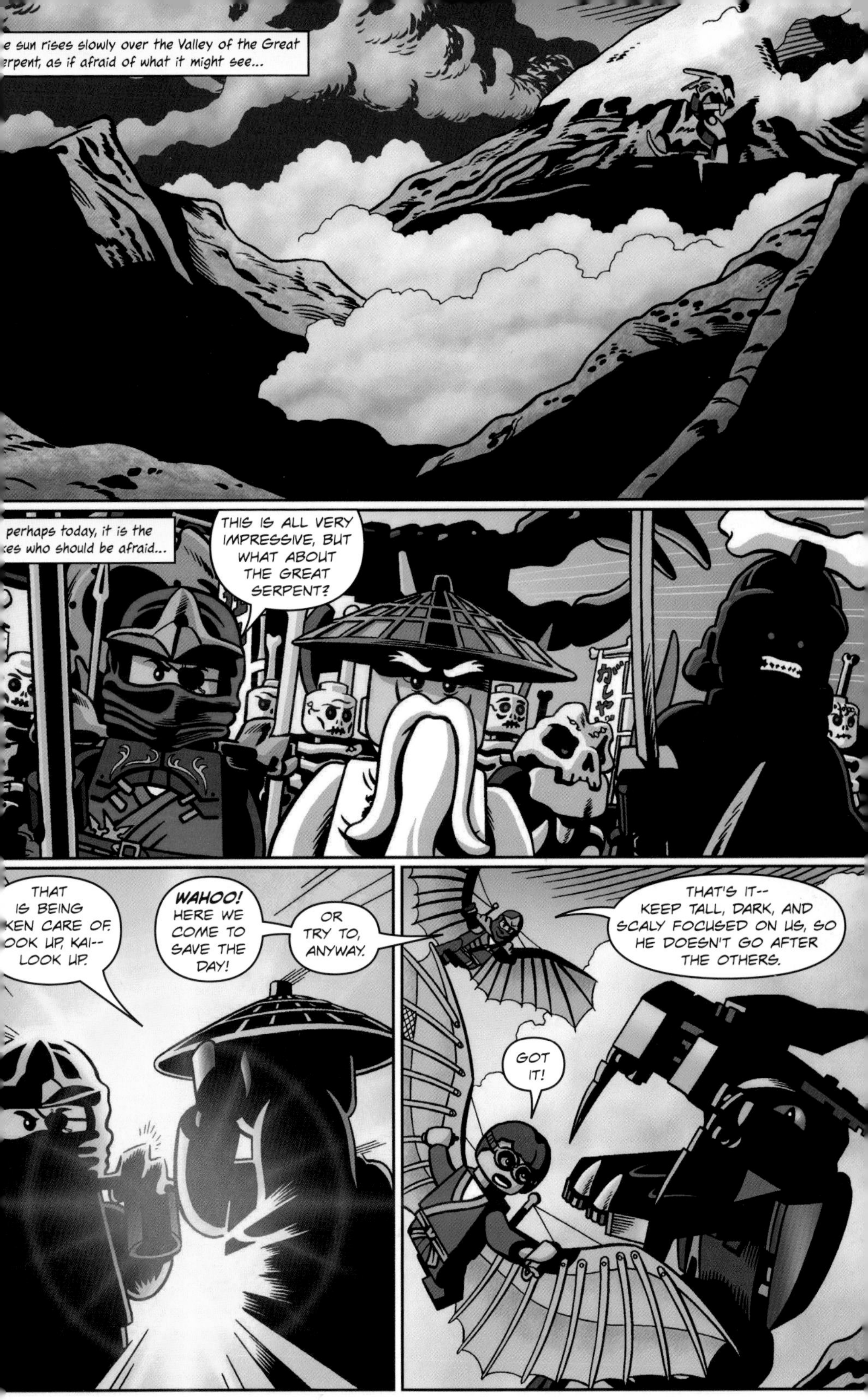
e sun rises slowly over the Valley of the Great
erpent, as if afraid of what it might see...
perhaps today, it is the
es who should be afraid...
THIS IS ALL VERY IMPRESSIVE, BUT WHAT ABOUT THE GREAT SERPENT?
THAT IS BEING KEN CARE OF. OOK UP, KAI-- LOOK UP.
WAHOO! HERE WE COME TO SAVE THE DAY!
OR TRY TO, ANYWAY.
THAT'S IT-- KEEP TALL, DARK, AND SCALY FOCUSED ON US, SO HE DOESN'T GO AFTER THE OTHERS.
GOT IT!

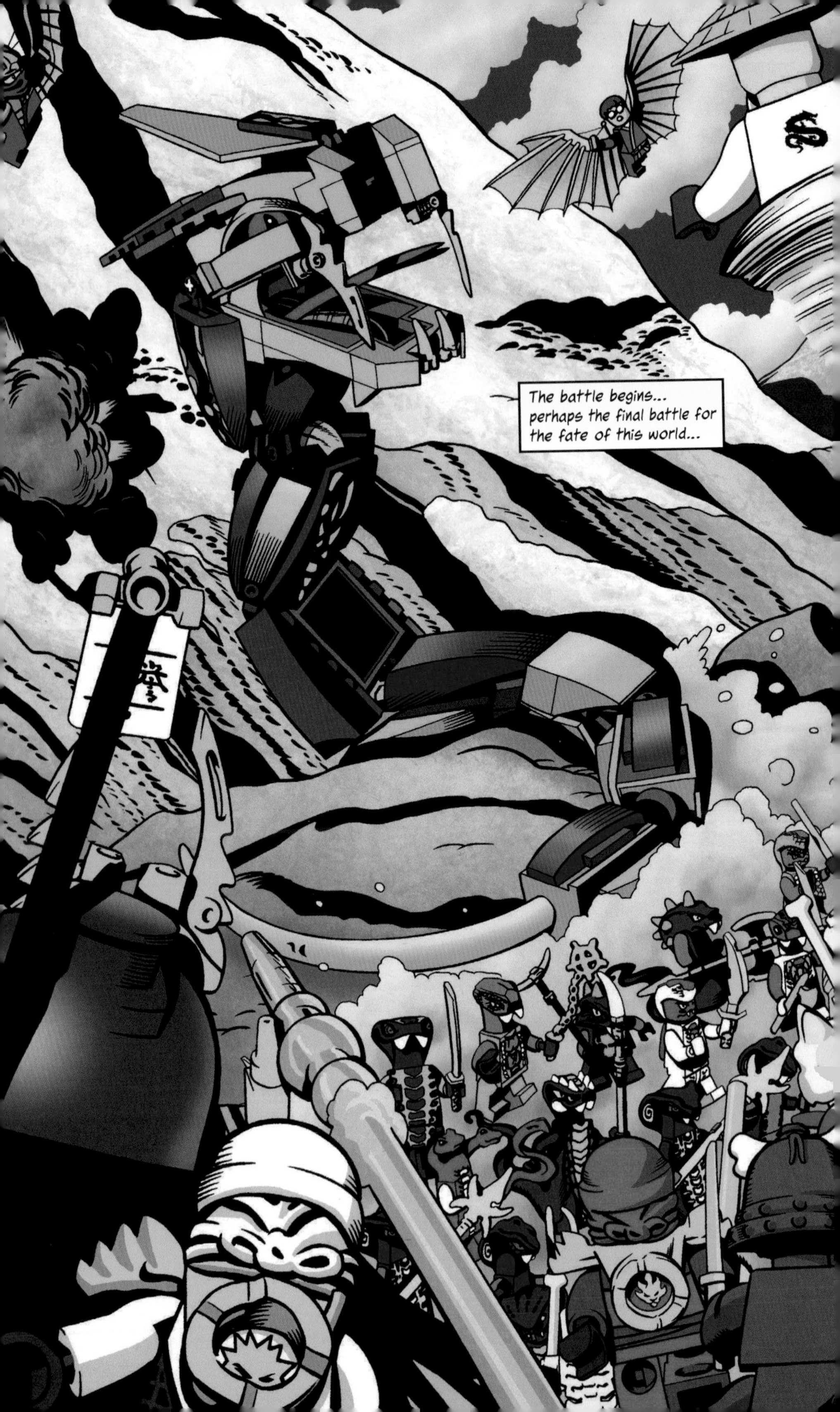
The battle begins... perhaps the final battle for the fate of this world...

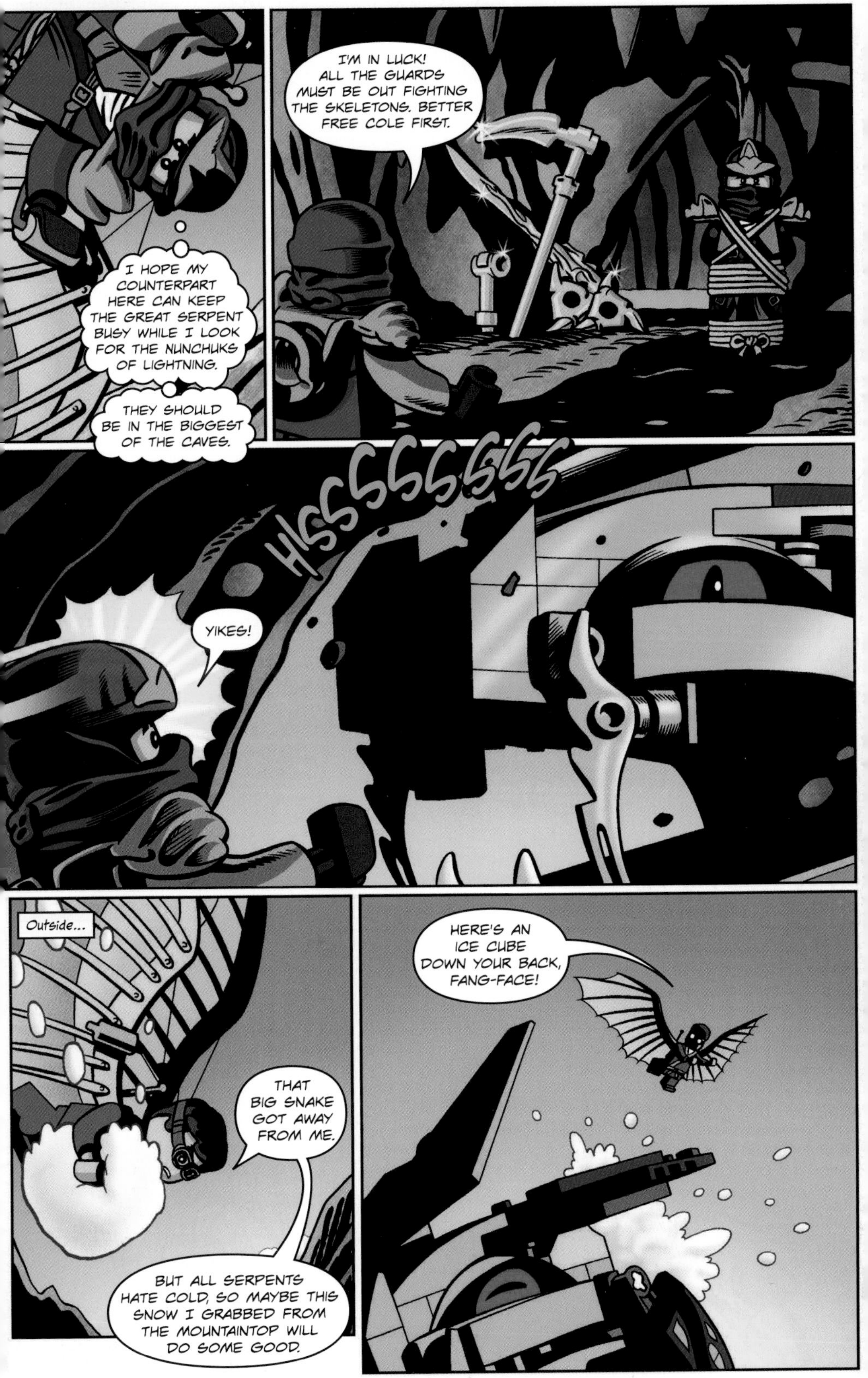
I HOPE MY COUNTERPART HERE CAN KEEP THE GREAT SERPENT BUSY WHILE I LOOK FOR THE NUNCHUKS OF LIGHTNING.
THEY SHOULD BE IN THE BIGGEST OF THE CAVES.
I'M IN LUCK! ALL THE GUARDS MUST BE OUT FIGHTING THE SKELETONS. BETTER FREE COLE FIRST.
HISSSSSSSSS
YIKES!
Outside...
THAT BIG SNAKE GOT AWAY FROM ME.
BUT ALL SERPENTS HATE COLD, SO MAYBE THIS SNOW I GRABBED FROM THE MOUNTAINTOP WILL DO SOME GOOD.
HERE'S AN ICE CUBE DOWN YOUR BACK, FANG-FACE!

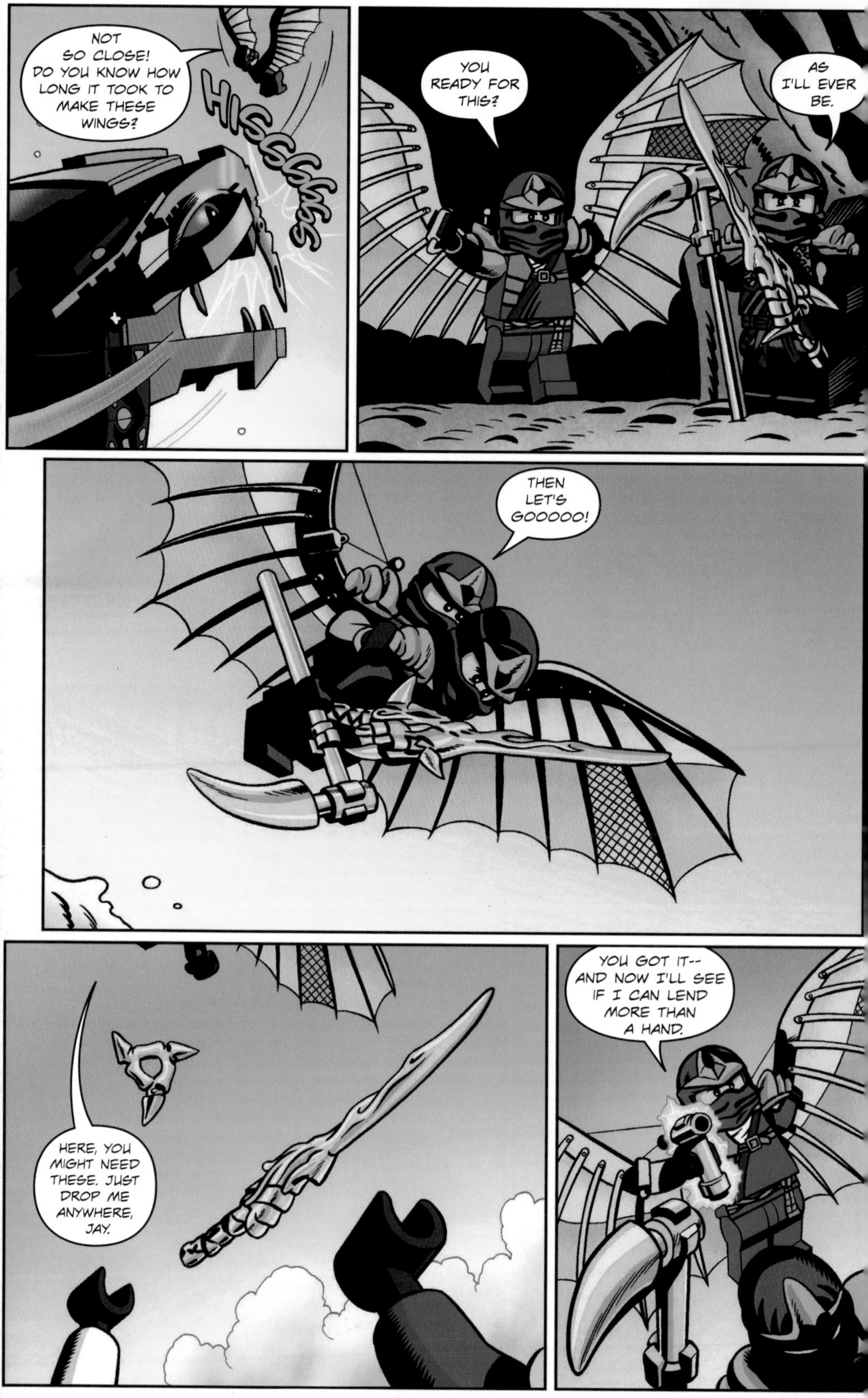
NOT SO CLOSE! DO YOU KNOW HOW LONG IT TOOK TO MAKE THESE WINGS?
HISSSSSSS
YOU READY FOR THIS?
AS I'LL EVER BE.
THEN LET'S GOOOOO!
HERE, YOU MIGHT NEED THESE. JUST DROP ME ANYWHERE, JAY.
YOU GOT IT-- AND NOW I'LL SEE IF I CAN LEND MORE THAN A HAND.

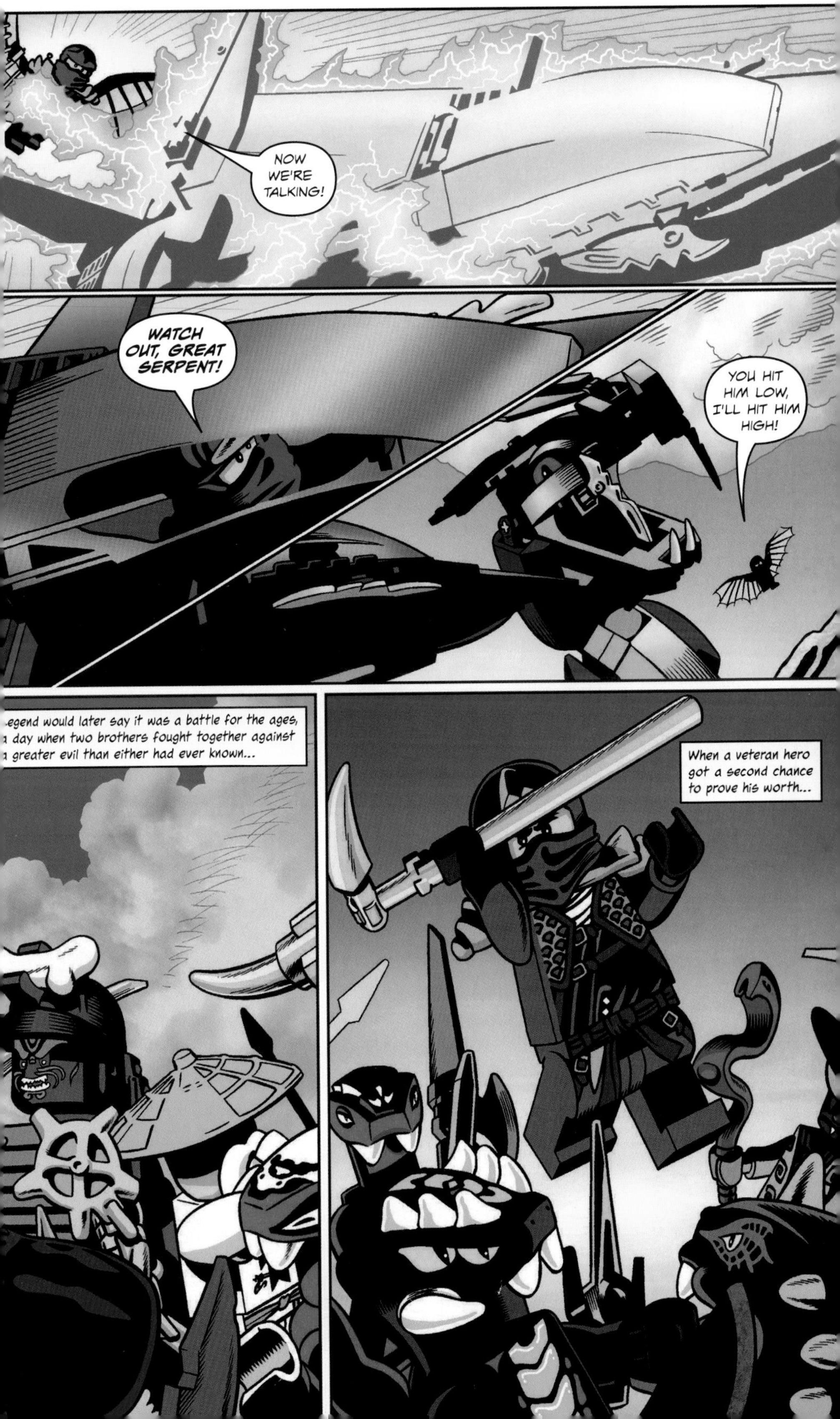

NOW WE'RE TALKING!
WATCH OUT, GREAT SERPENT!
YOU HIT HIM LOW, I'LL HIT HIM HIGH!
egend would later say it was a battle for the ages, day when two brothers fought together against greater evil than either had ever known...
When a veteran hero got a second chance to prove his worth...

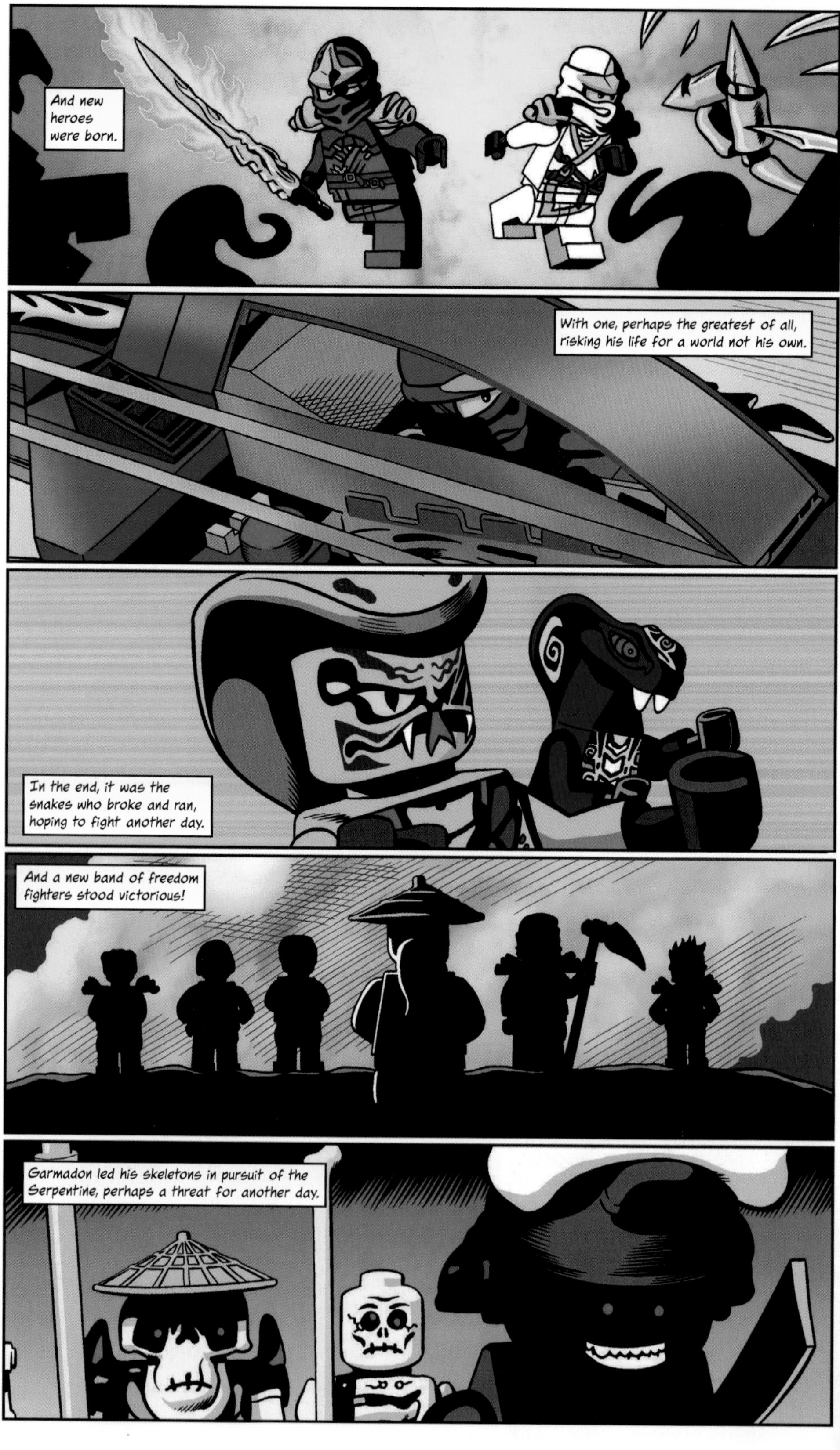
And new heroes were born.
With one, perhaps the greatest of all, risking his life for a world not his own.
In the end, it was the snakes who broke and ran, hoping to fight another day.
And a new band of freedom fighters stood victorious!
Garmadon led his skeletons in pursuit of the Serpentine, perhaps a threat for another day.

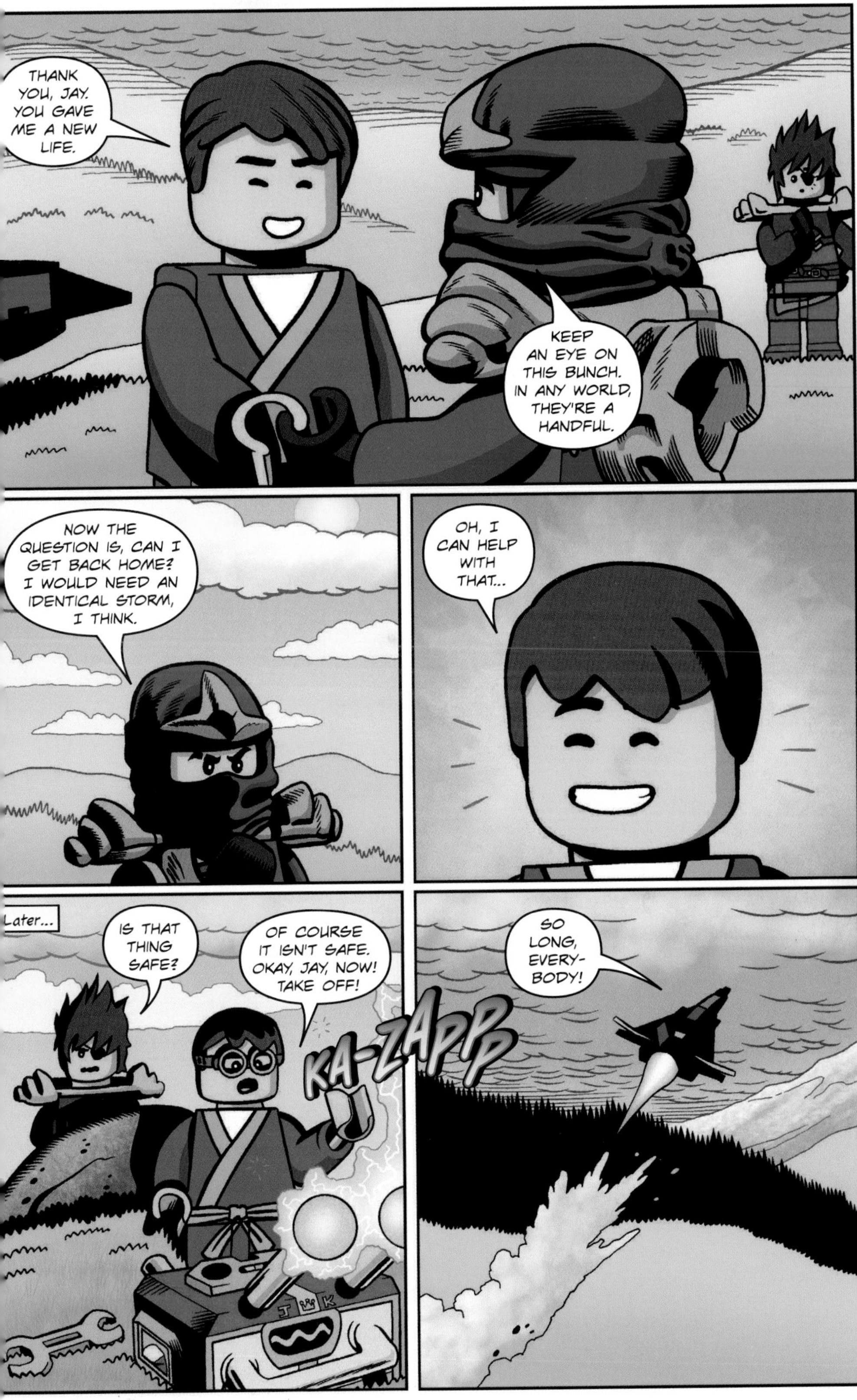
THANK YOU, JAY. YOU GAVE ME A NEW LIFE.
KEEP AN EYE ON THIS BUNCH. IN ANY WORLD, THEY'RE A HANDFUL.
NOW THE QUESTION IS, CAN I GET BACK HOME? I WOULD NEED AN IDENTICAL STORM, I THINK.
OH, I CAN HELP WITH THAT...
Later...
IS THAT THING SAFE?
OF COURSE IT ISN'T SAFE. OKAY, JAY, NOW! TAKE OFF!
KA-ZAPPP
SO LONG, EVERY-BODY!

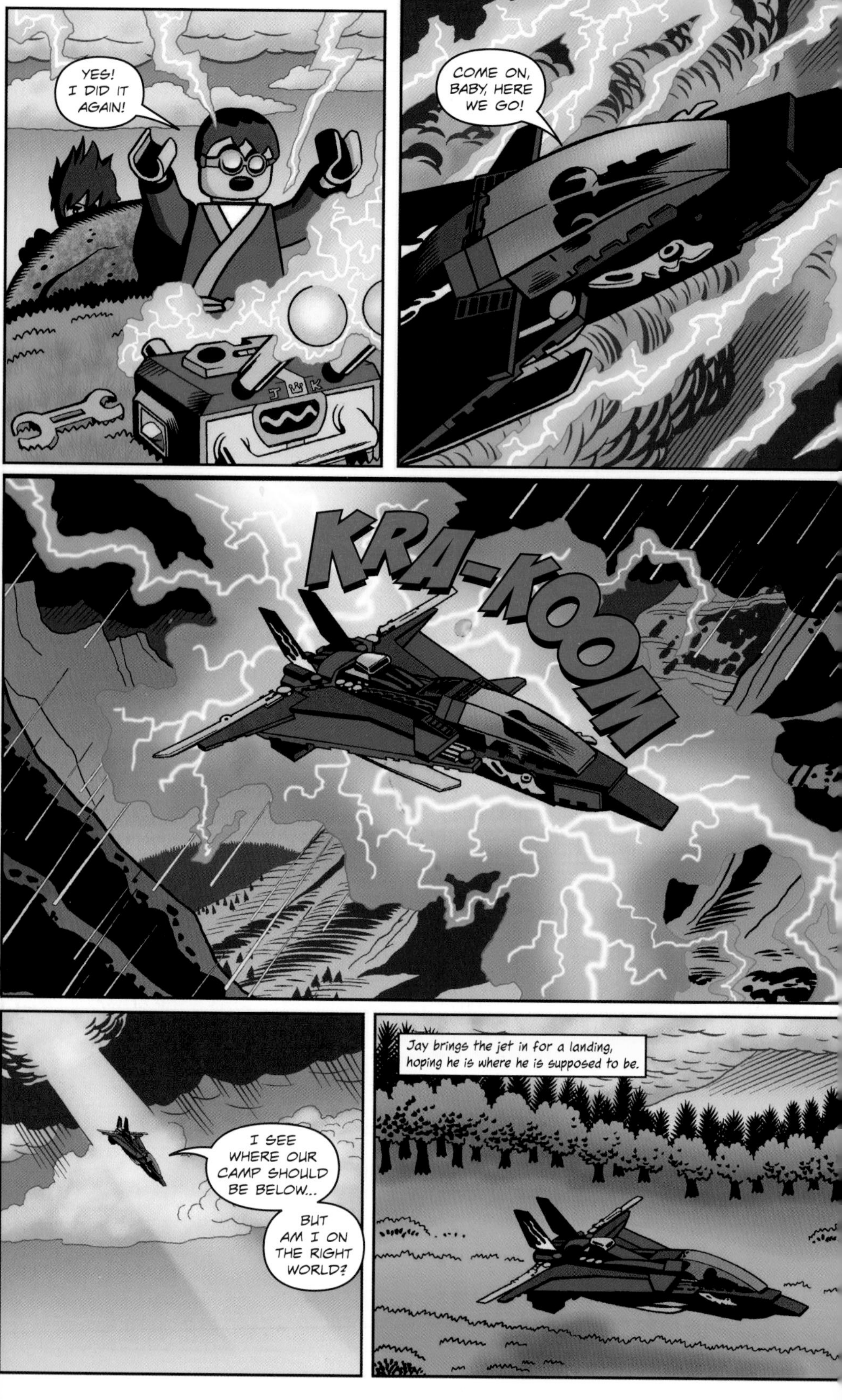
YES! I DID IT AGAIN!
COME ON, BABY, HERE WE GO!
KRA-KOOM
I SEE WHERE OUR CAMP SHOULD BE BELOW...
BUT AM I ON THE RIGHT WORLD?
Jay brings the jet in for a landing, hoping he is where he is supposed to be.

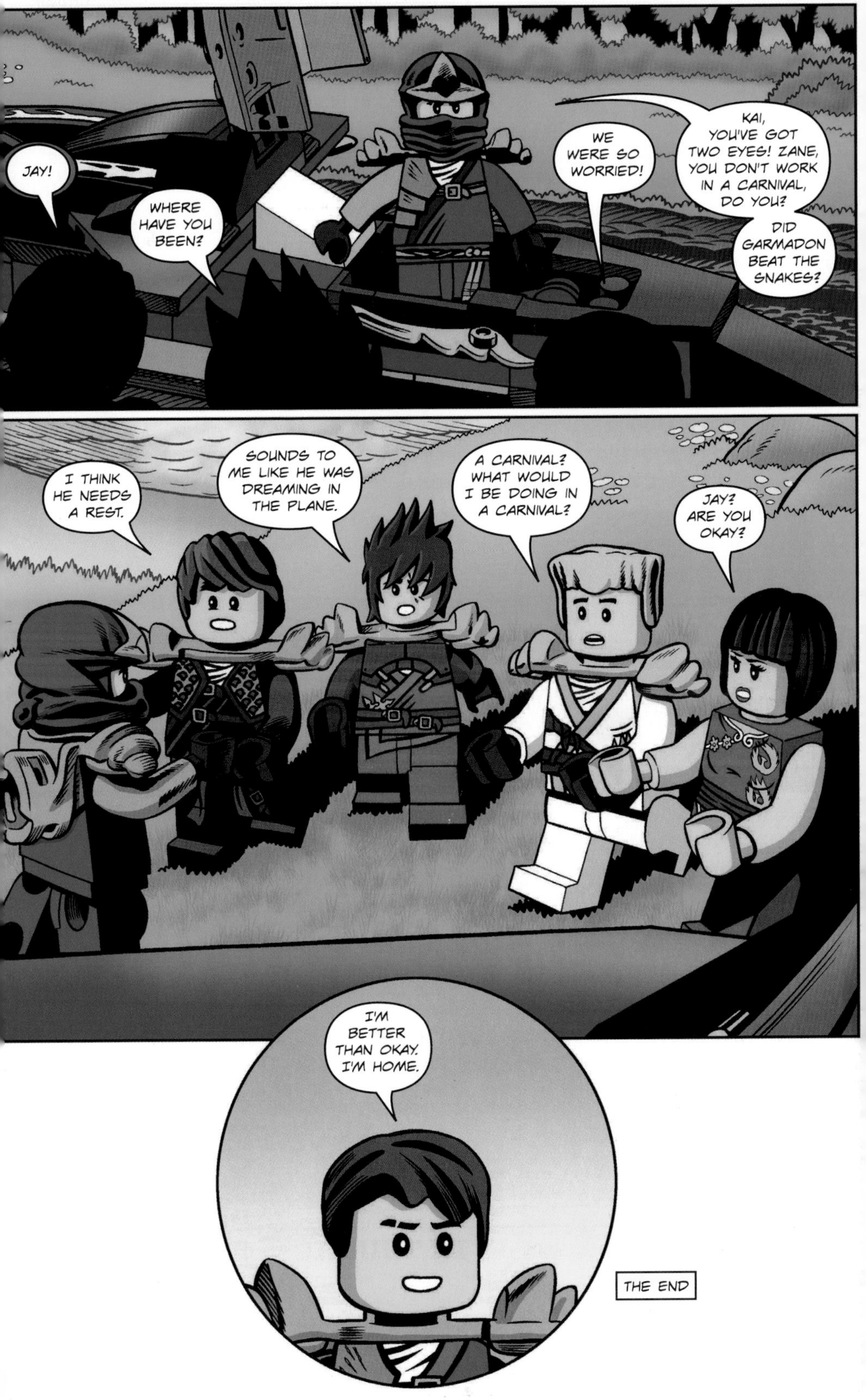

JAY!
WHERE HAVE YOU BEEN?
WE WERE SO WORRIED!
KAI, YOU'VE GOT TWO EYES! ZANE, YOU DON'T WORK IN A CARNIVAL, DO YOU?
DID GARMADON BEAT THE SNAKES?
I THINK HE NEEDS A REST.
SOUNDS TO ME LIKE HE WAS DREAMING IN THE PLANE.
A CARNIVAL? WHAT WOULD I BE DOING IN A CARNIVAL?
JAY? ARE YOU OKAY?
I'M BETTER THAN OKAY. I'M HOME.
THE END

WATCH OUT FOR PAPERCUTZ™

Welcome to the thrilling third LEGO® NINJAGO SPECIAL EDITION graphic novel from Papercutz, the guys dedicated to publishing great graphic novels for all ages. I'm Jim Salicrup, the Editor-in-Chief of Papercutz. Ever since the release of LEGO NINJAGO #1 we' been struggling to meet the voracious demand for more and more LEGO NINJAGO graph novels! As demand still hasn't let up, we decided to combine volumes of the original LEG NINJAGO graphic novels to create LEGO NINJAGO SPECIAL EDITIONS, to make it easier, less expensive, for fans just joining us to catch up on all the previous volumes.

Speaking of just joining us (and no, we're not coming apart!), if you've only watched the a ventures of LEGO NINJAGO on the Cartoon Network or picked up the Scholastic novels (a by Greg Farshtey) you may think that the Papercutz graphic novels are adaptations of sto you've already seen. Nope! In fact, these stories are all-new and haven't been told anywhe else other than in the graphic novels! In "Kingdom of the Snakes," we encounter a world v much like Ninjago, except in this world Sensei Wu decided not to put together his team of Spinjitzu Masters, and as a result, the Snakes took over! Fortunately, back on the Ninjago all know and love, the snakes have long been defeated...

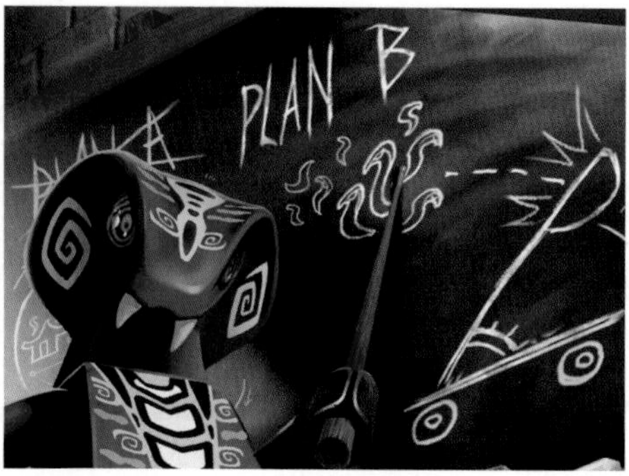
PLAN B

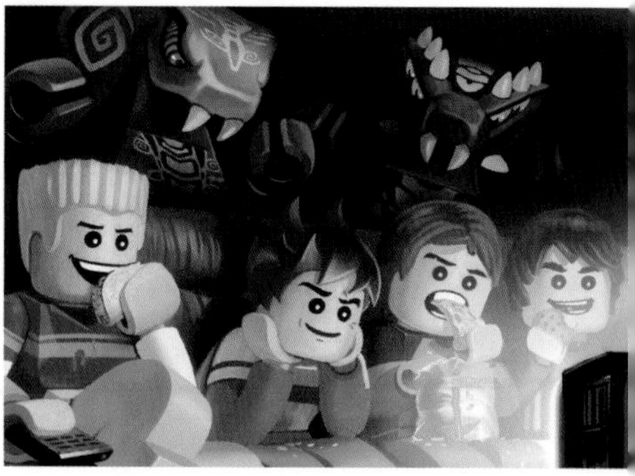

Or have they?!

Be that as it may, "Warriors of Stone" is actually a tale that takes place before Jay, Cole, Zane, and Kai ever met the real Stone Warriors! And right now, Papercutz is getting ready release LEGO NINJAGO #8, the first story to appear anywhere that takes place after the e Stone Warriors saga! That's right, Jay, Cole, Zane, and Kai, along with Sensei Wu, Garmadc (not to be confused with Gargamel, who appears in the THE SMURFS graphic novels from Papercutz), and Lloyd are all back together, and starring in LEGO NINJAGO #8 "Destiny of Doom"!

So, if you haven't been following the LEGO NINJAGO graphic novels from Papercutz, ther are plenty of great adventures just waiting for you to enjoy! And if you have been following the graphic novels—it's not over yet! There's still more LEGO NINJAGO greatness yet t come!

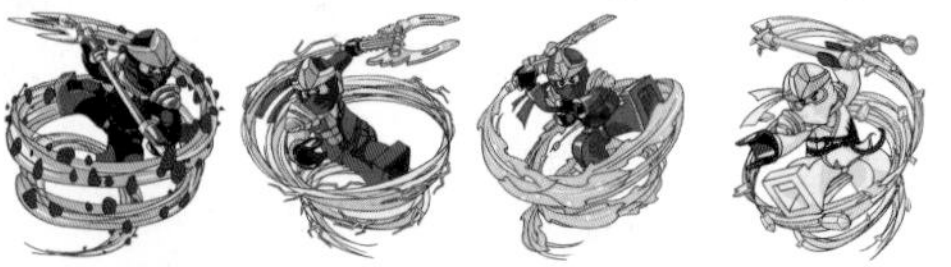

Thanks,

Jim

STAY IN TOUCH!

EMAIL:	salicrup@papercutz.com
WEB:	www.papercutz.com
TWITTER:	@papercutzgn
FACEBOOK:	PAPERCUTZGRAPHICNOVELS
SNAIL MAIL:	Papercutz, 160 Broadway, Suite 700, East Wing, New York, NY 10038

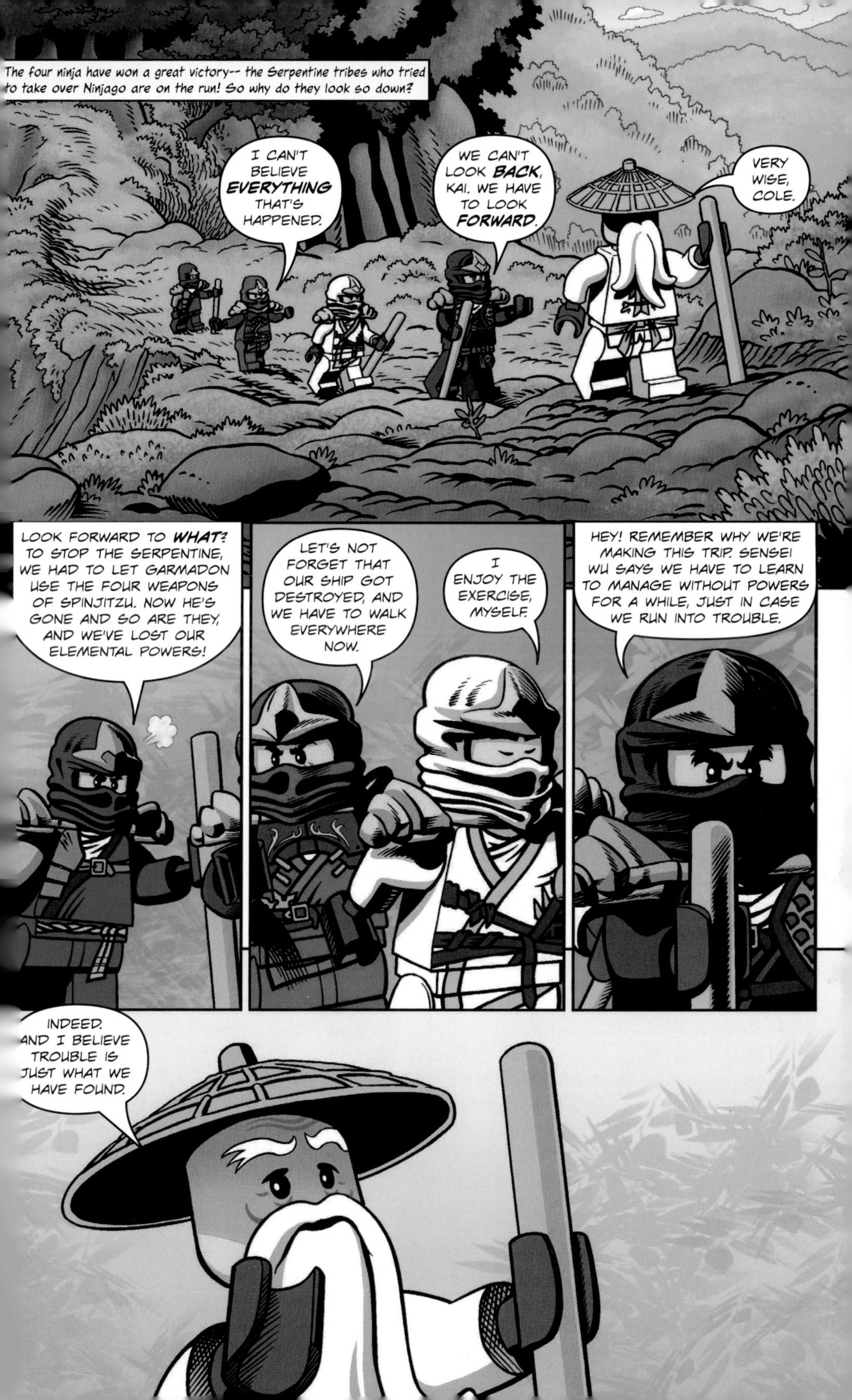
The four ninja have won a great victory-- the Serpentine tribes who tried to take over Ninjago are on the run! So why do they look so down?
I CAN'T BELIEVE EVERYTHING THAT'S HAPPENED.
WE CAN'T LOOK BACK, KAI. WE HAVE TO LOOK FORWARD.
VERY WISE, COLE.
LOOK FORWARD TO WHAT? TO STOP THE SERPENTINE, WE HAD TO LET GARMADON USE THE FOUR WEAPONS OF SPINJITZU. NOW HE'S GONE AND SO ARE THEY, AND WE'VE LOST OUR ELEMENTAL POWERS!
LET'S NOT FORGET THAT OUR SHIP GOT DESTROYED, AND WE HAVE TO WALK EVERYWHERE NOW.
I ENJOY THE EXERCISE, MYSELF.
HEY! REMEMBER WHY WE'RE MAKING THIS TRIP. SENSEI WU SAYS WE HAVE TO LEARN TO MANAGE WITHOUT POWERS FOR A WHILE, JUST IN CASE WE RUN INTO TROUBLE.
INDEED. AND I BELIEVE TROUBLE IS JUST WHAT WE HAVE FOUND.

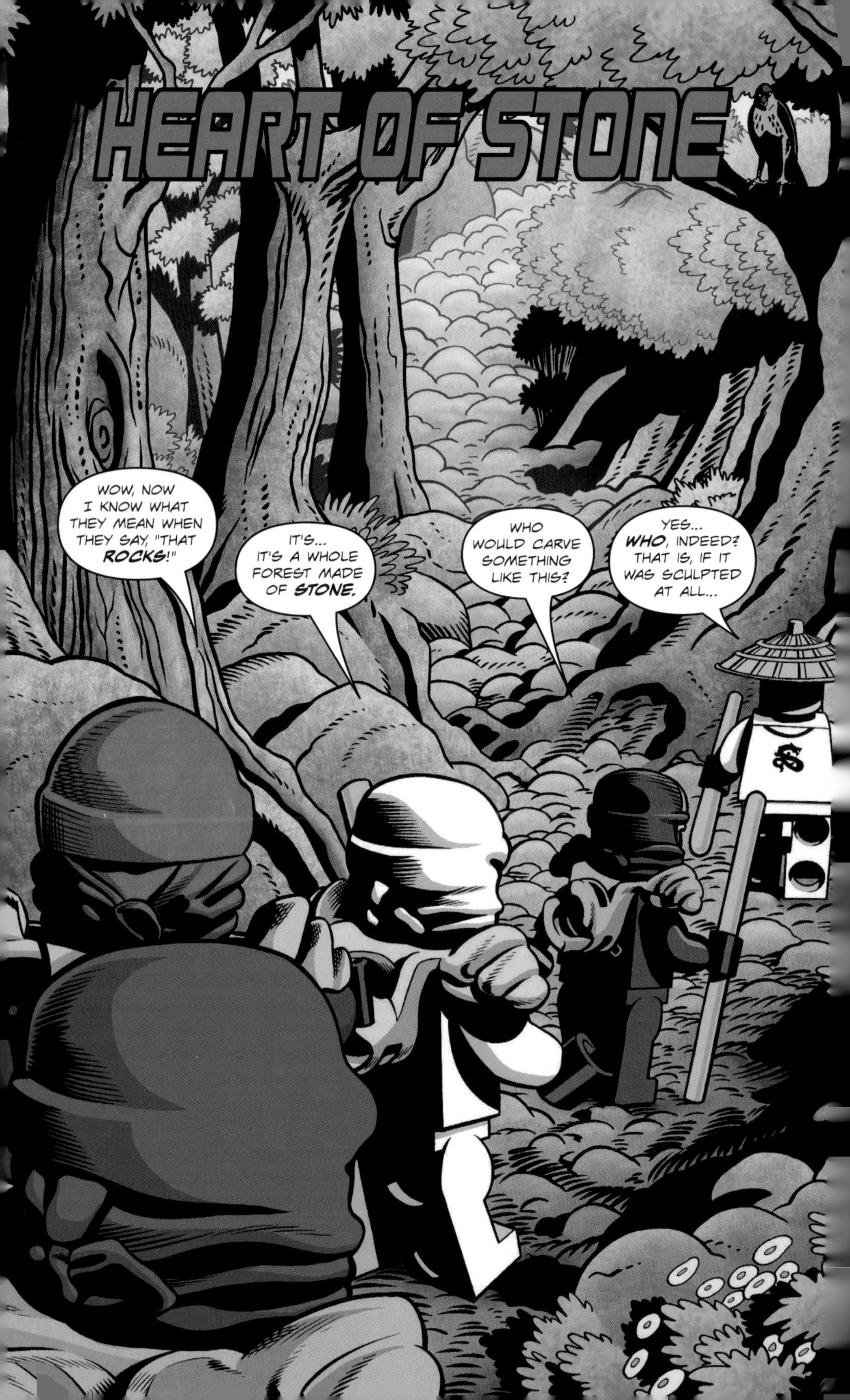
HEART OF STONE
WOW, NOW I KNOW WHAT THEY MEAN WHEN THEY SAY, "THAT ROCKS!"
IT'S... IT'S A WHOLE FOREST MADE OF STONE.
WHO WOULD CARVE SOMETHING LIKE THIS?
YES... WHO, INDEED? THAT IS, IF IT WAS SCULPTED AT ALL...

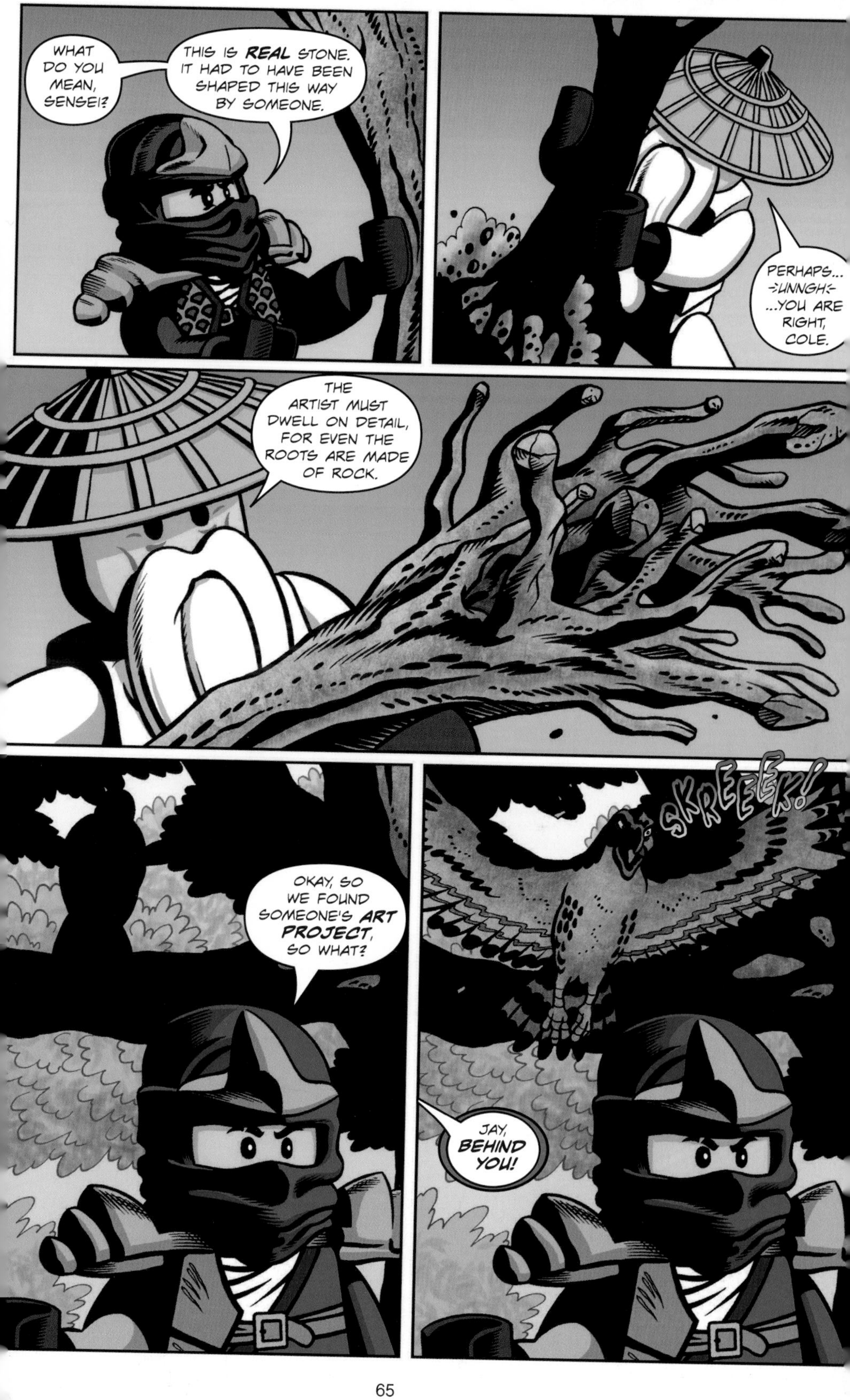
WHAT DO YOU MEAN, SENSEI?
THIS IS REAL STONE. IT HAD TO HAVE BEEN SHAPED THIS WAY BY SOMEONE.
PERHAPS... -UNNGH- ...YOU ARE RIGHT, COLE.
THE ARTIST MUST DWELL ON DETAIL, FOR EVEN THE ROOTS ARE MADE OF ROCK.
OKAY, SO WE FOUND SOMEONE'S ART PROJECT, SO WHAT?
SKREEEK!
JAY, BEHIND YOU!

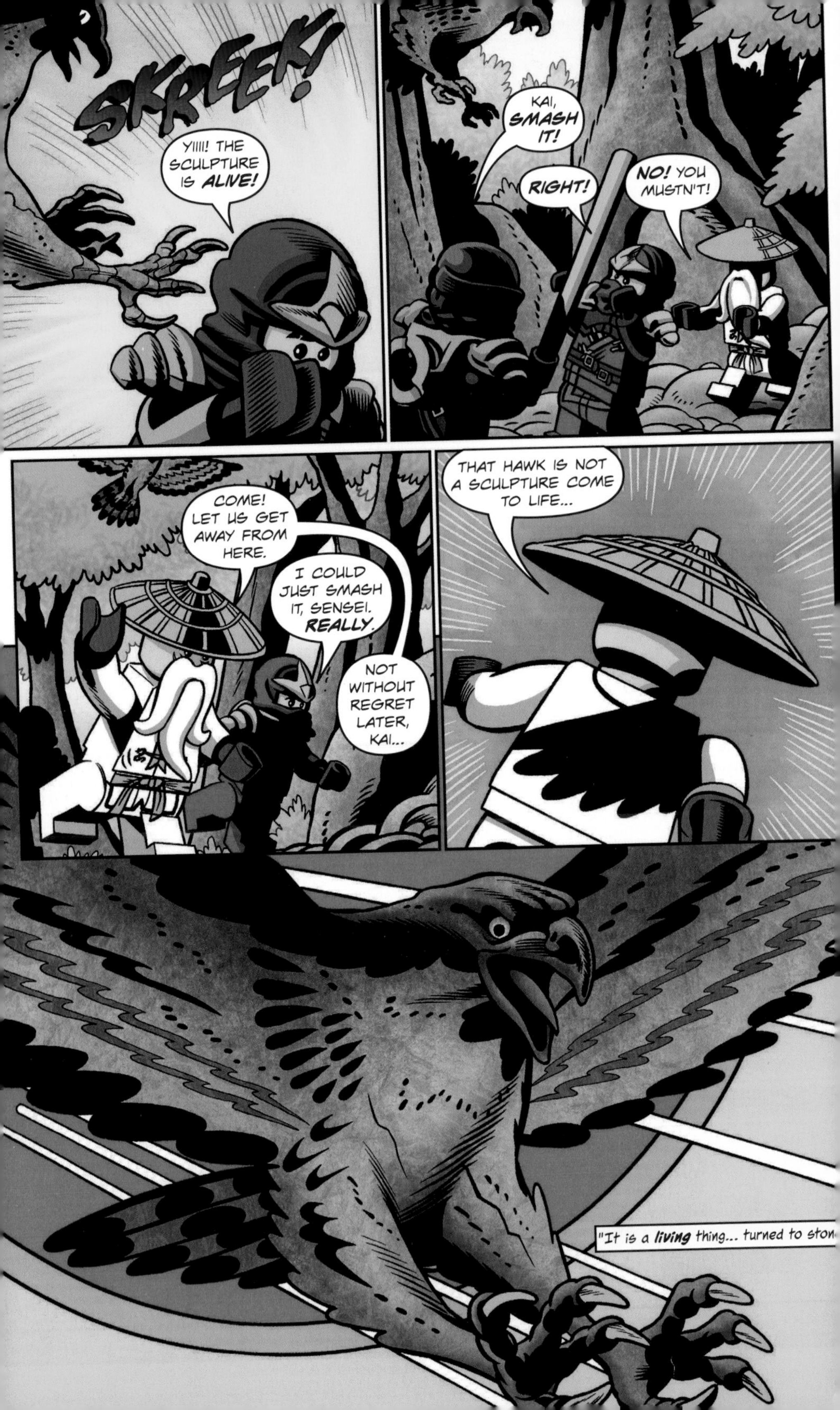
SKREEK!
YIIII! THE SCULPTURE IS ALIVE!
KAI, SMASH IT!
RIGHT!
NO! YOU MUSTN'T!
COME! LET US GET AWAY FROM HERE.
I COULD JUST SMASH IT, SENSEI. REALLY.
NOT WITHOUT REGRET LATER, KAI...
THAT HAWK IS NOT A SCULPTURE COME TO LIFE...
"It is a living thing... turned to ston

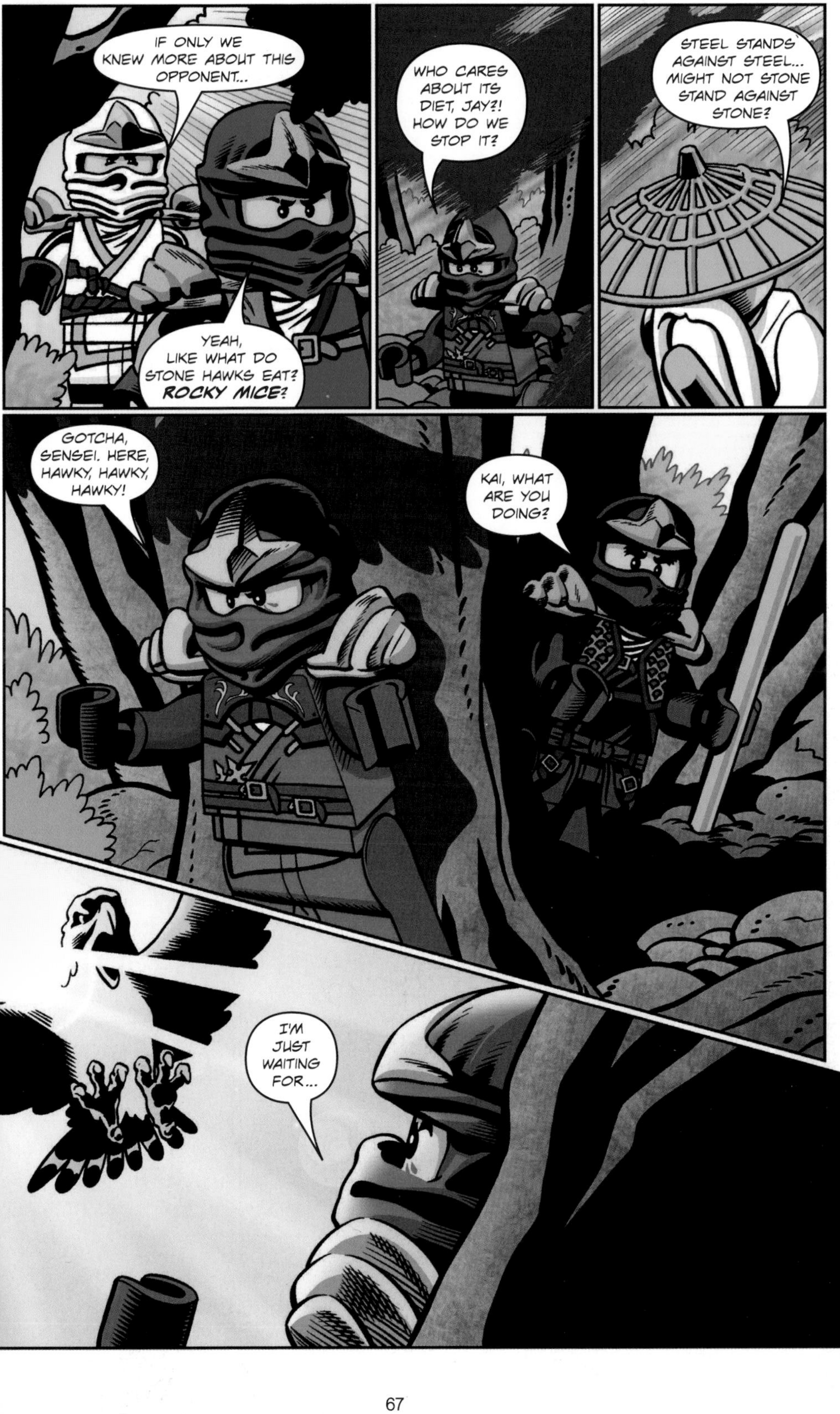
IF ONLY WE KNEW MORE ABOUT THIS OPPONENT...
YEAH, LIKE WHAT DO STONE HAWKS EAT? ROCKY MICE?
WHO CARES ABOUT ITS DIET, JAY?! HOW DO WE STOP IT?
STEEL STANDS AGAINST STEEL... MIGHT NOT STONE STAND AGAINST STONE?
GOTCHA, SENSEI. HERE, HAWKY, HAWKY, HAWKY!
KAI, WHAT ARE YOU DOING?
I'M JUST WAITING FOR...

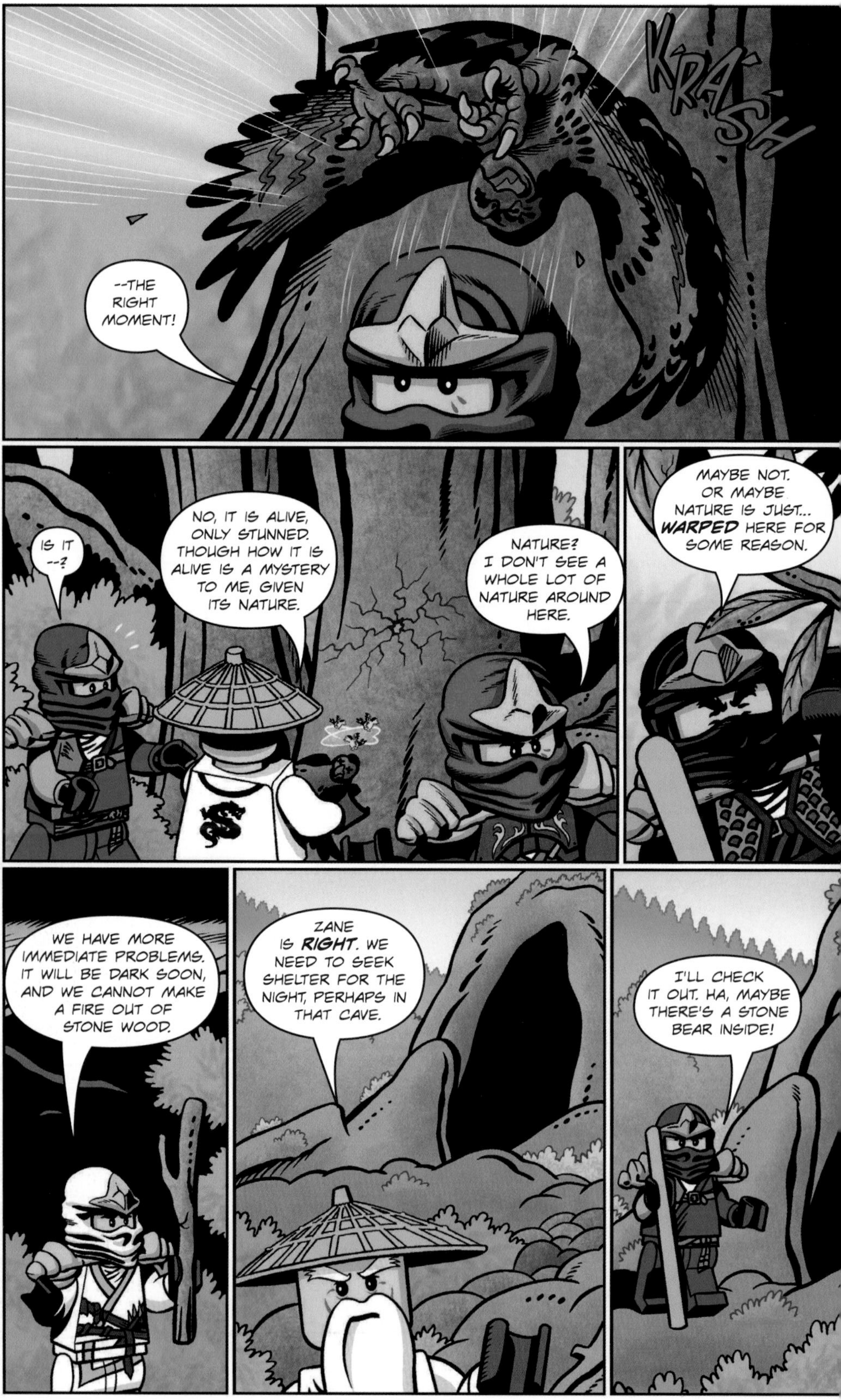
KRASH
--THE RIGHT MOMENT!
IS IT --?
NO, IT IS ALIVE, ONLY STUNNED. THOUGH HOW IT IS ALIVE IS A MYSTERY TO ME, GIVEN ITS NATURE.
NATURE? I DON'T SEE A WHOLE LOT OF NATURE AROUND HERE.
MAYBE NOT. OR MAYBE NATURE IS JUST... WARPED HERE FOR SOME REASON.
WE HAVE MORE IMMEDIATE PROBLEMS. IT WILL BE DARK SOON, AND WE CANNOT MAKE A FIRE OUT OF STONE WOOD.
ZANE IS RIGHT. WE NEED TO SEEK SHELTER FOR THE NIGHT, PERHAPS IN THAT CAVE.
I'LL CHECK IT OUT. HA, MAYBE THERE'S A STONE BEAR INSIDE!

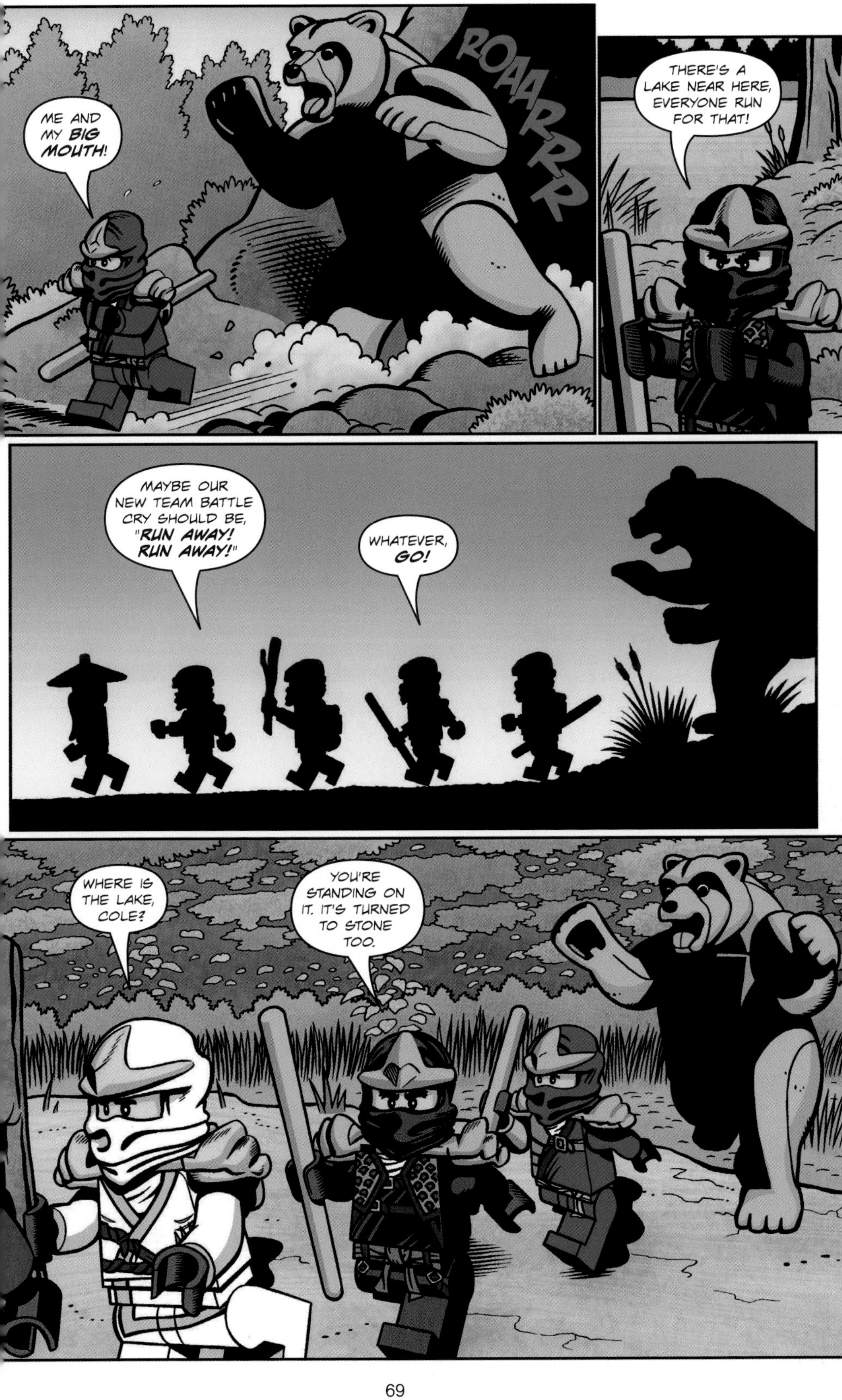
ROAAARRR
ME AND MY BIG MOUTH!
THERE'S A LAKE NEAR HERE, EVERYONE RUN FOR THAT!
MAYBE OUR NEW TEAM BATTLE CRY SHOULD BE, "RUN AWAY! RUN AWAY!"
WHATEVER, GO!
WHERE IS THE LAKE, COLE?
YOU'RE STANDING ON IT. IT'S TURNED TO STONE TOO.

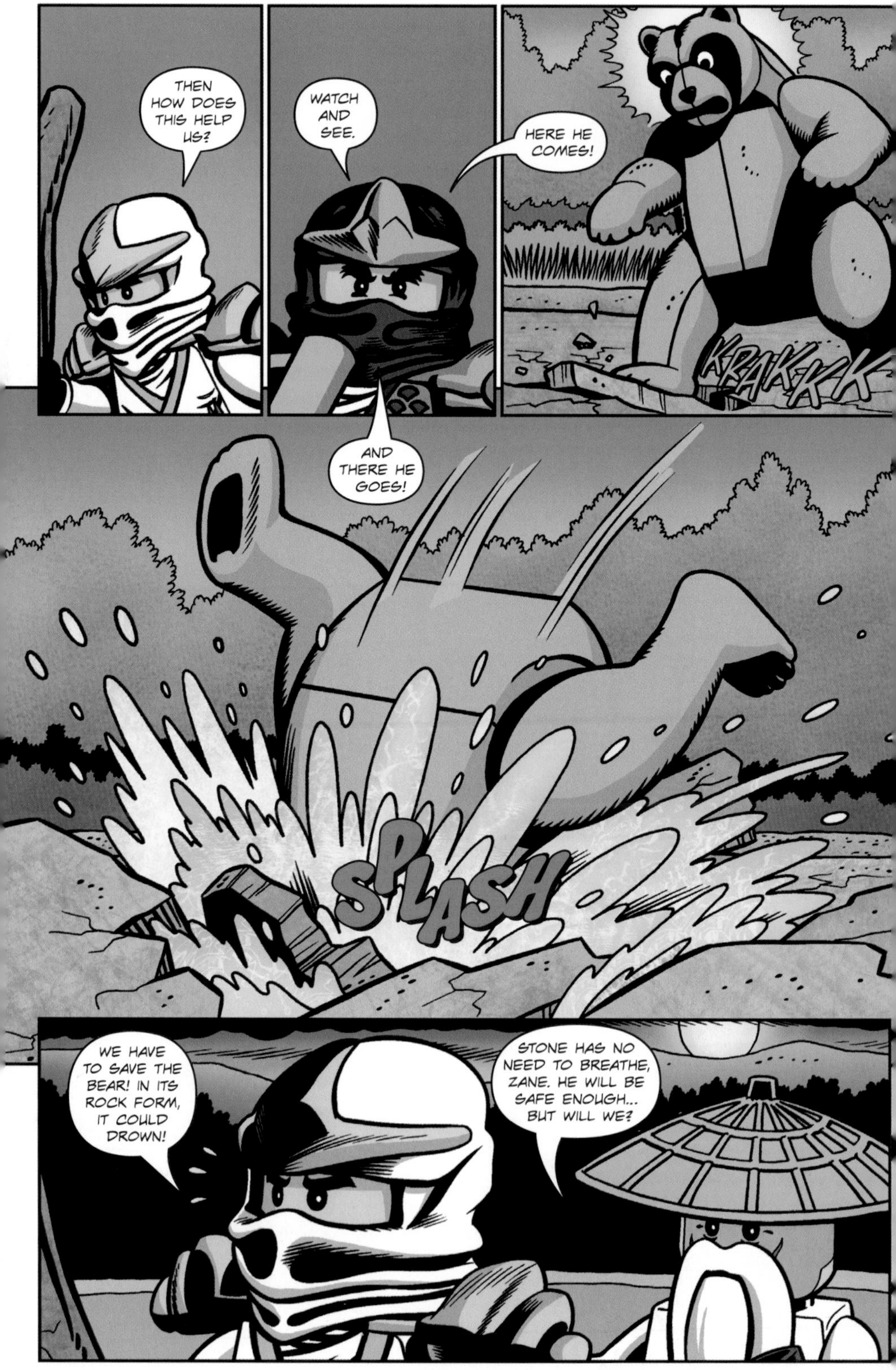

THEN HOW DOES THIS HELP US?
WATCH AND SEE.
HERE HE COMES!
KRAKKKK
AND THERE HE GOES!
SPLASH
WE HAVE TO SAVE THE BEAR! IN ITS ROCK FORM, IT COULD DROWN!
STONE HAS NO NEED TO BREATHE, ZANE. HE WILL BE SAFE ENOUGH... BUT WILL WE?

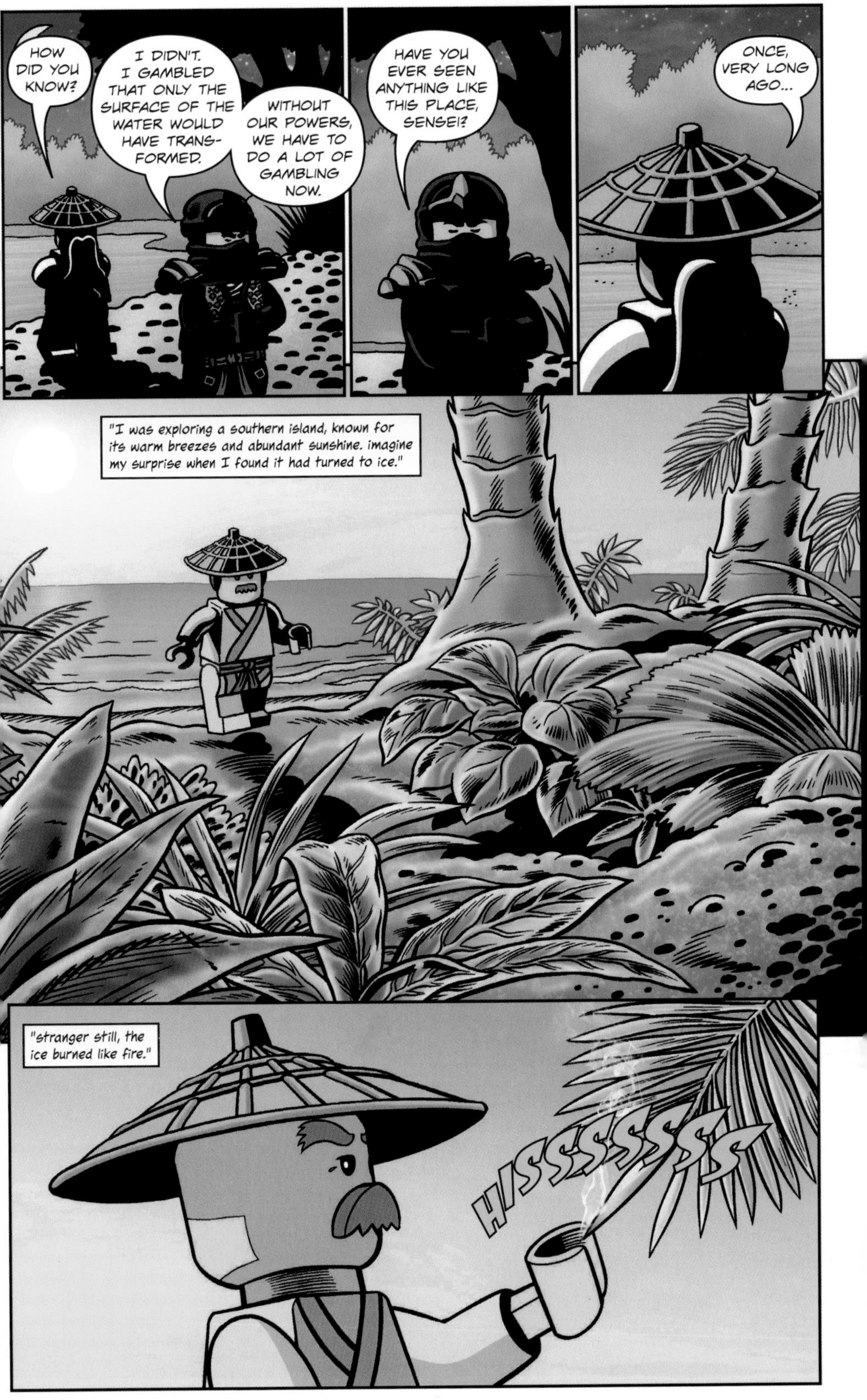
HOW DID YOU KNOW?
I DIDN'T. I GAMBLED THAT ONLY THE SURFACE OF THE WATER WOULD HAVE TRANS-FORMED.
WITHOUT OUR POWERS, WE HAVE TO DO A LOT OF GAMBLING NOW.
HAVE YOU EVER SEEN ANYTHING LIKE THIS PLACE, SENSEI?
ONCE, VERY LONG AGO...
"I was exploring a southern island, known for its warm breezes and abundant sunshine. imagine my surprise when I found it had turned to ice."
"stranger still, the ice burned like fire."
HISSSSSSSS

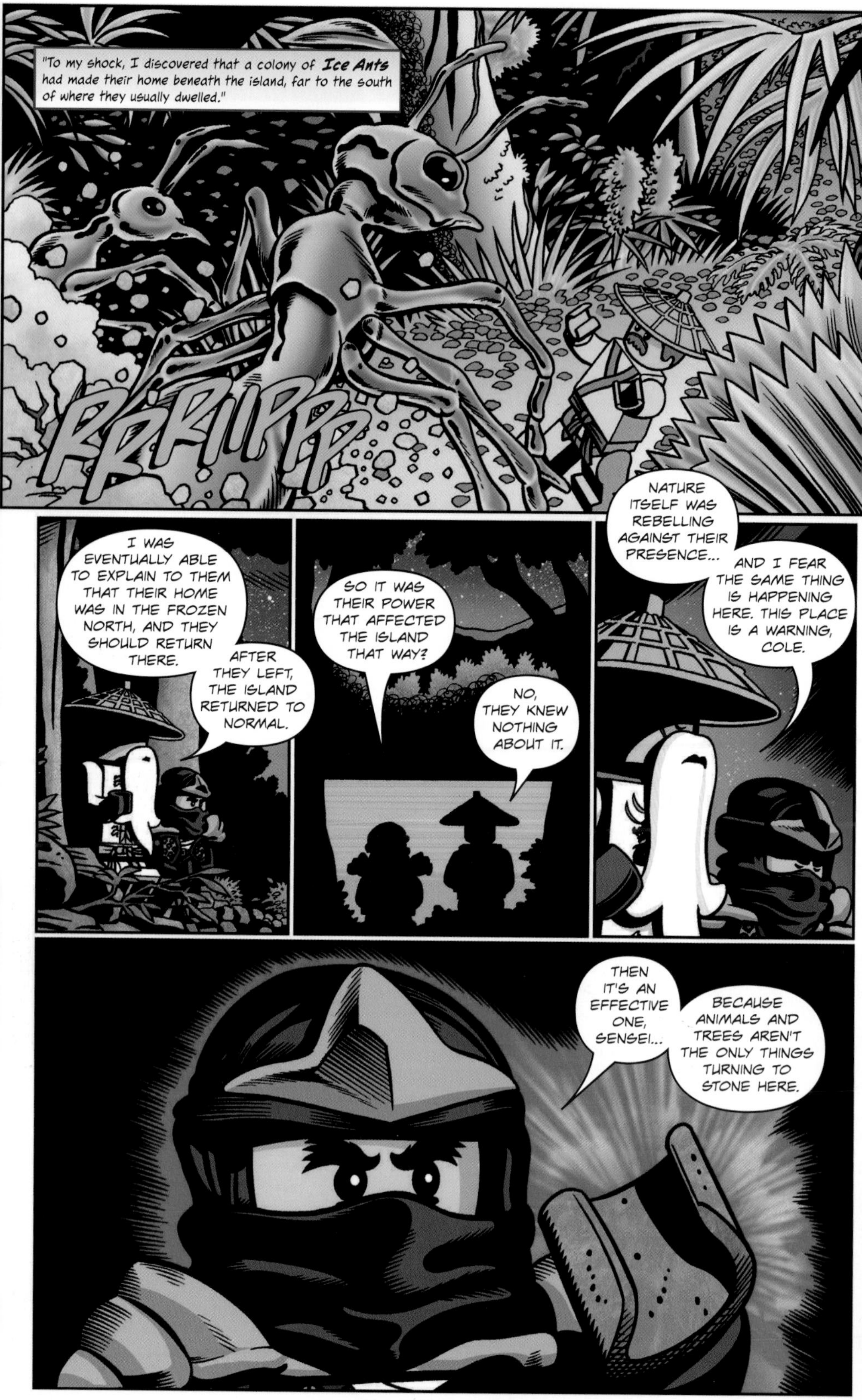

"To my shock, I discovered that a colony of **Ice Ants** had made their home beneath the island, far to the south of where they usually dwelled."
RRRIIIPPP
I WAS EVENTUALLY ABLE TO EXPLAIN TO THEM THAT THEIR HOME WAS IN THE FROZEN NORTH, AND THEY SHOULD RETURN THERE.
AFTER THEY LEFT, THE ISLAND RETURNED TO NORMAL.
SO IT WAS THEIR POWER THAT AFFECTED THE ISLAND THAT WAY?
NO, THEY KNEW NOTHING ABOUT IT.
NATURE ITSELF WAS REBELLING AGAINST THEIR PRESENCE...
AND I FEAR THE SAME THING IS HAPPENING HERE. THIS PLACE IS A WARNING, COLE.
THEN IT'S AN EFFECTIVE ONE, SENSEI...
BECAUSE ANIMALS AND TREES AREN'T THE ONLY THINGS TURNING TO STONE HERE.

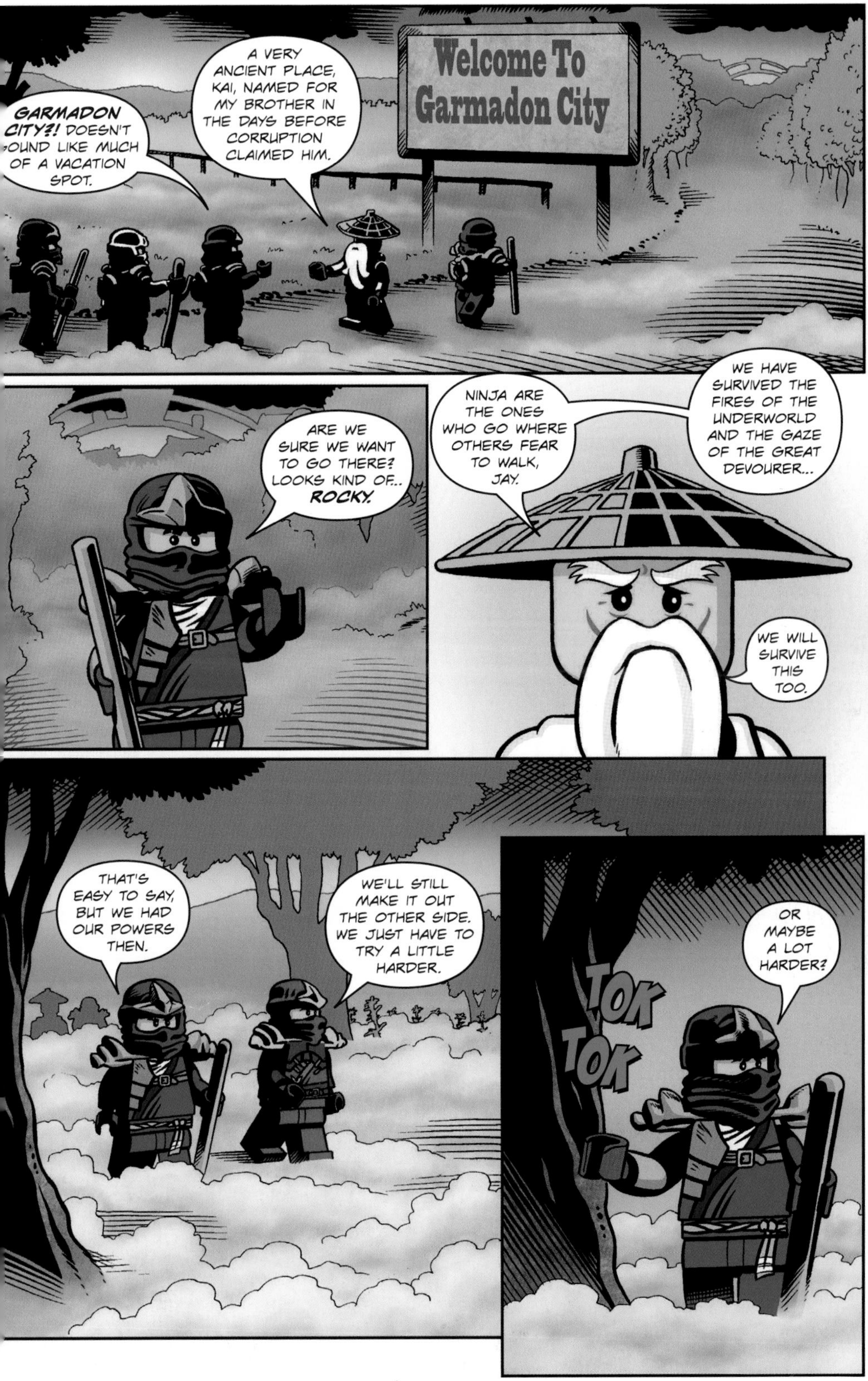
Welcome To Garmadon City
GARMADON CITY?! DOESN'T SOUND LIKE MUCH OF A VACATION SPOT.
A VERY ANCIENT PLACE, KAI, NAMED FOR MY BROTHER IN THE DAYS BEFORE CORRUPTION CLAIMED HIM.
ARE WE SURE WE WANT TO GO THERE? LOOKS KIND OF... ROCKY.
NINJA ARE THE ONES WHO GO WHERE OTHERS FEAR TO WALK, JAY.
WE HAVE SURVIVED THE FIRES OF THE UNDERWORLD AND THE GAZE OF THE GREAT DEVOURER...
WE WILL SURVIVE THIS TOO.
THAT'S EASY TO SAY, BUT WE HAD OUR POWERS THEN.
WE'LL STILL MAKE IT OUT THE OTHER SIDE. WE JUST HAVE TO TRY A LITTLE HARDER.
TOK TOK
OR MAYBE A LOT HARDER?

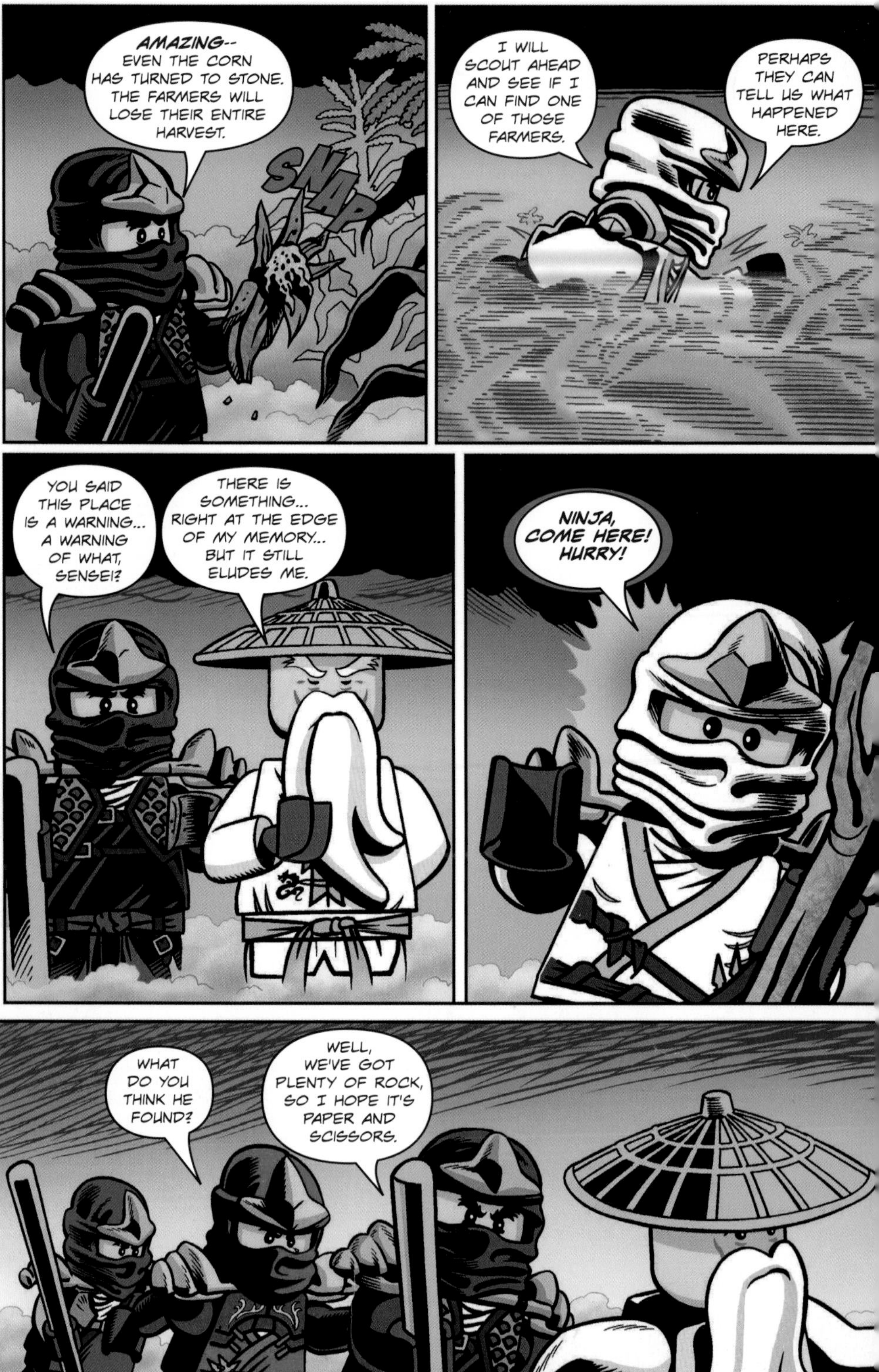
AMAZING-- EVEN THE CORN HAS TURNED TO STONE. THE FARMERS WILL LOSE THEIR ENTIRE HARVEST.
SNAP
I WILL SCOUT AHEAD AND SEE IF I CAN FIND ONE OF THOSE FARMERS.
PERHAPS THEY CAN TELL US WHAT HAPPENED HERE.
YOU SAID THIS PLACE IS A WARNING... A WARNING OF WHAT, SENSEI?
THERE IS SOMETHING... RIGHT AT THE EDGE OF MY MEMORY... BUT IT STILL ELUDES ME.
NINJA, COME HERE! HURRY!
WHAT DO YOU THINK HE FOUND?
WELL, WE'VE GOT PLENTY OF ROCK, SO I HOPE IT'S PAPER AND SCISSORS.

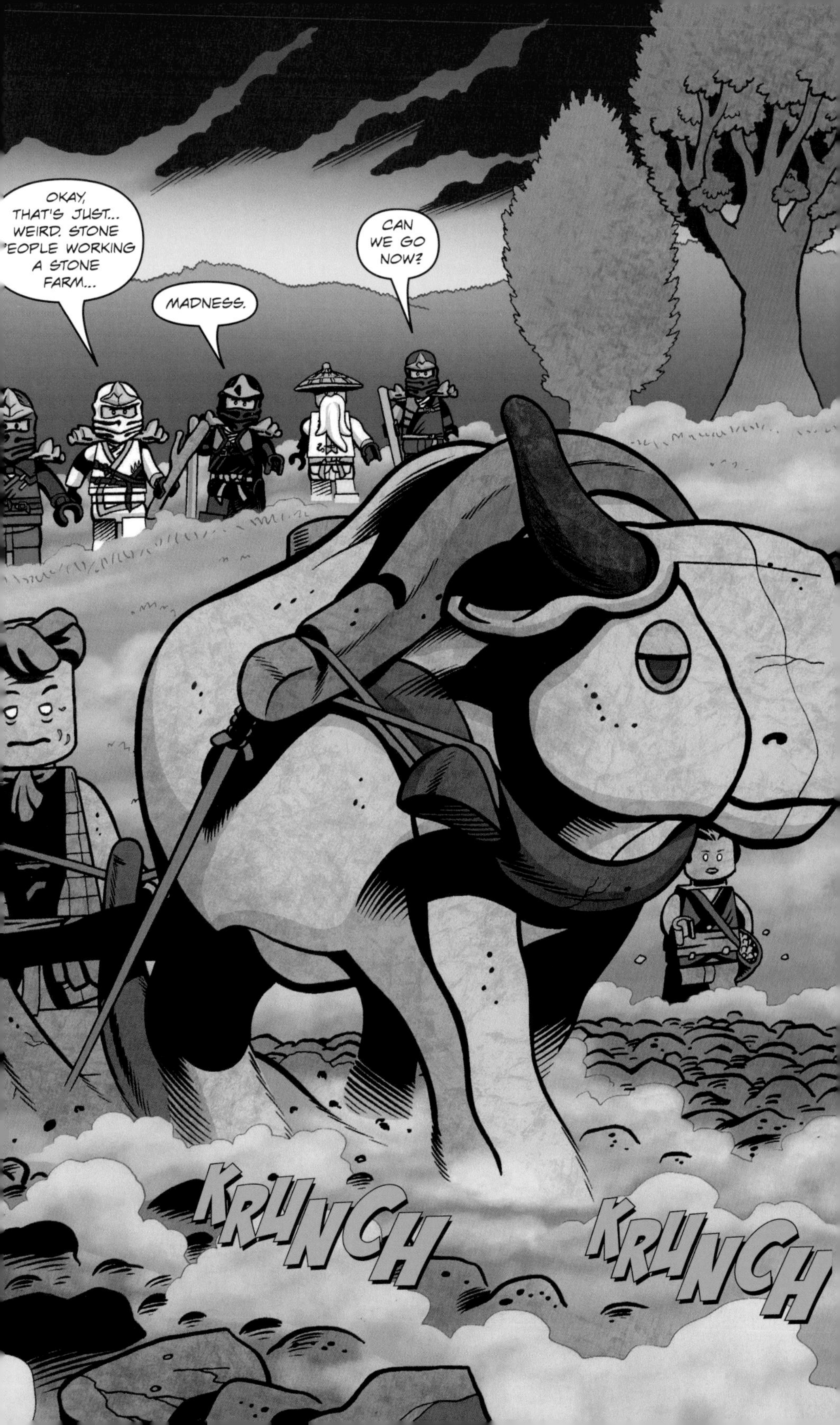
OKAY, THAT'S JUST... WEIRD. STONE 'EOPLE WORKING A STONE FARM...
MADNESS.
CAN WE GO NOW?
KRUNCH
KRUNCH

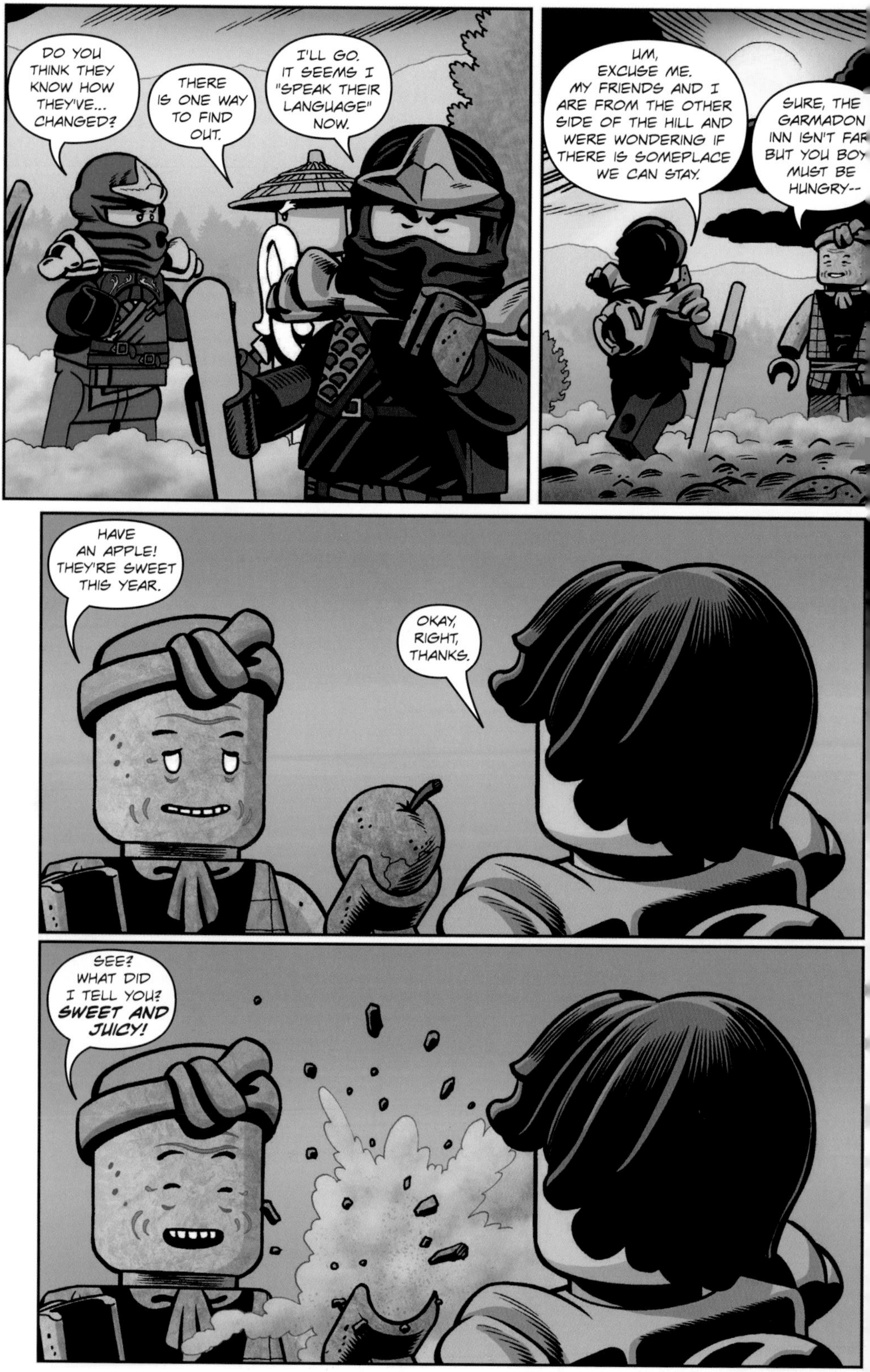
DO YOU THINK THEY KNOW HOW THEY'VE... CHANGED?
THERE IS ONE WAY TO FIND OUT.
I'LL GO. IT SEEMS I "SPEAK THEIR LANGUAGE" NOW.
UM, EXCUSE ME. MY FRIENDS AND I ARE FROM THE OTHER SIDE OF THE HILL AND WERE WONDERING IF THERE IS SOMEPLACE WE CAN STAY.
SURE, THE GARMADON INN ISN'T FAR BUT YOU BOYS MUST BE HUNGRY--
HAVE AN APPLE! THEY'RE SWEET THIS YEAR.
OKAY, RIGHT, THANKS.
SEE? WHAT DID I TELL YOU? **SWEET AND JUICY!**

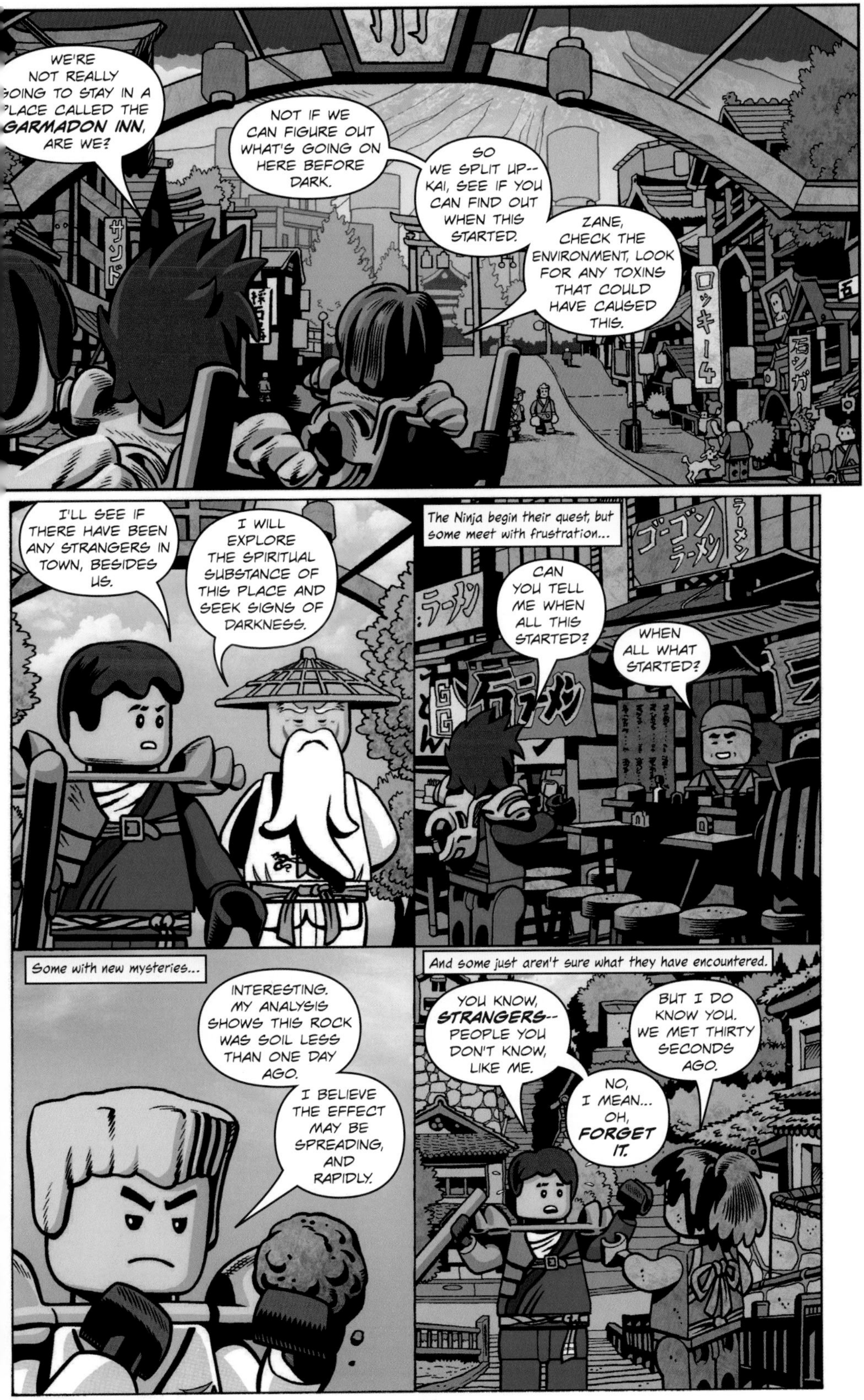
WE'RE NOT REALLY GOING TO STAY IN A PLACE CALLED THE **GARMADON INN**, ARE WE?
NOT IF WE CAN FIGURE OUT WHAT'S GOING ON HERE BEFORE DARK.
SO WE SPLIT UP-- KAI, SEE IF YOU CAN FIND OUT WHEN THIS STARTED.
ZANE, CHECK THE ENVIRONMENT, LOOK FOR ANY TOXINS THAT COULD HAVE CAUSED THIS.
I'LL SEE IF THERE HAVE BEEN ANY STRANGERS IN TOWN, BESIDES US.
I WILL EXPLORE THE SPIRITUAL SUBSTANCE OF THIS PLACE AND SEEK SIGNS OF DARKNESS.
The Ninja begin their quest, but some meet with frustration...
CAN YOU TELL ME WHEN ALL THIS STARTED?
WHEN ALL WHAT STARTED?
Some with new mysteries...
INTERESTING. MY ANALYSIS SHOWS THIS ROCK WAS SOIL LESS THAN ONE DAY AGO.
I BELIEVE THE EFFECT MAY BE SPREADING, AND RAPIDLY.
And some just aren't sure what they have encountered.
YOU KNOW, **STRANGERS**-- PEOPLE YOU DON'T KNOW, LIKE ME.
BUT I DO KNOW YOU. WE MET THIRTY SECONDS AGO.
NO, I MEAN... OH, **FORGET IT.**

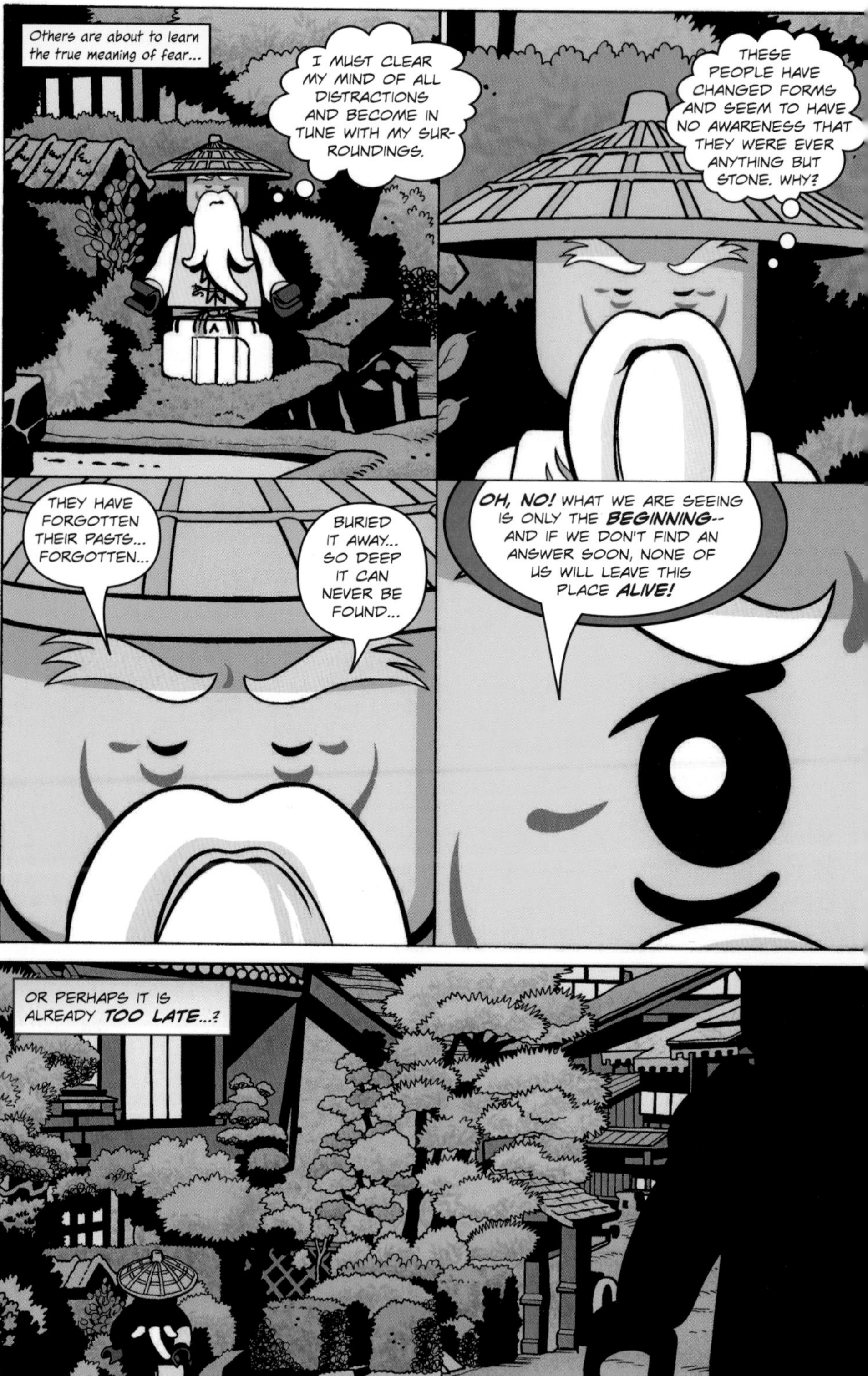
Others are about to learn the true meaning of fear...
I MUST CLEAR MY MIND OF ALL DISTRACTIONS AND BECOME IN TUNE WITH MY SURROUNDINGS.
THESE PEOPLE HAVE CHANGED FORMS AND SEEM TO HAVE NO AWARENESS THAT THEY WERE EVER ANYTHING BUT STONE. WHY?
THEY HAVE FORGOTTEN THEIR PASTS... FORGOTTEN...
BURIED IT AWAY... SO DEEP IT CAN NEVER BE FOUND...
OH, NO! WHAT WE ARE SEEING IS ONLY THE BEGINNING-- AND IF WE DON'T FIND AN ANSWER SOON, NONE OF US WILL LEAVE THIS PLACE ALIVE!
OR PERHAPS IT IS ALREADY TOO LATE...?

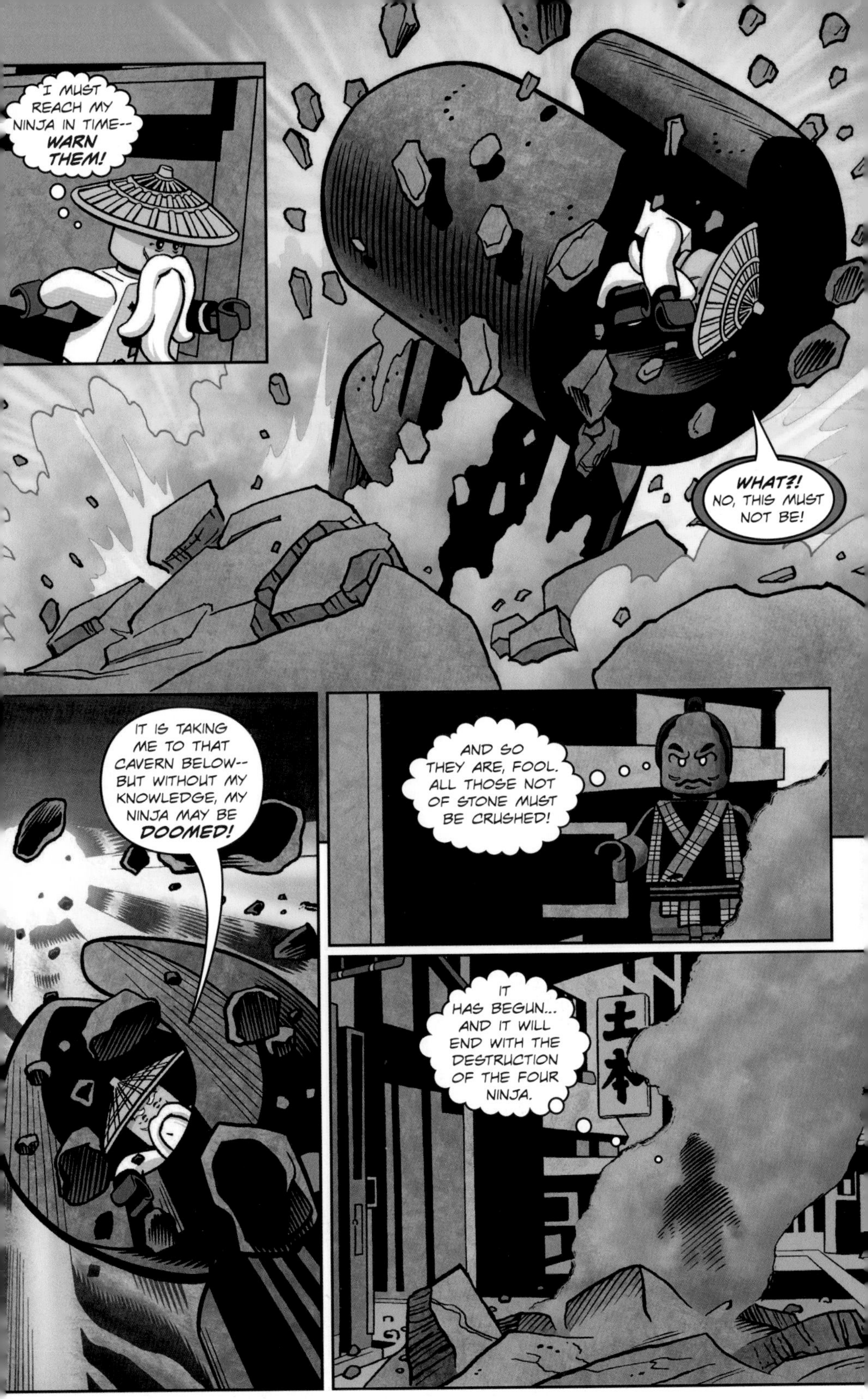
I MUST REACH MY NINJA IN TIME-- WARN THEM!
WHAT?! NO, THIS MUST NOT BE!
IT IS TAKING ME TO THAT CAVERN BELOW-- BUT WITHOUT MY KNOWLEDGE, MY NINJA MAY BE DOOMED!
AND SO THEY ARE, FOOL. ALL THOSE NOT OF STONE MUST BE CRUSHED!
IT HAS BEGUN... AND IT WILL END WITH THE DESTRUCTION OF THE FOUR NINJA.
土本

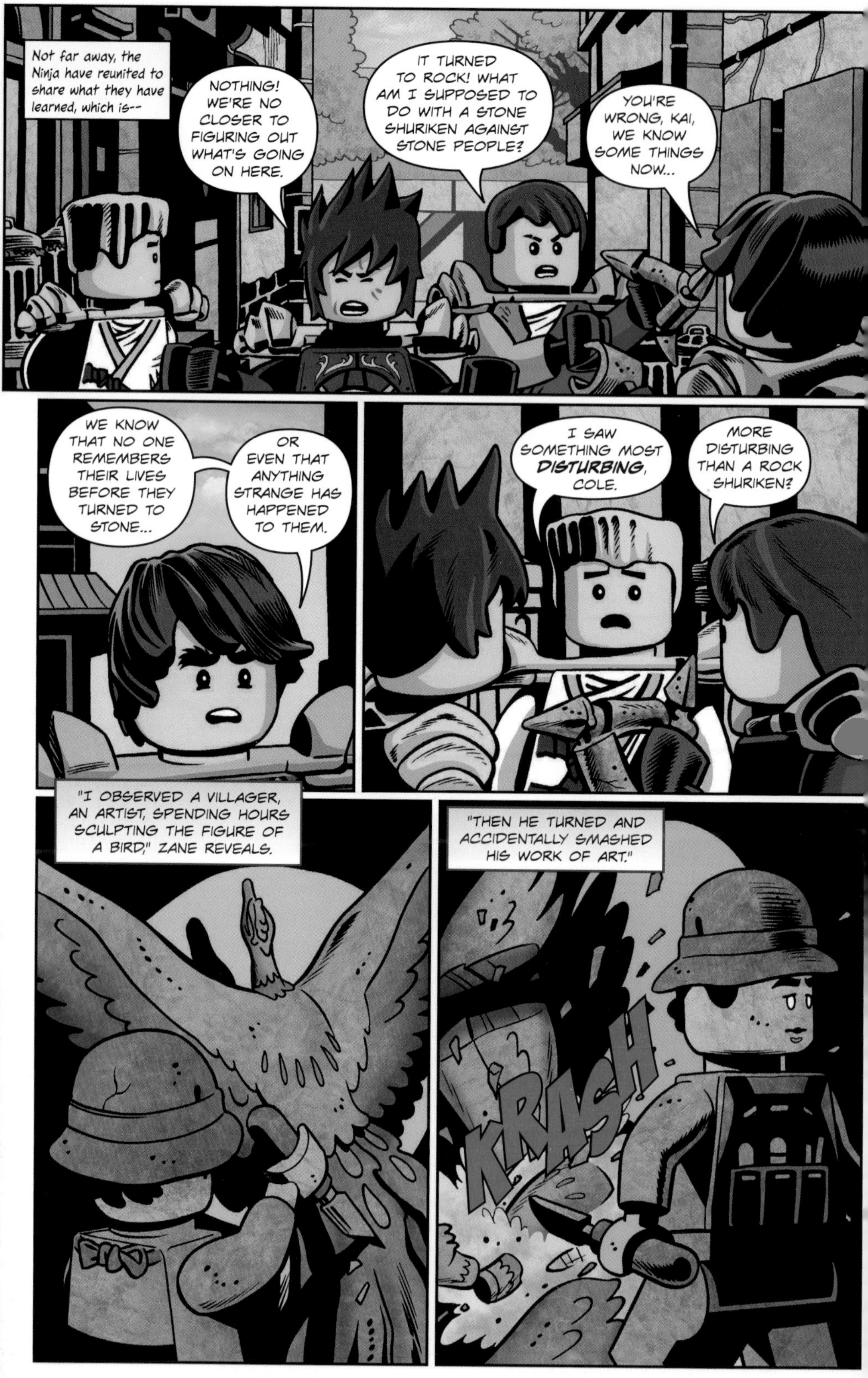
Not far away, the Ninja have reunited to share what they have learned, which is--
NOTHING! WE'RE NO CLOSER TO FIGURING OUT WHAT'S GOING ON HERE.
IT TURNED TO ROCK! WHAT AM I SUPPOSED TO DO WITH A STONE SHURIKEN AGAINST STONE PEOPLE?
YOU'RE WRONG, KAI, WE KNOW SOME THINGS NOW...
WE KNOW THAT NO ONE REMEMBERS THEIR LIVES BEFORE THEY TURNED TO STONE...
OR EVEN THAT ANYTHING STRANGE HAS HAPPENED TO THEM.
I SAW SOMETHING MOST **DISTURBING**, COLE.
MORE DISTURBING THAN A ROCK SHURIKEN?
"I OBSERVED A VILLAGER, AN ARTIST, SPENDING HOURS SCULPTING THE FIGURE OF A BIRD," ZANE REVEALS.
"THEN HE TURNED AND ACCIDENTALLY SMASHED HIS WORK OF ART."
KRASH

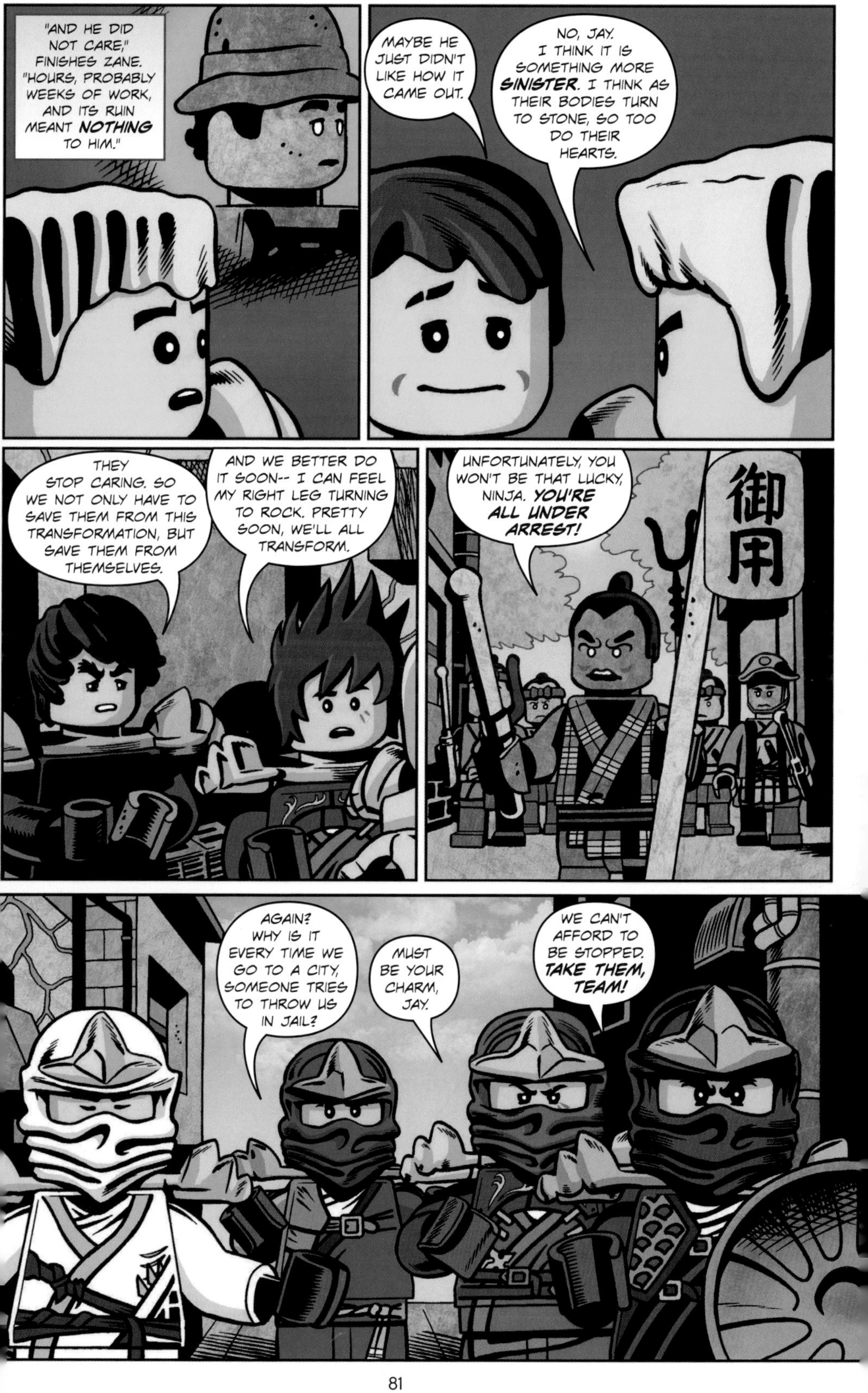
"AND HE DID NOT CARE," FINISHES ZANE. "HOURS, PROBABLY WEEKS OF WORK, AND ITS RUIN MEANT **NOTHING** TO HIM."
MAYBE HE JUST DIDN'T LIKE HOW IT CAME OUT.
NO, JAY. I THINK IT IS SOMETHING MORE **SINISTER**. I THINK AS THEIR BODIES TURN TO STONE, SO TOO DO THEIR HEARTS.
THEY STOP CARING. SO WE NOT ONLY HAVE TO SAVE THEM FROM THIS TRANSFORMATION, BUT SAVE THEM FROM THEMSELVES.
AND WE BETTER DO IT SOON-- I CAN FEEL MY RIGHT LEG TURNING TO ROCK. PRETTY SOON, WE'LL ALL TRANSFORM.
UNFORTUNATELY, YOU WON'T BE THAT LUCKY, NINJA. ***YOU'RE ALL UNDER ARREST!***
御用
AGAIN? WHY IS IT EVERY TIME WE GO TO A CITY, SOMEONE TRIES TO THROW US IN JAIL?
MUST BE YOUR CHARM, JAY.
WE CAN'T AFFORD TO BE STOPPED. ***TAKE THEM, TEAM!***

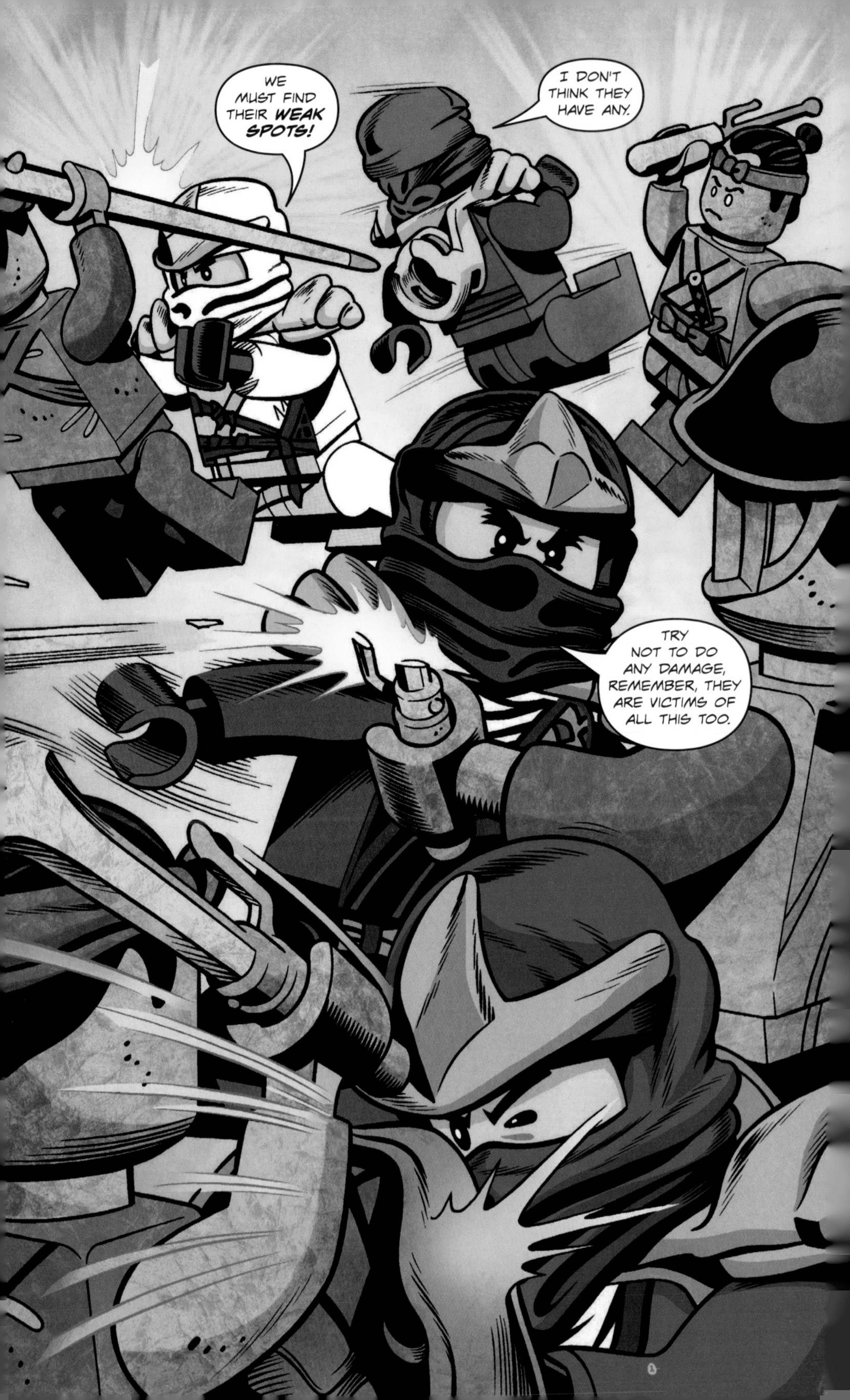
WE MUST FIND THEIR WEAK SPOTS!
I DON'T THINK THEY HAVE ANY.
TRY NOT TO DO ANY DAMAGE, REMEMBER, THEY ARE VICTIMS OF ALL THIS TOO.

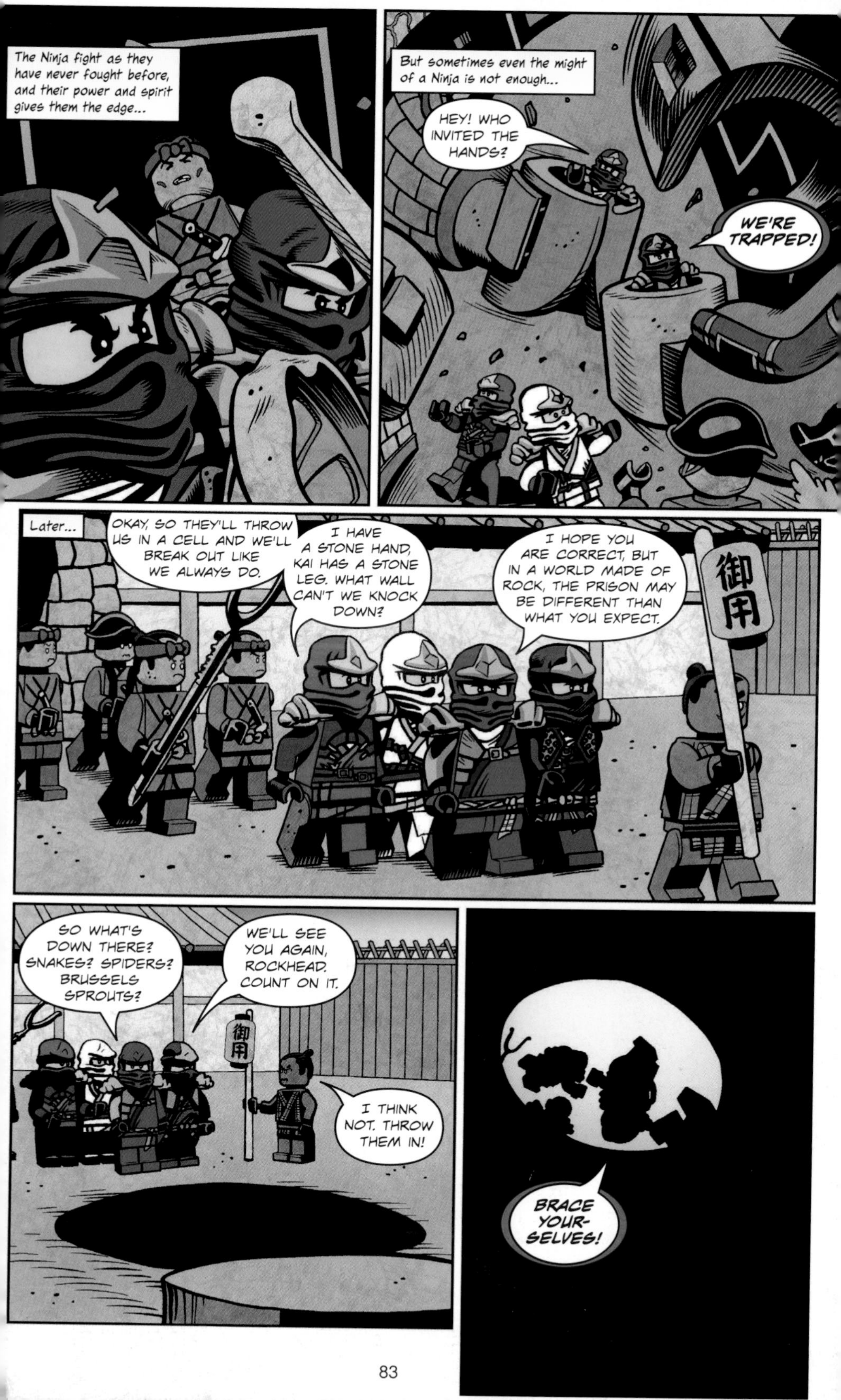

The Ninja fight as they have never fought before, and their power and spirit gives them the edge...
But sometimes even the might of a Ninja is not enough...
HEY! WHO INVITED THE HANDS?
WE'RE TRAPPED!
Later...
OKAY, SO THEY'LL THROW US IN A CELL AND WE'LL BREAK OUT LIKE WE ALWAYS DO.
I HAVE A STONE HAND, KAI HAS A STONE LEG. WHAT WALL CAN'T WE KNOCK DOWN?
I HOPE YOU ARE CORRECT, BUT IN A WORLD MADE OF ROCK, THE PRISON MAY BE DIFFERENT THAN WHAT YOU EXPECT.
御用
SO WHAT'S DOWN THERE? SNAKES? SPIDERS? BRUSSELS SPROUTS?
WE'LL SEE YOU AGAIN, ROCKHEAD. COUNT ON IT.
御用
I THINK NOT. THROW THEM IN!
BRACE YOUR-SELVES!

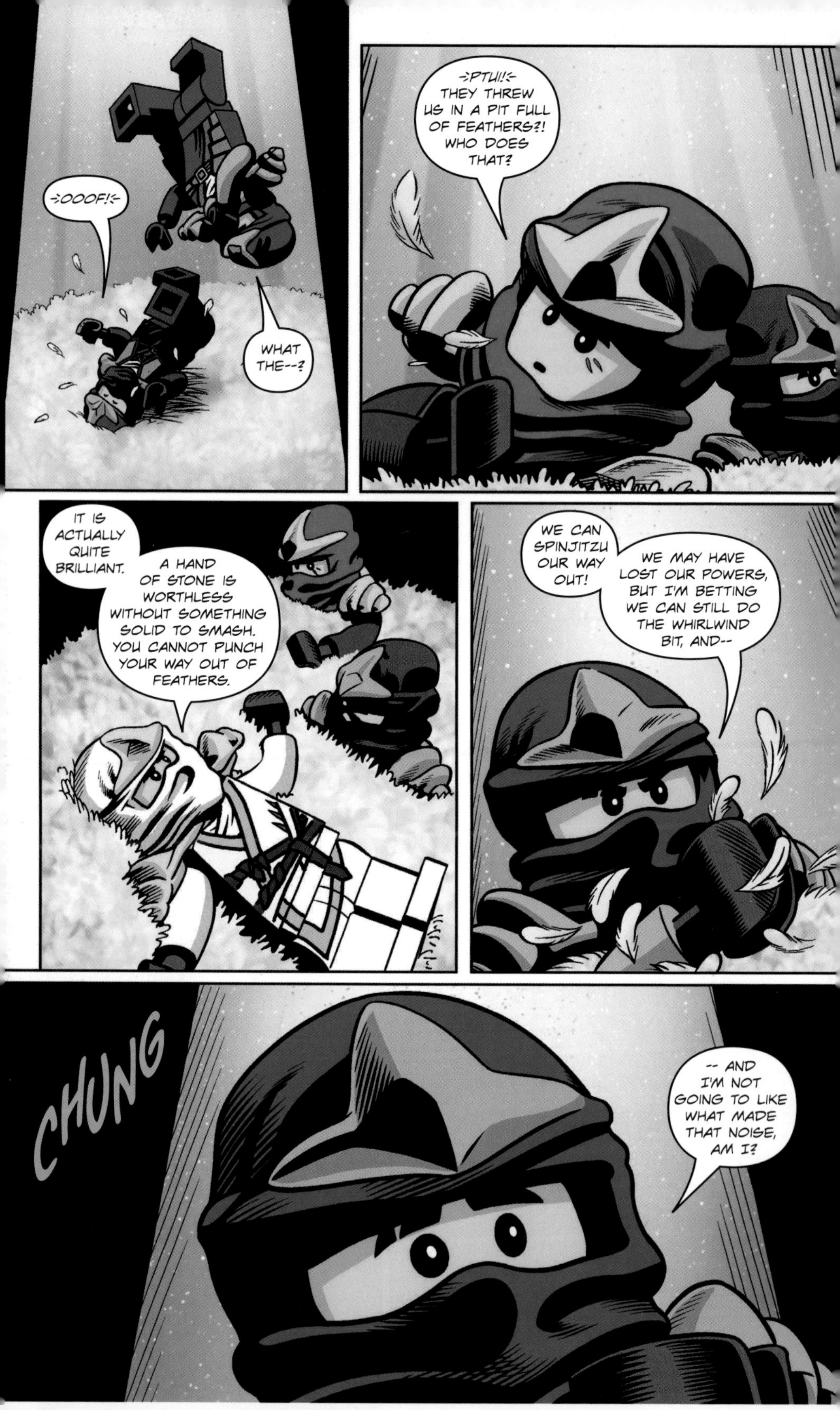

⚟OOOF!⚞
WHAT THE--?
⚟PTUI!⚞ THEY THREW US IN A PIT FULL OF FEATHERS?! WHO DOES THAT?
IT IS ACTUALLY QUITE BRILLIANT.
A HAND OF STONE IS WORTHLESS WITHOUT SOMETHING SOLID TO SMASH. YOU CANNOT PUNCH YOUR WAY OUT OF FEATHERS.
WE CAN SPINJITZU OUR WAY OUT!
WE MAY HAVE LOST OUR POWERS, BUT I'M BETTING WE CAN STILL DO THE WHIRLWIND BIT, AND--
CHUNG
-- AND I'M NOT GOING TO LIKE WHAT MADE THAT NOISE, AM I?

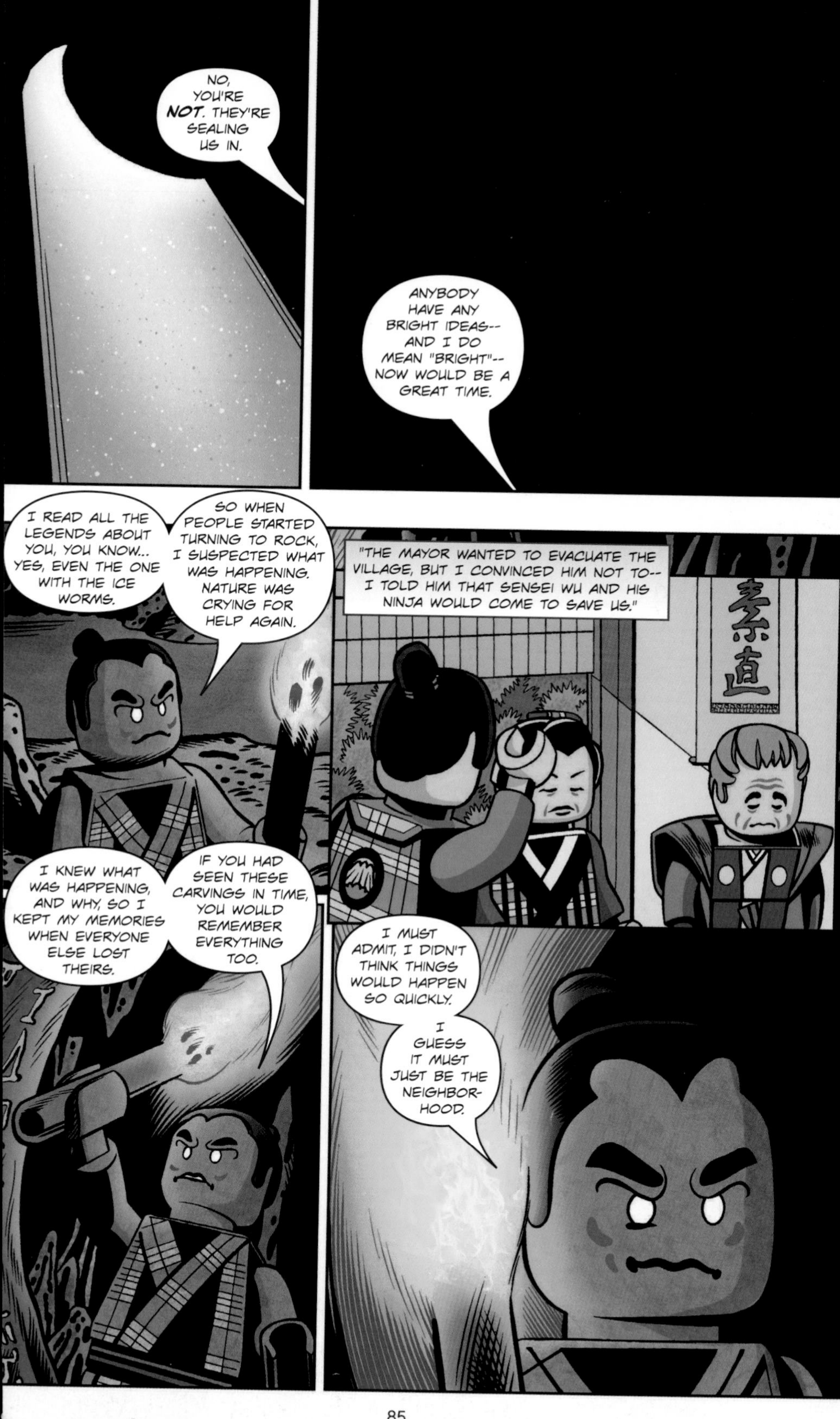
NO, YOU'RE NOT. THEY'RE SEALING US IN.
ANYBODY HAVE ANY BRIGHT IDEAS-- AND I DO MEAN "BRIGHT"-- NOW WOULD BE A GREAT TIME.
I READ ALL THE LEGENDS ABOUT YOU, YOU KNOW... YES, EVEN THE ONE WITH THE ICE WORMS.
SO WHEN PEOPLE STARTED TURNING TO ROCK, I SUSPECTED WHAT WAS HAPPENING. NATURE WAS CRYING FOR HELP AGAIN.
"THE MAYOR WANTED TO EVACUATE THE VILLAGE, BUT I CONVINCED HIM NOT TO-- I TOLD HIM THAT SENSEI WU AND HIS NINJA WOULD COME TO SAVE US."
I KNEW WHAT WAS HAPPENING, AND WHY, SO I KEPT MY MEMORIES WHEN EVERYONE ELSE LOST THEIRS.
IF YOU HAD SEEN THESE CARVINGS IN TIME, YOU WOULD REMEMBER EVERYTHING TOO.
I MUST ADMIT, I DIDN'T THINK THINGS WOULD HAPPEN SO QUICKLY.
I GUESS IT MUST JUST BE THE NEIGHBOR-HOOD.

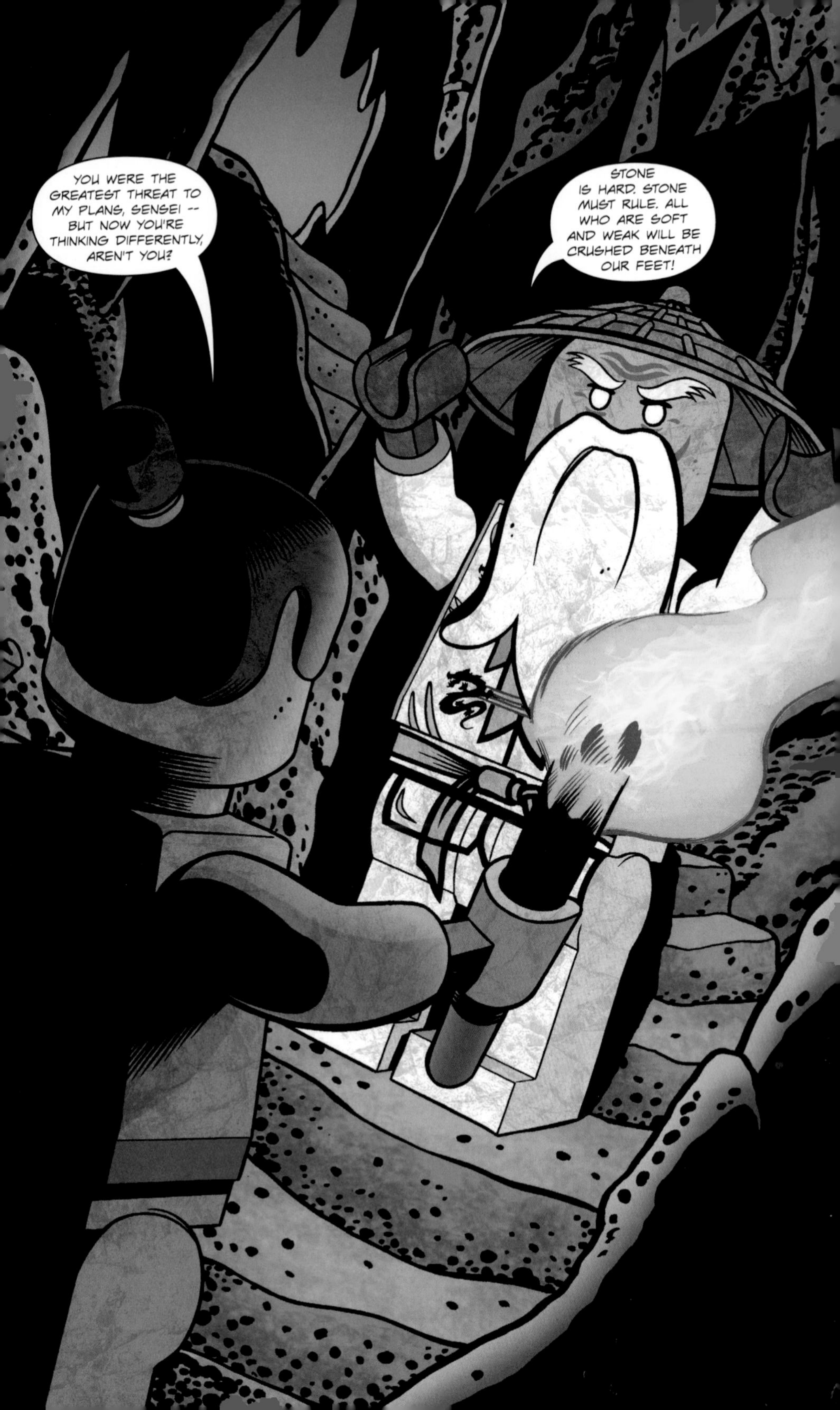
YOU WERE THE GREATEST THREAT TO MY PLANS, SENSEI -- BUT NOW YOU'RE THINKING DIFFERENTLY, AREN'T YOU?
STONE IS HARD. STONE MUST RULE. ALL WHO ARE SOFT AND WEAK WILL BE CRUSHED BENEATH OUR FEET!

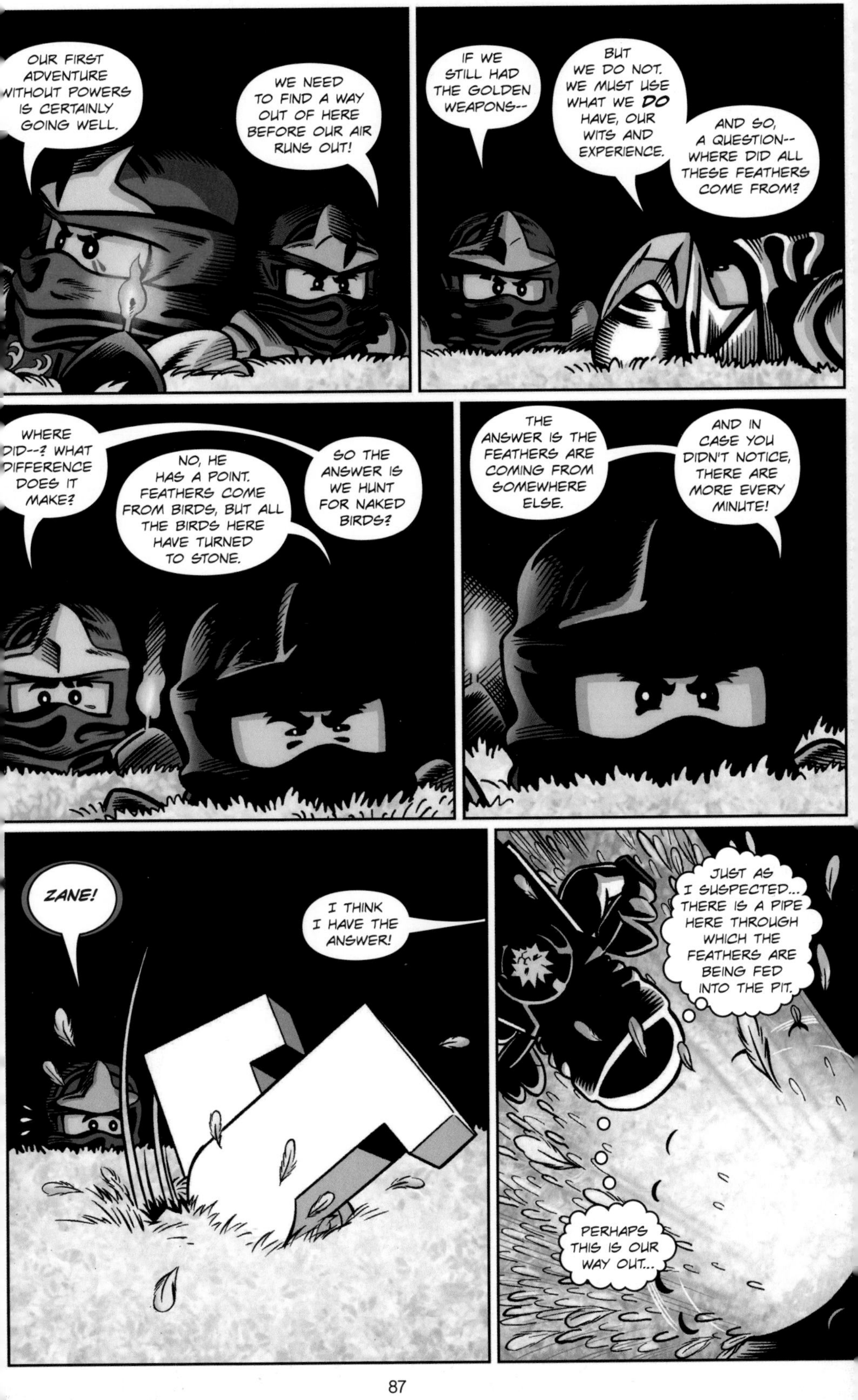

OUR FIRST ADVENTURE WITHOUT POWERS IS CERTAINLY GOING WELL.
WE NEED TO FIND A WAY OUT OF HERE BEFORE OUR AIR RUNS OUT!
IF WE STILL HAD THE GOLDEN WEAPONS--
BUT WE DO NOT. WE MUST USE WHAT WE **DO** HAVE, OUR WITS AND EXPERIENCE.
AND SO, A QUESTION-- WHERE DID ALL THESE FEATHERS COME FROM?
WHERE DID--? WHAT DIFFERENCE DOES IT MAKE?
NO, HE HAS A POINT. FEATHERS COME FROM BIRDS, BUT ALL THE BIRDS HERE HAVE TURNED TO STONE.
SO THE ANSWER IS WE HUNT FOR NAKED BIRDS?
THE ANSWER IS THE FEATHERS ARE COMING FROM SOMEWHERE ELSE.
AND IN CASE YOU DIDN'T NOTICE, THERE ARE MORE EVERY MINUTE!
ZANE!
I THINK I HAVE THE ANSWER!
JUST AS I SUSPECTED... THERE IS A PIPE HERE THROUGH WHICH THE FEATHERS ARE BEING FED INTO THE PIT.
PERHAPS THIS IS OUR WAY OUT...

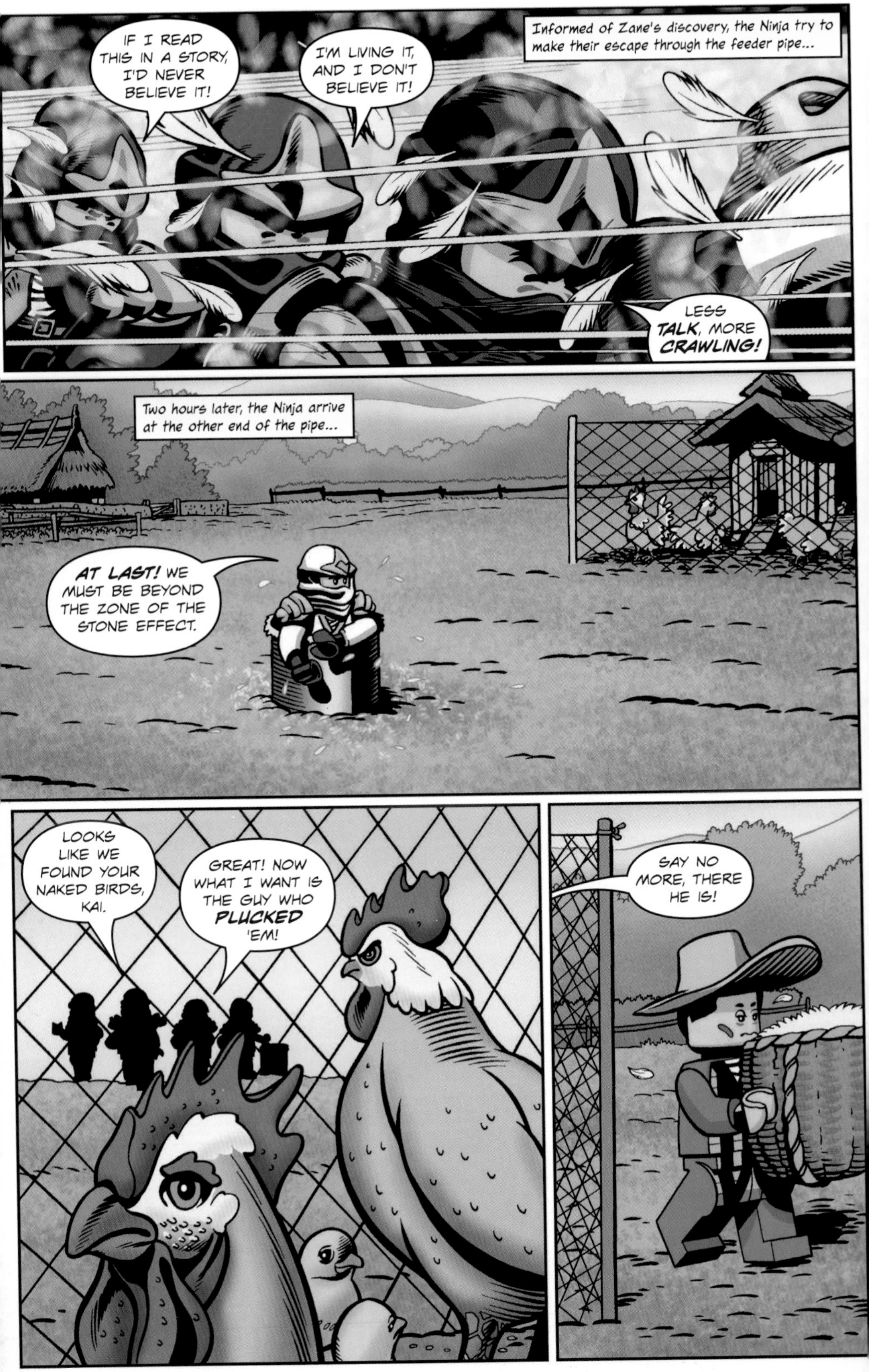
Informed of Zane's discovery, the Ninja try to make their escape through the feeder pipe...
IF I READ THIS IN A STORY, I'D NEVER BELIEVE IT!
I'M LIVING IT, AND I DON'T BELIEVE IT!
LESS TALK, MORE CRAWLING!
Two hours later, the Ninja arrive at the other end of the pipe...
AT LAST! WE MUST BE BEYOND THE ZONE OF THE STONE EFFECT.
LOOKS LIKE WE FOUND YOUR NAKED BIRDS, KAI.
GREAT! NOW WHAT I WANT IS THE GUY WHO PLUCKED 'EM!
SAY NO MORE, THERE HE IS!

HEY, YOU!

YIIII! WHO'S THAT?

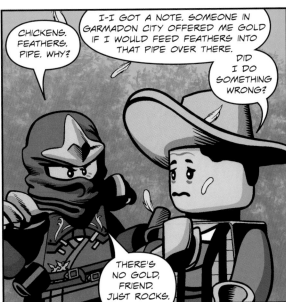

CHICKENS. FEATHERS. PIPE. WHY?

I-I GOT A NOTE. SOMEONE IN GARMADON CITY OFFERED ME GOLD IF I WOULD FEED FEATHERS INTO THAT PIPE OVER THERE.

DID I DO SOMETHING WRONG?

THERE'S NO GOLD, FRIEND. JUST ROCKS.

WELL, HAT GOT US NO-WHERE.

WRONG. WHOEVER SENT THE FARMER THAT NOTE KNEW THAT FARM WOULDN'T TURN TO STONE, AT LEAST NOT ANYTIME SOON.

THAT MEANS SOMEONE IN GARMADON CITY KNOWS WHAT'S GOING ON.

WE'VE GOT A LONG WALK AHEAD OF US-- AND A PLAN TO MAKE.

ime, when the Ninja enter Garmadon City, e not asking questions, but giving answers...

DON'T WORRY ABOUT THE WHOLE ROCK THING, FOLKS-- WE FIGURED IT ALL OUT.

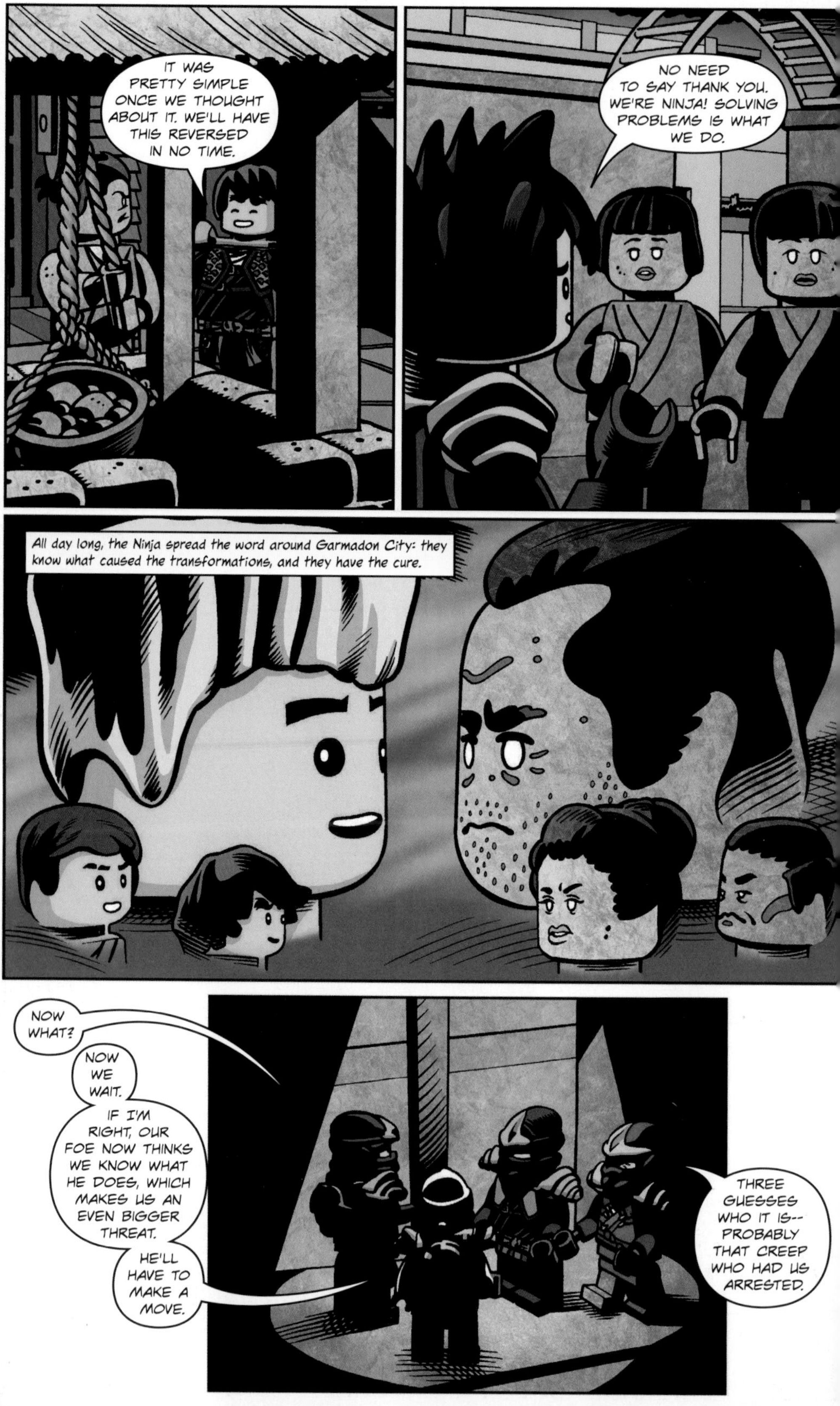
IT WAS PRETTY SIMPLE ONCE WE THOUGHT ABOUT IT. WE'LL HAVE THIS REVERSED IN NO TIME.
NO NEED TO SAY THANK YOU. WE'RE NINJA! SOLVING PROBLEMS IS WHAT WE DO.
All day long, the Ninja spread the word around Garmadon City: they know what caused the transformations, and they have the cure.
NOW WHAT?
NOW WE WAIT.
IF I'M RIGHT, OUR FOE NOW THINKS WE KNOW WHAT HE DOES, WHICH MAKES US AN EVEN BIGGER THREAT.
HE'LL HAVE TO MAKE A MOVE.
THREE GUESSES WHO IT IS-- PROBABLY THAT CREEP WHO HAD US ARRESTED.

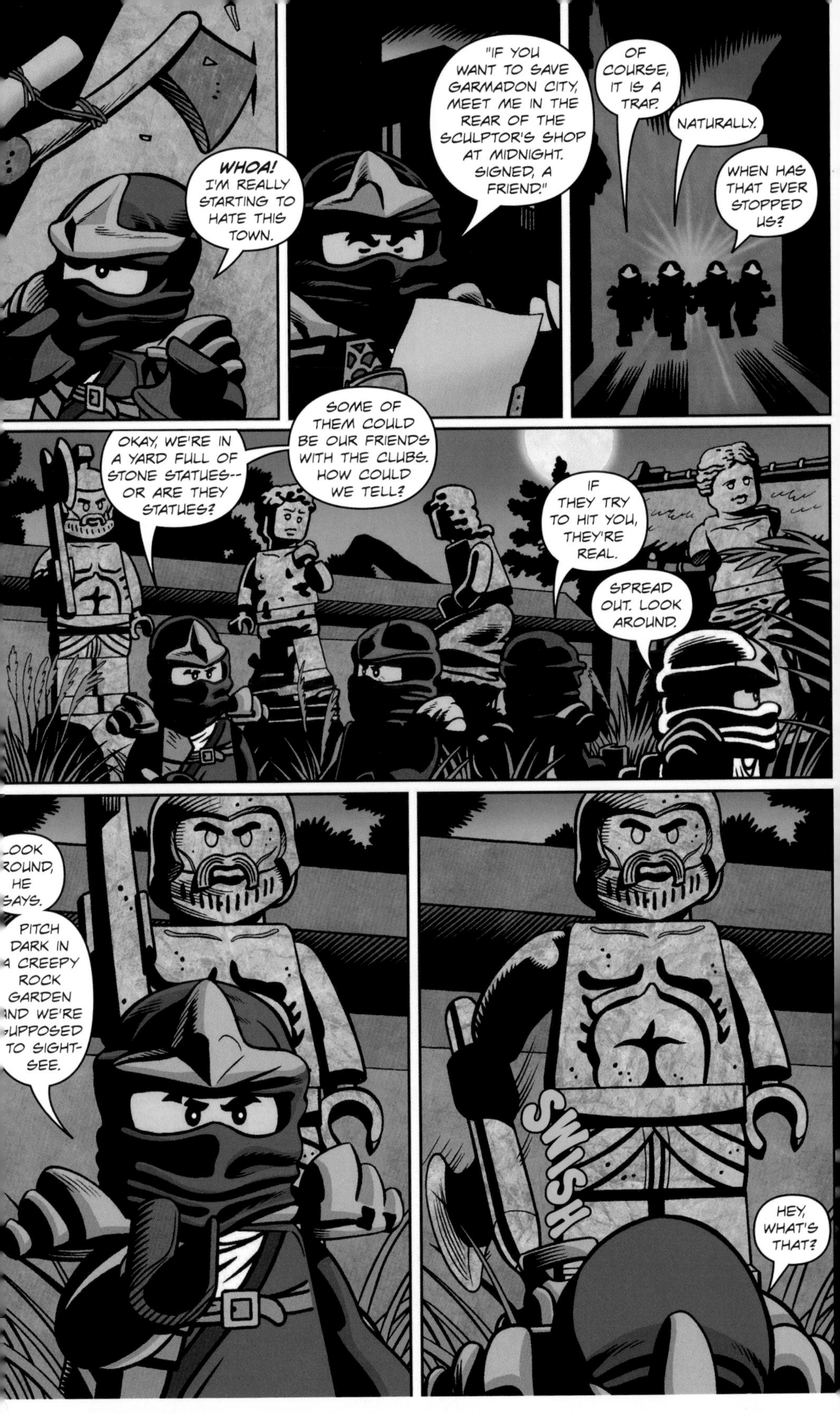
WHOA! I'M REALLY STARTING TO HATE THIS TOWN.
"IF YOU WANT TO SAVE GARMADON CITY, MEET ME IN THE REAR OF THE SCULPTOR'S SHOP AT MIDNIGHT. SIGNED, A FRIEND."
OF COURSE, IT IS A TRAP.
NATURALLY.
WHEN HAS THAT EVER STOPPED US?
OKAY, WE'RE IN A YARD FULL OF STONE STATUES--OR ARE THEY STATUES?
SOME OF THEM COULD BE OUR FRIENDS WITH THE CLUBS. HOW COULD WE TELL?
IF THEY TRY TO HIT YOU, THEY'RE REAL.
SPREAD OUT. LOOK AROUND.
LOOK ROUND, HE SAYS.
PITCH DARK IN A CREEPY ROCK GARDEN AND WE'RE SUPPOSED TO SIGHT-SEE.
SWISH
HEY, WHAT'S THAT?

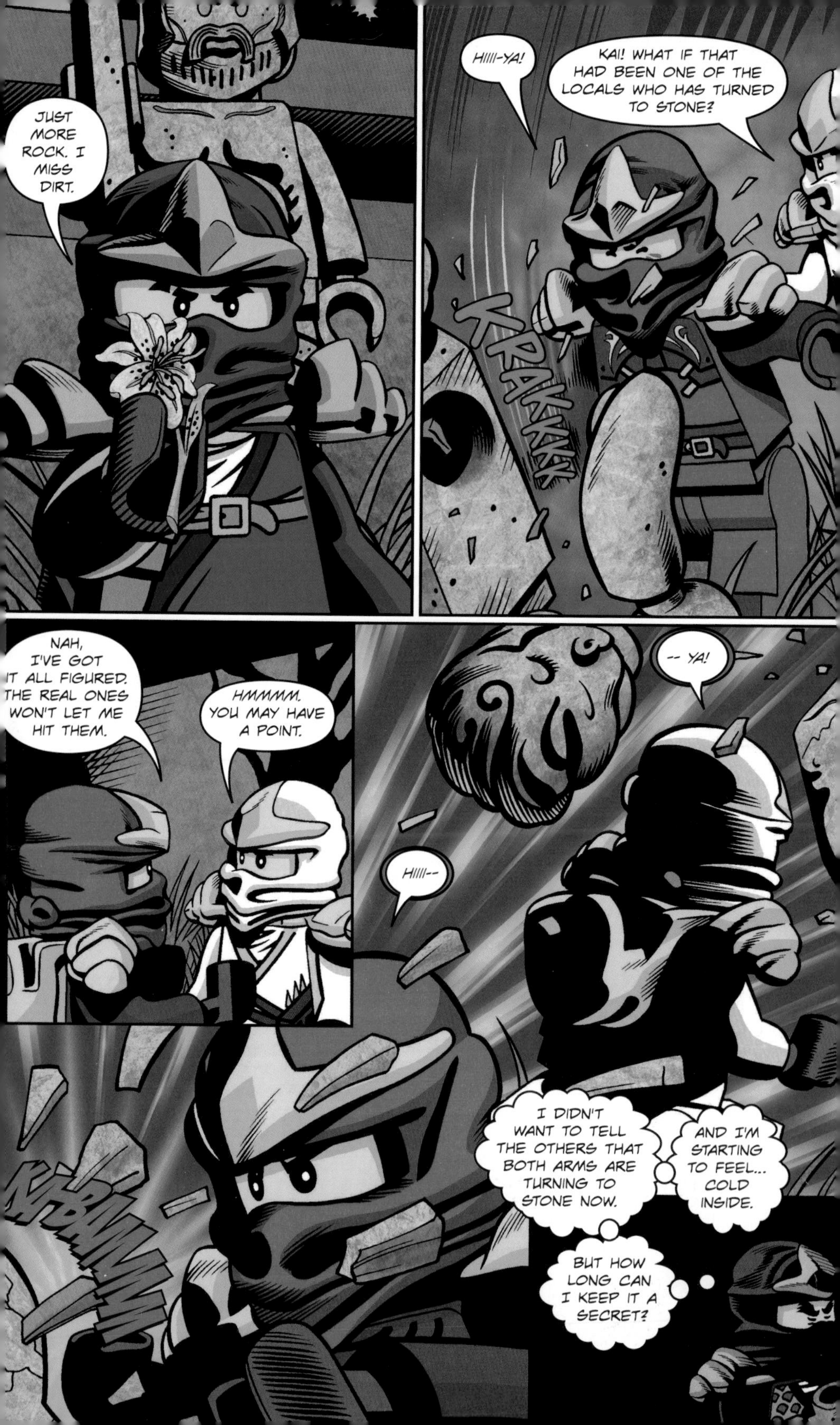
JUST MORE ROCK. I MISS DIRT.
HIIII-YA!
KAI! WHAT IF THAT HAD BEEN ONE OF THE LOCALS WHO HAS TURNED TO STONE?
KRAKKKK
NAH, I'VE GOT IT ALL FIGURED. THE REAL ONES WON'T LET ME HIT THEM.
HMMMM. YOU MAY HAVE A POINT.
HIIII--
-- YA!
I DIDN'T WANT TO TELL THE OTHERS THAT BOTH ARMS ARE TURNING TO STONE NOW.
AND I'M STARTING TO FEEL... COLD INSIDE.
BUT HOW LONG CAN I KEEP IT A SECRET?

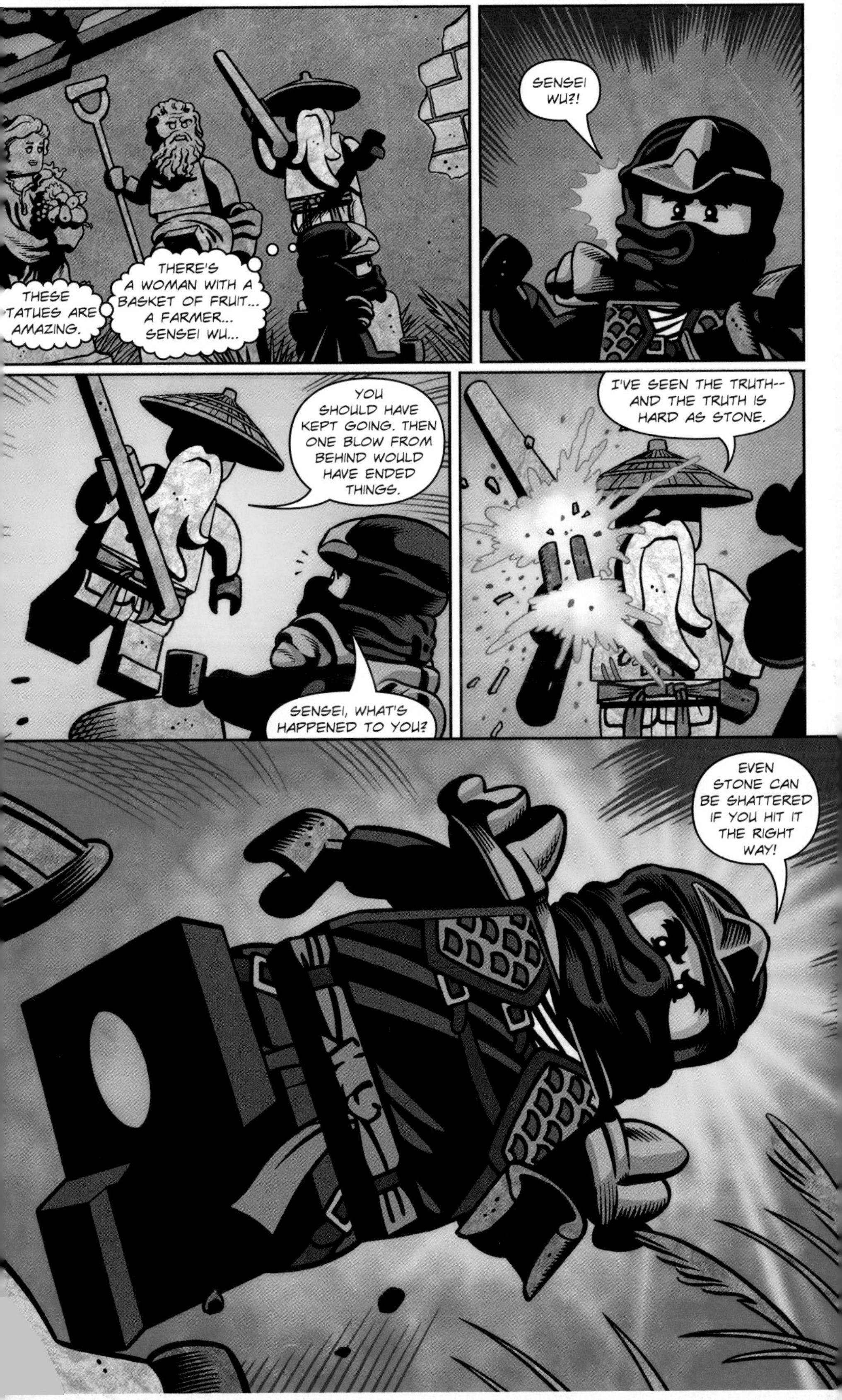
THESE STATUES ARE AMAZING.
THERE'S A WOMAN WITH A BASKET OF FRUIT... A FARMER... SENSEI WU...
SENSEI WU?!
YOU SHOULD HAVE KEPT GOING. THEN ONE BLOW FROM BEHIND WOULD HAVE ENDED THINGS.
SENSEI, WHAT'S HAPPENED TO YOU?
I'VE SEEN THE TRUTH-- AND THE TRUTH IS HARD AS STONE.
EVEN STONE CAN BE SHATTERED IF YOU HIT IT THE RIGHT WAY!

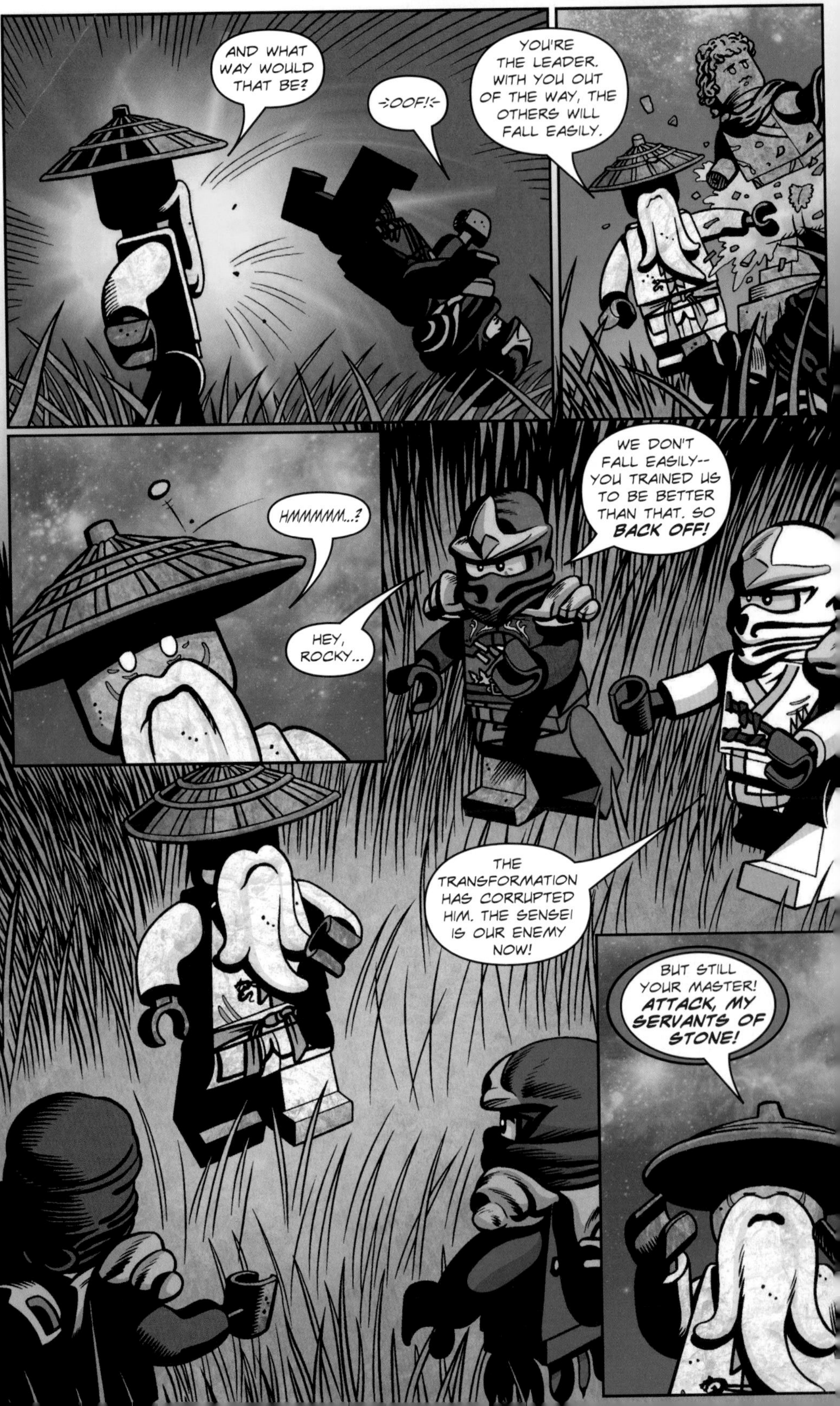
AND WHAT WAY WOULD THAT BE?
OOF!
YOU'RE THE LEADER. WITH YOU OUT OF THE WAY, THE OTHERS WILL FALL EASILY.
HMMMMM...?
HEY, ROCKY...
WE DON'T FALL EASILY-- YOU TRAINED US TO BE BETTER THAN THAT. SO BACK OFF!
THE TRANSFORMATION HAS CORRUPTED HIM. THE SENSEI IS OUR ENEMY NOW!
BUT STILL YOUR MASTER! ATTACK, MY SERVANTS OF STONE!

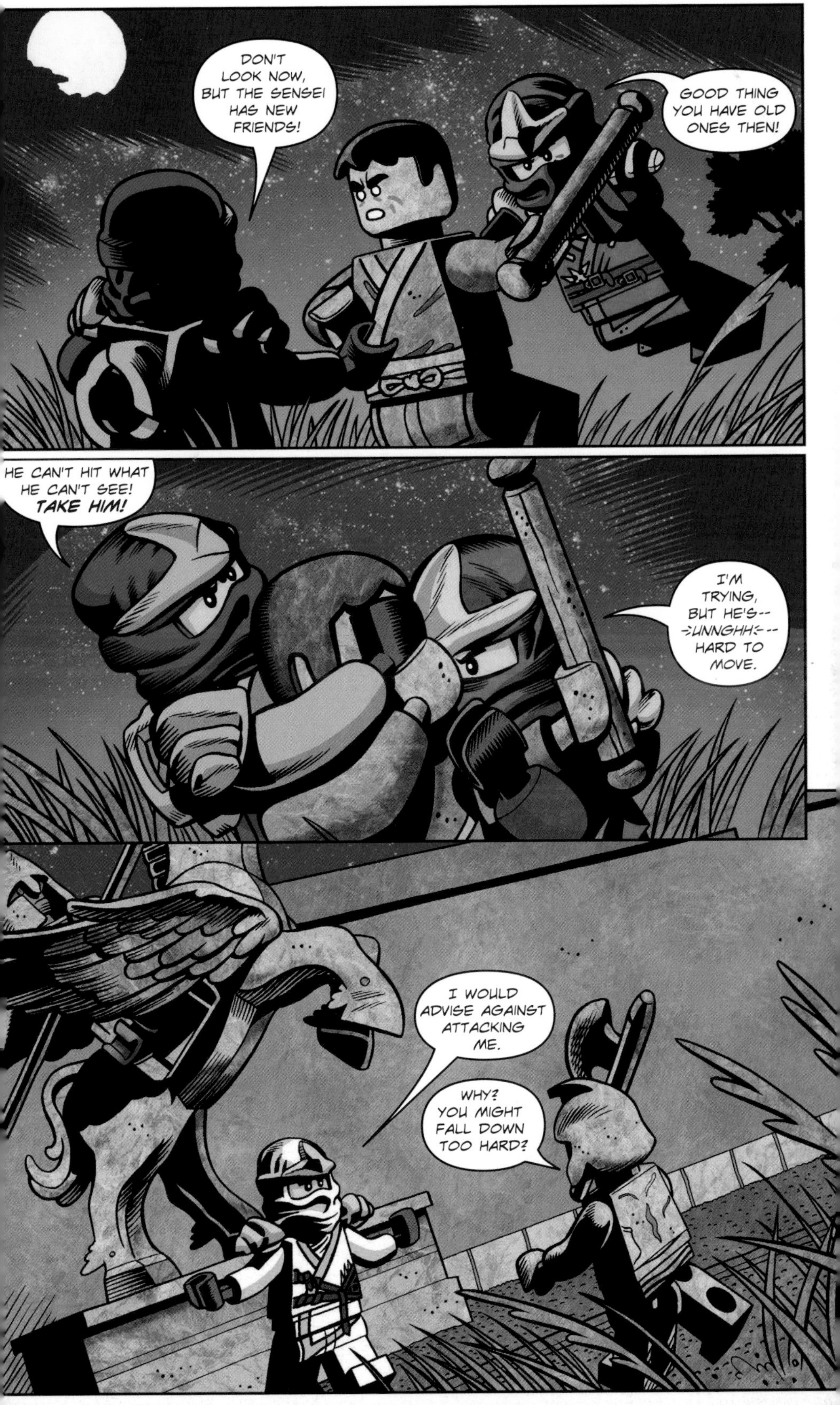
DON'T LOOK NOW, BUT THE SENSEI HAS NEW FRIENDS!
GOOD THING YOU HAVE OLD ONES THEN!
HE CAN'T HIT WHAT HE CAN'T SEE! TAKE HIM!
I'M TRYING, BUT HE'S-- -UNNGHH- -- HARD TO MOVE.
I WOULD ADVISE AGAINST ATTACKING ME.
WHY? YOU MIGHT FALL DOWN TOO HARD?

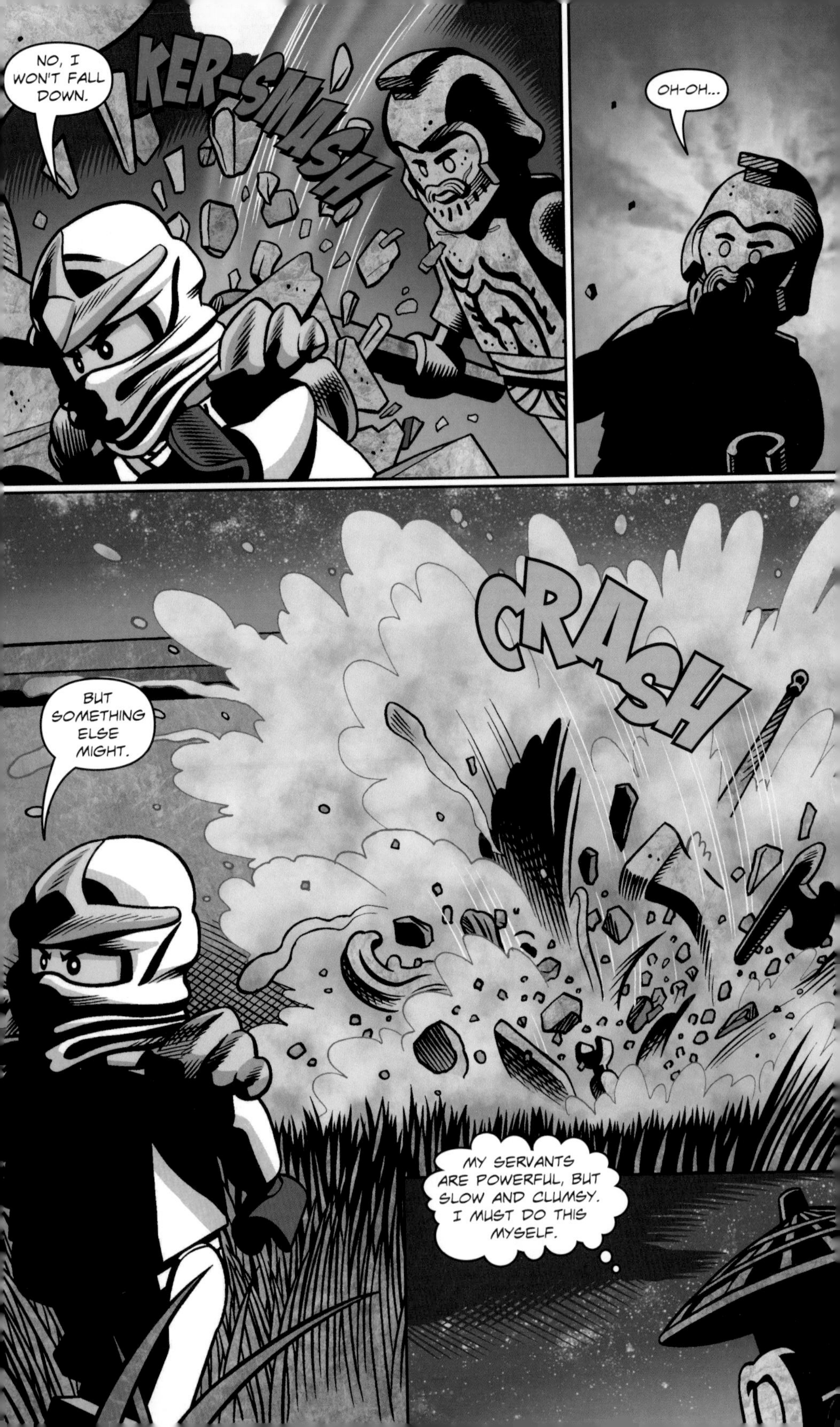
NO, I WON'T FALL DOWN.
KER-SMASH
OH-OH...
BUT SOMETHING ELSE MIGHT.
CRASH
MY SERVANTS ARE POWERFUL, BUT SLOW AND CLUMSY. I MUST DO THIS MYSELF.

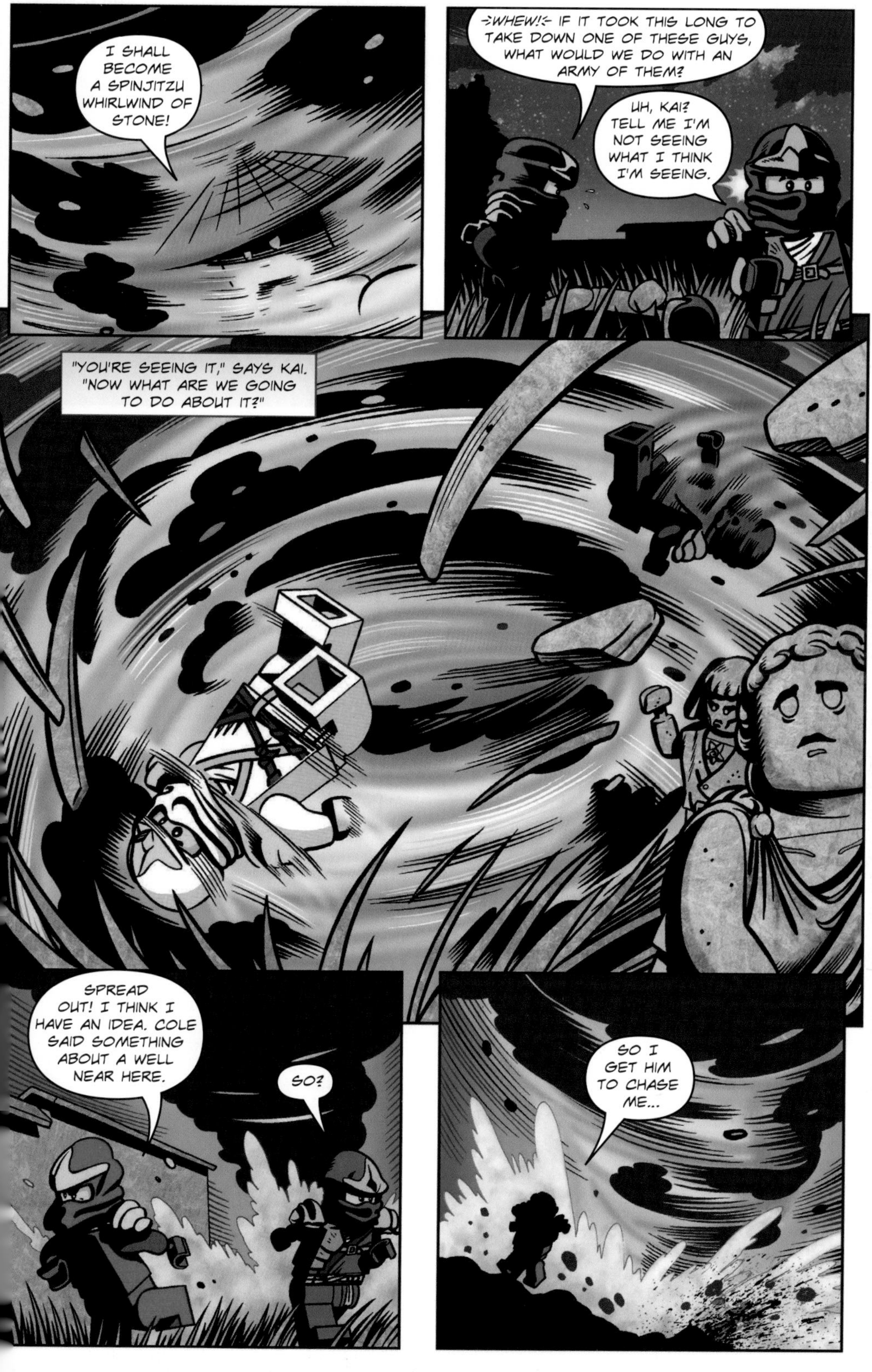
I SHALL BECOME A SPINJITZU WHIRLWIND OF STONE!
>WHEW!< IF IT TOOK THIS LONG TO TAKE DOWN ONE OF THESE GUYS, WHAT WOULD WE DO WITH AN ARMY OF THEM?
UH, KAI? TELL ME I'M NOT SEEING WHAT I THINK I'M SEEING.
"YOU'RE SEEING IT," SAYS KAI. "NOW WHAT ARE WE GOING TO DO ABOUT IT?"
SPREAD OUT! I THINK I HAVE AN IDEA. COLE SAID SOMETHING ABOUT A WELL NEAR HERE.
SO?
SO I GET HIM TO CHASE ME...

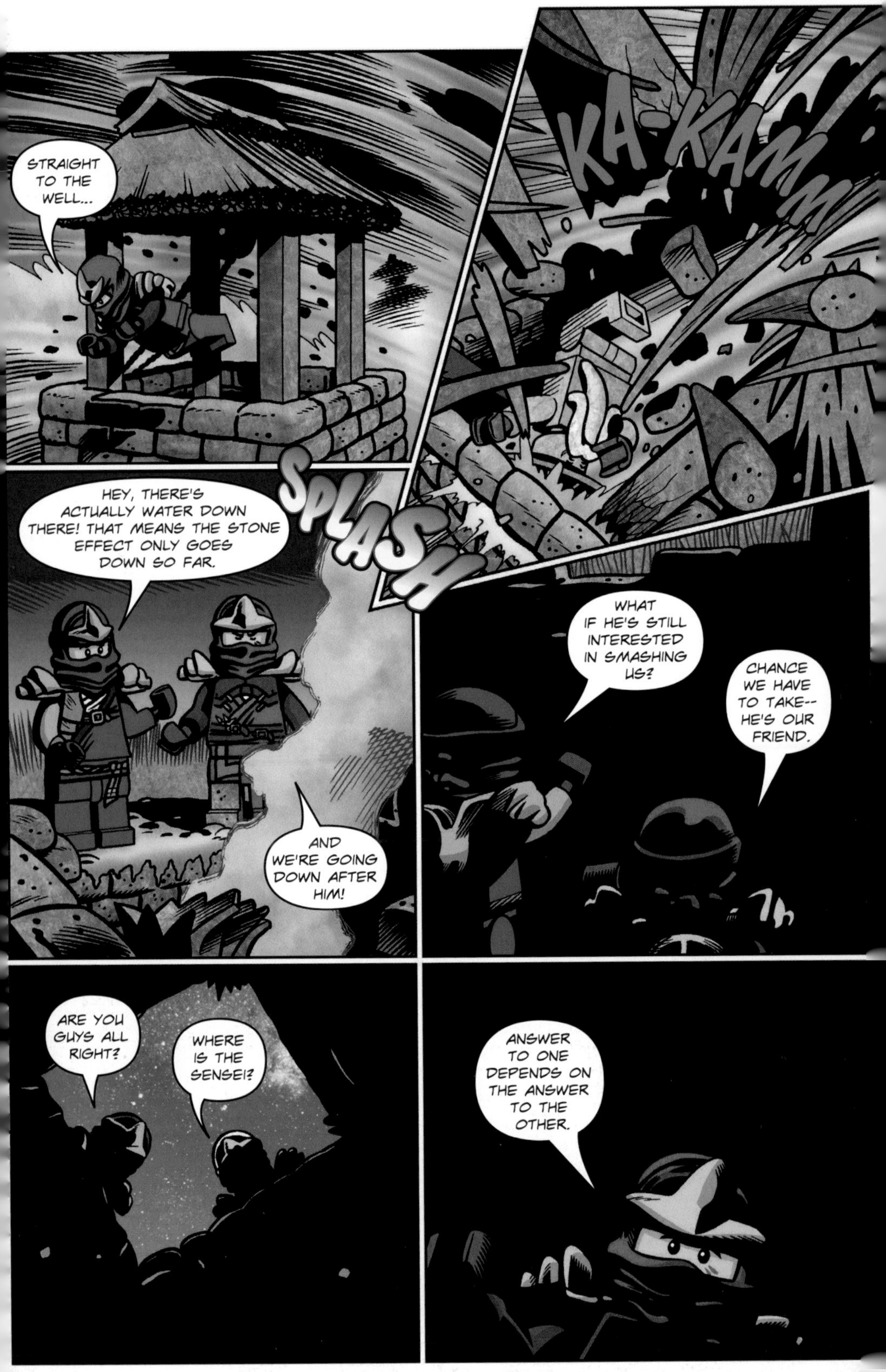
STRAIGHT TO THE WELL...
KA-KAMM
SPLASH
HEY, THERE'S ACTUALLY WATER DOWN THERE! THAT MEANS THE STONE EFFECT ONLY GOES DOWN SO FAR.
AND WE'RE GOING DOWN AFTER HIM!
WHAT IF HE'S STILL INTERESTED IN SMASHING US?
CHANCE WE HAVE TO TAKE-- HE'S OUR FRIEND.
ARE YOU GUYS ALL RIGHT?
WHERE IS THE SENSEI?
ANSWER TO ONE DEPENDS ON THE ANSWER TO THE OTHER.

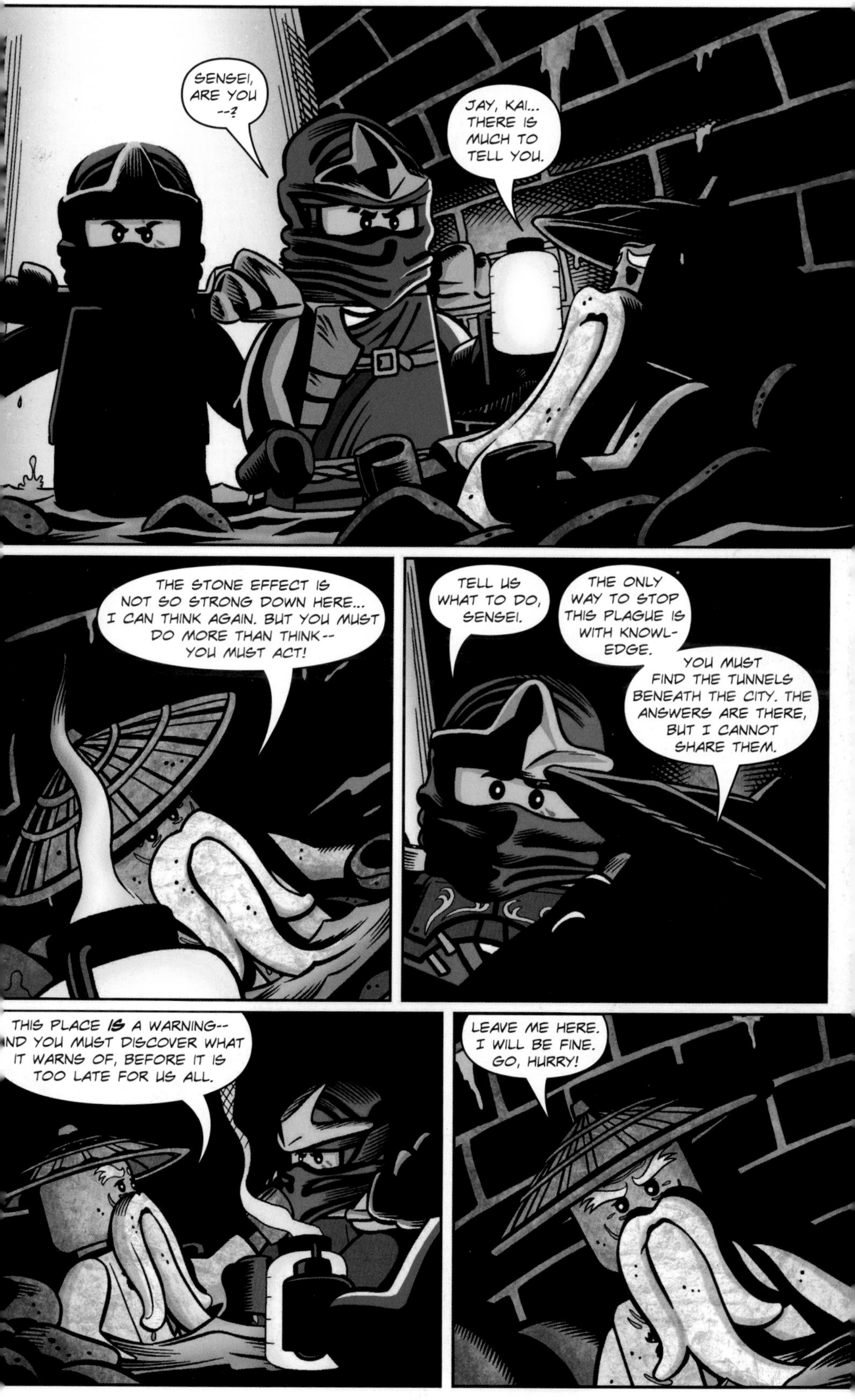
SENSEI, ARE YOU --?
JAY, KAI... THERE IS MUCH TO TELL YOU.
THE STONE EFFECT IS NOT SO STRONG DOWN HERE... I CAN THINK AGAIN. BUT YOU MUST DO MORE THAN THINK-- YOU MUST ACT!
TELL US WHAT TO DO, SENSEI.
THE ONLY WAY TO STOP THIS PLAGUE IS WITH KNOWL- EDGE.
YOU MUST FIND THE TUNNELS BENEATH THE CITY. THE ANSWERS ARE THERE, BUT I CANNOT SHARE THEM.
THIS PLACE IS A WARNING-- ND YOU MUST DISCOVER WHAT IT WARNS OF, BEFORE IT IS TOO LATE FOR US ALL.
LEAVE ME HERE. I WILL BE FINE. GO, HURRY!

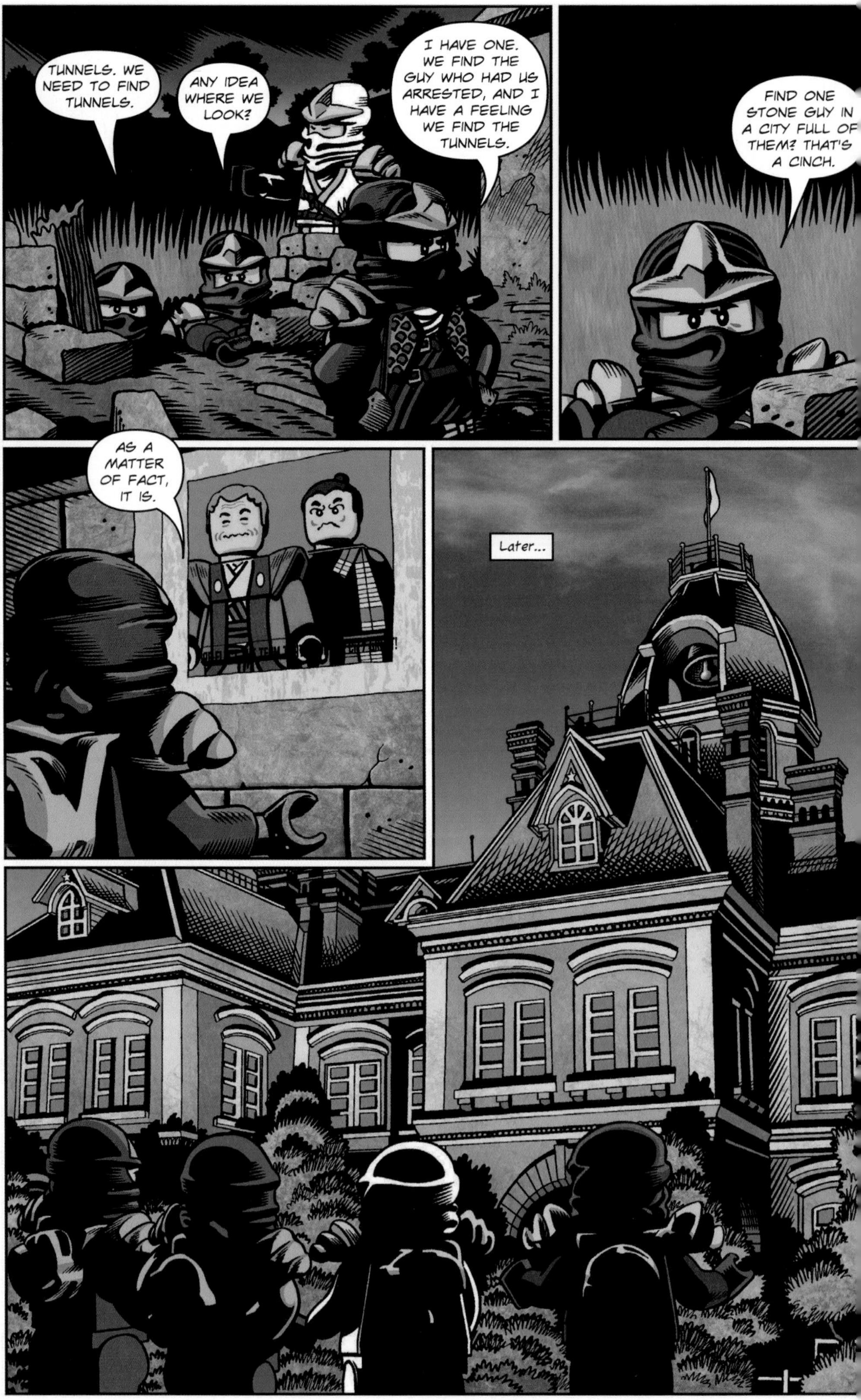
TUNNELS. WE NEED TO FIND TUNNELS.
ANY IDEA WHERE WE LOOK?
I HAVE ONE. WE FIND THE GUY WHO HAD US ARRESTED, AND I HAVE A FEELING WE FIND THE TUNNELS.
FIND ONE STONE GUY IN A CITY FULL OF THEM? THAT'S A CINCH.
AS A MATTER OF FACT, IT IS.
Later...

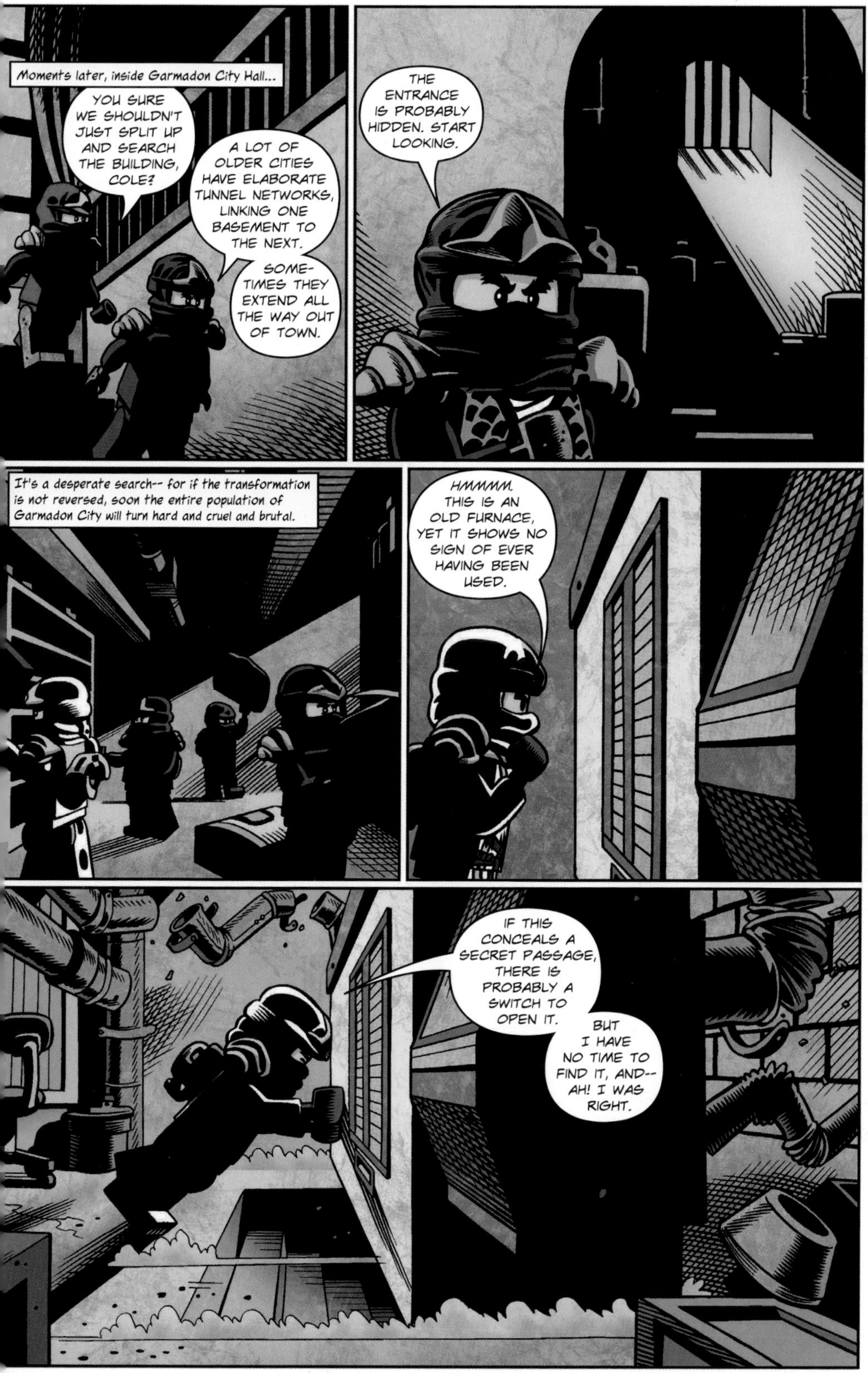
Moments later, inside Garmadon City Hall...
YOU SURE WE SHOULDN'T JUST SPLIT UP AND SEARCH THE BUILDING, COLE?
A LOT OF OLDER CITIES HAVE ELABORATE TUNNEL NETWORKS, LINKING ONE BASEMENT TO THE NEXT.
SOME-TIMES THEY EXTEND ALL THE WAY OUT OF TOWN.
THE ENTRANCE IS PROBABLY HIDDEN. START LOOKING.
It's a desperate search-- for if the transformation is not reversed, soon the entire population of Garmadon City will turn hard and cruel and brutal.
HMMMM. THIS IS AN OLD FURNACE, YET IT SHOWS NO SIGN OF EVER HAVING BEEN USED.
IF THIS CONCEALS A SECRET PASSAGE, THERE IS PROBABLY A SWITCH TO OPEN IT.
BUT I HAVE NO TIME TO FIND IT, AND-- AH! I WAS RIGHT.

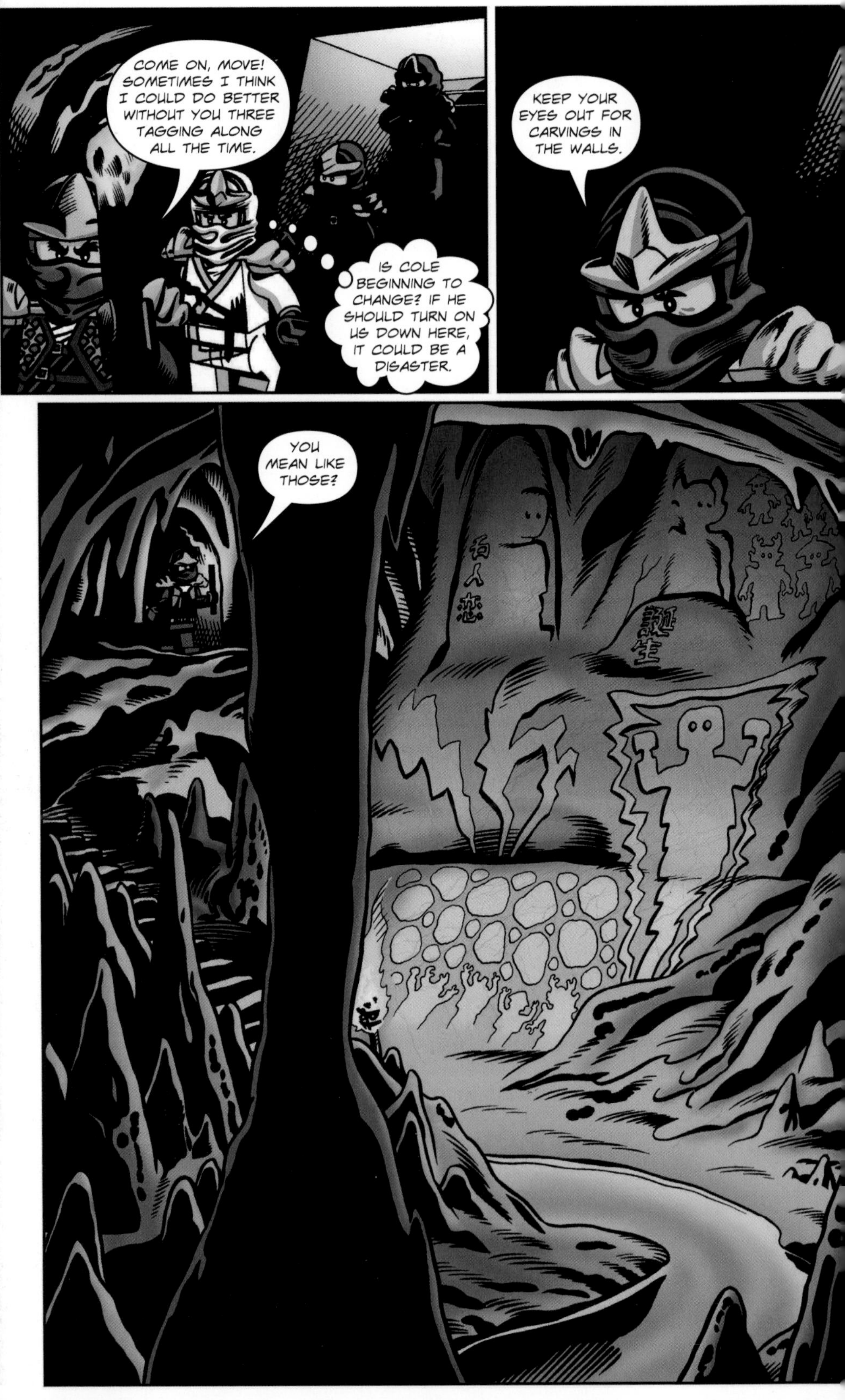
COME ON, MOVE! SOMETIMES I THINK I COULD DO BETTER WITHOUT YOU THREE TAGGING ALONG ALL THE TIME.
IS COLE BEGINNING TO CHANGE? IF HE SHOULD TURN ON US DOWN HERE, IT COULD BE A DISASTER.
KEEP YOUR EYES OUT FOR CARVINGS IN THE WALLS.
YOU MEAN LIKE THOSE?

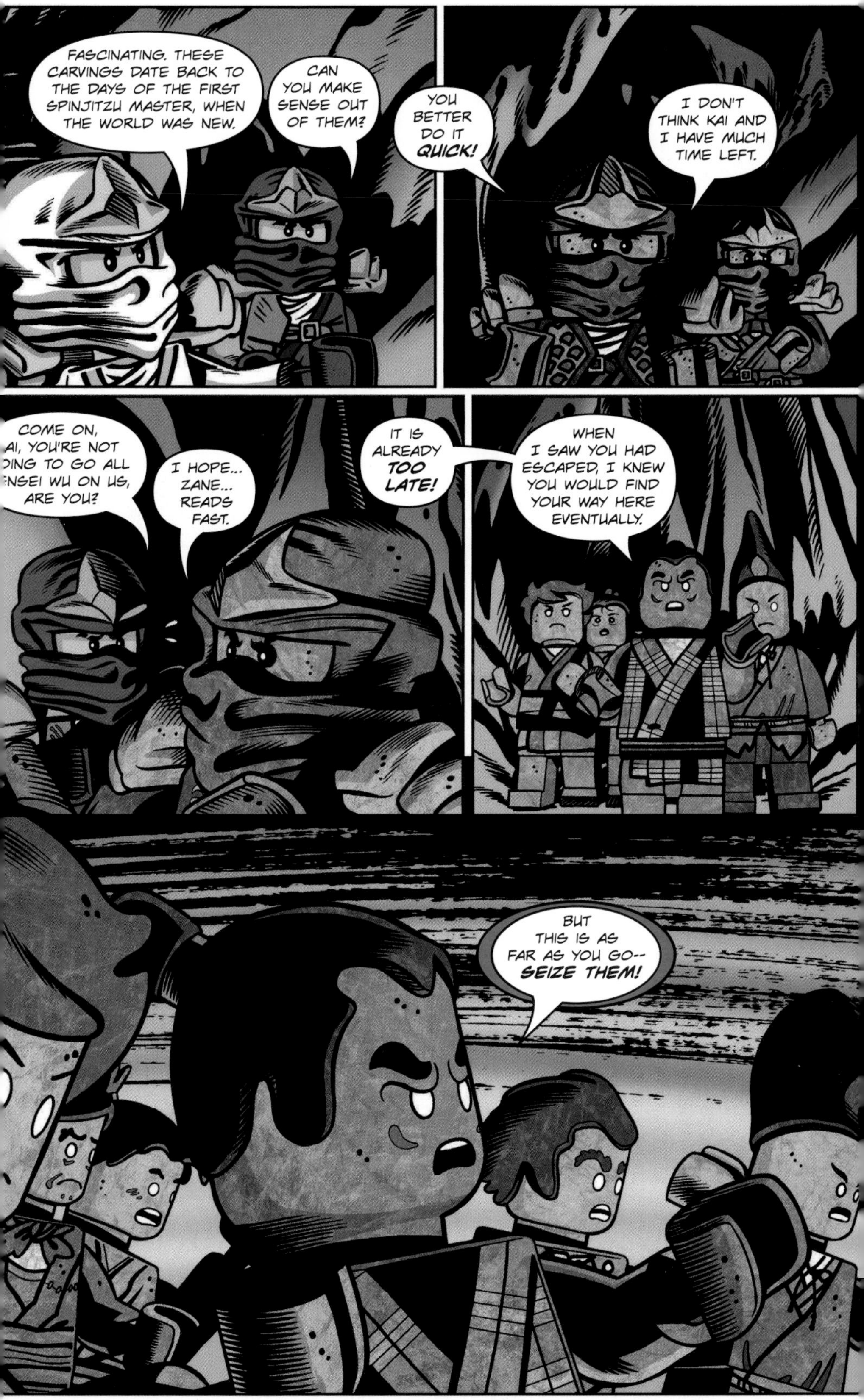
FASCINATING. THESE CARVINGS DATE BACK TO THE DAYS OF THE FIRST SPINJITZU MASTER, WHEN THE WORLD WAS NEW.
CAN YOU MAKE SENSE OUT OF THEM?
YOU BETTER DO IT QUICK!
I DON'T THINK KAI AND I HAVE MUCH TIME LEFT.
COME ON, AI, YOU'RE NOT OING TO GO ALL NSEI WU ON US, ARE YOU?
I HOPE... ZANE... READS FAST.
IT IS ALREADY TOO LATE!
WHEN I SAW YOU HAD ESCAPED, I KNEW YOU WOULD FIND YOUR WAY HERE EVENTUALLY.
BUT THIS IS AS FAR AS YOU GO-- SEIZE THEM!

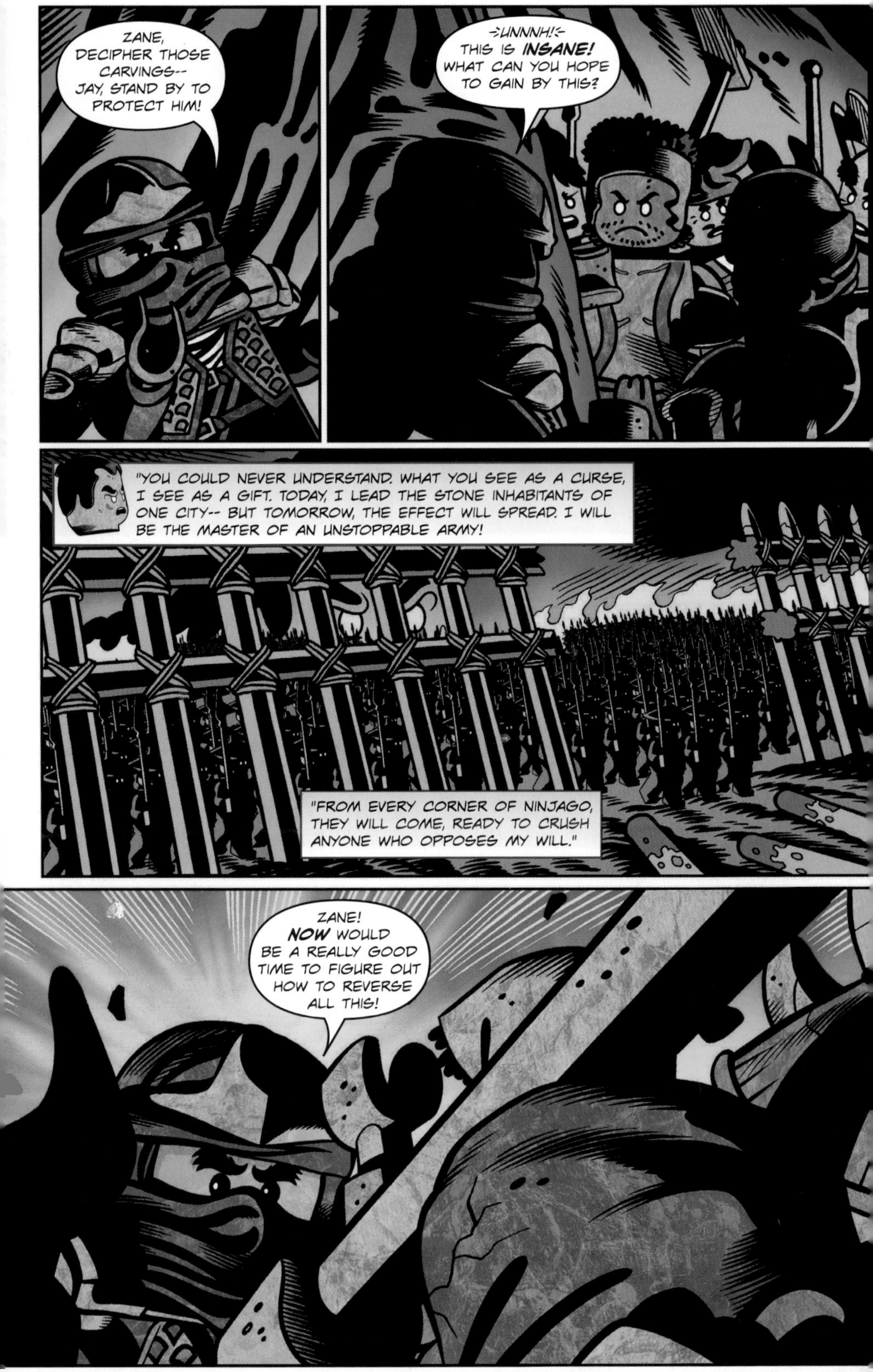
ZANE, DECIPHER THOSE CARVINGS-- JAY, STAND BY TO PROTECT HIM!
-UNNNH!- THIS IS INSANE! WHAT CAN YOU HOPE TO GAIN BY THIS?
"YOU COULD NEVER UNDERSTAND. WHAT YOU SEE AS A CURSE, I SEE AS A GIFT. TODAY, I LEAD THE STONE INHABITANTS OF ONE CITY-- BUT TOMORROW, THE EFFECT WILL SPREAD. I WILL BE THE MASTER OF AN UNSTOPPABLE ARMY!
"FROM EVERY CORNER OF NINJAGO, THEY WILL COME, READY TO CRUSH ANYONE WHO OPPOSES MY WILL."
ZANE! NOW WOULD BE A REALLY GOOD TIME TO FIGURE OUT HOW TO REVERSE ALL THIS!

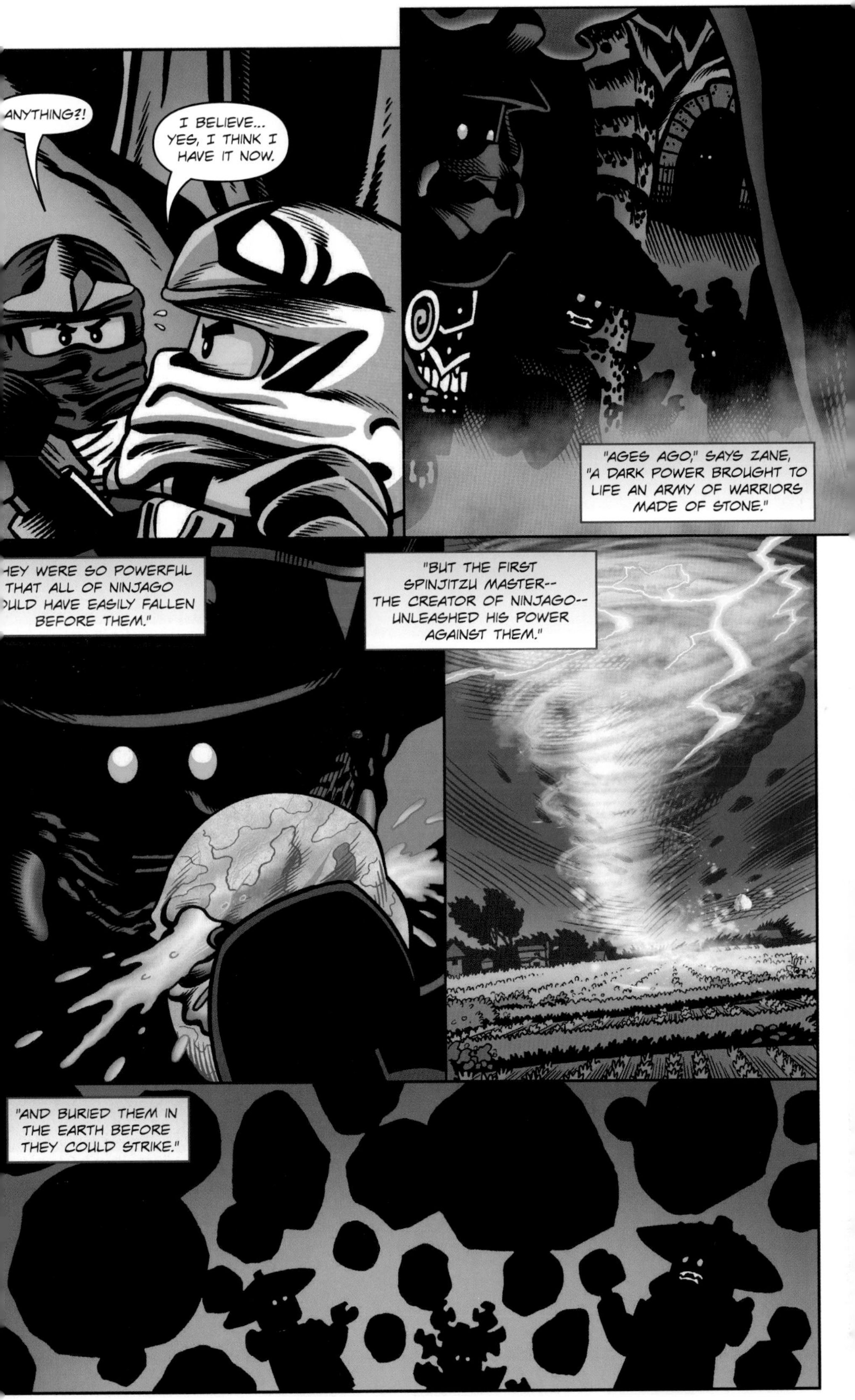
ANYTHING?!
I BELIEVE... YES, I THINK I HAVE IT NOW.
"AGES AGO," SAYS ZANE, "A DARK POWER BROUGHT TO LIFE AN ARMY OF WARRIORS MADE OF STONE."
HEY WERE SO POWERFUL THAT ALL OF NINJAGO OULD HAVE EASILY FALLEN BEFORE THEM."
"BUT THE FIRST SPINJITZU MASTER-- THE CREATOR OF NINJAGO-- UNLEASHED HIS POWER AGAINST THEM."
"AND BURIED THEM IN THE EARTH BEFORE THEY COULD STRIKE."

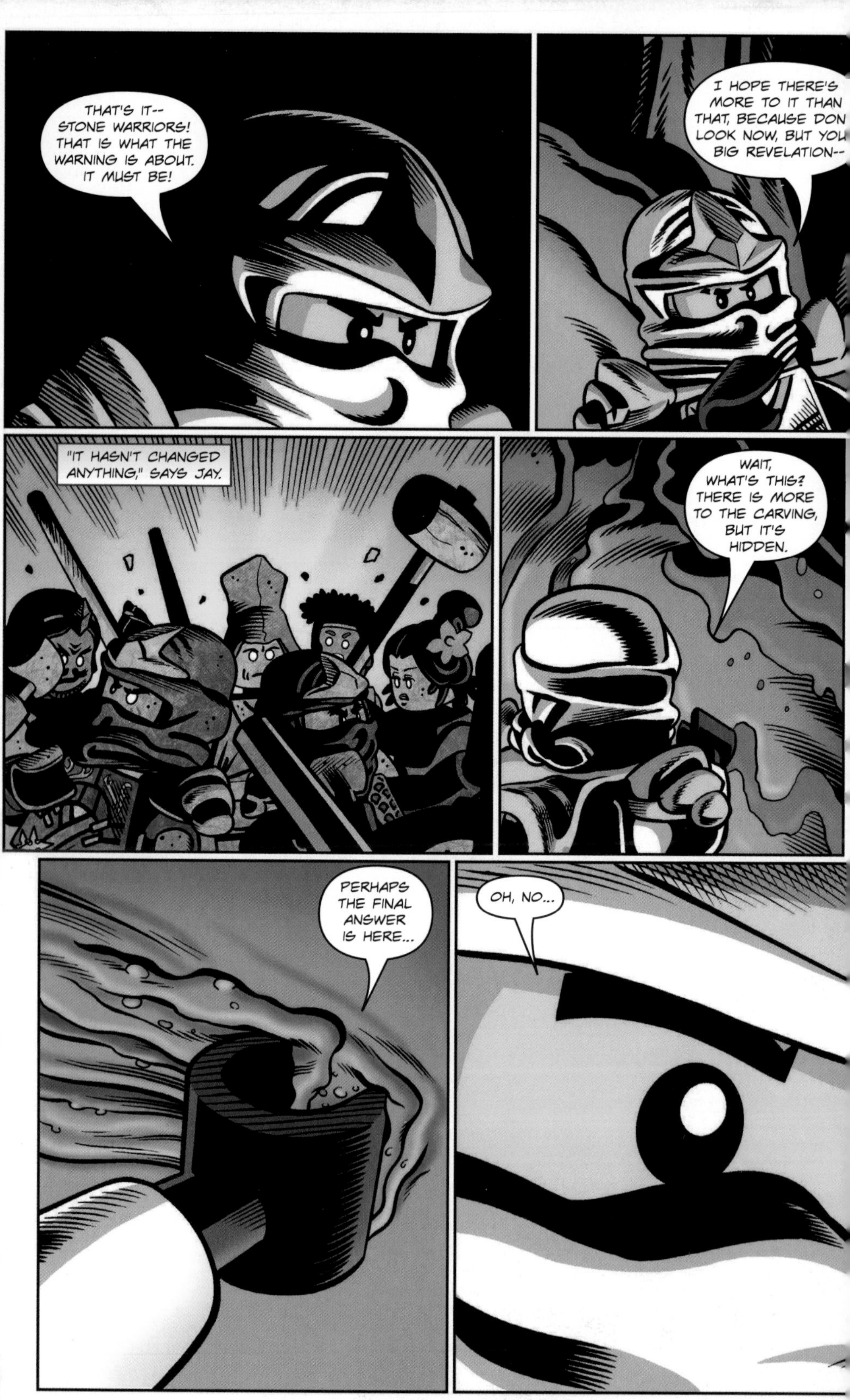
THAT'S IT--
STONE WARRIORS!
THAT IS WHAT THE
WARNING IS ABOUT.
IT MUST BE!
I HOPE THERE'S MORE TO IT THAN THAT, BECAUSE DON LOOK NOW, BUT YOU BIG REVELATION--
"IT HASN'T CHANGED ANYTHING," SAYS JAY.
WAIT, WHAT'S THIS? THERE IS MORE TO THE CARVING, BUT IT'S HIDDEN.
PERHAPS THE FINAL ANSWER IS HERE...
OH, NO...

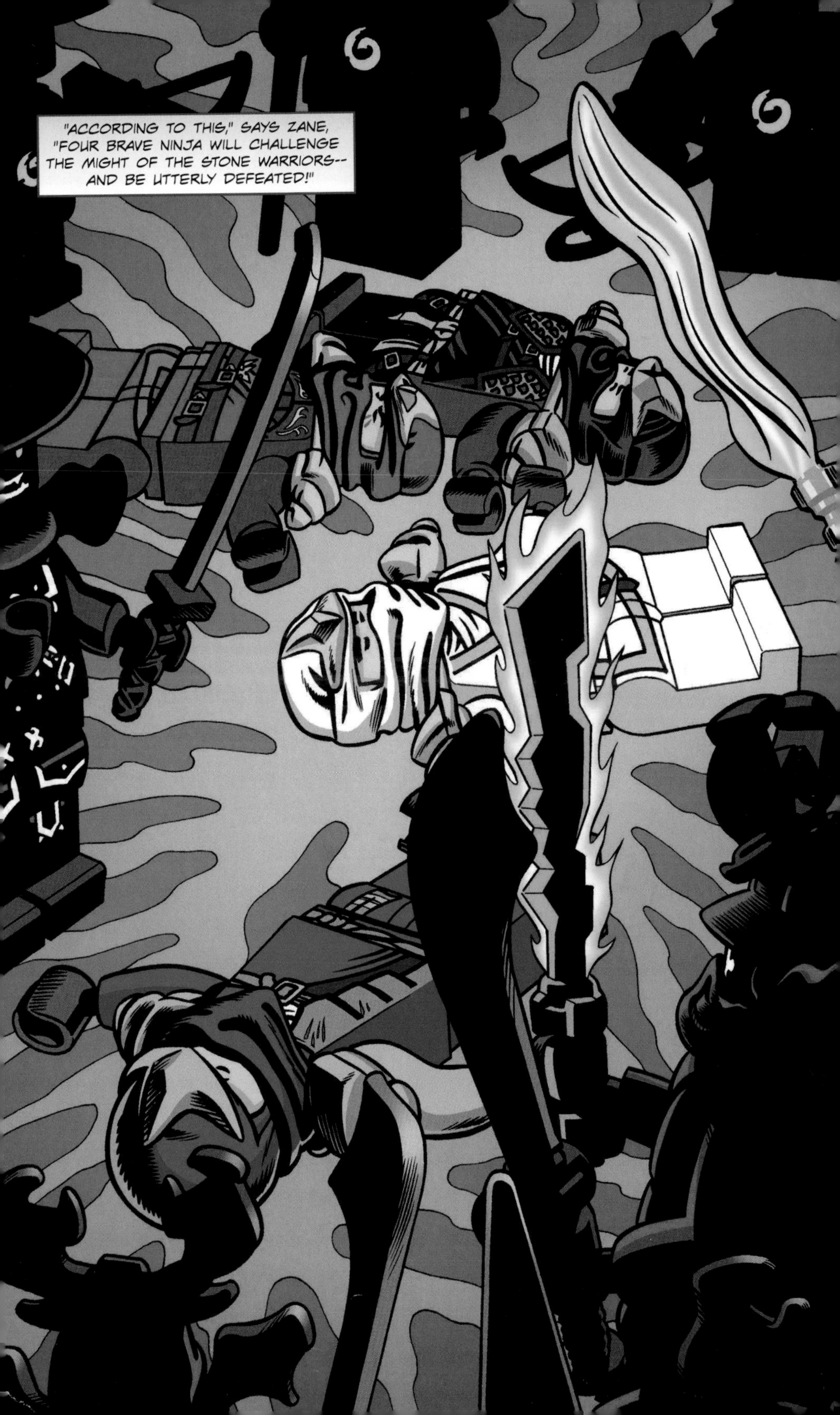
"ACCORDING TO THIS," SAYS ZANE, "FOUR BRAVE NINJA WILL CHALLENGE THE MIGHT OF THE STONE WARRIORS-- AND BE UTTERLY DEFEATED!"

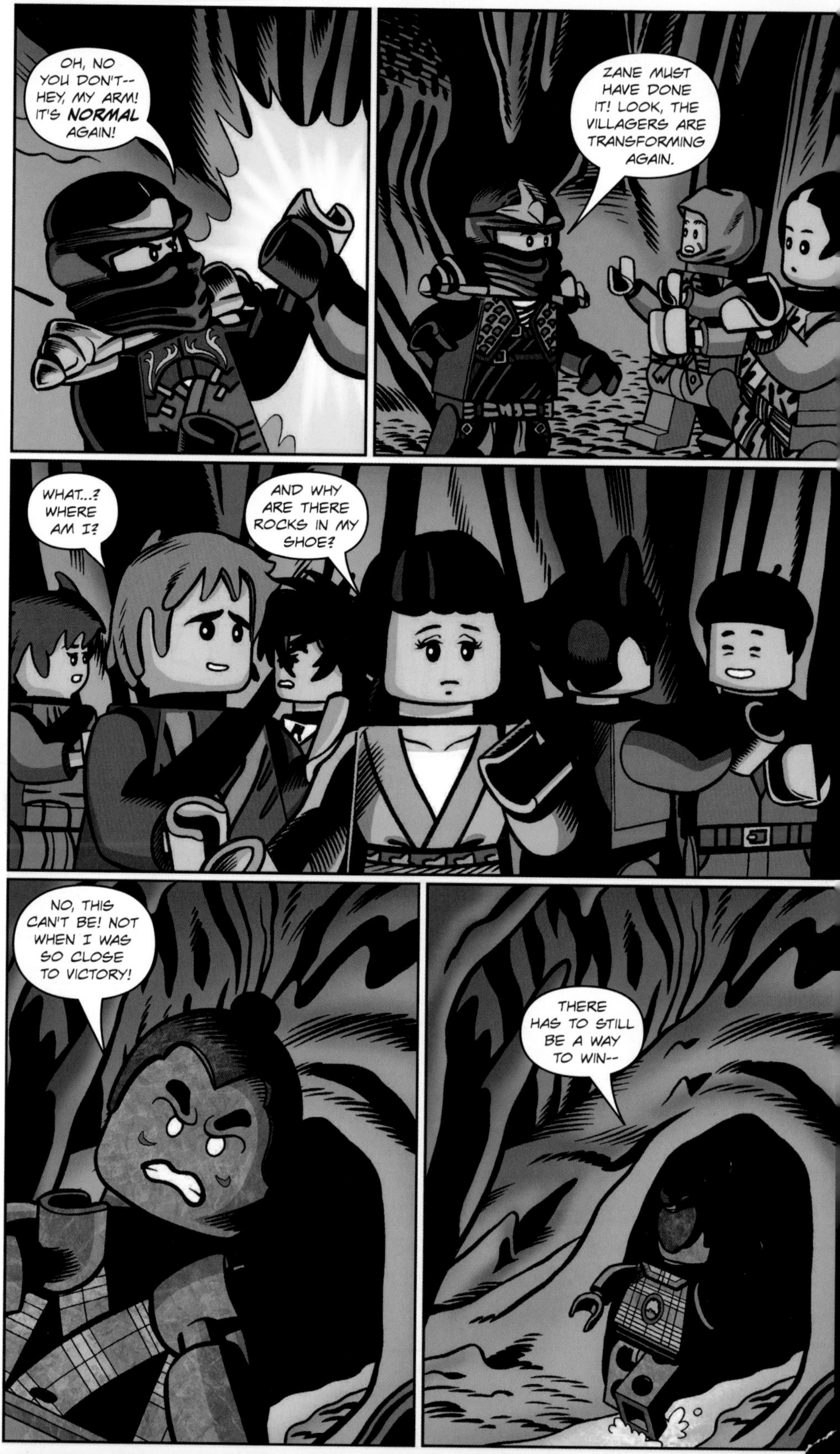
OH, NO YOU DON'T-- HEY, MY ARM! IT'S **NORMAL** AGAIN!
ZANE MUST HAVE DONE IT! LOOK, THE VILLAGERS ARE TRANSFORMING AGAIN.
WHAT...? WHERE AM I?
AND WHY ARE THERE ROCKS IN MY SHOE?
NO, THIS CAN'T BE! NOT WHEN I WAS SO CLOSE TO VICTORY!
THERE HAS TO STILL BE A WAY TO WIN--

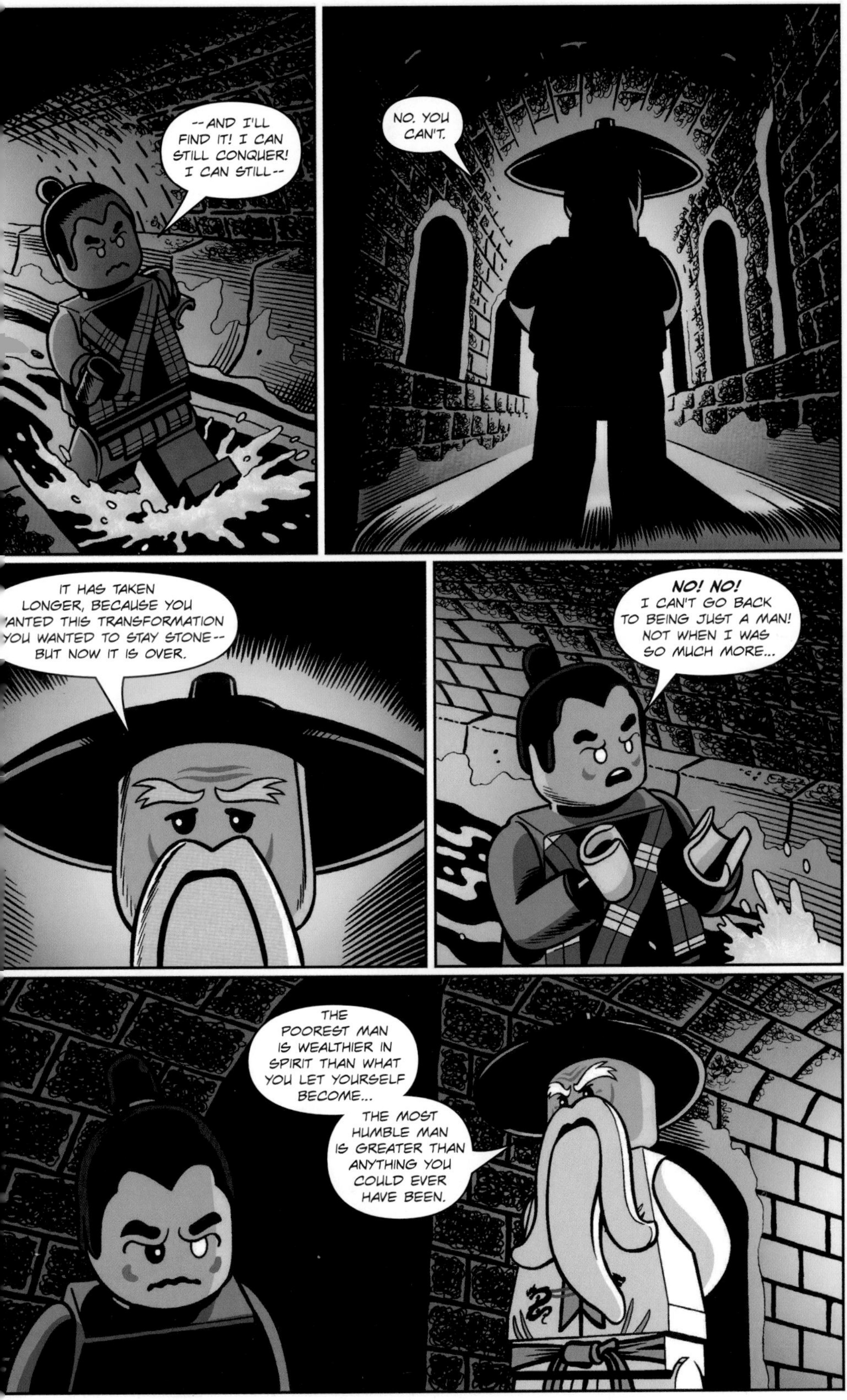
--AND I'LL FIND IT! I CAN STILL CONQUER! I CAN STILL--
NO. YOU CAN'T.
IT HAS TAKEN LONGER, BECAUSE YOU ANTED THIS TRANSFORMATION YOU WANTED TO STAY STONE-- BUT NOW IT IS OVER.
NO! NO! I CAN'T GO BACK TO BEING JUST A MAN! NOT WHEN I WAS SO MUCH MORE...
THE POOREST MAN IS WEALTHIER IN SPIRIT THAN WHAT YOU LET YOURSELF BECOME...
THE MOST HUMBLE MAN IS GREATER THAN ANYTHING YOU COULD EVER HAVE BEEN.

Morning comes to Garmadon City, where the only things made of rock... are rocks.

SO IT REALLY WAS JUST LIKE YOUR OLD CASE, SENSEI?

IN A SENSE, YES.

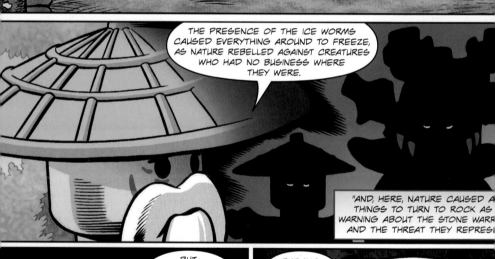

THE PRESENCE OF THE ICE WORMS CAUSED EVERYTHING AROUND TO FREEZE, AS NATURE REBELLED AGAINST CREATURES WHO HAD NO BUSINESS WHERE THEY WERE.

"AND, HERE, NATURE CAUSED A THINGS TO TURN TO ROCK AS WARNING ABOUT THE STONE WARR AND THE THREAT THEY REPRES

BUT IF THE STONE WARRIORS WERE BURIED BY THE FIRST SPINJITZU MASTER, WHAT IS THERE TO BE WORRIED ABOUT?

BURYING SOMETHING IS ONE THING... HAVING IT STAY BURIED IS QUITE ANOTHER.

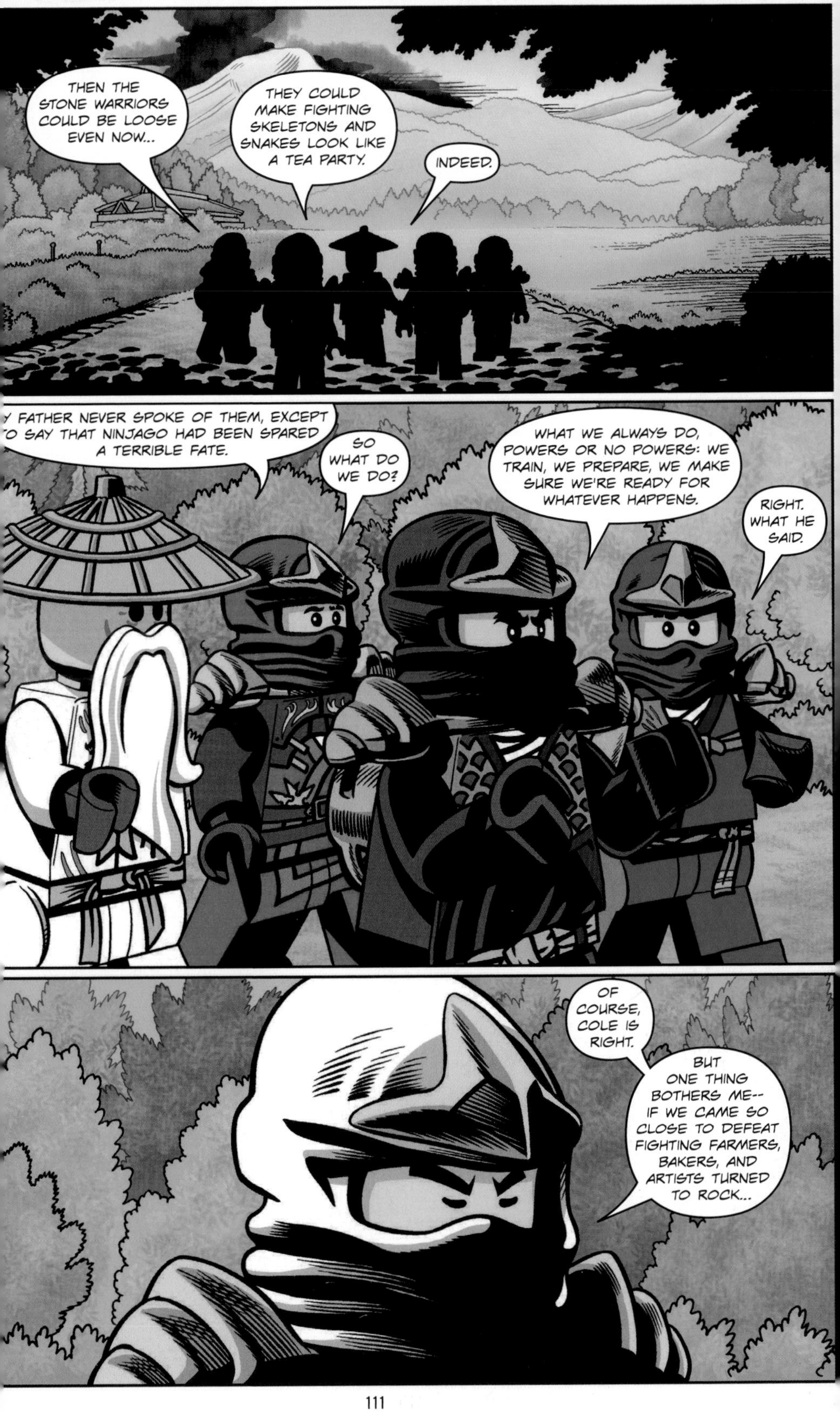

THEN THE STONE WARRIORS COULD BE LOOSE EVEN NOW...
THEY COULD MAKE FIGHTING SKELETONS AND SNAKES LOOK LIKE A TEA PARTY.
INDEED.
Y FATHER NEVER SPOKE OF THEM, EXCEPT O SAY THAT NINJAGO HAD BEEN SPARED A TERRIBLE FATE.
SO WHAT DO WE DO?
WHAT WE ALWAYS DO, POWERS OR NO POWERS: WE TRAIN, WE PREPARE, WE MAKE SURE WE'RE READY FOR WHATEVER HAPPENS.
RIGHT. WHAT HE SAID.
OF COURSE, COLE IS RIGHT.
BUT ONE THING BOTHERS ME-- IF WE CAME SO CLOSE TO DEFEAT FIGHTING FARMERS, BAKERS, AND ARTISTS TURNED TO ROCK...

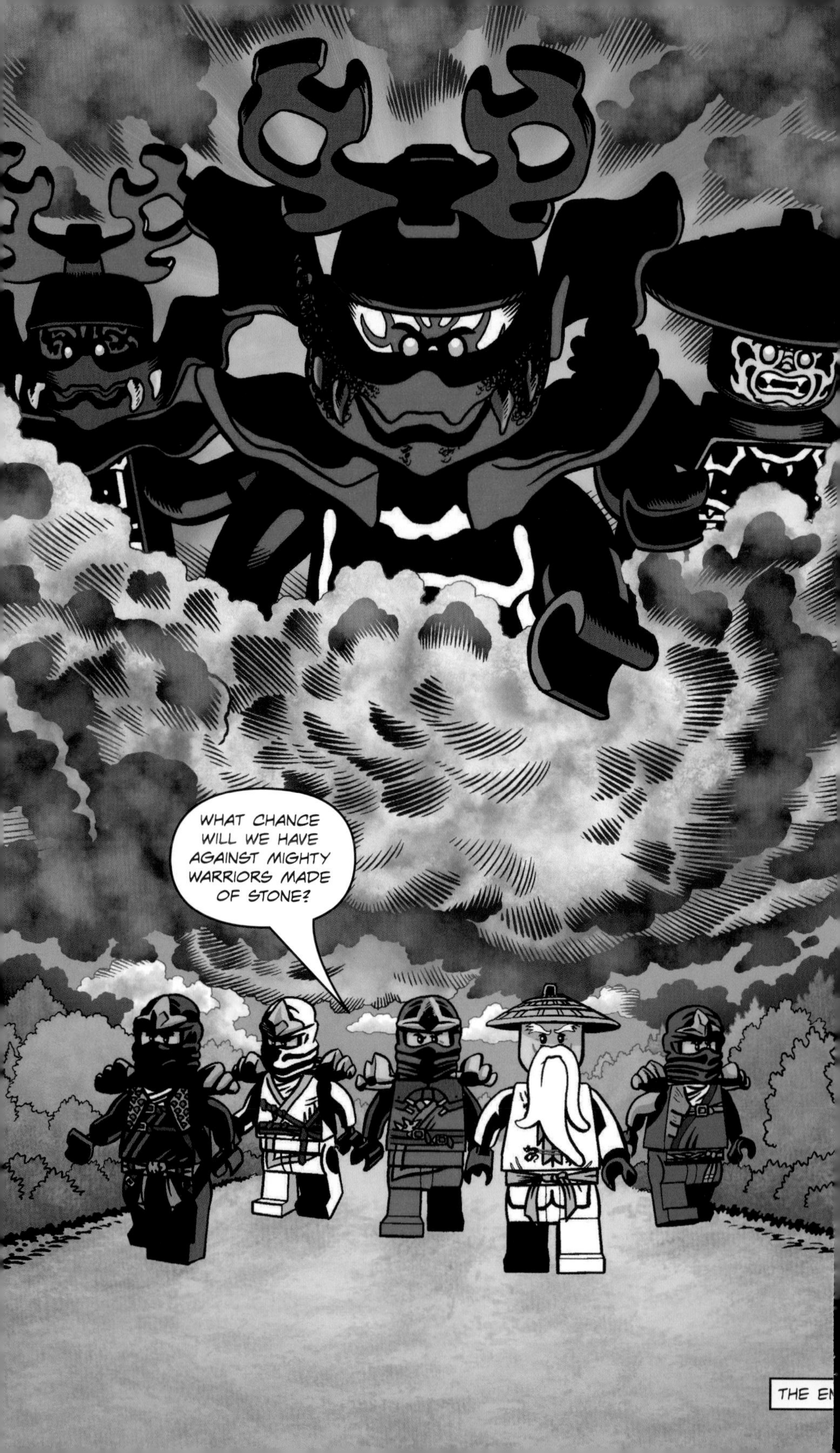
WHAT CHANCE WILL WE HAVE AGAINST MIGHTY WARRIORS MADE OF STONE?
THE EN